SPIRIT BOUND

SPIRIT BOUND

RICHELLE MEAD

AN IMPRINT OF PENGUIN GROUP (USA) INC.

Spirit Bound

RAZORBILL

Published by the Penguin Group
Penguin Young Readers Group
345 Hudson Street, New York, New York 10014, U.S.A.
Penguin Group (USA) Inc., 375 Hudson Street, New York, New York 10014, U.S.A.
Penguin Group (Canada), 90 Eglinton Avenue East, Suite 700, Toronto, Ontario, Canada M4P 2Y3 (a division of Pearson Penguin Canada Inc.)
Penguin Books Ltd, 80 Strand, London WC2R 0RL, England
Penguin Ireland, 25 St Stephen's Green, Dublin 2, Ireland (a division of Penguin Books Ltd)
Penguin Group (Australia), 250 Camberwell Road, Camberwell, Victoria 3124, Australia (a division of Pearson Australia Group Pty Ltd)
Penguin Books India Pvt Ltd, 11 Community Centre, Panchsheel Park, New Delhi – 110 017, India
Penguin Group (NZ), 67 Apollo Drive, Mairangi Bay, Auckland 1311, New Zealand (a division of Pearson New Zealand Ltd)
Penguin Books (South Africa) (Pty) Ltd, 24 Sturdee Avenue, Rosebank, Johannesburg 2196, South Africa

Penguin Books Ltd, Registered Offices: 80 Strand, London WC2R 0RL, England

10 9 8 7 6 5 4 3 2

Library of Congress Cataloging-in-Publication Data is available

Printed in the United States of America

Vampire Academy novels
by Richelle Mead:

Vampire Academy
Frostbite
Shadow Kiss
Blood Promise
Spirit Bound

For my agent, Jim McCarthy.

Thanks for doing all the hard stuff.

These books couldn't happen

without you!

ONE

THERE'S A BIG DIFFERENCE BETWEEN death threats and love letters—even if the person writing the death threats still claims to actually love you. Of course, considering *I* once tried to kill someone I loved, maybe I had no right to judge.

Today's letter had been perfectly timed, not that I should have expected any less. I'd read it four times so far, and even though I was running late, I couldn't help but read it a fifth time.

My dearest Rose,

One of the few downsides to being awakened is that we no longer require sleep; therefore we also no longer dream. It's a shame, because if I could dream, I know I'd dream about you. I'd dream about the way you smell and how your dark hair feels like silk between my fingers. I'd dream about the smoothness of your skin and the fierceness of your lips when we kiss.

Without dreams, I have to be content with my own imagination—which is almost as good. I can picture all of those things perfectly, as well as how it'll be when I take your life from this world. It's something I regret having to do, but you've made my choice inevitable. Your refusal to join me in eternal life and love leaves no other course of action, and I can't allow someone as dangerous as you to live. Besides, even if I forced your awakening, you now have so many enemies among the Strigoi that one of them would kill you. If you must die, it'll be by my hand. No one else's.

Nonetheless, I wish you well today as you take your trials—not that you need any luck. If they're actually making you take them, it's a waste of everyone's time. You're the best in that group, and by this evening you'll wear your promise mark. Of course, that means you'll be all that much more of a challenge when we meet again—which I'll definitely enjoy.

And we will *be meeting again. With graduation, you'll be turned out of the Academy, and once you're outside the wards, I'll find you. There is no place in this world you can hide from me. I'm watching.*

Love,

Dimitri

Despite his "warm wishes" I didn't really find the letter inspiring as I tossed it onto my bed and blearily left the room. I tried not to let his words get to me, though it was kind of impossible to not be creeped out by something like that. *There is no place in this world you can hide from me.*

I didn't doubt it. I knew Dimitri had spies. Since my former instructor-turned-lover had been turned into an evil, undead vampire, he'd also become a sort of leader among them—something I'd helped speed along when I killed off his former boss. I suspected a lot of his spies were humans, watching for me to step outside my school's borders. No Strigoi could have stayed on a twenty-four-hour stakeout. Humans could, and I'd recently learned that plenty of humans were willing to serve the Strigoi in exchange for the promise of being turned someday. Those humans considered eternal life worth corrupting their souls and killing off others to survive. Those humans made me sick.

But the humans weren't what made my steps falter as I walked through grass that had turned bright green with summer's touch. It was Dimitri. Always Dimitri. Dimitri, the man I'd loved. Dimitri, the Strigoi I wanted to save. Dimitri, the monster I'd most likely have to kill. The love we'd shared always burned within me, no matter how often I told myself to move on, no matter how much the world did think I'd moved on. He was always with me, always on my mind, always making me question myself.

"You look like you're ready to face an army."

I shifted out of my dark thoughts. I'd been so fixated on Dimitri and his letter that I'd been walking across campus, oblivious to the world, and hadn't noticed my best friend, Lissa, falling into step with me, a teasing smile on her face. Her catching me by surprise was a rarity because we shared a psychic bond, one that always kept me aware of her presence and feelings. I had to be pretty distracted to not notice her, and if ever there was a distraction, it was someone wanting to kill me.

I gave Lissa what I hoped was a convincing smile. She knew what had happened to Dimitri and how he was now waiting to kill me after I'd tried—and failed—to kill him. Nonetheless, the letters I got from him every week worried her, and she had enough to deal with in her life without my undead stalker to add to the list.

"I kind of *am* facing an army," I pointed out. It was early evening, but late summer still found the sun up in the Montana sky, bathing us in golden light as we walked. I loved it, but as a Moroi—a peaceful, living vampire—Lissa would eventually grow weak and uncomfortable in it.

She laughed and tossed her platinum hair over one shoulder. The sun lit up the pale color into angelic brilliance. "I suppose. I didn't think you'd really be all that worried."

I could understand her reasoning. Even Dimitri had said these would be a waste of my time. After all, I'd gone to Russia to search for him and had faced real Strigoi—killing a number of them on my own. Maybe I shouldn't have been afraid of the upcoming tests, but all the fanfare and expectation suddenly pressed in upon me. My heart rate increased. What if I couldn't do it? What if I wasn't as good as I thought I was? The guardians who would challenge me out here might not be true Strigoi, but they were skilled and had been fighting a lot longer than me. Arrogance could get me into a lot of trouble, and if I failed, I'd be doing it in front of all the people who cared about me. All the people who had such faith in me.

One other thing also concerned me.

"I'm worried about how these grades will affect my future," I said. That was the truth. The trials were the final exam for a novice guardian like me. They ensured I could graduate from St. Vladimir's Academy and take my place with true guardians who defended Moroi from the Strigoi. The trials pretty much decided which Moroi a guardian would be assigned to.

Through our bond, I felt Lissa's compassion—and her

worry. "Alberta thinks there's a good chance we can stay together—that you'll still be my guardian."

I grimaced. "I think Alberta was saying that to keep me in school." I'd dropped out to hunt Dimitri a few months ago and then returned—something that didn't look good on my academic record. There was also the small fact that the Moroi queen, Tatiana, hated me and would probably be going out of her way to influence my assignment—but that was another story. "I think Alberta knows the only way they'd let me protect you is if I was the last guardian on earth. And even then, my odds would still be pretty slim."

Ahead of us, the roar of a crowd grew loud. One of the school's many sports fields had been transformed into an arena on par with something from Roman gladiatorial days. The bleachers had been built up, expanded from simple wooden seats to luxuriously cushioned benches with awnings to shade the Moroi from the sun. Banners surrounded the field, their bright colors visible from here as they whipped in the wind. I couldn't see them yet, but I knew there would be some type of barracks built near the stadium's entrance where novices waited, nerves on edge. The field itself would have turned into an obstacle course of dangerous tests. And from the sound of those deafening cheers, plenty were already there to witness this event.

"I'm not giving up hope," Lissa said. Through the bond, I knew she meant it. It was one of the wonderful things about her—a steadfast faith and optimism that weathered the most terrible ordeals. It was a sharp contrast to my recent cynicism.

"And I've got something that might help you out today."

She came to a stop and reached into her jeans pocket, producing a small silver ring scattered with tiny stones that looked like peridots. I didn't need any bond to understand what she was offering.

"Oh, Liss . . . I don't know. I don't want any, um, unfair advantage."

Lissa rolled her eyes. "That's not the problem, and you know it. This one's fine, I swear."

The ring she offered me was a charm, infused with the rare type of magic she wielded. All Moroi had control of one of five elements: earth, air, water, fire, or spirit. Spirit was the rarest—so rare, it had been forgotten over the centuries. Then Lissa and a few others had recently surfaced with it. Unlike the other elements, which were more physical in nature, spirit was tied into the mind and all sorts of psychic phenomena. No one fully understood it.

Making charms with spirit was something Lissa had only recently begun to experiment with—and she wasn't very good at it. Her best spirit ability was healing, so she kept trying to make healing charms. The last one had been a bracelet that singed my arm.

"This one works. Only a little, but it'll help keep the darkness away during the trial."

She spoke lightly, but we both knew the seriousness of her words. With all of spirit's gifts came a cost: a darkness that showed itself now as anger and confusion, and eventually led to insanity. Darkness that sometimes bled over into me through our bond. Lissa and I had been told that with charms and her healing, we could fight it off. That was also something we had yet to master.

I gave her a faint smile, moved by her concern, and accepted the ring. It didn't scald my hand, which I took as a promising sign. It was tiny and only fit on my pinky. I felt nothing whatsoever as it slid on. Sometimes that happened with healing charms. Or it could mean the ring was completely ineffectual. Either way, no harm done.

"Thanks," I said. I felt delight sweep through her, and we continued walking.

I held my hand out before me, admiring the way the green stones glittered. Jewelry wasn't a great idea in the kind of physical ordeals I'd be facing, but I would have gloves on to cover it.

"Hard to believe that after this, we'll be done here and out in the real world," I mused aloud, not really considering my words.

Beside me, Lissa stiffened, and I immediately regretted speaking. "Being out in the real world" meant Lissa and I were going to undertake a task she'd—unhappily—promised to help me with a couple months ago.

While in Siberia, I'd learned there might be a way to restore Dimitri back to being a dhampir like me. It was a long shot—possibly a lie—and considering the way he was fixated on killing me, I had no illusions that I would have any other choice but to kill him if it came down to him or me. But if there was a way I might save him before that happened, I had to find out.

Unfortunately, the only lead we had to making this miracle come true was through a criminal. Not just any criminal either: Victor Dashkov, a royal Moroi who had tortured Lissa and committed all sorts of other atrocities that had made our lives hell. Justice had been served, and Victor was locked away in prison, which complicated things. We'd learned that so long as he was destined for a life behind bars, he saw no reason to share what he knew about his half-brother—the only person who had once allegedly saved a Strigoi. I'd decided—possibly illogically—that Victor might give up the information if we offered him the one thing no one else could: freedom.

This idea was not foolproof, for a number of reasons. First, I didn't know if it would work. That was kind of a big thing. Second, I had no idea how to stage a prison break, let alone where his prison even was. And finally, there was the fact that we would be releasing our mortal enemy. That was devastating enough to me, let alone Lissa. Yet as much as the idea troubled her—and believe me, it did—she'd firmly sworn she would help me. I'd offered to free her from the promise dozens of times in the last couple months, but she'd stood firm. Of course, considering we had no way to even find the prison, her promise might not matter in the end.

I tried to fill the awkward silence between us, explaining instead that I'd really meant we'd be able to celebrate her birthday in style next week. My attempts were interrupted by Stan, one of my longtime instructors. "Hathaway!" he barked, coming from the direction of the field. "Nice of you to join us. Get in there now!"

Thoughts of Victor vanished from Lissa's mind. Lissa gave me a quick hug. "Good luck," she whispered. "Not that you need it."

Stan's expression told me that this ten-second goodbye was ten seconds too long. I gave Lissa a grin by way of thanks, and then she headed off to find our friends in the stands while I scurried after Stan.

"You're lucky you aren't one of the first ones," he growled. "People were even making bets about whether you'd show."

"Really?" I asked cheerfully. "What kind of odds are there on that? Because I can still change my mind and put down my own bet. Make a little pocket money."

His narrowed eyes shot me a warning that needed no words as we entered the waiting area adjacent to the field, across from the stands. It had always amazed me in past years how much work went into these trials, and I was no less impressed now as I saw it up close. The barrack that novices waited in was constructed out of wood, complete with a roof. The structure looked as though it had been part of the stadium forever. It had been built with remarkable speed and would be taken down equally quickly once the trials were over. A doorway about three people wide gave a partial glimpse onto the field, where one of my classmates was waiting anxiously for her name to be called. All sorts of obstacles were set up there, challenges to test balance and coordination while still having to battle and elude the adult guardians who would be lurking around objects and corners. Wooden walls had been constructed on one end of the field, creating a dark and confusing maze. Nets and shaky platforms hung across other areas, designed to test just how well we could fight under difficult conditions.

A few of the other novices crowded the doorway, hoping to get an advantage by watching those who went ahead of them. Not me. I would go in there blind, content to take on whatever they threw before me. Studying the course now would simply make me overthink and panic. Calm was what I needed now.

So I leaned against one of the barrack walls and watched those around me. It appeared that I really had been the last to show up, and I wondered if people had actually lost money betting on me. Some of my classmates whispered in clusters. Some were doing stretches and warm-up exercises. Others stood with instructors who had been mentors. Those teachers spoke intently to their students, giving last-minute words of advice. I kept hearing words like *focus* and *calm down*.

Seeing the instructors made my heart clench. Not so long ago, that was how I'd pictured this day. I'd imagined Dimitri and me standing together, with him telling me to take this seriously and not to lose my cool when I was out on the field. Alberta had done a fair amount of mentoring for me since I'd returned from Russia, but as captain, she was out on the field herself now, busy with all sorts of responsibilities. She had no time to come in here and hold my hand. Friends of mine who might have offered comfort—Eddie, Meredith, and others—were wrapped up in their own fears. I was alone.

Without her or Dimitri—or, well, anyone—I felt a surprising ache of loneliness flow through me. This wasn't right. I shouldn't have been alone. Dimitri should have been here with me. That's how it was supposed to have been. Closing my eyes, I allowed myself to pretend he was really there, only inches away as we spoke.

"Don't worry, comrade. I can do this blindfolded. Hell, maybe I actually will. Do you have anything I can use? If you're nice to me, I'll even let you tie it on." Since this fantasy would have taken place after we'd slept together, there was a strong possibility that he would have later helped me take off that blindfold—among other things.

I could perfectly picture the exasperated shake of his head that would earn me. "Rose, I swear, sometimes it feels like every day with you is my own personal trial."

But I knew he'd smile anyway, and the look of pride and encouragement he'd give me as I headed toward the field would be all I needed to get through the tests—

"Are you meditating?"

I opened my eyes, astonished at the voice. "Mom? What are you doing here?"

My mother, Janine Hathaway, stood in front of me. She was just a few inches shorter than me but had enough fight in her for someone twice my size. The dangerous look on her tanned face dared anyone to bring on a challenge. She gave me a wry smile and put one hand on her hip.

"Did you honestly think I wouldn't come to watch you?"

"I don't know," I admitted, feeling kind of guilty for doubting her. She and I hadn't had much contact over the years, and it was only recent events—most of them bad—that had begun to reestablish our connection. Most of the time, I still didn't know how to feel about her. I oscillated between a little girl's need for her absent mother and a teenager's resentment over abandonment. I also wasn't entirely sure if I'd forgiven her for the time she "accidentally" punched me in a mock fight. "I figured you'd have, you know, more important things to do."

"There's no way I could miss this." She inclined her head toward the stands, making her auburn curls sway. "Neither could your father."

"*What?*"

I hurried toward the doorway and peered out onto the fields. My view of the stands wasn't fantastic, thanks to all the obstacles on the field, but it was good enough. There he was: Abe Mazur. He was easy to spot, with his black beard and mustache, as well as the emerald green scarf knotted over his dress shirt. I could even barely make out the glint of his gold earring. He had to be melting in this heat, but I figured it would take more than a little sweat for him to tame down his flashy fashion sense.

If my relationship with my mother was sketchy, my relationship with my father was practically nonexistent. I'd met him back in May, and even then, it wasn't until after I'd gotten back that I found out I was his daughter. All dhampirs had one Moroi parent, and he was mine. I still wasn't sure how I felt about him. Most of his background remained a mystery, but there were plenty of rumors that he was involved with illegal business. People also acted like he was the kneecap-breaking type, and though I'd seen little evidence of this, I didn't find it surprising. In Russia, they called him Zmey: the serpent.

While I stared at him in astonishment, my mom strolled over to my side. "He'll be happy you made it in time," she said. "He's running some big wager on whether you'd show. He put his money on you, if that makes you feel any better."

I groaned. "Of course. Of course he'd be the bookie behind the pool. I should have known as soon as—" My jaw dropped. "Is he talking to Adrian?"

Yup. Sitting beside Abe was Adrian Ivashkov—my more-or-less boyfriend. Adrian was a royal Moroi—and another spirit user like Lissa. He'd been crazy about me (and often just crazy) ever since we first met, but I'd had eyes only for Dimitri. After the failure in Russia, I'd returned and promised to give Adrian a shot. To my surprise, things had been . . . good between us. Great, even. He'd written me up a proposal of why dating him was a sound decision. It had included things like "I'll give up cigarettes unless I really, *really* need one" and "I'll unleash romantic surprises every week, such as: an impromptu picnic, roses, or a trip to Paris—but not actually any of those things because now they're not surprises."

Being with him wasn't like it had been with Dimitri, but then, I supposed, no two relationships could ever be exactly alike. They were different men, after all. I still woke up all the time, aching over the loss of Dimitri and our love. I tormented myself over my failure to kill him in Siberia and free him from his undead state. Still, that despair didn't mean my romantic life was over—something it had taken me a while to accept. Moving on was hard, but Adrian did make me happy. And for now, that was enough.

But that didn't necessarily mean I wanted him cozying up to my pirate mobster father either.

"He's a bad influence!" I protested.

My mother snorted. "I doubt Adrian will influence Abe that much."

"Not Adrian! *Abe*. Adrian's trying to be on good behavior. Abe will mess everything up." Along with smoking, Adrian had sworn he'd quit drinking and other vices in his dating proposal. I squinted at him and Abe across the crowded stands, trying to figure out what topic could be so interesting. "What are they talking about?"

"I think that's the least of your problems right now." Janine Hathaway was nothing if not practical. "Worry less about them and more about that field."

"Do you think they're talking about *me*?"

"Rose!" My mother gave me a light punch on the arm, and I dragged my eyes back to her. "You have to take this seriously. Keep calm, and don't get distracted."

Her words were so like what I'd imagined Dimitri saying that a small smile crept onto my face. I wasn't alone out here after all.

"What's so funny?" she asked warily.

"Nothing," I said, giving her a hug. She was stiff at first and then relaxed, actually hugging me back briefly before stepping away. "I'm glad you're here."

My mother wasn't the overly affectionate type, and I'd caught her off guard. "Well," she said, obviously flustered, "I told you I wouldn't miss this."

I glanced back at the stands. "Abe, on the other hand, I'm not so sure of."

Or . . . wait. An odd idea came to me. No, not so odd, actually. Shady or not, Abe had connections—ones extensive enough to slip a message to Victor Dashkov in prison. Abe had been the one to ask for info about Robert Doru, Victor's spirit-wielding brother, as a favor to me. When Victor had sent back the message saying he had no reason to help Abe with what he needed, I'd promptly written off my father's assistance and jumped to my prison-break idea. But now—

"Rosemarie Hathaway!"

It was Alberta who called me, her voice ringing loud and clear. It was like a trumpet, a call to battle. All thoughts of Abe and Adrian—and yes, even Dimitri—vanished from my mind. I think my mother wished me good luck, but the exact wording was lost on me as I strode toward Alberta and the field. Adrenaline surged through me. All my attention was now on what lay ahead: the test that would finally make me a guardian.

TWO

MY TRIALS WERE A BLUR.

You'd think, seeing as they were the most important part of my education at St. Vladimir's, that I'd remember everything in perfect, crystalline detail. Yet my earlier thoughts were kind of realized. How could these measure up to what I'd already faced? How could these mock fights compare to a mob of Strigoi descending on our school? I'd had to stand against overwhelming odds, not knowing if those I loved were alive or dead. And how could I fear a so-called battle with one of the school's instructors after having fought Dimitri? He'd been lethal as a dhampir and worse as a Strigoi.

Not that I meant to make light of the trials. They were serious. Novices failed them all the time, and I refused to be one of them. I was attacked on all sides, by guardians who'd been fighting and defending Moroi since before I was born. The arena wasn't flat, which complicated everything. They'd filled it with contraptions and obstacles, beams and steps that tested my balance—including a bridge that painfully reminded me of that last night I'd seen Dimitri. I'd pushed him after plunging a silver stake into his heart—a stake that had fallen out during his plummet to the river below.

The arena's bridge was a bit different from the solid wooden one upon which Dimitri and I had fought in Siberia. This one was rickety, a badly constructed path of wooden planks with only rope rails for support. Every step made the entire bridge swing and shake, and holes in the boards showed me where former classmates had (unfortunately for them) discovered weak spots. The test they assigned me on the bridge was probably the worst of all. My goal was to get a "Moroi" away from a group of "Strigoi" that were in pursuit. My Moroi was being played by Daniel, a new guardian who had come with others to the school to replace those killed in the attack. I didn't know him very well, but for this exercise, he was playing completely docile and helpless—even a little afraid, just as any Moroi I was guarding might have been.

He gave me a little resistance about stepping onto the bridge, and I used my calmest, most coaxing voice to finally get him to walk out ahead of me. Apparently they were testing people skills as well as combat skills. Not far behind us on the course, I knew the guardians acting as Strigoi were approaching.

Daniel stepped out, and I shadowed him, still giving him reassurances while all my senses stayed on alert. The bridge swung wildly, telling me with a jolt that our pursuers had joined us. I glanced back and saw three "Strigoi" coming after us. The guardians playing them were doing a remarkable job—moving with as much dexterity and speed as true Strigoi would. They were going to overtake us if we didn't get a move on.

"You're doing great," I told Daniel. It was hard to keep the right tone in my voice. Screaming at Moroi might put them into shock. Too much gentleness would make them think it wasn't serious. "And I know you can move faster. We need to keep ahead of them—they're getting closer. I know you can do this. *Come on.*"

I must have passed that persuasive part of the test because he did indeed pick up his speed—not quite enough to match that of our pursuers, but it was a start. The bridge shifted crazily again. Daniel yelped convincingly and froze, gripping the rope sides tightly. Ahead of him, I saw another guardian-as-Strigoi waiting on the opposite side of the bridge. I believed his name was Randall, another new instructor. I was sandwiched between him and the group at my back. But Randall stayed still, waiting on the first plank of the bridge so that he could shake it and make it harder for us.

"Keep going," I urged, my mind spinning. "You can do it."

"But there's a Strigoi there! We're trapped," Daniel exclaimed.

"Don't worry. I'll deal with him. Just move."

My voice was fierce this time, and Daniel crept forward, pushed on by my command. The next few moments required perfect timing on my part. I had to watch the "Strigoi" on both sides of us and keep Daniel in motion, all the while monitoring where we were on the bridge. When we were almost three quarters of the way across, I hissed, "Drop down on all fours right now! Hurry!"

He obeyed, coming to a halt. I immediately knelt, still speaking in an undertone: "I'm about to shout at you. Ignore it." In a louder voice, for the benefit of those coming after us, I exclaimed, "What are you doing? We can't stop!"

Daniel didn't budge, and I again spoke softly. "Good. See where the ropes connect the base to the rails? Grab them. Grab them as tightly as you can, and do *not* let go, no matter what happens. Wrap them around your hands if you have to. Do it now!"

He obeyed. The clock was ticking, and I didn't waste another moment. In one motion, while still crouched, I turned around and hacked at the ropes with a knife I'd been given along with my stake. The blade was sharp, thank God. The guardians running the trial weren't messing around. It didn't instantly slice the ropes, but I cut through them so quickly that the "Strigoi" on either side of us didn't have time to react.

The ropes snapped just as I again reminded Daniel to hold on. The two halves of the bridge swung toward the sides of wooden scaffolding, carried by the weight of the people on them. Well, ours did at least. Daniel and I had been prepared. The three pursuers behind us hadn't been. Two fell. One just barely managed to catch hold of a plank, slipping a bit before securing his grip. The actual drop was six feet, but I'd been told to regard it as fifty—a distance that would kill me and Daniel if we fell.

Against all odds, he was still clutching the rope. I was hanging on as well, and once the rope and wood were lying flat against the scaffolding's sides, I began scrambling up it like a ladder. It wasn't easy climbing over Daniel, but I did it, giving me one more chance to tell him to hang on. Randall, who'd been waiting ahead of us, hadn't fallen off. He'd had his feet on the bridge when I cut it, though, and had been surprised enough to lose his balance. Quick to recover, he was now shimmying up the ropes, trying to climb up to the solid surface above. He was much closer to it than me, but I just managed to grab his leg and stop him. I jerked him toward me. He maintained his grip on the bridge, and we struggled. I knew I probably couldn't pull him off, but I was able to keep getting closer. At last, I let go of the knife I'd been holding and managed to get the stake from my belt—something that tested my balance. Randall's ungainly position gave me a shot at his heart, and I took it.

For the trials, we had blunt-ended stakes, ones that wouldn't pierce skin but which could be used with enough force to convince our opponents that we knew what we were doing. My alignment was perfect, and Randall, conceding it would have been a killing blow, relinquished his hold and dropped off the bridge.

That left me the painful task of coaxing Daniel to climb up. It took a long time, but again, his behavior wasn't out of character with how a scared Moroi might behave. I was just grateful he hadn't decided a real Moroi would have lost his grip and fallen.

After that challenge came many more, but I fought on, never slowing down or letting exhaustion affect me. I slipped into battle mode, my senses focused on basic instincts: *fight, dodge, kill.*

And while staying tuned to those, I still had to be innovative and not fall into a lull. Otherwise, I wouldn't be able to react to a surprise like the bridge. I managed it all, battling on with no other thoughts beyond accomplishing the tasks before me. I tried not to think of my instructors as people I knew. I treated them like Strigoi. I pulled no punches.

When it finally ended, I almost didn't realize it. I was simply standing there in the middle of the field with no more attackers coming at me. I was alone. Slowly, I became more aware of the world's details. Crowds in the stands cheering. A few instructors nodding to each other as they joined in. The pounding of my own heart.

It wasn't until a grinning Alberta tugged at my arm that I realized it was over. The test I'd waited for my entire life, finished in what felt like a blink of an eye.

"Come on," she said, wrapping her arm around my shoulder and guiding me toward the exit. "You need to get some water and sit down."

Dazed, I let her lead me off the field, around which people were still cheering and crying my name. Behind us, I heard some people saying they had to take a break and fix the bridge. She led me back to the waiting area and gently pushed me onto a bench. Someone else sat beside me and handed me a bottle of water. I looked over and saw my mother. She had an expression on her face that I had never seen before: pure, radiant pride.

"That was it?" I asked at last.

She surprised me again with genuinely amused laughter. "That was it?" she repeated. "Rose, you were out there for almost an hour. You blew through that test with flying colors—probably one of the best trials this school's ever seen."

"Really? It just seemed . . ." *Easy* wasn't quite the right word. "It was a haze, that's all."

My mom squeezed my hand. "You were amazing. I'm so, so proud of you."

The realization of it all truly, truly hit me then, and I felt a smile of my own spreading over my lips. "Now what happens?" I asked.

"Now you become a guardian."

I'd been tattooed many times, but none of those events came close to the ceremony and fanfare that occurred while getting my promise mark. Before, I'd received *molnija* marks for kills I'd made in unexpected, tragic circumstances: fighting Strigoi in Spokane, the school attack and rescue—events that were cause for mourning, not celebration. After all those kills, we'd kind of lost count, and while guardian tattoo artists still tried to log every individual kill, they'd finally given me a star-shaped mark that was a fancy way of saying we'd lost count.

Tattooing isn't a fast process, even if you're getting a small one, and my entire graduating class had to get them. The ceremony took place in what was usually the Academy's dining room, a room they were able to remarkably transform into something as grand and elaborate as we'd find at the Royal Court. Spectators—friends, family, guardians—packed the room as Alberta called our names one at a time and read our scores as we approached the tattoo artist. The scores were important. They would be made public and, along with our overall school grades, influence our assignments. Moroi could request certain grads for their guardians. Lissa had requested me, of course, but even the best scores in the world might not compensate for all the black behavioral marks on my record.

There were no Moroi at this ceremony, though, aside from the handful who had been invited as guests by the new graduates. Everyone else gathered was a dhampir: either one of the established guardians or about-to-become-guardians like me. The guests sat in the back, and the senior guardians sat near the front. My classmates and I stood the whole time, maybe as some sort of last test of endurance.

I didn't mind. I'd changed out of my torn and dirty clothes into simple slacks and a sweater, an outfit that seemed dressy while still retaining a solemn feel. It was a good call because the air in the room was thick with tension, all faces a mix of joy at our success but also anxiety about our new and deadly role in the world. I watched with shining eyes as my friends were called up, surprised and impressed at many of the scores.

Eddie Castile, a close friend, got a particularly high score in one-on-one Moroi protection. I couldn't help a smile as I watched the tattooist give Eddie his mark. "I wonder how he got his Moroi over the bridge," I murmured in an undertone. Eddie was pretty resourceful.

Beside me, another friend of mine, Meredith, gave me a puzzled look. "What are you talking about?" Her voice was equally soft.

"When we were chased onto the bridge with a Moroi. Mine was Daniel." She still looked confused, and I elaborated. "And they put Strigoi on each side?"

"I crossed the bridge," she whispered, "but it was just me being chased. I took my Moroi through a maze."

A glare from a nearby classmate shut us up, and I hid my frown. Maybe I wasn't the only one who'd gone through the trial in a daze. Meredith had her facts screwed up.

When my name was called, I heard a few gasps as Alberta read my scores. I had the highest in the class by far. I was kind of glad she didn't read my academic grades. They would have totally taken away some of the glory of the rest of my performance. I'd always done well in my combat classes, but math and history . . . well, those were a bit lacking, particularly since I always seemed to be dropping in and out of school.

My hair was pulled tightly into a bun, with every stray wisp held with hairpins so that the artist would have nothing to interfere with his work. I leaned forward to give him a good view and heard him grunt in surprise. With the back of my neck covered in marks, he'd have to be tricky. Usually a new guardian provided a blank canvas. This guy was good, though, and managed to delicately place the promise mark in the center of the nape of my neck after all. The promise mark looked like a long, stretched-out *S*, with curly ends. He fit it in between the *molnija* marks, letting it wrap around them like an embrace. The process hurt, but I kept my face blank, refusing to flinch. I was shown the final results in a mirror before he covered it up with a bandage so it would heal cleanly.

After that, I rejoined my classmates and watched as the rest of them received their tattoos. It meant standing for another two hours, but I didn't mind. My brain was still reeling with everything that had happened today. I was a guardian. A real, honest-to-goodness guardian. And with that thought came questions. What would happen now? Would my scores be good enough to erase my record of bad behavior? Would I be Lissa's guardian? And what about Victor? What about Dimitri?

I shifted uneasily as the full impact of the guardian ceremony hit me. This wasn't just about Dimitri and Victor. This was about me—about the rest of my life. School was over. I would no longer have teachers tracking my every move or correcting me when I made mistakes. All decisions would be on me when I was out protecting someone. Moroi and younger dhampirs would look to me as the authority. And I would no longer have the luxury of practicing combat one minute and lounging in my room the next. There were no clear-cut classes anymore. I would be on duty all the time. The thought was daunting, the pressure almost too great. I'd always equated graduation with freedom. Now I wasn't so sure. What new shape was my life going to take? Who would decide? And how could I reach Victor if I was assigned to guard anyone besides Lissa?

Across the room, I met Lissa's eyes among the audience. They burned with a pride that matched my mother's, and she grinned when our gazes met.

Get that look off your face, she chastised through the bond. *You shouldn't look that anxious, not today. You need to celebrate.*

I knew she was right. I could handle what was to come.

My worries, which were many, could wait one more day—particularly since the exuberant mood of my friends and family ensured that I would celebrate. Abe, with that influence he always seemed to wield, had secured a small banquet room and thrown a party for me that seemed more suited to a royal debutante, not some lowly, reckless dhampir.

Before the event, I changed yet again. Prettier party clothes now seemed more appropriate than the formal *molnija* ceremony outfit. I put on a short-sleeved, emerald green wrap dress and hung my *nazar* around my neck, even though it didn't match. The *nazar* was a small pendant that looked like an eye, with different shades of blue circling it. In Turkey, where Abe came from, it was believed to offer protection. He'd given it to my mother years ago, and she'd in turn given it to me.

By the time I'd put on makeup and brushed out my tangled hair into long, dark waves (because my tattoo bandages didn't go with the dress *at all*), I hardly looked like someone capable of fighting monsters or even throwing a punch. No—that wasn't quite true, I realized a moment later. Staring into the mirror, I was surprised to see a haunted look in my brown eyes. There was pain there, pain and loss that even the nicest dress and makeup couldn't hide.

I ignored it and set off for the party, promptly running into Adrian as soon as I stepped outside my dorm. Without a word, he swept me into his arms and smothered me with a kiss. I was totally caught off guard. It figured. Undead creatures didn't surprise me, but one flippant royal Moroi could.

And it was quite the kiss, one that I almost felt guilty about sinking into. I'd had concerns when first dating Adrian, but many of them had disappeared over time. After watching him flirt shamelessly and take nothing seriously for so long, I'd never expected to see such devotion from him in our relationship. I also hadn't expected to find my feelings for him growing—which seemed so contradictory considering I still loved Dimitri and was concocting impossible ways to save him.

I laughed when Adrian set me down. Nearby, a few younger Moroi had stopped to watch us. Moroi dating dhampirs wasn't super uncommon at our age, but a notorious dhampir dating the Moroi queen's great-nephew? That was kind of out there—especially since it was widely known how much Queen Tatiana hated me. There had been few witnesses to my last meeting with her, when she'd screamed at me to stay away from Adrian, but word of that kind of thing always gets around.

"Like the show?" I asked our voyeurs. Realizing they'd been busted, the Moroi kids hastily continued on their way. I turned back to Adrian and smiled. "What was that? It was kind of a big kiss to throw on me in public."

"That," he said grandly, "was your reward for kicking so much ass in those trials." He paused. "It was also because you look totally hot in that dress."

I gave him a wry look. "Reward, huh? Meredith's boyfriend got her diamond earrings."

He caught hold of my hand and gave an unconcerned shrug as we began to walk to the party. "You want diamonds?

I'll give you diamonds. I'll shower you in them. Hell, I'll get you a gown made out of them. But it's going to be skimpy."

"I think I'll settle for the kiss after all," I said, imagining Adrian dressing me like a swimsuit model. Or a pole dancer. The jewelry reference also suddenly brought on an unwanted memory. When Dimitri had held me captive in Siberia, lulling me into blissful complacency with his bites, he'd showered me with jewelry too.

"I knew you were a badass," continued Adrian. A warm summer breeze ruffled the brown hair he so painstakingly styled each day, and with his free hand, he absentmindedly tried to arrange it back into place. "But I didn't realize just how much until I saw you dropping guardians out there."

"Does that mean you're going to be nicer to me?" I teased.

"I'm already nice to you," he said loftily. "Do you know how badly I want a cigarette right now? But no. I manfully suffer through nicotine withdrawal—all for you. But I think seeing you out there will make me a little more careful around you. That crazy dad of yours is kind of gonna make me cautious too."

I groaned, recalling how Adrian and Abe had been sitting together. "God. Did you really have to hang out with him?"

"Hey, he's awesome. A little unstable, but awesome. We got along great." Adrian opened the door to the building we were seeking. "And he's a badass in his way too. I mean, any other guy who wore scarves like that? He'd be laughed out of this school. Not Abe. He'd beat someone almost as badly as you would. In fact . . ." Adrian's voice turned nervous.

I gave him a surprised look.

"In fact what?"

"Well . . . Abe said he liked me. But he also made it clear what he'd do to me if I ever hurt you or did anything bad." Adrian grimaced. "In fact, he described what he'd do in very graphic detail. Then, just like that, he switched to some random, happy topic. I like the guy, but he's scary."

"He's out of line!" I came to a halt outside the party's room. Through the door, I heard the buzz of conversation. We were apparently among the last to arrive. I guessed that meant I'd be making a grand entrance fitting for the guest of honor. "He has no right to threaten my boyfriends. I'm eighteen. An adult. I don't need his help. I can threaten my boyfriends myself."

My indignation amused Adrian, and he gave me a lazy smile. "I agree with you. But that doesn't mean I'm not going to take his 'advice' seriously. My face is too pretty to risk."

His face *was* pretty, but that didn't stop me from shaking my head in exasperation. I reached for the door's handle, but Adrian pulled me back.

"Wait," he said.

He drew me into his arms again, our lips meeting in another hot kiss. My body pressed to his, and I found myself confused by my own feelings and the realization that I was reaching a point where I might want more than just kissing.

"Okay," said Adrian when we'd finally broken away. "*Now* we can go in."

He had that same light tone to his voice, but in his dark green eyes, I saw the kindling of passion. I wasn't the only one considering more than just kissing. So far, we'd avoided discussing sex, and he'd actually been very good about not pressuring me. I think he knew I just wasn't ready after Dimitri, but in moments like these, I could see just how difficult it was for Adrian to hold back.

It softened something inside of me, and standing on my tiptoes, I gave him another kiss. "What was that?" he asked a few moments later.

I grinned. "*Your* reward."

When we finally made it into the party, everyone in the room greeted me with cheers and proud smiles. A long time ago, I'd thrived on being the center of attention. That desire had faded a little, but now, I put on a confident face and accepted my loved ones' praise with swagger and happiness. I held up my hands triumphantly, earning more clapping and approval.

My party was almost as much of a blur as my trials. You never really realize how many people care about you until they all turn out to support you. It made me feel humble and *almost* a little teary. I kept that to myself, though. I could hardly start crying at my own victory party.

Everyone wanted to talk to me, and I was surprised and delighted each time some new person approached me. It wasn't often that I had all the people I loved best in one place, and, uneasily I realized this opportunity might never come again.

"Well, you've finally got a license to kill. It's about time."

I turned and met the amused eyes of Christian Ozera, a onetime annoyance who'd become a good friend. So good, in fact, that in my joyous zeal, I reached out and hugged him—something he clearly didn't expect. I was surprising everyone today.

"Whoa, whoa," he said backing up, flushing. "It figures. You're the only girl who'd get all emotional about the thought of killing. I don't even want to think about what goes on when you and Ivashkov are alone."

"Hey, look who's talking. You're itching to get out there yourself."

Christian shrugged by way of agreement. It was a standard rule in our world: Guardians protected Moroi. Moroi didn't get involved in battles. Yet after recent Strigoi attacks, a lot of Moroi—though hardly a majority—had begun to argue that it was time for Moroi to step up and start helping the guardians. Fire users like Christian were particularly valuable since burning was one of the best ways to kill a Strigoi (along with staking and decapitation). The movement to teach Moroi to fight was currently—and purposely—stalled in the Moroi government, but that hadn't stopped some Moroi from practicing in secret. Christian was one of them. Glancing beside him, I blinked in astonishment. There was someone with him, someone I'd hardly noticed.

Jill Mastrano hovered near him like a shadow. A Moroi freshman—well, soon to be a sophomore—Jill had come forward as someone who also wanted to fight. She had sort of become Christian's student.

"Hey Jill," I said, giving her a warm smile. "Thanks for coming."

Jill flushed. She was determined to learn to defend herself, but she grew flustered among others—particularly around "celebrities" like me. Rambling was her nervous reaction. "I had to," she said, brushing her long, light brown hair out of her face. Like always, it was a tangle of curls. "I mean, it's so cool what you did. At the trials. Everyone was amazed. I heard one of the guardians saying that they'd never seen anything like you, so when Christian asked if I wanted to come, *of course* I had to. Oh!" Her light green eyes went wide. "I didn't even tell you congratulations. Sorry. Congratulations."

Beside her, Christian struggled to keep a straight face. I made no such attempts and laughingly gave her a hug too. I was in serious danger of turning warm and fuzzy. I'd probably get my tough guardian status revoked if I kept this up. "Thanks. Are you two ready to take on a Strigoi army yet?"

"Soon," said Christian. "But we might need your backup." He knew as well as I did that Strigoi were way out of their league. His fire magic had helped me a lot, but on his own? That'd be a different story. He and Jill were teaching themselves to use magic offensively, and when I'd had time between classes, I'd taught them a few combat moves.

Jill's face fell a little. "It's going to stop once Christian's gone."

I turned to him. It was no surprise he'd be leaving. We'd *all* be leaving. "What are you going to do with yourself?" I asked.

He shrugged. "Go to Court with the rest of you. Aunt Tasha says we're going to have a 'talk' about my future." He grimaced. Whatever his plans were, it looked like they weren't the same as Tasha's. Most royal Moroi would head off to elite colleges. I wasn't sure what Christian had in mind.

It was standard practice after graduation for new guardians to go to the Moroi Royal Court for orientation and to get their assignments. We were all due to leave in a couple of days. Following Christian's gaze, I saw his aunt across the room, and so help me, she was talking to Abe.

Tasha Ozera was in her late twenties, with the same glossy black hair and ice blue eyes that Christian had. Her beautiful face was marred, however, by some terrible scarring on one side—the result of injuries inflicted by Christian's own parents. Dimitri had been turned into a Strigoi against his will, but the Ozeras had purposely chosen to turn for the sake of immortality. It had ironically cost them their lives when the guardians hunted them down. Tasha had raised Christian (when he wasn't at school) and was one of the main leaders in the movement supporting those Moroi who wanted to fight Strigoi.

Scar or not, I admired her and still thought she was beautiful. From my wayward father's attitude, it was clear he did too. He poured her a glass of champagne and said something that made her laugh. She leaned forward, like she was telling him a secret, and he laughed in return. My jaw dropped. Even from this far away, it was obvious they were flirting.

"Dear God," I said with a shudder, hastily turning back to Christian and Jill.

Christian seemed torn between smugness at my discomfort and his own unease at watching a woman he regarded as a mother get hit upon by a pirate mobster guy. A moment later, Christian's expression softened as he turned back to Jill and continued our conversation.

"Hey, you don't need me," he said. "You'll find others around here. You'll have your own superhero club before you know it."

I found myself smiling again, but my kindly feelings were suddenly shattered by a jolt of jealousy. It wasn't my own, though. It was Lissa's, coming through the bond. Startled, I glanced around and spotted her across the room, giving Christian the look of death as he spoke to Jill.

It's worth mentioning that Christian and Lissa used to date. More than date. They'd been deeply in love, and honestly, they kind of still were. Unfortunately, recent events had badly strained their relationship, and Christian had broken up with her. He'd loved her but had lost his trust in her. Lissa had spun out of control when another spirit user named Avery Lazar had sought to control her. We'd eventually stopped Avery, and she was currently locked away in a mental institution, last I'd heard. Christian now knew the reasons for Lissa's horrible behavior, but the damage was done. Lissa had initially been depressed, but her sorrow had now turned to anger.

She claimed she wanted nothing to do with him anymore, but the bond gave her away. She was always jealous of any girl he talked to—particularly Jill, whom he'd been spending a lot of time with lately. I knew for a fact there was nothing romantic going on there. Jill idolized him as some wise teacher, nothing more. If she had a crush on anyone, it was Adrian, who always treated her like a kid sister. We all kind of did, really.

Christian followed my gaze, and his expression hardened. Realizing she had his attention, Lissa immediately turned away and began talking to the first guy she found, a good-looking dhampir from my class. She turned on the flirtatious charm that came so easily to spirit users, and soon, both of them were laughing and chatting in a way similar to Abe and Tasha. My party had turned into a round of speed dating.

Christian turned back to me. "Well, looks like she's got plenty to keep her busy."

I rolled my eyes. Lissa wasn't the only one who was jealous. Just as she grew angry whenever he hung out with other girls, Christian became prickly when she spoke to other guys. It was infuriating. Rather than admit they still had feelings and just needed to patch things up, those two idiots just kept displaying more and more hostility toward each other.

"Will you stop already and actually try to talk to her like a rational person someday?" I groaned.

"Sure," he said bitterly. "The day *she* starts acting like a rational person."

"Oh my God. You guys are going to make me rip my hair out."

"It'd be a waste of nice hair," said Christian. "Besides, she's made her attitude perfectly clear."

I started to protest and tell him how stupid he was, but he had no intention of sticking around to hear a lecture I'd already given a dozen times.

"Come on, Jill," he said. "Rose needs to mingle more."

He quickly stepped away, and I had half a mind to go beat some sense into him when a new voice spoke.

"When are you going to fix that?" Tasha was standing next to me, shaking her head at Christian's retreat. "Those two need to be back together."

"I know that. You know that. But they can't seem to get it through their heads."

"Well, you'd better get on it," she said. "If Christian goes to college across the country, it'll be too late." There was a dry—and exasperated—note in her voice when she mentioned Christian going to college.

Lissa was going to Lehigh, a university near the Court, per an arrangement with Tatiana. Lissa would get to attend a bigger university than Moroi usually went to, in exchange for spending time at the Court and learning the royal trade.

"I know," I said in exasperation. "But why am *I* the one who has to fix it?"

Tasha grinned. "Because you're the only one forceful enough to make them see reason."

I decided to let Tasha's insolence go, mostly because her talking to me meant that she wasn't talking to Abe. Glancing across the room, I suddenly stiffened. He was now talking to *my mother*. Snatches of their conversation came to me through the noise.

"Janine," he said winningly, "you haven't aged a day. You could be Rose's sister. Do you remember that night in Cappadocia?"

My mother actually giggled. I had never heard her do that before. I decided I never wanted to again. "Of course. And

I remember how eager you were to help me when my dress strap broke."

"Dear God," I said. "He's unstoppable."

Tasha looked puzzled until she saw what I was talking about. "Abe? He's actually pretty charming."

I groaned. "Excuse me."

I headed toward my parents. I accepted that they'd once had a romance—one that led to my conception—but that didn't mean I wanted to watch them relive it. They were recounting some walk on the beach when I reached them. I promptly tugged Abe's arm away. He was standing way too close to her.

"Hey, can I talk to you?" I asked.

He looked surprised but shrugged. "Certainly." He gave my mother a knowing smile. "We'll talk more later."

"Is no woman safe around here?" I demanded as I led him away.

"What are you talking about?"

We came to a stop by the punch bowl. "You're flirting with every woman in this room!"

My chastising didn't faze him. "Well, there are so many lovely women here. . . . Is that what you wanted to talk to me about?"

"No! I wanted to talk to you about threatening my boyfriend. You had no right to do that."

His dark eyebrows shot up. "What, that? That was nothing. Just a father looking out for his daughter."

"Most fathers don't threaten to disembowel their daughters' boyfriends."

"That's not true. And anyway, that's not what I actually said. It was much worse."

I sighed. He seemed to delight in my exasperation.

"Think of it as a graduation gift. I'm proud of you. Everyone knew you'd be good, but no one knew you'd be *that* good." He winked. "They certainly didn't expect you to destroy their property."

"What property?"

"The bridge."

I frowned. "I had to. It was the most efficient way. God, that was a bitch of a challenge. What'd the other grads do? They didn't actually fight in the middle of that thing, did they?"

Abe shook his head, loving every minute of his superior knowledge. "No one else was put in that situation."

"Of course they were. We all face the same tests."

"Not you. While planning the trials, the guardians decided you needed something . . . extra. Something special. After all, you'd been out fighting in the real world."

"What?" The volume of my voice caught the attention of a few others. I lowered it, and Meredith's earlier words came back to me. "That's not fair!"

He didn't seem concerned. "You're superior to the others. Making you do easy things wouldn't have been fair."

I'd faced a lot of ridiculous things in my life, but this was pretty out there. "So they had me do that crazy bridge stunt instead? And if they were surprised I cut it, then what the hell else did they expect me to do? How else was I supposed to survive that?"

"Hmm." He stroked his chin absentmindedly. "I honestly don't think they knew."

"Oh, for God's sake. This is unbelievable."

"Why are you so mad? You passed."

"Because they put me in a situation they didn't even know how to get out of." I gave him a suspicious look. "And how do you even know about this? This is all guardian business."

An expression I didn't like at all came over his face. "Ah, well, I was with your mother last night and—"

"Whoa, okay. Just stop," I interrupted. "I do not want to hear what you and my mother were doing last night. I think that'd be worse than the bridge."

He grinned. "Both are in the past, so no need to worry now. Enjoy your success."

"I'll try. Just don't do me any more favors with Adrian, okay? I mean, I'm glad you came to support me, but that's more than enough."

Abe gave me a canny look, reminding me that underneath that swagger he was indeed a shrewd and dangerous man. "You were more than happy to have me do you a favor after your return from Russia."

I grimaced. He had a point, seeing as he *had* managed to get a message into a high-security prison. Even if it hadn't led to anything, he still got points.

"Okay," I admitted. "That was pretty amazing. And I'm grateful. I still don't know how you pulled that off." Suddenly, like a dream you recall a day later, I remembered the thought I'd had just before my trials. I lowered my voice. "You didn't actually go there, did you?"

He snorted. "Of course not. I wouldn't set foot in that place. I simply worked my network."

"Where *is* that place?" I asked, hoping I sounded bland.

He wasn't fooled. "Why do you want to know?"

"Because I'm curious! Convicted criminals always disappear without a trace. I'm a guardian now, and I don't even know anything about our own prison system. Is there just one prison? Are there lots?"

Abe didn't answer right away. He was studying me carefully. In his business, he suspected everyone of ulterior motives. As his daughter, I was probably doubly suspect. It was in the genes.

He must have underestimated my potential for insanity because he said at last, "There's more than one. Victor's in one of the worst. It's called Tarasov."

"Where is it?"

"Right now?" He considered. "In Alaska, I think."

"What do you mean, 'right now'?"

"It moves throughout the year. Right now it's in Alaska. Later, it'll be in Argentina." He gave me a sly smile, apparently wondering how astute I was. "Can you guess why?"

"No, I—wait. Sunlight." It made perfect sense. "Alaska's got almost nonstop daylight this time of year—but nonstop night in the winter."

I think he was prouder of my realization than of my trials. "Any prisoners trying to escape would have a hard time." In full sun, no Moroi fugitive would get very far. "Not that anyone can escape through that level of security anyway." I tried to ignore how foreboding that sounded.

"Seems like they'd put it pretty far north in Alaska then," I said, hoping to worm out the actual location indirectly. "You get more light that way."

He chuckled. "Even I can't tell you that. That's information the guardians keep close, buried in their headquarters."

I froze. *Headquarters . . .*

Abe, despite being usually observant, didn't notice my reaction. His eyes were watching something across the room. "Is that Renee Szelsky? My, my . . . she's grown lovely over the years."

I grudgingly waved him away, largely because I wanted to chase this new plan in my mind—and because Renee wasn't anyone I knew very well, which made him hitting on her less appalling. "Well, don't let me stop you. Go lure more women into your web."

Abe didn't need much prodding. Alone, I let my brain spin, wondering if my developing scheme had any chance of success. His words had sparked a new plan in my mind. It wasn't much crazier than most of my others. Across the room, I met Lissa's jade eyes again. With Christian out of sight, her mood had improved. She was enjoying herself and was excited about the adventures ahead of us, now that we were free and out in the world. My mind flashed back to the anxieties I'd felt earlier in the day. We might be free now, but reality would catch up with us soon. The clock was ticking. Dimitri was waiting, watching. I wondered briefly if I'd still get his weekly letters, now that I'd be leaving the school.

I smiled at her, feeling kind of bad that I'd be ruining her mood when I told her we might now have a very real chance of busting out Victor Dashkov.

THREE

THE NEXT COUPLE OF DAYS were strange. The other novices and I might have had the flashiest graduation, but we weren't the only ones finishing our education at St. Vladimir's. The Moroi had their own commencement ceremony, and campus grew packed with visitors. Then, almost as quickly as they came, parents disappeared—taking their sons and daughters with them. Royal Moroi left to spend their summers with their parents at luxury estates—many in the Southern Hemisphere, where the days were shorter this time of year. "Ordinary" Moroi left with their parents too, off to more modest homes, possibly getting summer jobs before college.

And of course, with school wrapping up for the summer, all the other students left too. Some with no family to go home to, usually dhampirs, stayed year-round, taking special electives, but they were the minority. Campus grew emptier each day as my classmates and I waited for the day when we'd be taken to the Royal Court. We made our farewells to others, Moroi moving on or younger dhampirs who'd soon be following in our footsteps.

One person I was sad to part with was Jill. I happened to catch her as I was walking toward Lissa's dorm the day before my Court trip. There was a woman with Jill, presumably her mother, and both were carrying boxes. Jill's face lit up when she saw me.

"Hey Rose! I said goodbye to everyone else but couldn't find you," she said excitedly.

I smiled. "Well, I'm glad you caught me."

I couldn't tell her that I'd been saying goodbye too. I'd spent my last day at St. Vladimir's walking all the familiar sites, starting with the elementary campus where Lissa and I had first met in kindergarten. I'd explored the halls and corners of my dorms, walked past favorite classrooms, and even visited the chapel. I'd also passed a lot of time in areas filled with bittersweet memories, like the training areas where I'd first gotten to know Dimitri. The track where he used to make me run laps. The cabin where we'd finally given in to each other. It had been one of the most amazing nights of my life, and thinking about it always brought me both joy and pain.

Jill didn't need to be burdened with any of that, though. I turned toward her mother and started to offer my hand until I realized she couldn't shake it while maneuvering the box. "I'm Rose Hathaway. Here, let me carry that."

I took it before she could protest because I was certain she would. "Thank you," she said, pleasantly surprised. I fell in step with them as they began walking again. "I'm Emily Mastrano. Jill's told me a lot about you."

"Oh yeah?" I asked, giving Jill a teasing smile.

"Not that much. Just how I hang out with you sometimes." There was a slight warning in Jill's green eyes, and it occurred to me that Emily probably didn't know her daughter practiced forbidden forms of Strigoi-killing magic in her free time.

"We like having Jill around," I said, not blowing her cover. "And one of these days, we're going to teach her to tame that hair."

Emily laughed. "I've been trying for almost fifteen years. Good luck."

Jill's mother was stunning. The two didn't resemble each other much, at least not superficially. Emily's lustrous hair was straight and black, her eyes deep blue and long-lashed. She moved with a willowy grace, very different from Jill's always self-conscious walk. Yet, I could see the shared genes here and there, the heart-shaped faces and lip shapes. Jill was still young, and as she grew into her features, she'd likely be a heartbreaker herself someday—something she was probably oblivious to right now. Hopefully her self-confidence would grow.

"Where's home for you guys?" I asked.

"Detroit," said Jill, making a face.

"It's not that bad," laughed her mom.

"There are no mountains. Just highways."

"I'm part of a ballet company there," Emily explained. "So we stay where we can pay the bills." I think I was more surprised that people went to the ballet in Detroit than that Emily was a ballerina. It made sense, watching her, and really, with their tall and slim builds, Moroi were ideal dancers as far as humans were concerned.

"Hey, it's a big city," I told Jill. "Enjoy the excitement while you can before you come back to the boring middle of nowhere." Of course, illicit combat training and Strigoi attacks were hardly boring, but I wanted to make Jill feel better. "And it won't be that long." Moroi summer vacations were barely two months. Parents were eager to return their children to the safety of the Academy.

"I guess," said Jill, not sounding convinced. We reached their car, and I loaded the boxes into the trunk.

"I'll e-mail you when I can," I promised. "And I bet Christian will too. Maybe I can even talk Adrian into it."

Jill brightened, and I was happy to see her return to her normal overexcited self. "Really? That would be great. I want to hear everything that goes on at Court. You'll probably get to do all sorts of cool things with Lissa and Adrian, and I bet Christian will find out all sorts of things . . . about things."

Emily didn't seem to notice Jill's lame editing attempt and instead fixed me with a pretty smile. "Thanks for your help, Rose. It was great to meet you."

"You too—umph!"

Jill had thrown herself into me with a hug. "Good luck with everything," she said. "You're so lucky—you're going to have such a great life now!"

I returned the hug, unable to explain how jealous of her I was. Her life was still safe and innocent. She might resent spending a summer in Detroit, but the stay would be brief, and soon she'd be back in the familiar and easy world of St. Vladimir's. She wouldn't be setting out into the unknown and its dangers.

It was only after she and her mother had driven off that I

could bring myself to respond to her comment. "I hope so," I murmured, thinking about what was to come. "I hope so."

My classmates and select Moroi flew out early the next day, leaving the rocky mountains of Montana behind for the rolling hills of Pennsylvania. The Royal Court was a lot like I remembered, with the same imposing, ancient feel that St. Vladimir's tried to impart with its towering buildings and intricate stone architecture. But the school also seemed to want to show off a wise, studious air, whereas the Court was more ostentatious. It was like the buildings themselves tried to make sure we all knew that this was the seat of power and royalty among the Moroi. The Royal Court wanted us to be amazed and maybe a little cowed.

And even though I'd been here before, I was still impressed. The doors and windows of the tan stone buildings were embossed and framed in pristine golden decorations. They were a far cry from the brightness I'd seen in Russia, but I realized now that the Court's designers had modeled these buildings off the old European ones—the fortresses and palaces of Saint Petersburg. St. Vladimir's had benches and paths in the quads and courtyards, but the Court went a step further. Fountains and elaborate statues of past rulers adorned the lawns, exquisite marble works that had previously been hidden in snow. Now, in the full throes of summer, they were bright and on display. And everywhere, everywhere were flowers on trees, bushes, paths—it was dazzling.

It made sense that new grads would visit the guardians'

central administration, but it occurred to me that there was another reason they brought new guardians here in the summer. They wanted my classmates and me to see all of this, to be overwhelmed and appreciative of the glory for which we were fighting. Looking at the faces of the new graduates, I knew the tactic was working. Most had never been here before.

Lissa and Adrian had been on my flight, and the three of us clustered together as we walked with the group. It was as warm as it had been in Montana, but the humidity here was much thicker. I was sweating after only a little light walking.

"You *did* bring a dress this time, right?" asked Adrian.

"Of course," I said. "They've got some fancy things they want us to go to, aside from the main reception. Although, they might give me my black-and-white for that."

He shook his head, and I noticed his hand start to move toward his pocket before hesitating and pulling back. He might have been making progress in quitting smoking, but I was pretty sure the subconscious urge to automatically reach for a pack when outdoors was hard to get rid of so quickly.

"I mean for tonight. For dinner."

I glanced questioningly at Lissa. Her schedule at Court always had assorted functions thrown into it that "average people" didn't attend. With my new and uncertain status, I wasn't sure if I'd be going with her. I sensed her puzzlement through the bond and could tell that she didn't have a clue about any special dinner plans.

"What dinner?" I asked.

"The one I set up with my family."

"The one you—" I came to an abrupt halt and stared wide-eyed, not liking the smirk on his face one bit. "Adrian!" A few of the new grads gave me curious looks and continued walking around us.

"Come on, we've been going out a couple months. Meeting parents is part of the dating ritual. I've met your mom. I even met your scary-ass dad. Now it's your turn. I guarantee none of my family's gonna make the kind of suggestions your dad did."

I'd actually kind of met Adrian's dad before. Or, well, I'd seen him at a party. I doubted he had any idea who I was—my crazy reputation aside. I knew almost nothing about Adrian's mother. He actually spoke very little about his family members—well, most of them.

"*Just* your parents?" I asked warily. "Any other family I should know about?"

"Well . . ." Adrian's hand twitched again. I think this time he wanted a cigarette as some sort of protection from the warning note in my voice. Lissa, I observed, seemed highly amused by all of this. "My favorite great-aunt might stop by."

"Tatiana?" I exclaimed. For the hundredth time, I wondered how I had lucked out with a guy related to the leader of the entire Moroi world. "She hates me! You know what happened the last time we talked." Her Royal Majesty had laid into me, yelling about how I was too trashy to hook up with her nephew and how she had great "plans" for him and Lissa.

"I think she's come around."

"Oh, come *on*."

"No, really." He almost looked like he was telling the truth. "I talked to my mom the other day, and . . . I don't know. Aunt Tatiana doesn't seem to hate you as much."

I frowned, and the three of us began to walk again. "Maybe she admires your recent vigilante work," mused Lissa.

"Maybe," I said. But I didn't really believe it. If anything, me going rogue should have made me more despicable in the queen's eyes.

I felt kind of betrayed that Adrian had sprung this dinner on me, but there was nothing to be done about it now. The only bright side was that I had the impression he was teasing me about his aunt stopping by. I told him I'd go, and my decision put him in a good enough mood that he didn't ask too many questions when Lissa and I said we were going to do "our own thing" that afternoon. My classmates were all getting a tour of the Court and its grounds as part of their indoctrination, but I'd seen it all before and was able to wiggle out of it. Lissa and I dropped our belongings off in our rooms and then set out to the far side of the Court, where the not-so-royal people lived.

"Are you going to tell me yet what this *other* part of your plan is?" asked Lissa.

Ever since Abe had explained about Victor's prison, I'd been making another mental list of the problems we'd have breaking into it. Mainly, there were two, which was one less than I'd initially had since talking to Abe. Not that things were really much easier. First, we had no clue *where* in Alaska this place was. Second, we didn't know what the prison's defenses and layout were like. We had no idea what we had to bust through.

Yet, something told me all of these answers could be found in one source, which meant I really only had one immediate problem: how to reach that source. Fortunately, I knew someone who might be able to help get us there.

"We're going to see Mia," I told her.

Mia Rinaldi was a former Moroi classmate of ours—a former enemy, actually. She was also the poster child for total personality makeovers. She'd gone from a scheming bitch who was willing to crush—and sleep with—anyone in her quest for popularity to a down-to-earth, confident girl eager to learn to defend herself and others from Strigoi. She lived here at Court with her father.

"You think Mia knows how to break into a prison?"

"Mia's good, but I don't think she's that good. She can probably help us get intel, though."

Lissa groaned. "I can't believe you just used the word *intel*. This really is turning into a spy movie." She spoke flippantly, but I could feel the worry within her. The light tone was masking her fear, the unease she still felt about freeing Victor, despite her promise to me.

Those non-royals who worked and did ordinary things at Court lived in apartments far from the queen's quarters and receiving hall. I'd gotten Mia's address in advance, and we set out across the perfectly manicured grounds, grumbling to each other along the way about the hot day. We found her at home, casually dressed in jeans and a T-shirt with a Popsicle in her hand. Her eyes widened when she saw us outside her door.

"Well, I'll be damned," she said.

I laughed. It was the kind of response I'd give. "Nice to see you too. Can we come in?"

"Of course." She stepped aside. "You want a Popsicle?"

Did I ever. I took a grape one and sat with her and Lissa in the small living room. The place was a far cry from the opulence of royal guest housing, but it was cozy and clean and undoubtedly well loved by Mia and her father.

"I knew the grads were coming," Mia said, brushing blond curls out of her face. "But I wasn't sure if you were with them or not. Did you even graduate?"

"I did," I said. "Got the promise mark and everything." I lifted my hair so she could see the bandage.

"I'm surprised they let you back in after you took off on your killing spree. Or did you get extra credit for that?"

Apparently, Mia had heard the same tall tale about my adventures that everyone else had. That was fine with me. I didn't want to talk about the truth. I didn't want to talk about Dimitri.

"Do you think anyone could stop Rose from doing what she wants?" asked Lissa with a smile. She was trying to keep us from getting into too much detail about my past whereabouts, for which I was grateful.

Mia laughed and crunched on a big chunk of lime ice. It was a wonder she didn't get brain freeze. "True." Her smile faded as she swallowed the bite. Her blue eyes, always shrewd, studied me in silence for a few moments. "And Rose wants something now."

"Hey, we're just happy to see you," I said.

"I believe you. But I also believe you've got an ulterior motive."

Lissa's smile grew. She was amused by me being caught in my spy game. "What makes you say that? Can you read Rose that well or do you just *always* assume she's got an ulterior motive?"

Now Mia smiled again. "Both." She scooted forward on the couch, fixing me with a serious look. When had she grown so perceptive? "Okay. No point in wasting time. What do you need my help with?"

I sighed, busted. "I need to get inside the guardians' main security office."

Beside me, Lissa made a sort of strangled noise. I felt kind of bad for her. While she could conceal her thoughts from me on occasion, there wasn't much she did or said that came as a true surprise. Me? I continually blindsided her. She had no clue what was coming half the time, but honestly, if we were planning on springing a renowned criminal out of prison, then breaking into a security office shouldn't have been that big of a shock.

"Wow," said Mia. "You don't waste time with the little stuff." Her grin twitched a bit. "Of course, you wouldn't come to me with little stuff. You could do that yourself."

"Can you get me—us—in there?" I asked. "You're friendly with some of the guardians here . . . and your dad has access to a lot of places. . . ." I didn't know Mr. Rinaldi's exact job, but I thought it was maintenance-related.

"What are you looking for?" she asked. She held up a

hand when I opened my mouth to protest. "No, no. I don't need details. Just a general idea so I can figure this out. I know you're not going there just to tour the place."

"I need some records," I explained.

Her eyebrows rose. "Personnel? Trying to get yourself a job?"

"I—no." Huh. That wasn't a bad idea, considering my precarious position with being assigned to Lissa. But no. One issue at a time. "I need some records about outside security at other places—schools, royal homes, prisons." I tried to keep my expression casual as I mentioned that last one. Mia was on board with some crazy things, but even she had her limits. "I figured they must keep that stuff there?"

"They do," she said. "But most of it's electronic. And no offense, but that might even be beyond your abilities. Even if we could get to one of their computers, everything's password protected. And if they walk away, they lock the computers. I'm guessing you haven't become a hacker since the last time I saw you."

No, certainly not. And unlike the heroes of those spy movies Lissa teased me about, I had no tech-savvy friends who could even come close to breaking that kind of encryption and security. Damn. I stared glumly at my feet, wondering if I had any chance at all of getting more information out of Abe.

"But," said Mia, "if the information you need isn't *too* current, they might still have paper copies."

I jerked my head up. "Where?"

"They've got mass storage rooms, tucked away in one of

the basements. Files and files. Still under lock and key—but probably easier to get to than fighting the computers. Again, depends on what you need. How old it is."

Abe had given me the impression that Tarasov Prison had been around for a while. Surely there was a record of it in these archives. I didn't doubt the guardians had gone digital a while ago, which meant we might not find up-to-the-minute details on the place's security, but I'd settle for a blueprint.

"It might be what we need. Can you get us in?"

Mia was quiet for several seconds, and I could see her mind whirring. "Possibly." She glanced at Lissa. "Can *you* still compel people into being your slaves?"

Lissa grimaced. "I don't like to think of it like that, but yeah, I can." It was another of spirit's perks.

Mia considered a few moments more and then gave a quick nod. "Okay. Come back around two, and we'll see what we can do."

Two in the afternoon for the rest of the world meant the middle of the night for Moroi, who ran on a nocturnal schedule. Being out in broad daylight didn't feel particularly sneaky, but I had to figure Mia's planning here was based on the fact that there would also be fewer people around that time of day.

I was trying to decide if we should socialize more or head out when a knock interrupted my thoughts. Mia flinched and suddenly looked uncomfortable. She rose to get the door, and a familiar voice drifted down the hall toward us.

"Sorry I'm early, but I—"

Christian stepped into the living room. He abruptly shut

up when he saw Lissa and me. Everyone seemed frozen, so it looked like it was up to me to pretend like this wasn't a horribly awkward situation.

"Hey, Christian," I said cheerfully. "How's it going?"

His eyes were on Lissa, and it took him a moment to drag them to me. "Fine." He glanced at Mia. "I can come back. . . ."

Lissa hastily stood up. "No," she said, voice cool and princesslike. "Rose and I have to go anyway."

"Yeah," I agreed, following her lead. "We have . . . stuff . . . to do. And we don't want to interrupt your . . ." Hell, I had no idea what they were going to do. Wasn't sure I wanted to.

Mia had found her voice. "Christian wanted to see some of the moves I've been practicing with the campus guardians."

"Cool." I kept the smile on my face as Lissa and I moved toward the door. She stepped as far around Christian as she could. "Jill will be jealous."

And not just Jill. After another round of goodbyes, Lissa and I left and set back off across the grounds. I could feel the anger and jealousy radiating through her bond.

"It's only their fight club, Liss," I said, having no need for her side of the conversation. "Nothing's going on. They're going to talk punches and kicking and other boring stuff." Well, actually that stuff was pretty sweet, but I wasn't about to glorify Christian and Mia hanging out.

"Maybe *now* nothing's going on," she growled, staring stonily ahead. "But who knows what could happen? They spend time together, practice some physical moves, one thing leads to another—"

"That's ridiculous," I said. "That kind of stuff isn't romantic at all." Another lie, seeing as that was exactly how my relationship with Dimitri had begun. Again, best not to mention that. "Besides, Christian can't be involved with *every* girl he hangs out with. Mia, Jill—no offense, but he's not really that much of a ladies' man."

"He's really good-looking," she argued, those dark feelings still seething within her.

"Yeah," I conceded, keeping my eyes carefully on the pathway. "But it takes more than that. And besides, I thought you didn't care what he did."

"I don't," she agreed, not even convincing herself, let alone me. "Not at all."

My attempts to distract her proved pretty useless for the rest of the day. Tasha's words came back to me: *Why haven't you fixed this?* Because Lissa and Christian were being too damned unreasonable, both caught up in their own pissed-off feelings—which were kind of pissing me off in return. Christian would have been pretty helpful in my illicit escapades, but I had to keep my distance for Lissa's sake.

I finally left her to her bad mood when dinner came around. Compared to her romantic situation, my relationship with a semi-spoiled royal playboy from a disapproving family seemed downright optimistic. What a sad and scary world this was becoming. I assured Lissa I'd head straight back after dinner and that we'd go see Mia together. The mention of Mia didn't make Lissa happy, but the thought of a potential break-in did distract her momentarily from Christian.

The dress I had for dinner was maroon, made of light, gauzy material that was great for summer weather. The neckline was decent, and little cap sleeves gave it a classy edge. With my hair in a low ponytail that did a decent job of hiding the healing tattoo, I almost looked like a respectable girlfriend—which only went to show how deceptive appearances were, seeing as I was part of a crazy scheme to bring my last boyfriend back from the dead.

Adrian surveyed me from head to toe when I arrived at his parents' town house. They kept a permanent residence here at the Court. The small smile on his face told me he liked what he saw.

"You approve?" I asked, spinning around.

He slipped an arm around my waist. "Unfortunately, yes. I was hoping you'd show up in something a lot sluttier. Something that would scandalize my parents."

"Sometimes it's like you don't even care about me as a person," I observed as we walked inside. "It's like you're just using me for shock value."

"It's both, little dhampir. I care about you, *and* I'm using you for shock value."

I hid a smile as the Ivashkovs' housekeeper led us toward the dining room. The Court actually had restaurants and cafés tucked away within its buildings, but royals like Adrian's parents would consider it classier to have a fancy dinner in their home. Me, I would have preferred being out in public. More escape options.

"You must be Rose."

My assessment of the exits was interrupted when a very tall, very elegant Moroi woman came into the room. She wore a long, dark green satin dress that immediately made me feel out of place and that perfectly matched the color of her—and Adrian's—eyes. Her dark hair was pulled into a bun, and she smiled down at me with genuine warmth as she took my hand.

"I'm Daniella Ivashkov," she said. "It's very nice to meet you at last."

Was it really? My hand automatically shook hers in return. "Nice to meet you too, Lady Ivashkov."

"Call me Daniella, please." She turned to Adrian and *tsk*ed as she straightened the collar of his button-up shirt. "Honestly, darling," she said. "Do you even look in a mirror before you walk out the door? Your hair's a mess."

He dodged her as she reached toward his head. "Are you kidding? I spent hours in front of the mirror to *make* it look this way."

She gave a tormented sigh. "Some days I can't decide if I'm lucky or not to have no other children." Behind her, quiet servants were setting food out on the table. Steam rose up from the platters, and my stomach rumbled. I hoped no one else heard. Daniella glanced off down the hall beyond her. "Nathan, will you hurry up? The food's getting cold."

A few moments later, heavy footsteps sounded on the ornate wood floor, and Nathan Ivashkov swept into the room. Like his wife, he was dressed formally, the blue satin of his tie gleaming next to the starkness of his heavy black suit coat. I was glad they had air-conditioning in here, or he'd have been melting in that heavy fabric. The feature on him that stood out the most was what I remembered from before: a distinctly silver head of hair and mustache. I wondered if Adrian's hair would look like that when he was older. Nah, I'd never find out. Adrian would probably dye his hair at the first sign of gray—or silver.

Adrian's father might be exactly as I remembered, but it was clear he had no clue who I was. In fact, he seemed genuinely startled to see me.

"This is Adrian's, ah, friend, Rose Hathaway," said Daniella gently. "You remember—he said he'd bring her tonight."

"It's nice to meet you, Lord Ivashkov."

Unlike his wife, he didn't offer to put us on a first-name basis, which relieved me a little. The Strigoi who had forcefully turned Dimitri had been named Nathan too, and it wasn't a name I wanted to speak aloud. Adrian's father looked me over, but it wasn't with the appreciation Adrian had shown earlier. It was more like I was an oddity. "Oh. The dhampir girl."

He wasn't rude exactly, just disinterested. I mean, it wasn't like he called me a blood whore or anything. We all sat down to eat, and although Adrian kept his typical devil-may-care smile on his face, I again got the vibe that he really, *really* wanted a cigarette. Probably hard liquor, too. Being around his parents was not something he enjoyed. When one of the servants poured us all wine, Adrian looked immensely relieved and didn't hold back. I shot him a cautioning look that he ignored.

Nathan managed to rapidly devour his balsamic-glazed

pork medallions while still looking elegant and proper. "So," he said, attention focused on Adrian, "now that Vasilisa's graduated, what are you going to do with yourself? You aren't going to keep slumming with high school students, are you? There's no point in you being there anymore."

"I don't know," said Adrian lazily. He shook his head, further tousling his carefully mussed hair. "I kind of like hanging out with them. They think I'm funnier than I really am."

"Unsurprising," his father replied. "You aren't funny at all. It's time you do something productive. If you aren't going to go back to college, you should at least start sitting in on some of the family business meetings. Tatiana spoils you, but you could learn a lot from Rufus."

I knew enough about royal politics to recognize the name. The oldest member of each family was usually its "prince" or "princess" and held a Royal Council position—and was eligible to become king or queen. When Tatiana had taken the crown, Rufus had become prince of the Ivashkov family since he was the next oldest.

"True," said Adrian deadpan. He wasn't eating so much as pushing his food around. "I'd really like to know how he keeps his two mistresses a secret from his wife."

"Adrian!" snapped Daniella, a flush spilling over her pale cheeks. "Don't say things like that at our dinner table—and certainly not in front of a guest."

Nathan seemed to notice me again and gave a dismissive shrug. "She doesn't matter." I bit my lip on that, repressing the urge to see if I could throw my china plate Frisbee style and hit him in the head. I decided against it. Not only would it ruin dinner, but the plate probably wouldn't get the lift I needed. Nathan turned his scowl back to Adrian. "But *you* do. I'm not going to have you sitting around doing nothing—and using our money to fund it."

Something told me I should stay out of this, but I couldn't stand to see Adrian dressed down by his annoying father. Adrian *did* sit around and waste money, but Nathan didn't have the right to make fun of him for it. I mean, sure, I did all the time. But that was different.

"Maybe you could go to Lehigh with Lissa," I offered. "Keep studying spirit with her and then . . . do whatever else you were doing the last time you were in college. . . ."

"Drinking and skipping classes," said Nathan.

"Art," said Daniella. "Adrian took art classes."

"Really?" I asked, turning to him in surprise. Somehow, I could imagine him as an artistic type. It fit his erratic personality. "Then this would be perfect. You could pick it up again."

He shrugged and finished his second glass of wine. "I don't know. This college would probably have the same problem the last one did."

I frowned. "What's that?"

"Homework."

"Adrian," growled his father.

"It's okay," said Adrian breezily. He rested his arm casually on the table. "I don't really need a job or extra money. After Rose and I get married, the kids and I'll just live off of her guardian paycheck."

We all froze, even me. I knew perfectly well that he was joking. I mean, even if he harbored fantasies of marriage and kids (and I was *pretty* sure he didn't), the meager salary a guardian made would *never* be enough to keep him in the luxurious life he required.

Adrian's father, however, clearly did *not* think he was joking. Daniella seemed undecided. Me, I was just uncomfortable. It was a very, very bad topic to bring up at a dinner like this, and I couldn't believe Adrian had gone there. I didn't even think the wine was to blame. Adrian just liked tormenting his father that much.

The awful silence grew thicker and thicker. My gut instinct to fill conversation voids was raging, but something told me to stay quiet. The tension increased. When the doorbell rang, all four of us nearly jumped out of our chairs.

The housekeeper, Torrie, scurried off to answer it, and I breathed a mental sigh of relief. An unexpected visitor would help ease the tension.

Or maybe not.

Torrie cleared her throat when she returned, clearly flustered as she looked from Daniella to Nathan. "Her Royal Majesty Queen Tatiana is here."

No. Way.

All three Ivashkovs stood up abruptly, and a half second later, I joined them. I hadn't believed Adrian earlier when he said Tatiana might come. From his face, he seemed pretty surprised now too. But sure enough, there she was. She swept into the room, elegant in what must have been business casual for her: tailored black slacks and jacket with a red silk and lace blouse underneath. Little jeweled barrettes gleamed in her dark hair, and those imperious eyes peered down at us all as we offered hasty bows. Even her own family followed formalities.

"Aunt Tatiana," said Nathan, forcing what looked like a smile onto his face. I don't think he did it very often. "Won't you join us for dinner?"

She waved a hand dismissively. "No, no. I can't stay. I'm on my way to meet with Priscilla but thought I'd stop by when I heard Adrian had returned." Her gaze fell on him. "I can't believe you've been here all day and didn't come visit." Her voice was cool, but I swear there was an amused twinkle in her eyes. It was scary. She wasn't someone I thought of as warm and fuzzy. The whole experience of seeing her outside of one of her ceremonial rooms was totally unreal.

Adrian grinned at her. He was clearly the most comfortable person in the room right now. For reasons I never understood, Tatiana loved and spoiled Adrian. That wasn't to say that she didn't love her other family members; it was just clear that he was her favorite. It had always surprised me, considering what a scoundrel he was sometimes.

"Aw, I figured you had more important things to do than see me," he told her. "Besides, I quit smoking, so now we won't be able to go sneak cigarettes out behind the throne room together."

"Adrian!" chastised Nathan, turning bright red. It occurred to me then that I could have based a drinking game around how many times he exclaimed his son's name disapprovingly. "Auntie, I'm sor—"

Tatiana held up a hand again. "Oh, be silent, Nathan. No one wants to hear it." I almost choked. Being in the same room with the queen was horrid, but it was almost worth it to see her verbally bitch-slap Lord Ivashkov. She turned back to Adrian, face thawing. "You've finally quit? It's about time. I suppose this is your doing?"

It took me a moment to realize she was speaking to me. Until that point, I'd kind of hoped she might not have even noticed me. It seemed the only explanation for her not screaming at them to remove the rebellious little blood whore. It was shocking. Her voice wasn't accusatory, either. It was . . . impressed.

"W-well, it wasn't me, Your Majesty," I said. My meekness was a far cry from my behavior at our last meeting. "Adrian was the one who had the, uh, determination to do it."

So help me, Tatiana chuckled. "Very diplomatic. They should assign you to a politician."

Nathan didn't like the attention on me. I wasn't sure I did either, semi-pleasant or not. "Are you and Priscilla doing business tonight? Or just having a friendly dinner?"

Tatiana dragged her gaze from me. "Both. There's been some inter-family squabbling going on. Not publicly, but it's getting out. People are making noise about security. Some are ready to start training up right now. Others are wondering if guardians can go without sleep." She rolled her eyes. "And those are the tamest of the suggestions."

No question about it. This visit had gotten a lot more interesting.

"I hope you're going to shut those would-be militants up," growled Nathan. "Us fighting alongside guardians is absurd."

"What's *absurd*," said Tatiana, "is having strife among the royal classes. That's what I want to 'shut up.'" Her tone grew lofty, very queenlike. "We're the leaders among the Moroi. We have to set an example. We need to be unified to survive."

I studied her curiously. What did that mean? She hadn't agreed or disagreed with Nathan's stance on Moroi fighting. She'd only mentioned establishing peace among her people. But how? Was her method to encourage the new motion or squash it? Security was a huge concern for everyone after the attack, and it fell on her to figure it out.

"Sounds pretty hard to me," said Adrian, playing oblivious to the seriousness of the matter. "If you still want a cigarette afterward, I'll make an exception."

"I'll settle for you coming to make a proper visit tomorrow," she said dryly. "Leave the cigarettes at home." She glanced at his empty wineglass. "And other things." A flash of steely resolve crossed her gaze, and even though it melted as quickly as it had come, I felt almost relieved. There was the icy Tatiana I knew.

He saluted. "Noted."

Tatiana gave the rest of us brief glances. "Have a good evening," was her only farewell. We bowed again, and then she headed back toward the front door. As she did, I heard scuffling and murmured voices. She'd been traveling with a retinue, I realized, and had left them all in the foyer while she came to say hello to Adrian.

Dinner was quiet after that. Tatiana's visit had kind of left us all astonished. At least it meant I didn't have to hear Adrian and his father bicker anymore. Daniella mostly maintained what little conversation there was, attempting to inquire about my interests, and I realized she hadn't said a word during Tatiana's brief visit. Daniella had married into the Ivashkovs, and I wondered if she found the queen intimidating.

When the time came for us to leave, Daniella was all smiles while Nathan retired to his study.

"You need to come by more often," she told Adrian, smoothing his hair in spite of his protests. "And you're welcome anytime, Rose."

"Thank you," I said, dumbfounded. I kept studying her face to see if she was lying, but I didn't think she was. It made no sense. Moroi didn't approve of long-term relationships with dhampirs. Royal Moroi especially didn't. And royal Moroi related to the queen *especially* didn't, at least if past experience was any indication.

Adrian sighed. "Maybe if he's not around. Oh, damn. That reminds me. I left my coat here last time—I wanted to get out too fast."

"You've got, like, fifty coats," I remarked.

"Ask Torrie," said Daniella. "She'll know where it is."

Adrian went off to find the housekeeper, leaving me with his mother. I should have made polite, inconsequential small talk, but my curiosity was getting the better of me.

"Dinner was really great," I told her honestly. "And I hope you won't take this the wrong way . . . but I mean . . . well, you seem okay with Adrian and me dating."

She nodded serenely. "I am."

"And . . ." Well, it had to be said. "Tat—Queen Tatiana kind of seemed okay with it too."

"She is."

I made sure my jaw didn't drop to the floor. "But . . . I mean, the last time I talked to her, she was really mad. She kept telling me over and over how she'd never allow us to be together in the future or get married or anything like that." I cringed, recalling Adrian's joke. "I figured you'd feel the same. Lord Ivashkov does. You can't really want your son to be with a dhampir forever."

Daniella's smile was kind but wry. "Do *you* plan on being with him forever? Do *you* plan on marrying him and settling down?"

The question totally caught me off guard. "I . . . no . . . I mean, no offense to Adrian. I just never—"

"Planned on settling down at all?" She nodded wisely. "That's what I thought. Believe me, I know Adrian wasn't serious earlier. Everyone's jumping to conclusions that haven't even happened. I've heard of you, Rose—everyone has. And I admire you. And based on what I've learned, I'm guessing you aren't the type who would quit being a guardian to be a housewife."

"You're right," I admitted.

"Then I don't see the problem. You're both young. You're

entitled to have fun and do what you want now, but I—you and I—know that even if you see Adrian off and on for the rest of your life, you aren't going to get married or settle down. And it has nothing to do with what Nathan or anyone says. It's the way of the world. It's the kind of person you are. I can see it in your eyes. Tatiana's realized it too, and that's why she eased up. You need to be out there fighting, and that's what you'll do. At least if you truly intend to be a guardian."

"I do." I was staring at her in wonder. Her attitude was amazing. She was the first royal I'd met who hadn't immediately freaked out and gone crazy over the idea of a Moroi and dhampir match. If other people shared her view, it would make a lot of others' lives easier. And she was right. It didn't matter what Nathan thought. It wouldn't have even mattered if Dimitri had been around. The bottom line was that Adrian and I wouldn't be together for the rest of our lives because I'd always be on guardian duty, not lounging around like he did. Realizing that freed things up . . . yet it made me a little sad too.

Behind her, I could see Adrian approaching down the hall. Daniella leaned forward, pitching her voice low for me. There was a wistful note to her words when she spoke, the tone of a concerned mother. "But Rose? While I'm fine with you two dating and being happy, please try not to break his heart *too* much when the time comes."

FOUR

I DECIDED IT'D BE BEST not to mention my conversation with Adrian's mother to him. I didn't need psychic powers to sense his mixed mood as we walked back to guest housing. His father had annoyed him, but his mother's seeming acceptance had cheered him up. I didn't want to damage that by letting Adrian know she was only okay with our dating because she figured it was a temporary, fun thing.

"So you're going off with Lissa?" he asked when we reached my room.

"Yup, sorry. You know—girl stuff." And by girl stuff, I meant breaking and entering.

Adrian seemed a little disappointed, but I knew he didn't begrudge our friendship. He gave me a small smile and wrapped his arms around my waist, leaning down to kiss me. Our lips met, and that warmth that always surprised me spread through me. After a few sweet moments, we broke apart, but the look in his eyes said it wasn't easy for him.

"See you later," I said. He gave me one more quick kiss and then headed off to his own room.

I immediately sought out Lissa, who was hanging out in her own room. She was staring intently at a silver spoon, and through our bond, I could sense her intent. She was attempting to infuse it with spirit's compulsion, so that whoever held it would cheer up. I wondered if she intended it for herself or was just randomly experimenting. I didn't probe her mind to find out.

"A spoon?" I asked with amusement.

She shrugged and set it down. "Hey, it's not easy to keep getting a hold of silver. I have to take what I can get."

"Well, it'd make for happy dinner parties."

She smiled and put her feet upon the ebony coffee table that sat in the middle of her little suite's living room. Each time I saw it, I couldn't help but be reminded of the glossy black furniture that had been in my own prison suite back in Russia. I had fought Dimitri with a stake made from a chair's leg of similar style.

"Speaking of which . . . how was *your* dinner party?"

"Not as bad as I thought," I admitted. "I never realized what an asshole Adrian's dad was, though. His mom was actually pretty cool. She didn't have a problem with us dating."

"Yeah, I've met her. She is nice . . . though I never thought she was nice enough to be okay with scandalous dating. I don't suppose Her Royal Majesty showed up?" Lissa was joking, so my response floored her.

"She did, and . . . it wasn't awful."

"What? Did you say 'wasn't'?"

"I know, I know. It was so crazy. It was this really quick visit to see Adrian, and she acted like me being there was no big deal." I didn't bother delving into the politics of Tatiana's views on Moroi training for battle. "Of course, who knows what would have happened if she stayed? Maybe she would have turned into her old self. I would have needed a whole set of magic silverware then—to stop me from pulling a knife on her."

Lissa groaned. "Rose, you *cannot* make those kinds of jokes."

I grinned. "I say the things you're too afraid to."

This made her smile in return. "It's been a long time since I've heard that," she said softly. My trip to Russia had fractured our friendship—which had ended up showing me just how much it really meant to me.

We spent the rest of the time hanging out, talking about Adrian and other gossip. I was relieved to see she'd gotten over her earlier mood about Christian, but as the day progressed, her anxiety grew about our pending mission with Mia.

"It's going to be okay," I told her when the time came. We were heading back across the Court grounds, dressed in comfortable jeans and T-shirts. It was nice to be free of school curfew, but again, being out in the bright sunlight didn't make me feel very covert. "This'll be easy."

Lissa cut me a look but said nothing. The guardians were the security force in our world, and this was their headquarters. Breaking in was going to be anything but easy.

Mia looked determined when we reached her, though, and I felt encouraged by her attitude—and that she was wearing all black. True, it wouldn't do much in sunlight, but it made this all feel more legitimate. I was dying to know what had happened with Christian, and Lissa was too. Again, it was one of those topics best left unexplained.

Mia did, however, explain her plan to us, and I honestly felt it had about a 65 percent chance of working. Lissa was uneasy about her role since it involved compulsion, but she was a trooper and agreed to do it. We went over everything in detail a few more times and then set out to the building that housed guardian operations. I'd been there once before, when Dimitri had taken me to see Victor in the holding cells adjacent to the guardians' HQ. I'd never spent much time in the main offices before, and as Mia had predicted, they were lightly staffed this time of the day.

When we walked in, we were immediately met by a reception area like you'd find in any other administrative office. A stern guardian sat at a desk with a computer, filing cabinets and tables all around him. He probably didn't have much to do at this time of night, but he was still clearly on high alert. Beyond him was a door, and it held my attention. Mia had explained that it was a gateway to all the guardian secrets, to their records and main offices—and surveillance areas that monitored high-risk regions of the Court.

Stern or not, the guy had a small smile for Mia. "Isn't it a little late for you? You aren't here for lessons, are you?"

She grinned back. He must have been one of the guardians she'd grown friendly with during her time at Court. "Nah, just up with some friends and wanted to show them around."

He arched an eyebrow as he took in me and Lissa. He gave a slight nod of acknowledgment. "Princess Dragomir.

Guardian Hathaway." Apparently our reputations preceded us. It was the first time I'd been addressed by my new title. It startled me—and made me feel slightly guilty about betraying the group I'd just become a member of.

"This is Don," explained Mia. "Don, the princess has a favor to ask." She looked meaningfully at Lissa.

Lissa took a deep breath, and I felt the burnings of compulsion magic through our bond as she focused her gaze upon him. "Don," she said firmly, "give us the keys and codes to the records archives downstairs. And then make sure the cameras in those areas are turned off."

He frowned. "Why would I—" But as her eyes continued to hold his, I could see the compulsion seize him. The lines on his face smoothed into compliance, and I breathed a sigh of relief. Plenty of people were strong enough to resist compulsion—particularly that of ordinary Moroi. Lissa's was much stronger because of spirit, though you never knew if someone might break through.

"Of course," he said, standing up. He opened a desk drawer and handed Mia a set of keys that she promptly gave to me. "The code is 4312578."

I committed it to memory, and he beckoned us through the all-powerful door. Beyond it, corridors spread in all directions. He pointed to one on our right. "Down there. Take a left at the end, go downstairs two flights, and it's the door on the right."

Mia glanced at me to make sure I understood. I nodded, and she turned back to him. "Now make sure the surveillance is off."

"Take us there," said Lissa firmly.

Don couldn't resist her command, and she and Mia followed him, leaving me on my own. This part of the plan was all on me, and I hurried down the hall. The facility might be lightly staffed, but I could still run into someone—and would have no compulsion to help me talk my way out of trouble.

Don's directions were spot-on, but I still wasn't prepared when I punched in the code and entered the vault. Rows and rows of filing cabinets stretched down a huge hall. I couldn't see the end of it. Drawers were stacked five high, and the faint fluorescent lighting and eerie silence gave it all a spooky, almost haunted feel. All the guardians' information from before the digital age. God only knew how far back these records went. To medieval days in Europe? I suddenly felt daunted and wondered if I could pull this off.

I walked to the first cabinet on my left, relieved to see it was labeled. AA1 it read. Below it was AA2 and so forth. Oh dear. It was going to take me several cabinets to even get out of the As. I was grateful the organization was as simple as alphabetical order, but I now understood why these cabinets went on forever. I had to go back more than three quarters of the way down the room to get to the Ts. And it wasn't until I got to the TA27 drawer that I found the file for Tarasov Prison.

I gasped. The file was thick, filled with all sorts of documents. There were pages on the prison's history and its migration patterns, as well as floor plans for each of its locations. I could hardly believe it. So much information . . . but what did I need? What would be useful? The answer came quickly: *all of it*. I shut the drawer and tucked the folder under my arm. Okay. Time to get out of here.

I turned around and began heading for the exit at a light jog. Now that I had what I needed, the urgency of escape was pressing on me. I was almost there when I heard a soft click, and the door opened. I froze as a dhampir I didn't recognize stepped through. He froze as well, clearly astonished, and I took it as a small blessing that he didn't immediately pin me against the wall and start interrogating me.

"You're Rose Hathaway," he said. Good lord. Was there anyone who didn't know who I was?

I tensed, unsure what to expect now, but spoke as though us meeting here made perfect sense. "So it would seem. Who are you?"

"Mikhail Tanner," he said, still puzzled. "What are you doing here?"

"Running an errand," I said breezily. I indicated the file. "The guardian on duty down here needed something."

"You're lying," he said. "*I'm* the guardian on archive duty. If someone needed something, they would have sent me."

Oh, shit. Talk about best-laid plans failing. Yet as I stood there, a strange thought came to me. His appearance wasn't familiar at all: curly brown hair, average height, late twenties. Pretty good-looking, really. But his name . . . something about his name . . .

"Ms. Karp," I gasped. "You're the one . . . you were involved with Ms. Karp."

He stiffened, blue eyes narrowing warily. "What do you

know about that?"

I swallowed. What I'd done—or tried to do for Dimitri—wasn't without precedent. "You loved her. You went out to kill her after she . . . after she turned."

Ms. Karp had been a teacher of ours a few years ago. She'd been a spirit user, and as the effects of it began to drive her insane, she'd done the only thing she could to save her mind: become a Strigoi. Mikhail, her lover, had done the only thing *he'd* known to end that evil state: search for and kill her. It occurred to me that I was standing face-to-face with the hero of a love story nearly as dramatic as my own.

"But you never found her," I said softly. "Did you?"

He took a long time in answering, his eyes weighing me heavily. I wondered what he was thinking about. Her? His own pain? Or was he analyzing me?

"No," he said finally. "I had to stop. The guardians needed me more."

He spoke in that calm, controlled way that guardians excelled at, but in his eyes, I saw grief—a grief I more than understood. I hesitated before taking a shot at the only chance I had to not get busted and end up in a jail cell.

"I know . . . I know you have every reason to drag me out of here and turn me in. You should. It's what you're supposed to do—what I'd do too. But the thing is, this . . ." I again nodded at the folder. "Well, I'm kind of trying to do what you did. I'm trying to save someone."

He remained quiet. He could probably guess who I meant and assumed "save" meant "kill." If he knew who I was, he'd know who my mentor had been. Few knew about my romantic relationship with Dimitri, but me caring about him would have been a foregone conclusion.

"It's futile, you know," Mikhail said at last. This time, his voice cracked a little. "I tried . . . I tried so hard to find her. But when they disappear . . . when they don't want to be found . . ." He shook his head. "There's nothing we can do. I understand why you want to do it. Believe me, I do. But it's impossible. You'll never find him if he doesn't want you to."

I wondered how much I could tell Mikhail—how much I should. It occurred to me then that if there was anyone else in this world who understood what I was going through, it would be this man. Besides, I didn't have a lot of options here.

"The thing is, I think I can find him," I said slowly. "He's looking for me."

"What?" Mikhail's eyebrows rose. "How do you know?"

"Because he, um, sends me letters about it."

That fierce warrior look immediately returned. "If you know this, if you *can* find him . . . you should get backup to kill him."

I flinched at those last words and again feared what I had to say next. "Would you believe me if I said there was a way to save him?"

"You mean by destroying him."

I shook my head. "No . . . I mean really save. A way to restore him to his original state."

"No," Mikhail said swiftly. "That's impossible."

"It might not be. I know someone who did it—who turned

a Strigoi back." Okay, that was a small lie. I didn't actually know the person, but I wasn't going to get into the string of knowing-someone-who-knew-someone . . .

"That's impossible," Mikhail repeated. "Strigoi are dead. Undead. Same difference."

"What if there was a chance?" I said. "What if it could be done? What if Ms. Karp—if Sonya—could become Moroi again? What if you could be together again?" It'd also mean she'd be crazy again, but that was a technicality for later.

It felt like an eternity before he answered, and my anxiety grew. Lissa couldn't compel forever, and I'd told Mia I would be fast. This plan would fall apart if I didn't get out soon. Yet, watching him deliberate, I could see his mask falter. After all this time, he still loved his Sonya.

"If what you're saying is true—and I don't believe it—then I'm coming with you."

Whoa, no. Not in the plan. "You can't," I said swiftly. "I've already got people in place." Another small lie. "Adding more might ruin things. I'm not doing it alone," I said, cutting off what I figured would be his next argument. "If you really want to help me—really want to take a chance on bringing her back—you need to let me go."

"There's no way it can be true," he repeated. But there was doubt in his voice, and I played on it.

"Can you take that chance?"

More silence. I was starting to sweat now. Mikhail closed his eyes for a moment and took a deep breath. Then he stepped aside and gestured to the door. "Go."

I nearly sagged in relief and immediately grabbed the door handle. "Thank you. Thank you so much."

"I could get in a lot of trouble for this," he said wearily. "And I still don't believe it's possible."

"But you hope it is." I didn't need a response from him to know I was right. I opened the door, but before going through, I paused and glanced at him. This time, he no longer hid the grief and pain in his face. "If you mean it . . . if you want to help . . . there might be a way you can."

Another piece of the puzzle had unraveled itself for me, another way we might pull this off. I explained what I needed from him and was surprised at how quickly he agreed. He really was like me, I realized. We both knew the idea of bringing back Strigoi was impossible . . . and yet we so, so wanted to believe it could be done

I slipped back upstairs alone after that. Don wasn't at his desk, and I wondered what Mia had done with him. I didn't wait to find out and instead headed outside, off to a small courtyard that we'd established as our rendezvous point. Mia and Lissa were both waiting there, pacing. No longer distracted with anxiety, I opened myself to the bond and felt Lissa's agitation.

"Thank God," she said when she saw me. "We thought you'd been caught."

"Well . . . it's a long story." One I didn't bother with. "I got what I needed. And . . . I actually got a whole lot more. I think we can do this."

Mia gave me a look that was both wry and wistful. "I sure

do wish I knew what you guys were doing."

I shook my head as the three of us walked away. "No," I replied. "I'm not sure that you do."

FIVE

I DECIDED IT'D BE BEST if Lissa and I stayed up late when we returned to her room, poring over the documents. She was a jumble of feelings when I told her about my encounter with Mikhail—which I hadn't mentioned to Mia. Lissa's initial reaction was surprise, but there were other things too. Fear over the trouble I could have gotten into. A bit of warm romanticism over what both Mikhail and I were willing to do for those we loved. Wonder if she would do the same if Christian were in that situation. She decided instantly that she would; her love for him was still that strong. Then she told herself that she actually didn't care about him anymore, which I would have found annoying if I wasn't so distracted.

"What's wrong?" she asked.

I'd sighed aloud in dismay without realizing it while I read her thoughts. Not wanting her to know I'd been perusing her mind, I pointed at the papers spread out on her bed. "Just trying to make sense of this." Not entirely that far off from the truth.

The prison's layout was complex. The cells occupied two floors and were tiny—only one prisoner per cell. The papers didn't explain why, but the reason was obvious. It went along with what Abe had said about keeping criminals from turning Strigoi. If I'd been locked away in prison for years, I could understand the temptation of cracking and killing my roommate to become Strigoi and escape. The cells were also kept housed in the very center of the building, surrounded by guards, offices, "exercise rooms," a kitchen, and a feeders' room. The documents explained guard rotations, as well as prisoner feeding schedules. They were apparently escorted to the feeders one at a time, heavily guarded, and only allowed very short spurts of blood. Again, everything kept the prisoners weak and prevented them from turning Strigoi.

It was all good information, but I had no reason to believe any of it was up-to-date, since the file was five years old. It was also likely the prison had all sorts of new surveillance equipment in place. Probably the only things we could count on being the same were the prison's location and the building's layout.

"How good are you feeling about your charm-making skills?" I asked Lissa.

Although she hadn't been able to put as much spirit healing into my ring as a woman I knew named Oksana could, I had noticed my darkness-induced temper soothed a little. Lissa'd made a ring for Adrian too, though I couldn't say for sure if it was what was helping him control his vices lately—vices he usually indulged in to control spirit.

She shrugged and rolled over onto her back. Exhaustion filled her, but she was trying to stay awake for my sake. "Getting better. Wish I could meet Oksana."

"Maybe someday," I said vaguely. I didn't think Oksana

would ever leave Siberia. She'd run off with her guardian and wanted to keep a low profile. Besides, I didn't want Lissa over there anytime soon after my ordeals. "Have you been able to put in anything besides healing?" A moment later, I answered my own question. "Oh, right. The spoon."

Lissa grimaced, but it turned into a yawn. "I don't think it worked so well."

"Hmm."

"Hmm?"

I glanced back at the blueprints. "I'm thinking if you could make a few more compulsion charms, it would go a long way to help with this. We need to make people see what we want them to see." Surely if Victor—whose powers of compulsion were nowhere near hers—had managed a lust charm, she could do what I needed. She just needed more practice. She understood the basic principles but had trouble making her desired effects last. The only problem was that in asking her to do this, I was making her use more spirit. Even if the side effects didn't show up right away, they would likely come back to haunt her in the future.

She glanced at me curiously, but when I saw her yawn again, I told her not to worry about it. I'd explain tomorrow. She offered no argument, and after a quick hug, we each retired to our own beds. We weren't going to get much sleep, but we had to get what we could. Tomorrow was a big day.

I'd worn a variation of the guardians' formal black-and-white outfit when I went to Victor's trial. In normal bodyguard situations, we wore ordinary clothes. But for fancy events, they wanted us looking crisp and professional. The morning after our daring break-in, I got my first true taste of guardian fashion.

I'd worn hand-me-down clothes at Victor's trial but now had an official guardian outfit, tailored exactly to my measurements: straight-legged black slacks, a white button-up blouse, and a black dress jacket that fit me perfectly. It certainly wasn't meant to be sexy, but the way it hugged my stomach and hips did good things for my body. I felt satisfied with my reflection in the mirror, and after several minutes of thought, I pulled my hair into a neatly braided bun that showed off my *molnija* marks. The skin was still irritated, but at least the bandage was gone. I looked very . . . professional. I was actually kind of reminded of Sydney. She was an Alchemist—a human who worked with Moroi and dhampirs to hide the existence of vampires from the world. With her proper sense of fashion, she always looked ready for a business meeting. I kept wanting to send her a briefcase for Christmas.

If ever there was a time for me to show off, today was the day. After the trials and graduation, this was the next biggest step in becoming a guardian. It was a luncheon that all new grads attended. Moroi eligible for new guardians would also attend, hoping to scope out the candidates. Our scores from school and the trials would have been made public knowledge by now, and this was a chance for Moroi to meet us and put in bids for who they wanted to guard them. Naturally, most guests would be royal, but a few other important Moroi would also qualify.

I really had no interest in showing off and hooking a posh family. Lissa was the only one I wanted to guard. Still, I had to make a good impression. I needed to make it clear that *I* was the one who should be with her.

She and I walked over to the royal ballroom together. It was the only place large enough to hold us all, since more than just St. Vladimir's grads were in attendance. All the American schools had sent their new recruits, and for a moment, I found the sea of black and white dizzying. Bits of color—royals dressed up in their finest clothing—livened the palette up a little. Around us, soft watercolor murals made the walls seem to glow. Lissa hadn't worn a ball gown or anything, but she looked very elegant in a formfitting teal dress made of raw silk.

The royals mingled with the social ease they'd been raised with, but my classmates moved about uneasily. No one seemed to mind. It wasn't our job to seek out others; we would be approached. The grads all wore name tags—engraved metal ones. There were no HELLO, MY NAME IS . . . stickers here. The tags made us identifiable so that the royals could come and do their interrogations.

I didn't expect anyone except my friends to talk to me, so Lissa and I headed straight for the buffet and then occupied a quiet corner to munch on our canapés and caviar. Well, Lissa ate caviar. It reminded me too much of Russia.

Adrian, of course, sought us out first. I gave him a crooked grin. "What are you doing here? I know you aren't eligible for a guardian."

With no concrete plans for his future, it was assumed Adrian would simply live at Court. As such, he'd need no outside protection—though he'd certainly qualify if he chose to strike out into the world.

"True, but I could hardly miss a party," he said. He held a glass of champagne in his hand, and I wondered if the effects of the ring Lissa had given him were wearing off. Of course, the occasional drink really wasn't the end of the world, and the dating proposal's language had been loose in that area. It was mostly the smoking I wanted him to stay away from. "Have you been approached by a dozen hopeful people?"

I shook my head. "Who wants reckless Rose Hathaway? The one who drops out without warning to do her own thing?"

"Plenty," he said. "I sure do. You kicked ass in the battle, and remember—everyone thinks you went off on some Strigoi-killing spree. Some might think it's worth your crazy personality."

"He's right," a voice suddenly said. I looked up and saw Tasha Ozera standing near us, a small smile on her scarred face. In spite of the disfigurement, I thought she looked beautiful today—more royal than I'd ever seen her. Her long black hair gleamed, and she wore a navy skirt and lacy tank top. She even had on high heels and jewelry—something I was certain I'd never seen her wearing.

I was happy to see her; I hadn't known she'd come to Court. An odd thought occurred to me. "Have they finally let you have a guardian?" The royals had a lot of quiet, polite ways of shunning those who were in disgrace. In the Ozeras' case, their guardian allotment had been cut in half as kind of a punishment for what Christian's parents had done. It was totally unfair. The Ozeras deserved the same rights as any other royal family.

She nodded. "I think they're hoping it'll shut me up about Moroi fighting with dhampirs. Kind of a bribe."

"One you won't fall for, I'm sure."

"Nope. If anything, it'll just give me someone to practice with." Her smile faded, and she cast uncertain looks among us. "I hope you won't be offended . . . but I put in a request for you, Rose."

Lissa and I exchanged startled glances. "Oh." I didn't know what else to say.

"I hope they'll give you to Lissa," Tasha added hastily, clearly uncomfortable. "But the queen seems pretty dead-set on her own choices. If that's the case . . ."

"It's okay," I said. "If I can't be with Lissa, then I really would rather be with you." It was the truth. I wanted Lissa more than anyone else in the world, but if they kept us apart, then I'd absolutely prefer Tasha to some snobby royal. Of course, I was pretty sure my odds of getting assigned to her were as bad as those of getting assigned to Lissa. Those who were angry at me for running off would go out of their way to put me in the most unpleasant situation possible. And even if she was being granted a guardian, I had a feeling Tasha's preferences wouldn't be high priority either. My future was still a big question mark.

"Hey," exclaimed Adrian, offended that I hadn't named

him as my second choice.

I shook my head at him. "You know they'd assign me to a woman anyway. Besides, you've got to do something with your life to earn a guardian."

I meant it jokingly, but a small frown made me think I might have actually hurt his feelings. Tasha, meanwhile, looked relieved. "I'm glad you don't mind. In the meantime, I'll do what I can to help you two." She rolled her eyes. "Not that my opinion counts for much."

Sharing my misgivings about getting assigned to Tasha seemed pointless. Instead, I started to thank her for the offer, but we were then joined by yet another visitor: Daniella Ivashkov. "Adrian," she chastised gently, a small smile on her face, "you can't keep Rose and Vasilisa all to yourself." She turned to Lissa and me. "The queen would like to see you both."

Lovely. We both stood up, but Adrian remained sitting, having no desire to visit his aunt. Tasha apparently didn't either. Seeing her, Daniella gave a curt, polite nod. "Lady Ozera." She then walked away, assuming we'd follow. I found it ironic that Daniella seemed willing to accept me but still held that typical aloof Ozera-prejudice. I guess her niceness only went so far.

Tasha, however, had long since grown immune to that sort of treatment. "Have fun," she said. She looked over at Adrian. "More champagne?"

"Lady Ozera," he said grandly, "you and I are two minds with a single thought."

I hesitated before following Lissa to Tatiana. I'd taken in

Tasha's grand appearance but only now really paid attention to something. "Is all your jewelry silver?" I asked.

She absentmindedly touched the opal necklace around her neck. Her fingers were adorned with three rings. "Yes," she said, confused. "Why?"

"This is going to sound really weird . . . well, maybe not compared to my normal weirdness. But could we, um, borrow all of those?"

Lissa shot me a look and immediately guessed my motives. We needed more charms and were short on silver. Tasha arched an eyebrow, but like so many of my friends, she had a remarkable ability to roll with weird ideas.

"Sure," she said. "But can I give them to you later? I don't really want to strip my jewelry in the middle of this party."

"No problem."

"I'll have them sent to your room."

With that settled, Lissa and I walked over to where Tatiana was surrounded by admirers and those wanting to suck up. Daniella had to be mistaken in saying Tatiana wanted to see *both* of us. The memory of her yelling at me over Adrian still burned in my head, and dinner at the Ivashkovs' hadn't fooled me into thinking the queen and I were suddenly best friends.

Yet, astonishingly, when she caught sight of Lissa and me, she was all smiles. "Vasilisa. And Rosemarie." She beckoned us closer, and the group parted. I approached with Lissa, my steps tentative. Was I going to get yelled at in front of all these people?

Apparently not. There were always new royals to meet,

and Tatiana first introduced Lissa to all of them. Everyone was curious about the Dragomir princess. I was introduced as well, though the queen didn't go out of her way to sing my praises as she did Lissa's. Still, being acknowledged at all was incredible.

"Vasilisa," said Tatiana, once the formalities were finished, "I was thinking you should visit Lehigh soon. Arrangements are being made for you to go in, oh, maybe a week and a half. We thought it would be a nice treat for your birthday. Serena and Grant will accompany you, naturally, and I'll send a few others." Serena and Grant were the guardians who had replaced Dimitri and me as Lissa's future protection. Of course they'd be going with her. Then, Tatiana said the most startling thing of all. "And you can go too, if you'd like, Rose. Vasilisa could hardly celebrate without you."

Lissa lit up. Lehigh University. The lure that had made her accept a life at Court. Lissa yearned for as much knowledge as she could get, and the queen had given her a chance at it. The prospect of a visit totally filled her with eagerness and excitement—especially if she could celebrate her eighteenth birthday there with me. It was enough to distract her from Victor and Christian, which was saying something.

"Thank you, Your Majesty. That'd be great."

There was a strong possibility, I knew, that we might not be around for this scheduled visit—not if my plan for Victor worked. But I didn't want to ruin Lissa's happiness—and I could hardly mention it in this royal crowd. I was also kind of stunned that I'd been invited at all. After issuing the invite, the queen said nothing else to me and continued speaking with the others around her. Yet, she'd been pleasant—for *her*, at least—while addressing me, just as she had at the Ivashkov home. Not best-friend nice but certainly not raving-bitch insane, either. Maybe Daniella had been right.

More pleasantries followed as everyone chatted and tried to impress the queen, and it soon became clear that I was no longer needed. Glancing around the room, I found someone I needed to talk to and meekly separated myself from the group, knowing Lissa could fend for herself.

"Eddie," I called, reaching the other side of the ballroom. "Alone at last."

Eddie Castile, a longtime friend of mine, grinned when he saw me. He too was a dhampir, tall with a long, narrow face that still had a cute, boyish look to it. He had tamed his dark, sandy-blond hair for a change. Lissa had once hoped Eddie and I would date, but he and I were strictly just friends. His best friend had been Mason, a sweet guy who'd been crazy about me and who had been murdered by Strigoi. After his death, Eddie and I had adopted protective attitudes toward each other. He'd later been kidnapped during the attack at St. Vladimir's, and his experiences had made him a serious and determined guardian—sometimes a little *too* serious. I wanted him to have more fun and was delighted to see the happy glint in his hazel eyes now.

"I think every royal in the room's been trying to bribe you," I teased. It wasn't entirely a joke. I'd been keeping an eye on him throughout the party, and there'd always been someone with him. His record was stellar. Surviving the awful events in his life might have scarred him, but they reflected well on his skills. He had great grades and ratings from the trial. Most importantly, he didn't have my reckless reputation. He was a good catch.

"Kind of seems that way." He laughed. "I didn't really expect it."

"You're so modest. You're the hottest thing in this room."

"Not compared to you."

"Yeah. As shown by the people lining up to talk to me. Tasha Ozera's the only one who wants me as far as I know. And Lissa, of course."

Lines of thought creased Eddie's face. "Could be worse."

"It will be worse. No way will I get either of them."

We fell silent, and a sudden anxiety filled me. I'd come to ask a favor of Eddie, and it no longer seemed like a good idea. Eddie was on the verge of a shining career. He was a loyal friend, and I'd been certain he'd help with what I needed . . . but I suddenly didn't think I could ask. Like Mia, however, Eddie was observant.

"What's wrong, Rose?" His voice was concerned—that protective nature kicking in.

I shook my head. I couldn't do it. "Nothing."

"*Rose,*" he said warningly.

I looked away, unable to meet his eyes. "It's not important. Really." I'd find another way, someone else.

To my surprise, he reached out to touch my chin and tip my head back up. His gaze caught mine, allowing no escape. "What do you need?"

I stared at him for a long time. I was so selfish, risking the lives and reputations of friends I cared about. If Christian and Lissa weren't on the outs, I'd be asking him, too. But Eddie was all that was left to me.

"I need something . . . something that's pretty extreme."

His face was still serious, but his lips tugged into a wry smile. "Everything you do is extreme, Rose."

"Not like this. This is . . . well, it's something that could ruin everything for you. Get you in big trouble. I can't do that to you."

That half smile vanished. "It doesn't matter," he said fiercely. "If you need me, I'll do it. No matter what it is."

"You don't know what it is."

"I trust you."

"It's kind of illegal. Treasonous, even."

That took him aback for a moment, but he stayed resolute. "Whatever you need. I don't care. I've got your back." I'd saved Eddie's life twice, and I knew he meant what he said. He felt indebted to me. He would go wherever I asked, not out of romantic love, but out of friendship and loyalty.

"It's illegal," I repeated. "You'd have to sneak out of Court . . . tonight. And I don't know when we'd be back." It was entirely possible that we *wouldn't* come back. If we had a run-in with prison guards . . . well, they might take lethal measures to do their duty. It was what all of us had trained for. But I couldn't pull this breakout off with Lissa's compulsion alone. I needed another fighter at my back.

"Just tell me when."

And that was all there was to it. I didn't tell him the full extent of our plan, but I gave him that night's rendezvous location and told him what he would need to bring. He never questioned me. He said he'd be there. New royals came to talk to him just then, and I left him, knowing he'd show up later. It was hard, but I pushed aside my guilt over possibly endangering his future.

Eddie arrived, just as he'd promised, when my plan unfolded later that night. Lissa did too. Again, *night* meant "broad daylight." I felt that same anxiety I did when we'd sneaked around with Mia. Light exposed everything, but then, most people were asleep. Lissa, Eddie, and I still moved through the Court's grounds as covertly as we could, meeting Mikhail in a section of the compound that held all sorts of garaged vehicles. The garages were big metal, industrial-looking buildings set on the fringes of Court, and no one else was out.

We slipped into the garage he'd indicated last night, and I was relieved to find no one else there. He surveyed the three of us, looking surprised at my "strike team," but he offered no questions and made no further attempts to join us. More guilt surged up within me. Here was someone else who was risking his future for me.

"Gonna be a tight fit," he mused.

I forced a smile. "We're all friends here."

Mikhail didn't laugh at my joke but instead popped the trunk of a black Dodge Charger. He wasn't kidding about the tight fit. It was a newer one, which was kind of a shame. An older model would have been bigger, but guardians only kept top-of-the-line stuff around.

"Once we're far enough away, I'll pull over and let you out," he said.

"We'll be fine," I assured him. "Let's do this."

Lissa, Eddie, and I crawled into the trunk. "Oh God," muttered Lissa. "I hope no one's claustrophobic."

It was like a bad game of Twister. The trunk was large enough for some luggage but not intended for three people. We were squeezed together, and personal space was nonexistent. We were all up close and personal. Satisfied we were all snug, Mikhail closed the trunk and darkness engulfed us. The engine started a minute later, and I felt the car move.

"How long until you think we stop?" asked Lissa. "Or die from carbon monoxide poisoning?"

"We haven't even left the Court yet," I noted. She sighed.

The car drove off, and not too long afterward, we came to a stop. Mikhail must have reached the gates and been chatting with the guards. He'd told me earlier that he'd come up with some excuse or other to run an errand, and we had no reason to believe the guards would question him or search the car. The Court wasn't worried about people sneaking out, like our school had been. The biggest concern here was people getting inside.

A minute passed, and I uneasily wondered if there was a problem. Then the car moved again, and all three of us exhaled in relief. We picked up speed, and after what I suspected was a mile or so, the car veered sideways and came to a stop. The trunk popped open, and we spilled out of it. I'd never been so grateful for fresh air. I got in the passenger seat beside Mikhail, and Lissa and Eddie took the back. Once we were settled, Mikhail continued driving without another word.

I allowed myself a few more moments of guilt over the people I'd involved but then let it go. It was too late to worry now. I also let go of my guilt about Adrian. He would have been a good ally, but I could hardly ask for his help in this.

And with that, I settled back and turned my thoughts to the job before us. It would take us about an hour to get to the airport, and from there, the three of us were off to Alaska.

SIX

"YOU KNOW WHAT WE NEED?"

I was sitting between Eddie and Lissa, on our flight from Seattle to Fairbanks. As the shortest—marginally—and the mastermind, I'd gotten stuck with the middle seat.

"A new plan?" asked Lissa.

"A miracle?" asked Eddie.

I paused and glared at them both before responding. Since when had they become the comedians here? "*No.* Stuff. We need cool gadgets if we're going to pull this off." I tapped the prison blueprint that had been on my lap for almost every part of our trip so far. Mikhail had dropped us off at a small airport an hour away from the Court. We'd caught a commuter flight from there to Philadelphia, and from there to Seattle and now Fairbanks. It reminded me a little of the crazy flights I'd had to take from Siberia back to the U.S. That journey had also gone via Seattle. I was starting to believe that city was a gateway to obscure places.

"I thought the only tools we needed were our wits," mused Eddie. He might be serious about his guardian work most of the time, but he could also turn on his dry humor when relaxed. Not that he was totally at ease with our mission here, now that he knew more of (but not all) the details. I knew he'd snap back into readiness once we landed. He'd been understandably shocked when I'd revealed we were freeing Victor Dashkov. I hadn't told Eddie anything about Dimitri or spirit, only that getting Victor out played a larger role in the greater good. Eddie's trust in me was so implicit that he'd taken me at my word and pursued the issue no further. I wondered how he'd react when he learned the truth.

"At the very least, we're going to need a GPS," I said. "There's only latitude and longitude on this thing. No real directions."

"Shouldn't be hard," said Lissa, turning a bracelet over and over in her hands. She'd opened her tray and spread out Tasha's jewelry across it. "I'm sure even Alaska has modern technology." She'd also turned on a droll attitude, even with anxiety radiating through the bond.

Eddie's good mood faded a little. "I hope you aren't thinking of guns or anything like that."

"No. Absolutely not. If this works how we want, no one will even know we're there." A physical confrontation was likely, but I hoped to minimize serious injury.

Lissa sighed and handed me the bracelet. She was worried because a lot of my plan depended on her charms—literally and figuratively. "I don't know if this'll work, but maybe it'll give you more resistance."

I took the bracelet and slipped it on my wrist. I felt nothing, but I only rarely did with charmed objects. I'd left Adrian a note saying that Lissa and I had wanted to escape for a "girls' getaway" before my assignment and her college visit. I knew he'd be hurt. The girl angle would carry a lot of weight, but he'd feel injured at not being invited along on a daring vacation—if he even believed we were on one. He probably knew me well enough by now to guess most of my actions had ulterior motives. My hope was that he'd spread the story to Court officials when our disappearance was noticed. We'd still get in trouble, but a wild weekend was better than a prison break. And honestly, how could things get worse for me? The one flaw here was that Adrian could visit my dreams and grill me on what was really going on. It was one of the more interesting—and occasionally annoying—spirit abilities. Lissa hadn't learned to walk dreams, but she had a crude understanding of the principle. Between that and compulsion, she'd tried to charm the bracelet in a way that would block Adrian when I slept later.

The plane began its descent into Fairbanks, and I gazed out the window at tall pines and stretches of green land. In Lissa's thoughts, I read how she'd been half-expecting glaciers and snowbanks, despite knowing it was full summer here. After Siberia, I'd learned to keep an open mind about regional stereotypes. My biggest concern was the sun. It had been full daylight when we'd left the Court, and as our travels took us west, the time zone change meant that the sun stayed with us. Now, though it was almost nine in the evening, we had a full, sunny blue sky, thanks to our northern latitude.

It was like a giant safety blanket. I hadn't mentioned this to Lissa or Eddie, but it seemed likely Dimitri would have spies everywhere. I was untouchable at St. Vladimir's and the

Court, but his letters had clearly stated he'd be waiting for me to leave those boundaries. I didn't know the extent of his logistics, but humans watching the Court in daylight wouldn't have surprised me. And even though I'd left hidden in a trunk, there was a strong possibility that Dimitri was already in pursuit. But the same light that guarded the prisoners would keep us safe too. We'd barely have a few hours of night to guard against, and if we pulled this off quickly, we'd be out of Alaska in hardly any time at all. Of course, that might not be such a good thing. We'd lose the sun.

Our first complication came after we landed and tried to rent a car. Eddie and I were eighteen, but none of the car companies would rent to anyone so young. After the third refusal, my anger began to grow. Who would have thought we'd be delayed by something so idiotic? Finally, at a fourth counter, the woman hesitantly told us that there was a guy about a mile from the airport who would likely rent us a car if we had a credit card and a big enough deposit.

We made the walk in pleasant weather, but I could tell the sun was starting to bother Lissa by the time we reached our destination. Bud—of Bud's Rental Cars—didn't seem *quite* as sleazy as expected and did indeed rent us a car when we produced enough money. From there, we got a room at a modest motel and went over our plans again.

All our information indicated that the prison ran on a vampire schedule, which meant this was their active time of the day. Our plan was to stay in the hotel until the following day, when the Moroi "night" came, and catch some sleep beforehand. It gave Lissa more time to work on her charms. Our room was easily defendable.

My sleep was Adrian-free, for which I was grateful, meaning he'd either accepted the girl trip or couldn't break through Lissa's bracelet. In the morning, we rustled up some doughnuts for breakfast and ate a little bleary-eyed. Running against our vampire schedule was throwing us all off a little.

The sugar helped kick-start us, though, and Eddie and I left Lissa around ten to go do some scouting. We bought my coveted GPS and a few other things at a sporting goods store along the way and used it to navigate remote country roads that seemed to lead nowhere. When the GPS claimed we were a mile from the prison, we pulled off to the side of a small dirt road and set off on foot across a field of tall grass that stretched endlessly before us.

"I thought Alaska was tundra," said Eddie, crunching through the tall stalks. The sky was blue and clear again, with only a few clouds that did nothing to keep the sun away. I'd started out in a light jacket but now had it tied around my waist as I sweated. Occasionally a welcome gust of wind would roll through, flattening the grass and whipping my hair around.

"I guess not all parts. Or maybe we have to go further north. Oh, hey. This looks promising."

We came to a stop before a high, barbwire fence with an enormous PRIVATE PROPERTY—NO UNAUTHORIZED PERSONNEL ALLOWED sign on it. The lettering was red, apparently to emphasize how serious they were. Personally, I would have added a skull and crossbones to really drive the message home.

Eddie and I studied the fence for a few moments, then gave each other resigned glances. "Lissa will heal up anything we get," I said hopefully.

Climbing barbed wire isn't impossible, but it's not fun. Tossing my jacket on the wires I had to grip went a long way to protect me, but I still ended up with some scratches and snagged clothing. Once I was at the top, I jumped down, preferring the jolting landing to another climb down. Eddie did the same, grimacing at the hard impact.

We walked a little farther, and then the dark line of a building came into sight. We both came to a halt as one and knelt down, seeking what coverage we could in the grass. The prison file had indicated that they had cameras on the outside, which meant we risked detection if we got too close. I'd bought high-power binoculars along with the GPS and took them out now, studying the building's exterior.

The binoculars were good—really good—as well they should have been for the price. The level of detail was amazing. Like so many Moroi creations, the building was a mixture of the old and the new. The walls were made of sinister gray stone blocks and almost entirely obscured the actual prison, whose roof just barely peeped above. A couple of figures paced along the top of the walls, living eyes to go with the cameras. The place looked like a fortress, impenetrable and inescapable. It deserved to be on a rocky cliff, with a sinister black sky behind it. The field and sun seemed out of place.

I handed the binoculars to Eddie. He made his own assessment and then gestured to the left. "There."

Squinting, I just barely made out a truck or SUV driving up toward the prison. It went around the back and vanished from sight. "Our only way in," I murmured, recalling the blueprint. We knew we had no shot of scaling the walls or even getting close enough on foot without being spotted. We needed to literally walk through the front door, and that's where the plan got a little sketchy.

Eddie lowered the binoculars and glanced over at me, brow furrowed. "I meant what I said before, you know. I trust you. Whatever reason you're doing this, I know it's a good one. But before things start moving, are you *sure* this is what you want?"

I gave a harsh laugh. "Want? No. But it's what we need to do."

He nodded. "Good enough."

We watched the prison a while longer, moving around to get different angles while still keeping a wide perimeter. The scenario was about what we'd expected, but having a 3-D visual was still helpful.

After about a half hour, we returned to the hotel. Lissa sat cross-legged on one of the beds, still working on the charms. The feelings coming through her were warm and content. Spirit always made her feel good—even if it had side effects later—and she thought she was making progress.

"Adrian called my cell phone twice," she told me when we entered.

"But you didn't answer?"

"Nope. Poor guy."

I shrugged. "It's better this way."

We gave her a rundown of what we'd seen, and her happy mood began to plummet. Our visit made what we were going to do later today more and more real, and working with so much spirit had already put her on edge. A few moments later, I sensed her swallowing her fear. She became resolved. She'd told me she would do this and she intended to stand by her word, even though she dreaded each second that brought her closer to Victor Dashkov.

Lunch followed, and then a few hours later, it was time to put the plan into motion. It was early evening for humans, which meant the vampiric night would be drawing to an end soon. It was now or never. Lissa nervously distributed the charms she'd made for us, worried they wouldn't work. Eddie dressed up in his newly bestowed black-and-white guardian formalwear while Lissa and I stayed in our street clothes—with a couple alterations. Lissa's hair was a mousy brown, the result of some wash-in temporary hair color. My hair was tightly bound up underneath a curly red wig that reminded me uncomfortably of my mother. We sat in the backseat of the car while Eddie drove us chauffeur style back along the remote road we'd followed earlier. Unlike before, we didn't pull over. We stayed on the road, driving right up to the prison—or, well, to its gatehouse. No one spoke as we drove, but the tension and anxiety within us all grew and grew.

Before we could even get near the outer wall, there was a checkpoint manned by a guardian. Eddie brought the car to a stop, and I tried to look calm. He lowered the window, and the guardian on duty walked over and knelt so that they were at eye level.

"What's your business here?"

Eddie handed over a piece of paper, his attitude confident and unconcerned, as though this were perfectly normal. "Dropping off new feeders."

The file had contained all sorts of forms and papers for prison business, including status reports and order forms for supplies—like feeders. We'd made a copy of one of the feeder requisition forms and filled it out.

"I wasn't notified of a delivery," the guardian said, not suspicious so much as puzzled. He peered at the paperwork. "This is an old form."

Eddie shrugged. "It's just what they gave me. I'm kind of new at this."

The man grinned. "Yeah, you barely look old enough to be out of school."

He glanced toward Lissa and me, and despite my practiced control, I tensed. The guardian frowned as he studied us. Lissa had given me a necklace, and she'd taken a ring, both charmed with a slight compulsion spell to make others think we were human. It would have been much easier to make her victim wear a charm and force them to think they were seeing humans, but that wasn't possible. The magic was harder this way. He squinted, almost like he was looking at us through a haze. If the charms had worked perfectly, he wouldn't have given us a second glance. The charms were a little flawed. They were changing our appearances but not quite as clearly as we'd hoped. That was why we'd gone to the trouble of altering our hair: if the human-illusion failed, we'd still have some identity protection. Lissa readied herself to work direct compulsion, though we'd hoped it wouldn't come to that with every person we met.

A few moments later, the guardian turned from us, apparently deciding we were human after all. I exhaled and unclenched my fists. I hadn't even realized I'd been holding them. "Hang on a minute, and I'll call this in," he told Eddie.

The guardian stepped away and picked up a phone inside his booth. Eddie glanced back at us. "So far so good?"

"Aside from the old form," I grumbled.

"No way to know if my charm's working?" asked Eddie.

Lissa had given him one of Tasha's rings, charmed to make him appear tan-skinned and black-haired. Since she wasn't altering his race, the magic only needed to blur his features. Like our human charms, I suspected it wasn't projecting the exact image she'd hoped for, but it should have altered his appearance enough that no one would identify Eddie later. With our resistance to compulsion—and knowing there was a charm in place, which negated its effects on us—Lissa and I couldn't say for certain what he looked like to others.

"I'm sure it's fine," said Lissa reassuringly.

The guardian returned. "They say go on in, and they'll sort it out there."

"Thanks," said Eddie, taking the form back.

The guard's attitude implied that he assumed this was a clerical error. He was still diligent, but the idea of someone sneaking feeders into a prison was hardly the kind of thing one would expect—or view as a security risk. Poor guy.

Two guardians greeted us when we arrived at the door in the prison's wall. The three of us got out and were led into the grounds between the wall and the prison itself. Whereas St. Vladimir's and the Court's grounds had been lush and filled with plants and trees, the land here was stark and lonely. Not even grass, just hard-packed earth. Was this what served as the prisoners' "exercise area"? Were they even allowed outside at all? I was surprised there wasn't a moat of some sort out here.

The inside of the building was as grim as its exterior. The holding cells at Court were sterile and cold, all metal and blank walls. I'd expected something similar. But whoever had designed Tarasov had foregone the modern look and instead emulated the kind of prison one might have found back in Romania in medieval days. The harsh stone walls continued down the hall, gray and foreboding, and the air was chill and damp. It had to make for unpleasant working conditions for the guardians assigned here. Presumably they wanted to ensure the intimidating façade extended everywhere, even for prisoners first entering the gates. According to our blueprint, there was a little section of dorms where employees lived. Hopefully those were nicer.

Dark Ages décor or not, we passed the occasional camera as we walked down the hallway. This place's security was in no way primitive. Occasionally we heard the heavy slamming of a door, but overall, there was a perfect, eerie silence that was almost creepier than shouts and screams.

We were taken to the warden's office, a room that still had the same gloomy architecture yet was filled with the usual administrative accessories: desk, computer, etc. It looked efficient, nothing more. Our escorts explained that we were going to see the assistant warden, since the senior one was still in bed. It figured. The subordinate would have gotten stuck with the night shift. I hoped that meant he was tired and unobservant. Probably not. That rarely happened to guardians, no matter their assignments.

"Theo Marx," said the assistant warden, shaking Eddie's hand. He was a dhampir not much older than us, and I wondered if he'd only been freshly assigned here.

"Larry Brown," replied Eddie. We'd come up with a boring name for him, one that wouldn't stand out, and had used it in the paperwork.

Theo didn't speak to Lissa and me, but he did give us that same puzzled glance the first guy had as the charm's glamour attempted its illusion. Another delay followed, but once more, we slipped through. Theo returned his attention to Eddie and took the requisition form.

"This is different from the usual one," he said.

"I have no clue," said Eddie apologetically. "This is my first time."

Theo sighed and glanced at the clock. "The warden'll be on duty in another couple hours. I think we're just going to have to wait until he's here to figure out what's going on. Sommerfield's usually got their act together."

There were a few Moroi facilities in the country that

gathered feeders—those on the fringes of human society who were content to spend their lives high on vampire endorphins—and then distributed them. Sommerfield was the name of one such facility, located in Kansas City.

"I'm not the only new person they just received," Eddie said. "Maybe someone got confused."

"Typical," snorted Theo. "Well, you might as well have a seat and wait. I can get coffee if you want."

"When are we getting a feeding?" I suddenly asked, using the whiniest, dreamiest voice I could. "It's been so long."

Lissa followed my lead. "They said we could when we got here."

Eddie rolled his eyes at what was typical feeder behavior. "They've been like this the whole time."

"I can imagine," said Theo. "Humph. Feeders." The door to his office was partially ajar and he called out of it. "Hey, Wes? Can you come here?"

One of the escort guardians stuck his head inside. "Yeah?"

Theo gave us a dismissive wave. "Take these two down to the feeding area so they don't drive us crazy. If someone's up, they can use them."

Wes nodded and beckoned us out. Eddie and I made the briefest of eye contact. His face betrayed nothing, but I knew he was nervous. Getting Victor out was our job now, and Eddie didn't like sending us to the dragon's lair.

Wes led us through more doors and security checkpoints as we went deeper into the prison. I realized that for every layer of security I crossed to get in, I was going to have to cross it again to escape. According to the blueprint, the feeding area was situated on the opposite side of the prison. I'd assumed we'd take some route along the periphery, but instead we cut right through the building's center—where the prisoners were kept. Studying had given me a sense of the layout, but Lissa didn't realize where we were headed until a sign alerted us: WARNING—NOW ENTERING PRISONER AREA (CRIMINAL). I thought that was an odd wording. Wasn't everyone in here a criminal?

Heavy double doors blocked this section off, and Wes used both an electronic code and a physical key to cross through. Lissa's pace didn't change, but I felt her anxiety increase as we entered a long corridor lined with bar-covered cells. I didn't feel any better about it myself, but Wes—while still alert—didn't display any sign of fear. He entered this area all the time, I realized. He knew its security. The prisoners might be dangerous, but passing by them was a routine activity for him.

Still, peeking inside the cells nearly made my heart stop. The little compartments were as dark and gloomy as anything, containing only bare-bones furnishings. Most of the prisoners were asleep, thankfully. A few, however, watched as we walked by. None of them said anything, but the silence was almost scarier. Some of the Moroi held there looked like ordinary people you'd pass on the street, and I wondered what they could have possibly done to end up here. Their faces were sad, devoid of all hope. I did a double take and realized that some of the prisoners weren't Moroi; they were dhampirs. It made sense but still caught me off guard. My own kind would have criminals that needed to be dealt with, too.

But not all of the prisoners appeared benign. Others looked like they definitely belonged in Tarasov. There was a malevolence about them, a sinister feel as their eyes locked onto us and didn't let go. They scrutinized our every detail, though for what reason, I couldn't say. Were they seeking out anything that might offer escape? Could they see through our façades? Were they simply hungry? I didn't know but felt grateful for the silent guardians posted throughout the hall. I was also grateful that I didn't see Victor and assumed he lived in a different hall. We couldn't risk being recognized yet.

We finally exited the prisoners' corridor through another set of double doors and at last reached the feeding area. It too felt like a medieval dungeon, but images had to be kept up for the sake of the prisoners. Décor aside, the feeding room's layout was similar to what St. Vladimir's had, except it was smaller. A few cubicles offered moderate privacy, and a bored-looking Moroi guy was reading a book at a desk but looked ready to fall asleep. There was only one feeder in the room, a scraggly-looking, middle-aged human who sat in a chair with a dopey smile on his face, staring at nothing.

The Moroi flinched when we entered, his eyes going wide. Clearly, we were the most exciting thing to happen to him all night. He didn't have that moment of disorientation when he glanced at us; he apparently had low compulsion resistance, which was good to know.

"What's this?"

"Two new ones just came in," said Wes.

"But we're not due," said the Moroi. "And we never get ones this young. They always give us the old, used-up ones."

"Don't ask me," said Wes, moving toward the door once he'd indicated seats for Lissa and me. It was clear he found escorting feeders beneath him. "Marx wants them here until Sullivan gets up. My guess is it's going to turn out to be a mistake, but they were complaining about needing a fix."

"Wonderful," groaned the Moroi. "Well, our next meal's due in fifteen minutes, so I can give Bradley over there a break. He's so gone, I doubt he'd notice if someone else gave blood instead of him."

Wes nodded. "We'll call down when we've got this straight."

The guardian left, and the Moroi picked up a clipboard with a sigh. I had the feeling everyone here was kind of tired of their jobs. I could understand why. This had to be a miserable place to work. Give me the wider world anytime.

"Who's due to feed in fifteen minutes?" I asked.

The Moroi's head jerked up in astonishment. It wasn't the kind of question a feeder asked. "What did you say?"

Lissa stood up and got him in her gaze. "Answer her question."

The man's face went slack. He *was* easy to compel. "Rudolf Kaiser."

No one either of us recognized. He could have been in here for mass murder or embezzlement for all I knew. "When's Victor Dashkov due?" asked Lissa.

"Two hours."

"Alter the schedule. Tell his guards there's been a

readjustment and he has to come now instead of Rudolf."

The Moroi's blank eyes—now as dazed looking as Bradley the feeder's, really—seemed to take a moment to process this. "Yes," he said.

"This is something that might happen normally. It won't raise suspicion."

"It won't raise suspicion," he repeated in a monotone.

"Do it," she ordered, voice hard. "Call them, set it up, and do not take your eyes off of me."

The Moroi complied. While speaking on the phone, he identified himself as Northwood. When he disconnected, the arrangements had been made. We had nothing to do but wait now. My entire body was tightly wound with tension. Theo had said we had over an hour until the warden was on duty. No one would ask questions until then. Eddie simply had to kill time with Theo and not raise suspicions behind a paperwork error. *Calm down, Rose. You can do this.*

While we waited, Lissa compelled Bradley the feeder into a heavy sleep. I didn't want any witnesses, even not drugged ones. Likewise, I turned the room's camera ever so slightly, so it no longer could see the bulk of the room. Naturally, we'd have to deal with the prison's entire surveillance system before we left, but for now, we needed no watching security personnel to catch sight of what was about to happen.

I had just settled into one of the cubicles when the door opened. Lissa had stayed in her chair near Northwood's desk, so that she could keep her compulsion on him. We'd instructed him that I would be the feeder. I was enclosed, but through

Lissa's sight, I saw the group enter: two guardians . . . and Victor Dashkov.

The same distress she'd felt when seeing him at her trial shot up within her. Her heart rate increased. Her hands shook. The only thing that had finally calmed her back at the trial was the resolution of it all, knowing Victor would be locked away forever and unable to hurt her again.

And now we were about to change all that.

Forcibly, Lissa shoved her fear out of her mind so that she could keep her hold on Northwood. The guardians beside Victor were stern and ready for action, though they didn't really need to be. The sickness that had plagued him for years—the one Lissa had temporarily healed him of—was starting to rear its head again. Lack of exercise and fresh air appeared to have taken a toll too, as had the limited blood prisoners were supposedly given. The guards had him clad in shackles as an extra precaution, and the heavy weight dragged him down, almost making him shuffle.

"Over there," said Northwood, pointing at me. "That one."

The guardians led Victor past Lissa, and he barely gave her a second glance. She was working double compulsion: keeping Northwood under her control and using a quick burst to make herself insignificant to Victor when he walked by. The guardians settled him into a chair beside me and then stepped back, still keeping him in sight. One of them struck up conversation with Northwood, noting our newness and youth. If I ever did this again, I'd have Lissa charm us into looking older.

Sitting beside me, Victor leaned toward me and opened his

mouth. Feedings were so second nature, the motions always the same, that he hardly had to think about what he did. It was like he didn't even see me.

Except, then . . . he did.

He froze, his eyes going wide. Certain characteristics marked the royal Moroi families, and light, jade-green eyes ran amongst both the Dashkovs and the Dragomirs. The weary, resigned look in his disappeared, and the cunning sharpness that so characterized him—the shrewd intellect I knew well—snapped into place. It reminded me eerily of some of the prisoners we'd passed earlier.

But he was confused. Like the other people we'd encountered, my charm was muddling his thoughts. His senses told him I was a human . . . yet the illusion wasn't perfect. There was also the fact that Victor, as a strong non–spirit compulsion wielder, was relatively resistant to it. And just as Eddie, Lissa, and I had been immune to one another's charms because we knew our true identities, Victor experienced the same effect. His mind might insist that I was human, but his eyes told him I was Rose Hathaway, even with my wig. And once that knowledge was solidified, the human illusion disappeared for him.

A slow, intrigued smile spread over his face, blatantly displaying his fangs. "Oh my. This might be the best meal I've ever had." His voice was barely audible, covered by the conversation of the others.

"Put your teeth anywhere near me and it'll be your last meal," I murmured, voice just as quiet. "But if you want any chance of getting out of here and seeing the world again, you'll do exactly what I say."

He gave me a questioning look. I took a deep breath, dreading what I had to say next.

"Attack me."

SEVEN

"NOT WITH YOUR TEETH," I added hastily. "Throw yourself at me. Swing your shackles. Whatever you can do."

Victor Dashkov was not a stupid man. Others might have hesitated or asked more questions. He did not. He might not know exactly what was going on, but he sensed that this was a shot at freedom. Possibly the only one he'd ever get. He was someone who had spent a large part of his life masterminding complicated plots, so he was a pro at slipping right into them.

Holding his hands up as much as he could manage, he lunged at me, making a good show of trying to choke me with the chain between his cuffs. As he did, I gave a bloodcurdling shriek. In an instant, the guardians were there to stop this crazy prisoner who was senselessly attacking a poor girl. But as they reached to subdue him, I leapt up and attacked *them*. Even if they'd expected me to be dangerous—and they hadn't—I had so much surprise on them that they had no time to react. I *almost* felt bad at how unfair it was to them.

I punched the first hard enough that he lost his grip on Victor and flew backward, hitting the wall near Lissa as she frantically compelled Northwood to stay calm and not call anyone in the midst of this chaos. The other guardian had slightly more time to react, but he was still slow in letting go of Victor and turning on me. I used the opening and got a punch in, forcing the two of us into a grappling match. He was big and formidable, and once he deemed me a threat, he didn't hold back. A blow to my shoulder sent shooting pain through my arm, and I responded with a swift knee in his stomach. Meanwhile, his counterpart was on his feet heading toward us. I had to end this fast, not only for my own sake but also because they would undoubtedly call for backup if given a moment's chance.

I grabbed the one closest to me and pushed him as hard as I could into a wall—headfirst. He staggered, dazed, and I did it again, just as his partner reached me. That first guardian slumped to the ground, unconscious. I hated doing that, but part of my training had been learning to differentiate between incapacitating and killing. He should only have a headache. I hoped. The other guardian was very much on the offensive, however, and he and I circled each other, getting in some shots and dodging others.

"I can't knock him out!" I called to Lissa. "We need him. Compel him."

Her response came through the bond. She could compel two people at the same time, but it took a lot of strength. We weren't out of this yet, and she couldn't risk burning herself out so soon. Frustration replaced fear within her.

"Northwood, go to sleep," she barked. "Right there. On your desk. You're exhausted and will sleep for hours."

Out of the corner of my eye, I saw Northwood slump, his head hitting the desk with a *thump*. Everyone who worked here would have a concussion by the time we were through. I threw myself at the guardian then, using my full weight to get him within Lissa's line of sight. She pushed her way into our fight. He glanced at her in surprise, and that was all she needed.

"Stop!"

He didn't respond as quickly as Northwood, but he did hesitate. This guy was more resistant.

"*Stop fighting!*" she repeated more forcefully, intensifying her will.

Strong or not, he couldn't stand against that much spirit. His arms fell to his sides, and he stopped wrestling me. I stepped back to catch my breath, straightening my wig back into place.

"Holding this one's going to be hard," Lissa told me.

"Hard as in five minutes or five hours?"

"Somewhere in the middle."

"Then let's move. Get Victor's key from him."

She demanded the guardian give her the key for the shackles. He told us the other guardian had it. Sure enough, I frisked the unconscious body—he was breathing steadily, thank God—and retrieved the key. Now I turned my full attention on Victor. Once the fight had started, he'd stepped out of the way and simply observed quietly while all sorts of new possibilities undoubtedly formed in his twisted mind.

I approached and put on my "scary face" as I held up the key. "I'm going to unlock your cuffs now," I told him, in a voice both sweet and menacing. "You're going to do exactly what we tell you to do. You're not going to run, start a fight, or in any way interfere with our plans."

"Oh? Are you using compulsion nowadays too, Rose?" he asked dryly.

"I don't need it." I unlocked the shackles. "I can render you unconscious as easily as that guy and drag you out. Makes no difference to me."

The heavy cuffs and chains fell to the floor. That sly, smug look stayed on his face, but his hands gently touched each wrist. I noticed then that there were welts and bruises on them. Those shackles weren't meant for comfort, but I refused to feel sorry for him. He glanced back up at us.

"How charming," he mused. "Out of all the people who would attempt to rescue me, I never would have expected you two . . . and yet, in retrospect, you're probably the most capable."

"We don't need your running commentary, Hannibal," I snapped. "And don't use the word *rescue*. It makes it sound like you're some wrongfully imprisoned hero."

He arched an eyebrow, like he believed that might indeed be the case. Instead of disputing me, he nodded toward Bradley, who had actually slept through the fight. In his drugged state, Lissa's compulsion had been more than enough to knock him out.

"Give him to me," said Victor.

"What?" I exclaimed. "We don't have time for this!"

"And I have no strength for whatever you have in mind,"

hissed Victor. That pleasant and all-knowing mask vanished, replaced by one vicious and desperate. "Imprisonment involves more than bars, Rose. They starve us of food and blood, trying to keep us weak. Walking here is the only exercise I get, and that's effort enough. Unless you really do plan on dragging me out of here, give me blood!"

Lissa interrupted any response I could make. "Be fast."

I stared at her in astonishment. I'd been about to deny Victor, but through the bond I felt an odd mix of feelings from her. Compassion and . . . understanding. Oh, she still hated him, absolutely. But she also knew what it was like to live on limited blood.

Mercifully, Victor was fast. His mouth was at the human's neck practically before Lissa finished speaking. Dazed or no, feeling teeth in his neck was enough to wake Bradley up. He woke with a start, his face soon moving into the delight feeders took from vampire endorphins. A short burst of blood was all Victor would need, but when Bradley's eyes started to go wide in surprise, I realized Victor was taking more than a quick drink. I leapt forward and jerked Victor away from the scattered feeder.

"What the hell are you doing?" I demanded, shaking Victor hard. It was something I'd wanted to do for a long time. "Did you think you could drain him and become Strigoi right in front of us?"

"Hardly," said Victor, wincing at the grip I had on him.

"That's not what he was doing," said Lissa. "He just lost control for a second."

His bloodlust satisfied, Victor's smooth demeanor had returned. "Ah, Vasilisa. Always so understanding."

"Don't make any assumptions," she growled.

I shot glares at both of them. "We have to go. Now." I turned to the compelled guardian. "Take us to the room where they monitor all security footage."

He didn't respond to me, and with a sigh, I looked expectantly at Lissa. She repeated my question, and he immediately began to leave the room. My adrenaline was running high from the fight, and I was anxious to finish all of this and get us out of here. Through the bond, I sensed her nervousness. She might have defended Victor's need for blood, but as we walked, she kept as far away from him as possible. The stark realization of who he was and what we were doing was creeping up on her. I wished I could comfort her, but there was no time.

We followed the guardian—Lissa asked his name; it was Giovanni—through more halls and security checkpoints. The route he led us on went around the prison's edge, not through the cells. I held my breath almost the entire time, terrified we'd run into someone. Too many other factors were working against us; we didn't need that too. Our luck held, though, and we ran into no one—again probably a result of doing this near the end of the night and not passing through a high-security zone.

Lissa and Mia had gotten the Court guardian to erase the security footage there too, but I hadn't witnessed it. Now, when Giovanni led us into the prison's surveillance room, I couldn't help a small gasp. Monitors covered the walls, and consoles with complex buttons and switches sat in front of them. Computer-covered desks were everywhere. I felt like this room had the power to blast off into space. Everything in the prison was in view: each cell, several halls, and even the warden's office, where Eddie sat making small talk with Theo. Two other guardians were in here, and I wondered if they'd seen us in the halls. But no—they were too fixated on something else: a camera that had been turned to face a blank wall. It was the one I'd adjusted in the feeding room.

They were leaning toward it, and one of them was saying how they should call someone to check down there. Then they both looked up and noticed us.

"Help her subdue them," Lissa ordered Giovanni.

Again, there was hesitation. We would have been better off with a "helper" with a weaker will, but Lissa had had no idea when she chose him. Like before, he eventually sprang into action. Also like before, surprise went a long way in subduing these two guardians. I was a stranger—immediately raising their guard—but still appeared as human. Giovanni was their coworker; they didn't expect an attack from him.

That didn't make them easy to take down, though. Having backup went a long way, and Giovanni was good at his job. We rendered one guardian unconscious pretty quickly, Giovanni using a choke hold to briefly cut off the guy's air until he collapsed. The other guard kept his distance from us, and I noticed his eyes continually shifting toward one of the walls. It had a fire extinguisher, a light switch, and a round silver button.

"That's an alarm!" exclaimed Victor, just as the guardian lunged for it.

Giovanni and I tackled him at the same time, stopping the guy just before his hand could brush the button and send a legion of guards down on us. A blow to the head knocked this guardian out too. With each person I took out in this prison break, a knot of guilt and nausea twisted tighter and tighter in my stomach. Guardians were the good guys, and I couldn't help but keep thinking I was fighting on the side of evil.

Now that we were left to ourselves, Lissa knew the next step. "Giovanni, disable all the cameras and erase the last hour's worth of footage."

There was a greater hesitation on his part this time. Getting him to fight his friends had required a lot of forceful compulsion on her part. She was keeping her control but growing weary, and it was only going to get harder making him obey our commands.

"Do it," growled Victor, coming to stand beside Lissa. She flinched at his proximity, but as his gaze joined hers, Giovanni complied with the order and began flipping switches on the consoles. Victor couldn't match Lissa's power by a long shot, but his small burst of compulsion had strengthened hers.

One by one, the monitors went black, and then Giovanni typed in a few commands on the computer that stored digital footage from the cameras. Red error lights were flashing on the consoles, but there was no one here now to fix them.

"Even if he erases it, there are those who might be able to recover it from the hard drive," noted Victor.

"It's a chance we'll have to take," I said irritably. "Reprogramming or whatever isn't really in my skill set."

Victor rolled his eyes. "Perhaps, but destruction certainly is."

It took me a moment to get what he meant, but then it clicked. With a sigh, I grabbed the fire extinguisher from the wall and beat the computer to a pulp until it was nothing more than a pile of plastic and metal fragments. Lissa winced at each blow and kept glancing at the door.

"I hope that's soundproof," she muttered.

"It looks sturdy," I said confidently. "And now it's time to go."

Lissa ordered Giovanni to return us to the warden's office at the front of the prison. He complied, leading us back through the maze we'd gone through earlier. His codes and security card got us through each checkpoint.

"I don't suppose you can compel Theo into letting us walk out?" I asked Lissa.

Her mouth was set in a grim line. She shook her head. "I don't even know how much longer I can hold Giovanni. I've never used someone as a puppet before."

"It's okay," I said, trying to reassure both of us. "We're almost done with this."

But we were going to have another fight on our hands. After beating up half the Strigoi in Russia, I still felt good about my own strength, but that guilty feeling wouldn't leave me. And if we ran into a dozen guardians, even my strength wasn't going to hold.

I'd lost my bearings from the blueprint, but it turned out that Giovanni's route back to the main office was taking us through a block of cells after all. Another sign read overhead WARNING—NOW ENTERING PRISONER AREA (PSYCHIATRIC).

"Psychiatric?" I asked in surprise.

"Of course," murmured Victor. "Where else do you think they send prisoners with mental problems?"

"To hospitals," I responded, holding back a joke about all criminals having mental problems.

"Well, that's not always—"

"Stop!"

Lissa interrupted him and came to an abrupt halt before the door. The rest of us nearly walked into her. She jerked away, taking several steps back.

"What's wrong?" I asked.

She turned to Giovanni. "Find another way to the office."

"This is the fastest way," he argued.

Lissa slowly shook her head. "I don't care. Find another, one where we won't run into others."

He frowned, but her compulsion held. He abruptly turned, and we scurried to keep up. "What's wrong?" I repeated. Lissa's mind was too tangled for me to pull out her reasoning. She grimaced.

"I felt spirit auras behind there."

"*What?* How many?"

"At least two. I don't know if they sensed me or not."

If not for Giovanni's clip and the urgency pressing on us, I would have come to a stop. "Spirit users . . ."

Lissa had looked so long and hard for others like her. Who'd have thought we'd find them here? Actually . . . maybe we should have expected this. We knew spirit users danced with insanity. Why wouldn't they end up in a place like this? And considering the trouble we'd gone through to learn about the prison, it was no wonder these spirit users had remained hidden. I doubted anyone working here even knew what they were.

Lissa and I exchanged brief glances. I knew how badly she wanted to investigate this, but now wasn't the time. Victor already looked too interested in what we'd said, so Lissa's next words were in my head: *I'm pretty sure any spirit users would see through my charms. We can't risk our real descriptions being discovered—even if they came from people who are allegedly crazy.*

I nodded my understanding, pushing aside curiosity and even regret. We'd have to check into this another time—say, like, the next time we decided to break into a maximum-security prison.

We finally reached Theo's office without further incident, though my heart pounded furiously the entire way as my brain kept telling me, *Go! Go! Go!* Theo and Eddie were chatting Court politics when our group entered. Eddie immediately leapt up and went for Theo, recognizing it was time to go. He had Theo in a choke hold as efficiently as Giovanni had managed earlier, and I was glad someone else was doing this dirty work besides me. Unfortunately, Theo managed a good yelp before passing out and falling to the ground.

Immediately, the two guardians who had escorted us in earlier charged the office. Eddie and I jumped into the fray, and Lissa and Victor got Giovanni in on it too. To make things more difficult, just after we subdued one of the guardians, Giovanni broke out of the compulsion and began fighting *against* us. Worse, he ran to the wall where I discovered—too late—there was another silver alarm button. He slammed his fist against it, and a piercing wail filled the air.

"Shit!" I yelled.

Lissa's skills weren't in physical fighting, and Victor wasn't much better. It was all on me and Eddie to finish these last two—and we had to do it *fast*. The second of the escort guardians went down, and then it was just us and Giovanni. He got a good hit in on me—one that knocked my head against the wall. It wasn't good enough to make me pass out, but the world spun and black and white spots danced before my eyes. It froze me up for a moment, but then Eddie was on him, and Giovanni was soon no longer a threat.

Eddie took my arm to steady me, and then the four of us immediately ran out of the room. I glanced back at the unconscious bodies, again hating myself for it. There was no time for guilt, though. We had to get out. Now. Every guardian in this prison would be here in less than a minute.

Our group ran to the front doors, only to discover them locked from the inside. Eddie swore and told us to wait. He ran back to Theo's office and returned with one of the security cards that Giovanni had often swiped at the doors. Sure enough, this one let us out, and we made a mad dash for the rental car. We piled in, and I was glad Victor kept up with all of us and made none of his annoying comments.

Eddie stepped on the gas and headed back toward the way

we'd come in. I sat beside him in the front. "I guarantee the gate guy's going to know about the alarm," I warned. Our original hope had been to simply leave and tell him there'd been a paperwork mix-up after all.

"Yup," Eddie agreed, face hard. Sure enough, the guardian stepped out of his gatehouse, arms waving.

"Is that a gun?" I exclaimed.

"I'm not stopping to find out." Eddie pushed hard on the gas, and when the guardian realized we were coming through regardless, he jumped out of the way. We crashed through the wooden arm that blocked the road, leaving it a mess of splinters.

"Bud's gonna keep our deposit," I said.

Behind us, I heard the sounds of gunshots. Eddie swore again, but as we sped away, the shots grew fainter, and soon, we were out of range. He exhaled. "If those had hit our tires or windows, we'd have had a lot more to worry about than a deposit."

"They're going to send people after us," said Victor from the backseat. Once again, Lissa had moved as far from him as she could. "Trucks are probably leaving right now."

"You don't think we guessed that?" I snapped. I knew he was trying to be helpful, but he was the last person I wanted to hear from at the moment. Even as I spoke, I peered back and saw the dark shapes of two vehicles speeding down the road after us. They were gaining quickly, leaving no question that the SUVs would soon catch up to our little compact car.

I looked at our GPS. "We need to turn soon," I warned

Eddie, not that he needed my advice.

We'd mapped out an escape route beforehand, one that took lots and lots of twisty turns on these remote back roads. Fortunately, there were a lot of them. Eddie made a hard left and then almost an immediate right. Still, the pursuing vehicles stayed with us in the rearview mirror. It wasn't until a few turns later that the road behind us stayed clear.

Tense silence filled the car as we waited for the guardians to catch up. They didn't. We'd made too many confusing turns, but it took nearly ten minutes for me to accept that we might have actually pulled this off.

"I think we lost them," said Eddie, the wonder in his voice matching my feelings. His face was still lined with worry, his hands gripping the wheel hard.

"We won't lose them until we clear Fairbanks," I said. "I'm sure they'll search it, and it's not that big."

"Where are we going?" asked Victor. "If I'm allowed to ask."

I squirmed around in my seat so that I could look him in the eye. "That's what you're going to tell us. As hard as it is to believe, we didn't do all that just because we missed your pleasant company."

"That *is* hard to believe."

I narrowed my eyes. "We want to find your brother. Robert Doru."

I had the satisfaction of momentarily catching Victor off guard. Then his sly look returned. "Of course. This is a follow-up to Abe Mazur's request, isn't it? I should have known he wouldn't take no for an answer. Of course, I never would have guessed you were in league with him."

Victor apparently didn't know I was actually in the familial league with Abe, and I wasn't about to enlighten him. "Irrelevant," I said coldly. "Now, you're going to take us to Robert. Where is he?"

"You forget, Rose," mused Victor. "You aren't the one with compulsion here."

"No, but I am the one who can tie you up by the side of the road and make an anonymous call back to the prison with your whereabouts."

"How do I know you won't get what you want from me and then turn me back in anyway?" he asked. "I have no reason to trust you."

"You're right. I sure as hell wouldn't trust me. But if things work out, there's a chance we might let you go afterward." No, there really wasn't. "Is this something you want to gamble on? You'll never get another opportunity like this, and you know it."

Victor had no witty quip for that. Score another one for me.

"So," I continued, "are you going to take us to him or not?"

Thoughts I couldn't read churned behind his eyes. No doubt he was scheming about how he could work this to his advantage, probably figuring out how to escape us before we even reached Robert. It was what I would have done.

"Las Vegas," Victor said at last. "We need to go to Las Vegas."

EIGHT

AFTER THE BITCHING I'D DONE to Abe about always going to remote, crappy places, I should have been excited about the prospect of going to Sin City. Alas, I had a few reservations about my next epic trip. First of all, somewhere like Las Vegas was the *last* place I would expect a semi-crazy recluse to be. From the bits and pieces I'd heard, Robert had dropped off the radar and wanted to be alone. A busy, tourist-filled city didn't really fit that description. Second, cities like that were perfect feeding grounds for Strigoi. Crowded. Reckless. Low inhibitions. Very easy for people to disappear—especially when most of them were out at night.

Part of me was certain it had to be a trick on Victor's part, but he swore up and down that it was true. So, with no other leads, Las Vegas became our next destination. We didn't have much time to debate the matter anyway, knowing the guardians would be searching Fairbanks for us. Admittedly, Lissa's charms had altered our appearances enough that they wouldn't be looking for people with our descriptions. They knew what Victor looked like, though, so the sooner we were out of Alaska, the better.

Unfortunately, we had a slight problem.

"Victor has no ID," said Eddie. "We can't take him on a plane."

It was true. All of Victor's possessions had been seized by prison authorities, and in the midst of disabling surveillance and taking out half a dozen guardians, we'd hardly had time to go searching for his personal stuff. Lissa's compulsion was phenomenal, but she was exhausted after wielding so much at the prison. Besides, guardians would likely be watching the airport.

Our "friend" Bud the car rental guy provided the solution. He hadn't been thrilled to see his car returned with all the scratches from Eddie's daredevil driving, but enough cash had finally stopped the human's muttering about "renting to a bunch of kids." It was Victor who thought of an alternative plan and suggested it to Bud.

"Is there a private airport nearby? With flights we might charter?"

"Sure," said Bud. "But it won't be cheap."

"It's not an issue," I said.

Bud eyed us askance. "Did you guys rob a bank or something?"

No, but we were packing a lot of currency. Lissa had a trust fund that doled her out monthly money until she was eighteen, as well as a high-limit credit card. I had a credit card of my own, leftover from when I'd sweet-talked Adrian into funding my Russian trip. I'd let go of the rest of my assets, like the huge bank account he'd set up. But, wrong or not, I'd decided to keep one card on hand, just in case of emergency.

This was certainly an emergency, so we used the card to pay for part of the private plane's cost. The pilot couldn't take us as far as Las Vegas, but he could take us to Seattle, where he was able to connect us with another pilot he knew who could go the rest of the way. More money.

"And Seattle again," I mused, just before the plane took off. The little jet's interior had a set of four seats, two on each side facing each other. I sat next to Victor, and Eddie sat across from him. We figured that was the best protective configuration.

"What about Seattle?" asked Eddie, puzzled.

"Never mind."

Little private jets aren't nearly as fast as big commercial ones, and our trip took a large part of the day. During it, I continued asking Victor about his brother's role in Las Vegas and finally got the answer I wanted. Victor would have had to tell us eventually, but I think he'd gotten a sadistic thrill out of prolonging the answer.

"Robert doesn't live in Las Vegas proper," he explained. "He has a small house—a cabin, I suppose—out by Red Rock Canyon, miles outside the city."

Ah. Now *that* was more what I'd expected. Lissa stiffened at the mention of a cabin, and I felt unease through the bond. When Victor had kidnapped her, he'd taken her to a cabin in the woods and tortured her there. I gave her as reassuring a look as I could. It was times like these I wished the bond worked both ways so that I could truly send her comfort.

"So we'll go out there?"

Victor snorted. "Certainly not. Robert values his privacy

too much. He wouldn't let strangers come to his home. But he'll come to the city if I ask."

Lissa eyed me. *Victor could be setting us up. He had lots of supporters. Now that he's out, he could call them instead of Robert to meet us.*

I gave her a tiny nod, again wishing I could respond back through the bond. I'd thought of this as well. It was imperative we never leave Victor alone to make unsupervised calls. And actually, this plan to meet in Las Vegas itself made me feel better. For our own safety from Victor's henchmen, it was better to be in the city than out in the middle of nowhere.

"Seeing as I've been so helpful," said Victor, "I have the right to know what you want with my brother." He glanced at Lissa. "Looking for spirit lessons? You had to have done some excellent investigative work to find out about him."

"You have no right to know about our plans," I retorted sharply. "And seriously? If you're keeping track of who's been the most helpful here, we are *totally* beating you on the scorecard. You've got a ways to go to catch up after what we did at Tarasov."

Victor's only response was a small smile.

Some of our flight time took place at night, which meant it was early morning when we landed in Las Vegas. The safety of sunlight. I was surprised to see how crowded the airport was. The private one in Seattle had had a fair amount of planes, but the Fairbanks airport had nearly been deserted. This strip was chock-full of little jets, many of them screaming "luxury." I shouldn't have been surprised. Las Vegas was the playground of celebrities and other wealthy people, many of whom probably couldn't lower themselves to fly commercial with ordinary passengers.

There were taxis there, sparing us the ordeal of another rental car. But when the driver asked us where we were going, we all stayed silent. I turned to Victor.

"The middle of the city, right? The Strip?"

"Yes," he agreed. He'd been certain Robert would want to meet strangers somewhere very public. Somewhere he could easily flee.

"The Strip's a big place," said the driver. "You got any place in particular or should I just drop you off in the middle of the street?"

Silence fell over us. Lissa shot me a meaningful look. "The Witching Hour?"

I considered it. Las Vegas was a favorite place for some Moroi. The bright sun made it less appealing for Strigoi, and the windowless casinos created comfortable, dark atmospheres. The Witching Hour was a hotel and casino we'd all heard of. While it had plenty of human customers, it was actually owned by Moroi, so it had lots of clandestine features to make it a great getaway for vampires. Feeders in back rooms. Special Moroi-only lounges. A fair number of guardians on patrol.

Guardians . . .

I shook my head and glanced sideways at Victor. "We can't take him there." Of all the hotels in Las Vegas, the Witching Hour was the last we'd want to go to. Victor's escape had to be breaking news all over the Moroi world. Taking him into Vegas's largest concentration of Moroi and guardians was probably the worst thing we could do at this point.

In the rearview mirror, the driver's face looked impatient. It was Eddie who finally piped up. "The Luxor."

He and I were in the backseat, with Victor between us, and I peered over. "Where did that come from?"

"It puts distance between us and the Witching Hour." Eddie suddenly looked a little sheepish. "And I've always wanted to stay there. I mean, if you're coming to Vegas, why not stay in a pyramid?"

"You can't fault that logic," said Lissa.

"The Luxor it is," I said to the driver.

We rode in silence, all of us—well, except for Victor—staring at the sights in awe. Even in the daytime, the streets of Las Vegas were teeming with people. The young and glamorous walked side by side with older couples from Middle America, who'd probably saved and saved to make this trip. The hotels and casinos we passed were huge, flashy, and inviting.

And when we reached the Luxor . . . yup. It was just like Eddie had said. A hotel shaped like a pyramid. I stared up at it when we got out of the car, trying hard not to let my jaw drop like the starry-eyed tourist I was. I paid the driver and we headed inside. I didn't know how long we'd be staying, but we definitely needed a room as our base of operation.

Stepping into the hotel was like being back in the nightclubs in Saint Petersburg and Novosibirsk. Flashing lights and the overwhelming scent of smoke. And noise. Noise, noise,

noise. The slot machines beeped and rang, chips fell, people yelled in dismay or delight, and the low thrum of conversation filled the room like humming bees. I grimaced. The stimuli grated on my senses.

We passed through the casino's edge to get to the front desk, where the attendant didn't even blink at three teenagers and an old man getting a room together. I had to imagine that around here, they saw it all. Our room was average-size, with two double beds, and somehow we'd lucked out with an amazing view. Lissa stood at the window, entranced by the sights of people and cars on the Strip below, but I jumped straight to business.

"Okay, call him," I ordered Victor. He'd settled down on one of the beds, hands crossed and expression serene, as though he truly were on vacation. Despite that smug smile, I could see the fatigue etched on his face. Even with his blood refill, the escape and long trip had been exhausting, and the effects of his slowly returning disease were naturally taking a toll on his physical strength.

Victor immediately reached for the hotel's phone, but I shook my head. "Liss, let him use your cell. I want a record of this number."

She gingerly handed the phone over, as though he might contaminate it. He took it and gave me a nigh-angelic look. "I don't suppose I could have some privacy? It's been so long since Robert and I have talked."

"No," I snapped. The harshness in my voice startled even me, and it occurred to me Lissa wasn't the only one suffering from all the spirit used today.

Victor gave a small shrug and began dialing. He'd told us on one of the flights that he had Robert's number memorized, and I had to take it on faith that that was who he was calling. I also had to hope Robert's number hadn't changed. Of course, even if Victor hadn't seen his brother in years, Victor had only been imprisoned a short while and had probably kept tabs on Robert beforehand.

Tension filled the room as we waited while the phone rang. A moment later, I heard a voice answer through the phone's speaker—though I couldn't make out the exact words.

"Robert," said Victor pleasantly, "it's Victor."

This received a frantic response on the other end. I only could hear half of the conversation, but it was intriguing. Victor first had to spend a lot of time convincing Robert that he was out of prison. Apparently, Robert wasn't so removed from Moroi society that he was out of touch with current news. Victor told him that the details would be revealed later and then began making his pitch for Robert to come meet us.

It took a long time. I got the feeling that Robert lived in fear and paranoia, which reminded me of Ms. Karp when she'd been in the advanced stages of spirit's insanity. Lissa's gaze stayed fixed on the scene outside the window during the entire call, but her feelings mirrored mine: fear that this could someday be her fate. Or mine as well, if I siphoned away spirit's effects. The image of the Tarasov sign flashed briefly through her mind: *WARNING—NOW ENTERING PRISONER AREA (PSYCHIATRIC).*

Victor's voice turned surprisingly cajoling as he spoke to

his brother, gentle even. I was reminded uneasily of the old days, before we'd known about Victor's demented plans for Moroi domination. Back then, he'd treated us kindly too and had practically been a member of Lissa's family. I wondered if at some point he'd been sincere or if it had all been an act.

Finally, after almost twenty minutes, Victor convinced Robert to come see us. The unintelligible words on the other end of the phone were filled with anxiety, and at this point, I felt convinced that Victor truly was talking to his crazy brother and not one of his accomplices. Victor set up a dinner meeting at one of the hotel's restaurants and at last disconnected.

"Dinner?" I asked when Victor set the phone down. "Isn't he worried about being out after dark?"

"It's an early dinner," Victor replied. "Four thirty. And the sun won't go down until almost eight."

"Four thirty?" I asked. "Good God. Are we getting the senior citizen special?"

But he made a good point about the time and sun. Without the safety of Alaska's nearly nonstop summer light, I was starting to feel suffocated by the pressure of sunrise and sunset boundaries, even though it was summer here. Unfortunately, a safe early dinner still meant we had hours to pass.

Victor leaned back on the bed, arms behind his head. I think he was attempting an unconcerned air, but my guess was that it was actually exhaustion driving him to seek the bed's comfort.

"Care to try your luck downstairs?" He glanced over at Lissa. "Spirit users make remarkably good card players. I don't have to tell you how good you are at reading people."

She made no response.

"Nobody's leaving this room," I said. I didn't like the idea of us all being cooped up here, but I couldn't risk an escape attempt or Strigoi lurking in the casino's dark corners.

After showering the dye from her hair, Lissa pulled up a chair by the window. She refused to get any closer to Victor. I sat cross-legged on the second bed, where there was plenty of room for Eddie to sit too, but he remained upright against a wall, in perfect guardian posture as he watched Victor. I had no doubt Eddie could maintain that position for hours, no matter how uncomfortable it got. We'd all been trained to endure harsh conditions. He did a good job at looking stern, but every once in a while, I'd catch him studying Victor curiously. Eddie had stood by me in this act of treason but still didn't know why I'd done it.

We'd been there a few hours when someone knocked at the door. I leapt up.

Eddie and I mirrored each other, both of us straightening to rigid attention, hands going for our stakes. We'd ordered lunch an hour ago, but room service had long since come and gone. It was too early for Robert, and besides, he didn't know the name our room was under. There was no nausea, though. No Strigoi at our door. I met Eddie's gaze, silent messages passing between us on what to do.

But it was Lissa who acted first, rising from her chair and taking a few steps across the room. "It's Adrian."

"What?" I exclaimed. "Are you sure?"

She nodded. Spirit users usually only saw auras, but they

could sense each other if they were close enough—just as she had at the prison. Still, none of us moved. She gave me a dry look.

"He knows I'm here," she pointed out. "He can feel me too."

I sighed, still keeping my hand on my stake, and strode to the door. I squinted through the peephole. Standing there, his expression amused and restless, was Adrian. I could see no one else, and with no indication of Strigoi to be found, I finally opened the door. His face lit with joy when he saw me. Leaning in, he gave me a quick kiss on the cheek before stepping into the room.

"You guys didn't really think you could go off on a party weekend without me, did you? Especially *here* of all places—"

He froze, and it was one of those rare moments when Adrian Ivashkov was caught totally and completely off guard.

"Did you know," he said slowly, "that Victor Dashkov is sitting on your bed?"

"Yeah," I said. "It was kind of a shock to us too."

Adrian dragged his gaze from Victor and glanced around the room, noticing Eddie for the first time. Eddie had been standing so still that he practically seemed like part of the furniture. Adrian turned to me.

"What the *hell* is going on? Everyone is out looking for him!"

Lissa's words spoke to me through my bond. *You might as well tell him. You know he won't leave now.*

She was right. I didn't know how Adrian had found us, but now that he had, there was no way he'd go. I glanced hesitantly at Eddie, who guessed my thoughts.

"We'll be fine," he said. "Go talk. I won't let anything happen."

And I'm strong enough again that I can compel him if he tries anything, Lissa added.

I sighed. "Okay. We'll be right back."

I took Adrian's arm and led him outside. As soon as we were in the hallway, he started in again. "Rose, what's—"

I shook my head. In our time here, I'd heard enough noise from other hotel guests in the hall to know that my friends would hear our conversation if we talked out there. Instead, Adrian and I took the elevator and headed downstairs, where the noise of the casino would mask our words. We found a slightly out-of-the-way corner, and Adrian practically pushed me against the wall, his expression dark. His light attitude annoyed me sometimes, but I preferred it to when he was upset, largely because I feared spirit would add an unstable edge.

"You leave me a note saying you're sneaking off for one last party weekend, and instead I find you holed up with one of the most notorious criminals ever? When I left Court, that's all everyone was talking about! Didn't that guy try to kill you?"

I answered his question with a question. "How did you even find us?"

"The credit card," he said. "I was waiting for you to use it."

My eyes widened. "You promised me when I got all those that you wouldn't go snooping!" Since my accounts and cards had come with his help, I'd known he had access to the records but had believed him when he'd said he'd respect my privacy.

"When you were in Russia, I kept that promise. This is different. I kept checking and checking with the company, and as soon as the activity with the charter plane showed up, I called and found out where you were going." Adrian's arrival here so soon after ours wasn't that unbelievable if he had been monitoring the card. Once he'd had the information he needed, he could have easily booked a flight. A nonstop commercial jet would have made up the time on our slower, multistop trip. "There was no way I could resist Vegas," he continued. "So I thought I'd surprise you and show up to join in the fun." I'd used my card for the room, I realized, again tipping off our location. No one else was linked to my or Lissa's cards, but the ease with which he'd tracked us made me nervous.

"You shouldn't have done that," I growled. "We might be together, but there are boundaries you've got to respect. This is none of your business."

"It's not like I was reading your diary! I just wanted to find my girlfriend and—" It was a sign of Adrian's distress that his mind was only now beginning to backtrack and put pieces together. "Oh lord. Rose, please tell me you guys aren't the ones who busted him out? They're all looking for two human girls and a dhampir guy. The descriptions don't match at all . . ." He groaned. "But it *was* you, wasn't it? Somehow, you broke into a maximum-security prison. With Eddie."

"Must not have been all that secure," I remarked lightly.

"Rose! This guy has fucked with both of your lives. Why would you free him?"

"Because . . ." I hesitated. How could I explain this to Adrian? How could I explain that which, by all evidence in our world, was impossible? And how could I explain what goal in particular was driving this? "Victor has information we need. Or, well, he has access to someone we need. This was the only way we could get it."

"What on earth could he possibly know to make you do all this?"

I swallowed. I walked into prisons and nests of Strigoi, but saying what I did next to Adrian filled me with apprehension. "Because there might be a way to save Strigoi. To turn them back to the way they were. And Victor . . . Victor knows someone who might have done this."

Adrian stared at me for several long seconds, and even in the midst of the casino's movement and noise, it was like the world grew still and silent.

"Rose, that's impossible."

"It might not be."

"If there was a way to do that, we would know."

"It involves spirit users. And we only just found out about them."

"That doesn't mean it's—oh. I see." His deep green eyes flashed, and this time, they were angry. "It's him, isn't it? This is your last crazy attempt to get to him. To Dimitri."

"Not just him," I said vaguely. "It could save all Strigoi."

"I thought this was over!" Adrian exclaimed. His voice was loud enough that a few people at nearby slot machines glanced over. "You told me it was over. You told me you could move on and be with me."

"I meant it," I said, surprised at the desperate note in my voice. "It's something we only just found out about. We had to try."

"And what then? What if this stupid fantasy works? You free Dimitri in some miraculous act, and you drop me like *that*." He snapped his fingers.

"I don't know," I said wearily. "We're just taking this one step at a time. I love being with you. Really. But I can't ignore this."

"Of course you can't." He turned his eyes heavenward. "Dreams, dreams. I walk them; I live them. I delude myself with them. It's a wonder I can spot reality anymore." The weird sound of his voice made me nervous. I could recognize one of his slightly crazy, spirit-induced lapses. Then, he turned from me with a sigh. "I need a drink."

Whatever pity I'd felt for him turned to anger. "Oh, good. That'll fix everything. I'm glad in a world gone mad, you've still got your old standbys."

I flinched at his glare. He didn't do it very often, and when he did, it was a powerful thing. "What do you expect me to do?" he asked.

"You could . . . you could . . ." Oh God. "Well, now that you're here, you could help us. Plus, this guy we're meeting. He's another spirit user."

Adrian didn't betray his thoughts, but I had a feeling that I had piqued his interest. "Yeah, that's exactly what I want. To help my girlfriend get her old boyfriend back." He turned away again, and I heard him mutter, "I need *two* drinks."

"Four thirty," I called after him. "We're meeting at four thirty."

There was no response, and Adrian melted into the crowd.

I returned to the room in a dark cloud that had to be obvious to everyone. Lissa and Eddie were smart enough not to ask questions, but Victor, of course, had no such reserves.

"What? Mr. Ivashkov isn't joining us? I'd so been looking forward to his company."

"Shut up," I said, crossing my arms and leaning against the wall near Eddie. "Don't speak unless you're spoken to."

The next couple hours dragged by. I was convinced that any minute, Adrian would come back and reluctantly agree to help us. We could use his compulsion if things went bad, even though he couldn't match Lissa. Surely . . . surely he loved me enough to come to my aid? He wouldn't abandon me? *You're an idiot, Rose.* It was my own voice that chastised me in my head, not Lissa's. *You've given him no reason to help. You just hurt him again and again. Just like you did Mason.*

When four fifteen came around, Eddie looked over at me. "Should we stake out a table?"

"Yeah." I was restless and upset. I didn't want to stay in this room any longer, trapped with dark feelings that wouldn't go away. Victor rose from the bed, stretching as though getting up from a relaxing nap. Still, I could have sworn there was an eager glint hidden in the depths of his eyes. By all accounts, he and his half-brother were close, though I'd seen no indication that Victor displayed love or loyalty to anyone. Who knew?

Maybe somewhere there was true affection for Robert.

We formed a sort of protective configuration with me in the front, Eddie in the back, and the two Moroi between us. I opened the room's door and came face-to-face with Adrian. His hand was raised as though he'd been about to knock. He arched an eyebrow.

"Oh, hey," he said. He had the standard laid-back Adrian expression on his face, though his voice was a bit strained. I knew he wasn't happy about any of this. I could see it in the tight set of his jaw and agitation in his eyes. Nonetheless, he was putting on a good front for the others, for which I was grateful. Most importantly, he'd come back. That was what mattered, and I could ignore the scent of alcohol and smoke wreathing him. "So . . . I hear there's some party going on. Mind if I join you?"

I gave him a weak, grateful smile. "Come on."

Our group now up to five, we headed down the hall toward the elevator. "I was cleaning up at poker, you know," Adrian added. "So this better be good."

"I don't know if it'll be good," I mused. The elevator doors opened. "But I think it'll be memorable."

We stepped inside, off to see Robert Doru. And what might be Dimitri's only salvation.

NINE

ROBERT DORU WAS EASY TO SPOT.

It wasn't because he looked like Victor. It wasn't even because of any dramatic running-toward-each-other reunion type thing between him and his brother. Rather, it was Lissa's mind that tipped me off. I saw Robert through her eyes, the golden aura of a spirit user lighting up his corner of the restaurant like a star. It caught her by surprise, and she stumbled briefly. Spirit users were too rare a sight for her to be fully used to them. Seeing auras was something she could tune in or out, and just before "turning his off," she noted that even though his had the brilliant gold she saw in Adrian, there was also a feel of instability to it. Sparks of other colors flashed there too, but they trembled and flickered. She wondered if it was a mark of spirit's insanity setting in.

His eyes lit up as Victor approached the table, but the two didn't hug or touch. Victor simply sat down beside his brother. The rest of us stood there awkwardly for a moment. The whole situation was too weird. But it was the reason we'd come, and after several more seconds, my friends and I joined the brothers at the table.

"Victor . . ." breathed Robert, eyes wide. Robert might have had some of the Dashkov facial features, but his eyes were brown, not green. His hands toyed with a napkin. "I can't believe it. . . . I've wanted to see you for so long. . . ."

Victor's voice was gentle, as it had been on the phone, as if he were talking to a child. "I know, Robert. I missed you too."

"Are you staying? Can you come back and stay with me?" Part of me wanted to snap that that was a ridiculous idea, but the desperation in Robert's voice sparked a tiny bit of pity in me. I remained silent, simply watching the drama before me unfold. "I'd hide you. It'd be great. Just the two of us."

Victor hesitated. He wasn't stupid. Despite my vague claims on the plane, he knew the odds of me letting him go were non-existent. "I don't know," he said quietly. "I don't know."

The waiter's arrival jolted us out of our haze, and we all ordered drinks. Adrian ordered a gin and tonic and wasn't even carded. I wasn't sure if it was because he looked twenty-one or was convincing enough with spirit. Regardless, I wasn't thrilled about it. Alcohol muted spirit. We were in a precarious situation, and I would have liked him at full strength. Of course, considering he'd been drinking earlier, it probably didn't matter now.

After the waiter left, Robert seemed to notice the rest of us. His eyes passed over Eddie quickly, sharpened at Lissa and Adrian, and lingered on me for a long time. I stiffened, not liking the scrutiny. He finally turned back to his brother.

"Who have you brought, Victor?" Robert still had that oblivious, scattered air to him but it was lit with suspicion now. Fear and paranoia. "Who are these children? Two spirit users and . . ." His gaze fell on me again. He was reading my aura. "One of the shadow-kissed?"

For a moment, I was astonished at his use of the term. Then I remembered what Mark, Oksana's husband, had told me. Robert had once been bonded to a dhampir—and that dhampir had died, drastically speeding up the deterioration of Robert's mind.

"They're friends," said Victor smoothly. "Friends who'd like to talk to you and ask you some questions."

Robert frowned. "You're lying. I can tell. And they don't consider you a friend. They're tense. They keep their distance from you."

Victor didn't deny the friend claim. "Nonetheless, they need your help, and I promised it to them. It was the price for me being allowed to visit you."

"You shouldn't have made promises for me." Robert's napkin was now in shreds. I kind of wanted to give him mine.

"But didn't you want to see me?" asked Victor winningly. His tone was warm, his smile *almost* genuine.

Robert looked troubled. Confused. I was again reminded of a child and was starting to have my doubts that this guy had ever transformed a Strigoi.

He was spared an answer yet again when our drinks arrived. None of us had even picked up our menus, much to the waiter's obvious annoyance. He left, and I opened mine without really seeing it.

Victor then introduced us to Robert, as formally as he might at any diplomatic function. Prison hadn't dulled his sense of royal etiquette. Victor gave first names only. Robert turned back to me, that frown still on his face, and glanced between Lissa and me. Adrian had said that whenever we were together, our auras showed that we were linked.

"A bond . . . I've almost forgotten what it was like . . . but Alden. I've never forgotten Alden . . ." His eyes grew dreamy and almost vacant. He was reliving a memory.

"I'm sorry," I said, surprised to hear the sympathy in my words. This was hardly the harsh interrogation I'd envisioned. "I can only imagine what it must have been like . . . losing him. . . ."

The dreamy eyes grew sharp and hard. "No. You cannot. It's like nothing you can imagine. *Nothing*. Right now . . . right now . . . you have the world. A universe of senses beyond those of others, an understanding of another person that no one can have. To lose that . . . to have that ripped away . . . it would make you wish for death."

Wow. Robert was pretty good at killing conversation, and we all kind of sat there hoping the waiter would return this time. When he did, we all made halfhearted attempts at ordering food—except Robert—most of us deciding on the spot. The restaurant served Asian cuisine, and I ordered the first thing I saw on the menu: an egg roll sampler.

With food ordered, Victor continued taking the firm hand with Robert that I seemed incapable of managing.

"Will you help them? Will you answer their questions?"

I had a feeling that Victor was pushing Robert on this not so much as a way to pay back us rescuing him, but rather because Victor's scheming nature was dying to know everyone's secrets and motivations.

Robert sighed. Whenever he looked at Victor, there was such a strong expression of devotion and even idol worship. Robert probably couldn't refuse his brother anything. He was the perfect type to play into Victor's plans, and I realized I should possibly be grateful that Robert had grown unstable. If he'd been in full control of his powers, Victor would never have bothered with Lissa last time. He would have already had his own private spirit wielder to use however he wanted.

"What do you want to know?" asked Robert blearily. He addressed me, apparently recognizing my leadership.

I glanced at my friends for moral support and received none. Neither Lissa nor Adrian approved of this mission in the first place, and Eddie still didn't know its purpose. I swallowed, steeling myself, and directed my full attention to Robert.

"We heard you freed a Strigoi once. That you were able to convert him—or her—back to their original state."

Surprise flashed on Victor's usually composed face. He certainly hadn't expected this.

"Where did you hear this?" demanded Robert.

"From a couple I met in Russia. Their names are Mark and Oksana."

"Mark and Oksana . . ." Again, Robert's gaze slipped away for a moment. I had a feeling this happened a lot, that he didn't spend much time in reality. "I didn't know they were still together."

"They are. They're doing really great." I needed him back

in the present. "Is it true? Did you do what they said? Is it possible?"

Robert's responses were always preceded by a pause. "Her."

"Huh?"

"It was a woman. I freed her."

I gasped in spite of myself, hardly daring to process his words.

"You're lying." It was Adrian who spoke, his tone harsh.

Robert glanced at him with an expression amused and scornful. "And who are you to say that? How can you tell? You've bruised and abused your powers so much, it's a wonder you can even touch the magic anymore. And all these things you do to yourself . . . it doesn't truly help, does it? Spirit's punishment still affects you . . . soon you won't be able to tell reality from dream. . . ."

The words stunned Adrian for a moment, but he kept going. "I don't need any physical signs to see that you're lying. I know you are because what you're describing is impossible. There's no way to save a Strigoi. When they're gone, they're gone. They're dead. Undead. Forever ."

"That which is dead doesn't always stay dead. . . ." Robert's words weren't directed at Adrian. They were spoken to me. I shivered.

"How? How did you do it?"

"With a stake. She was killed with a stake, and in doing so, was brought back to life."

"Okay," I said. "That *is* a lie. I've killed plenty of Strigoi with stakes, and believe me, they stay dead."

"Not just any stake." Robert's fingers danced along the edge of his glass. "A special stake."

"A stake charmed with spirit," said Lissa suddenly.

He lifted his eyes to her and smiled. It was a creepy smile. "Yes. You are a clever, clever girl. A clever, gentle girl. Gentle and kind. I can see it in your aura."

I stared off at the table, my mind in overdrive. A stake charmed with spirit. Silver stakes were charmed with the four main Moroi elements: earth, air, water, and fire. It was that infusion of life that destroyed the undead force within a Strigoi. With our recent discovery of how to charm objects with spirit, infusing a stake had never even occurred to us. Spirit healed. Spirit had brought me back from the dead. In joining with the other elements within a stake, was it truly possible that the twisted darkness that gripped Strigoi could be obliterated, thus restoring that person to their rightful state?

I was grateful for the food's arrival because my brain was still moving sluggishly. The egg rolls provided a welcome opportunity to think.

"Is it really that easy?" I asked at last.

Robert scoffed. "It's not easy at all."

"But you just said . . . you just said we need a spirit-charmed stake. And then I kill a Strigoi with it." Or well, not kill. The technicalities were irrelevant.

His smile returned. "Not you. You can't do it."

"Then who . . ." I stopped, the rest of my words dying on my lips. "No. *No.*"

"The shadow-kissed don't have the gift of life. Only the spirit-blessed," he explained. "The question is: Who's capable of doing it? Gentle Girl or Drunken Sod?" His eyes flicked between Lissa and Adrian. "My wager would be on Gentle Girl."

Those words were what snapped me out of my stunned state. In fact, they were what shattered this whole thing, this far-fetched dream of saving Dimitri.

"No," I repeated. "Even if it was possible—and I'm not sure if I believe you—she can't do it. I won't let her."

And in a turn of events almost as astonishing as Robert's revelation, Lissa spun toward me, anger flooding our bond. "And since when can *you* tell me what I can or can't do?"

"Since I don't recall you ever taking guardian training and learning to stake a Strigoi," I returned evenly, trying to keep my voice calm. "You only punched Reed, and that was hard enough." When Avery Lazar had tried to take over Lissa's mind, she'd sent her shadow-kissed brother to do some dirty work. With my help, Lissa had punched him and kept him away. It had been beautifully executed, but she'd hated it.

"I did it, didn't I?" she exclaimed.

"Liss, throwing a punch is *nothing* like staking a Strigoi. And that's not even counting the fact that you have to get near one in the first place. You think you could get in range before one bit you or snapped your neck? No."

"I'll learn." The determination in her voice and mind was admirable, but it took guardians decades to learn what we did—and plenty still got killed.

Adrian and Eddie looked uncomfortable in the midst of our bickering, but Victor and Robert seemed both intrigued and amused. I didn't like that. We weren't here for their entertainment.

I tried to deflect the dangerous topic by turning back to Robert. "If a spirit user brought back a Strigoi, then that person would become shadow-kissed." I didn't point out the obvious conclusion to Lissa. Part of what had driven Avery crazy (aside from normal spirit usage) had been bonding with more than one person. Doing so created a very unstable situation that rapidly led all people involved into darkness and insanity.

Robert's eyes grew dreamy as he stared beyond me. "Bonds form when someone dies—when their soul has actually left and moved onto the world of the dead. Bringing it back is what makes them shadow-kissed. Death's mark is upon them." His gaze suddenly snapped onto me. "Just as it is on you."

I refused to avoid his eyes, despite the chill his words sent through me. "Strigoi are dead. Saving one would mean its soul was brought back from the world of the dead too."

"No," he argued. "Their souls do not move on. Their souls linger . . . neither in this world nor the next. It's wrong and unnatural. It's what makes them what they are. Killing or saving a Strigoi sends the soul back to a normal state. There is no bond."

"Then there's no danger," Lissa said to me.

"Aside from a Strigoi killing you," I pointed out.

"Rose—"

"We'll finish this conversation later." I gave her a hard look.

We held each other's gazes a moment, and then she turned to Robert. There was still an obstinacy in the bond I didn't like.

"How do you charm the stake?" she asked him. "I'm still learning."

I again started to chastise her and then thought better of it. Maybe Robert was wrong. Maybe all it actually took to convert a Strigoi was a spirit-infused stake. He only thought a spirit user had to do it because *he* had done it. Allegedly. Besides, I'd much rather Lissa preoccupy herself with charming than fighting. If the charm part sounded too hard, she might have to give up altogether.

Robert glanced at me and then Eddie. "One of you must have a stake on you. I'll show you."

"You can't take a stake out in public," exclaimed Adrian, in what was a remarkably wise observation. "It might be weird for humans, but it's still obvious that it's a weapon."

"He's right," Eddie said.

"We could go back to the room after dinner," said Victor.

He had that perfectly pleasant and bland look on his face. I studied him, hoping my expression showed my distrust. Even with her zeal, I could sense the hesitation in Lissa too. She wasn't keen on following any suggestion of Victor's. We'd seen in the past how desperately far Victor would go in attempting to fulfill his plans. He'd convinced his own daughter to turn Strigoi and help him escape jail. For all we knew, he was planning the same for—

"That's it," I gasped, feeling my eyes go wide as I stared at him.

"That's what?" Victor asked.

"That's why you had Natalie turn. You thought . . . you knew about this. What Robert had done. You were going to use her Strigoi strength and then have him turn her back."

Victor's already pale face went paler, and he seemed to age before our eyes. His smug look disappeared, and he looked away. "Natalie is dead and long gone," he said stiffly. "There's no point in discussing her."

Some of us made an attempt to eat after that, but my egg roll seemed tasteless now. Lissa and I were thinking the same thing. Among all of Victor's sins, I'd always considered him convincing his own daughter to turn Strigoi to be the most awful. It was what had really sealed the deal for me about him being a monster. Suddenly, I was forced to reevaluate things—forced to reevaluate *him*. If he'd known he could bring her back, it made what he had done terrible—but not *as* terrible. He was still evil in my mind, no question. But if he had believed he could bring Natalie back, then that meant he believed in Robert's power. There was still no way I was letting Lissa near a Strigoi, but this incredible tale had become slightly more credible. I couldn't let it go without further investigation.

"We can go up to the room after this," I said at last. "But not for long." My words were to Victor and Robert. Robert seemed to have faded into his own world again, but Victor nodded.

I gave Eddie a quick glance and got a curt nod of a different sort from him. He understood the risk in taking the brothers to a private place. Eddie was telling me he would be extra-vigilant—not that he wasn't already.

By the time we finished dinner, Eddie and I were both rigid and tense. He walked near Robert, and I stayed by Victor. We kept Lissa and Adrian between the brothers. Yet, even keeping close, it was hard as we cut through the crowded casino. People stopped in our path, walked around us, through us . . . it was chaos. Twice, our group got split by oblivious tourists. We weren't too far from the elevators, but I was getting uneasy about the possibility of Victor or Robert running off through the mob of people

"We need to get out of this crowd," I shouted over to Eddie.

He gave me another of his quick nods and took an abrupt left that caught me by surprise. I steered Victor in that same direction, and Lissa and Adrian sidestepped to keep up with us. I was puzzled until I saw that we were approaching a hall with an EMERGENCY EXIT sign on it. Away from the busy casino, the noise level dimmed.

"Figure there are probably stairs here," Eddie explained.

"Crafty guardian." I flashed him a smile.

Another turn showed us a janitorial closet on our right and ahead of us: a door with a symbol for stairs. The door appeared to lead both outside and to upper floors.

"Brilliant," I said.

"You're, like, on the tenth floor," pointed out Adrian. It was the first time he'd spoken in a while.

"Nothing like a little exercise to—damn." I came to an abrupt halt in front of the door. It had a small warning sign saying that an alarm would go off if the door was opened. "Figures."

"Sorry," said Eddie, like he was personally responsible.

"Not your fault," I said, turning. "Back we go." We'd have to take our chances in the crowd. Maybe the roundabout detour had tired Victor and Robert out enough to make escape unappealing. Neither of them was that young anymore, and Victor was still in bad shape.

Lissa was too tense to think much about being led around, but Adrian gave me a look that clearly said he thought this traipsing was a waste of his time. Of course, he thought this whole Robert thing was a waste of time. I was honestly surprised he was coming with us at all back to the room. I would have expected him to stay in the casino with his cigarettes and another drink.

Eddie, leading our group, took a few steps back toward the casino down the hallway. And then it hit me.

"Stop!" I screamed.

He responded instantly, coming to a halt in the narrow space. A bit of confusion followed. Victor stumbled into Eddie in surprise, and then Lissa stumbled into Victor. Instinct made Eddie reach for his stake, but mine was already out. I'd grabbed it as soon as the nausea had swept me.

There were Strigoi between us and the casino.

TEN

AND ONE OF THEM. . . ONE OF THEM . . .

"No," I breathed, even as I sprang toward the one closest to me—a woman. There appeared to be three Strigoi around us.

Eddie was in motion too, and both of us were trying to shove the Moroi behind us. They didn't need much urging. At the sight of Strigoi, the Moroi had begun to back up—creating sort of a bottleneck. Between Eddie's instant reflexes and the Moroi panic, I was pretty sure no one had noticed what I already had spotted.

Dimitri was among them.

No, no, no, I said, this time to myself. He'd warned me. Over and over, he'd said in his letters that as soon as I was out of the safety of the wards, he would be coming for me. I'd believed him and yet . . . seeing the reality of it was a totally different thing. It had been three months, but in that instant, a million memories ran through my mind in crystal clear sharpness. My captivity with Dimitri. The way his mouth—so, so warm, despite his cold skin—had kissed mine. The feel of his fangs pressing into my neck and the sweet bliss that followed . . .

He looked exactly the same too, with that chalky white pallor and red-ringed eyes that so conflicted with the soft, chin-length brown hair and otherwise gorgeous lines of his face. He even had a leather duster on. It had to be a new one, seeing as his previous coat had gotten pretty torn up in our last fight on the bridge. Where did he keep getting them?

"Get out!" I yelled. My words were to the Moroi, even as my stake bit into the female Strigoi's heart. The momentary confusion with all of us in the hall had been more of a detriment to her than me. I got a good line of sight on her, and it was clear that she hadn't expected me to be so fast. I'd killed a lot of Strigoi because they'd underestimated me.

Eddie didn't have my luck. He stumbled when Victor shoved past him, allowing the other Strigoi—a guy—near the front to backhand Eddie against the wall. Still, that was the kind of thing we faced all the time, and Eddie responded beautifully. He immediately came back from the hit, and with the Moroi out of the way now, Eddie was able to lunge toward the Strigoi and engage him fully.

And me? My attention was on Dimitri.

I stepped over the fallen Strigoi without even looking at her. Dimitri had hovered near the back, sending his minions into the front lines of battle. Maybe it was because I knew Dimitri so well, but I suspected he wasn't surprised that I'd take out the one so quickly and that Eddie was giving the other a tough time. I doubted Dimitri cared whether they lived or died. They were just distractions for him to get to me.

"I told you," said Dimitri, eyes both amused and sharp. He was watching my every move, each of us subconsciously mirroring the other as we waited for an opening to attack.

"I told you I'd find you."

"Yeah," I said, trying to ignore the grunts of Eddie and the other Strigoi. Eddie could take him. I knew he could. "I got the memos."

A ghost of a smile curled up Dimitri's lips, showing the fangs that somehow triggered a mix of both longing and loathing in me. Instantly, I shoved those feelings aside. I'd hesitated before with Dimitri and nearly died because of it. I'd refused to let it happen again, and the adrenaline pumping through my body served as a good reminder that this was a do-or-die situation.

He made the first move, but I dodged it—almost having sensed it coming. That was the problem with us. We knew each other too well—knew each other's moves too well. Of course, that hardly meant we were an even match. Even in life, he'd had more experience than me, and his Strigoi abilities tipped the scale.

"Yet here you are," he said, still smiling. "Foolishly stepping outside when you should have stayed in the safety of Court. I couldn't believe it when my spies told me."

I said nothing, instead attempting a swipe with my stake. He saw that coming too and sidestepped it. His having spies didn't surprise me—even in the daytime. He controlled a network of Strigoi and humans alike, and I'd known he had eyes and ears observing Court. The question was: How the hell had he gotten into this hotel in the middle of the day? Even with human watchers at the airport or monitoring credit cards as Adrian had done, Dimitri and his Strigoi friends should have had to wait until nightfall to get here.

No, not necessarily, I realized a moment later. Strigoi occasionally had work-arounds. Trucks and vans with dark, completely sealed cabins. Underground entrances. Moroi wanting to casino-jump from the Witching Hour knew about secret tunnels connecting certain buildings. Dimitri would have known about all this too. If he'd been waiting for me to come outside of wards, he would have done whatever it took to get to me. I knew better than anyone else how resourceful he was.

I also knew he was trying to distract me with talking.

"And strangest of all," he continued, "you didn't come alone. You brought Moroi. You've always taken risks with your own life, but I didn't expect you to be so hasty with theirs."

Something occurred to me then. Aside from the faint hum of the casino on the other end of the hallway and the sounds of our fight, everything else was silent. We were missing an important noise. Say, like, the alarm from a fire door.

"Lissa!" I yelled. "Get the hell out of here! Get them *all* out of here."

She should have known better. They all should have known better. That door led to the upper floors—and outdoors. The sun was still out. It didn't matter if the alarm brought hotel security down on us. Hell, that might scare the Strigoi off. What mattered was that the Moroi fled to safety.

But a quick check of my bond told me the problem. Lissa was frozen. Stunned. She'd suddenly seen who I was fighting, and the shock of it was too much. Knowing Dimitri was a

Strigoi was one thing. Seeing it—really, really seeing it—well, that was different. I knew from personal experience. Even after being prepared, his appearance still unnerved me. She was blindsided, unable to think or move.

It only took me a heartbeat to assess her feelings, but in a fight with a Strigoi, a single second could be the difference between life and death. Dimitri's chatter had worked, and although I watched him and thought I had my guard up, he got through and shoved me against the wall, hands pinning my arms so painfully that I lost my grip on the stake.

He put his face right up to mine, so close that our foreheads touched. "Roza . . ." he murmured. His breath was warm and sweet against my skin. It seemed like it should have smelled like death or decay, but it didn't. "Why? Why did you have to be so difficult? We could have spent eternity together . . ."

My heart thundered in my chest. I was afraid, terrified of the death that I knew had to be seconds away. And at the same time, I was filled with sorrow over having lost him. Seeing the features of his face, hearing that same accented voice that even now wrapped around me like velvet . . . I felt my heart breaking all over again. Why? Why had this happened to us? Why was the universe so cruel?

I managed to flip the switch again, once more shutting out the fact that this was Dimitri. We were predator and prey—and I was in danger of being eaten.

"Sorry," I said through gritted teeth, shoving hard—and failing—to break his grip. "My eternity doesn't involve being part of the undead mafia."

"I know," he said. I could have sworn there was sadness in his face but later convinced myself I must have imagined it. "Eternity will be lonely without you."

A piercing shriek suddenly rang in my ears. Both of us winced. Noises intended to startle humans were hell on sensitive hearing like we had. Yet I couldn't help but feel relief. The fire door. Finally, those idiots—and yes, I had no qualms about calling my friends idiots when they were acting that way—had left the building. I felt sunlight through the bond and took comfort in that as Dimitri's fangs neared the artery that would spill the life's blood from my neck.

I hoped the alarm would distract him, but he was too good. I struggled once more, hoping I could use surprise on him, but it was to no avail. What *did* surprise him was Eddie's stake plunging into the side of his stomach.

Dimitri snarled in pain and let go of me, turning on Eddie. Eddie's face was hard, unblinking. If seeing Dimitri fazed him, my friend didn't show it. For all I knew, Eddie wasn't even registering this as Dimitri. Probably all he saw was a Strigoi. It was the way we were trained. See monsters, not people.

Dimitri's attention was off me for the moment. He wanted to draw out my death. Eddie was simply an annoyance he needed to rid us of so that he could continue the game.

Eddie and Dimitri engaged in a dance similar to the one I'd been in with Dimitri earlier, except that Eddie didn't know Dimitri's moves like I did. So Eddie wasn't able to completely avoid Dimitri grabbing him by the shoulder and shoving him to the wall. The maneuver had been intended to crush Eddie's skull, but Eddie managed to shift enough so that it was his body that took the brunt of the impact. It still hurt, but he was alive.

All of this took place in milliseconds. And in those fleeting moments, my perspective shifted. When Dimitri had been looming over me, about to bite me, I had managed to overcome that impulse to think of him *as* Dimitri, the person I'd once known and loved. Continually forced into a victim position, with my life about to end, I had kept kicking myself into *fight-fight-fight* mode.

Now, watching someone else battle Dimitri . . . seeing Eddie's stake snake out at him . . . well, suddenly, I lost that cool objectivity. I remembered why I'd come here. I remembered what we'd just learned from Robert.

Fragile. It was still all so fragile. I'd sworn to myself that if we reached a moment where Dimitri was about to kill me and I hadn't learned more about saving Strigoi, I would do it. I would kill him. And this was my chance. Between Eddie and me, we could take Dimitri down. We could end this evil state, just as he'd once wanted.

Yet . . . less than a half hour ago, I'd been given a small piece of hope that a Strigoi could be saved. True, that part about a spirit user doing it was absurd, but Victor had believed. And if someone like him had believed . . .

I couldn't do it. Dimitri couldn't die. Not yet.

I shot out with my stake, a hard strike that raked the silver point against the back of Dimitri's head. He let out a roar of rage and managed to turn and push me off while still fending

Eddie away. Dimitri was that good. But Eddie's stake was getting closer to Dimitri's heart, and my friend's gaze was unwavering, intent on his kill.

Dimitri's attention flitted between the two of us, and in one small lapse—only half a breath long—I saw Eddie get his stake in the zone, ready to take a shot at Dimitri's heart. A shot that looked like it might succeed where mine had failed.

And that was why, in one smooth motion, I struck out with my stake, swiping it across Dimitri's face and knocking Eddie's arm aside as I did. It was a beautiful face. I hated to mar it but knew Dimitri would heal. As I made that attack, I pushed past him, shoving into Eddie so that he and I stumbled toward the fire door that was still shrieking its warning. Eddie's stony face registered surprise, and for a moment we were deadlocked: me pushing him to the door and him pushing back toward Dimitri. I saw the hesitation, though. The positioning was off, and Eddie was on the verge of shoving me into a Strigoi, which his training wouldn't allow.

Dimitri was already seizing the opportunity, though. His hand reached out and grabbed my shoulder, trying to jerk me back. Eddie caught hold of my arm and pulled me forward. I cried out in surprise and pain. It felt like they were going to rip me in two. Dimitri was by far the strongest, but even stuck in the middle, my weight played a role, and I lent my force to Eddie's, which helped us gain some ground. Still, it was slow going. Like walking in honey. For each step I managed forward, Dimitri dragged me back.

But Eddie and I were making slow—and very, very

painful—progress toward the wailing door. A few moments later, I heard the clatter of feet and voices. "Security," grunted Eddie, giving me a tug.

"Shit," I said.

"You can't win," Dimitri hissed. He'd managed to get both hands on my shoulders now and was overpowering us.

"Oh yeah? We're about to have the entire Luxor Attack Squad here."

"We're about to have a pile of bodies here. Humans," he said dismissively.

Those humans reached us. I'm not sure what their impressions were. Some guy attacking teenagers? They shouted about us all letting go and facing them, directions the three of us ignored in our epic tug-of-war match. Then they must have laid hands on Dimitri. He was still gripping me, but his hold slackened enough that one huge pull from Eddie and a near-leap on my part broke me free. Eddie and I didn't even look back, though the security guards were now shouting at us too.

They weren't the only ones shouting. Just before I pushed open the door, I heard Dimitri calling to me. There was laughter in his voice. "It's not over, Roza. Do you really think there's anywhere you can go in this world where I can't find you?" The same warning, always the same warning.

I did my best to ignore the fear those words inspired. Eddie and I burst into smoggy desert air, as well as sunshine that was still hanging in there, despite being early evening. We were in the Luxor's parking lot—which wasn't crowded enough for us to hide in. With no spoken communication, he and I tore off toward the busy Strip, knowing our physical abilities would surpass those of any human pursuers and let us get lost in the mobs of people.

It worked. I never saw how many followed us. My guess was the security staff were devoting their attention to the tall guy killing people in their hotel. The voices shouting after us faded, and Eddie and I finally slowed to a stop in front of New York-New York, and again, without even talking, we immediately turned inside the hotel. It had a twisted layout and was more crowded than the Luxor, and we easily blended in until we could find an empty spot of wall on the far side of the hotel's casino.

The run had been hard even for us, and it took us a moment to catch our breath as we stood there. I knew things were serious when Eddie finally turned on me, and anger lit his features. Eddie was always the picture of calm and control, ever since his first abduction by Strigoi last year. It had toughened him, made him more determined to face any challenge. But oh, was he mad at me now.

"What the hell was that?" exclaimed Eddie. "You let him go!"

I put on my best tough face, but he seemed to be outdoing me today. "What, did you miss the part where I was slashing him with my stake?"

"I had his heart! I had a shot, and you stopped me!"

"Security was coming. We didn't have time. We had to get out of there, and we couldn't let them see *us* do the killing."

"I don't think any of them are left to report seeing anything,"

Eddie replied evenly. He seemed to be trying to regain his composure. "Dimitri left a pile of corpses there. You know it. People died because *you* wouldn't let me stake him."

I flinched, realizing Eddie was right. It should have ended there. I hadn't gotten a good look at the number of security guards. How many had died? It wasn't relevant. Only the fact that innocent people had died mattered. Even one was too many. And it was my fault.

My silence caused Eddie to press his advantage. "How could you of all people forget that lesson? I know he used to be your instructor—*used to be*. But he's not the same. They drilled that into us over and over. Don't hesitate. Don't think of him as a real person."

"I love him," I blurted out, without meaning to. Eddie hadn't known. Only a handful of people knew about my romantic relationship with Dimitri and what had happened in Siberia.

"What?" Eddie exclaimed with a gasp. His outrage had transformed to shock.

"Dimitri . . . he's more than my instructor . . ."

Eddie continued staring at me for several heavy seconds. "Was," he said at last.

"Huh?"

"He *was* more than your instructor. You *loved* him." Eddie's momentary confusion was gone. He was back to hard guardian now, no sympathy. "I'm sorry, but it's in the past, whatever was between you. You have to know that. The person you loved is gone. The guy we just saw? Not the same."

I slowly shook my head. "I . . . I know. I know it's not him. I know he's a monster, but we can save him . . . if we can do what Robert was telling us about. . . ."

Eddie's eyes widened, and for a moment, he was dumbstruck. "*That's* what this is about? Rose, that's ridiculous! You can't believe that. Strigoi are dead. They're gone to us. Robert and Victor were feeding you a bunch of crap."

Now I grew surprised. "Then why are you even here? Why have you stuck with us?"

He threw his hands up in exasperation. "Because you're my *friend*. I stayed with you through all of this . . . breaking out Victor, listening to his crazy brother . . . because I knew you needed me. You all did, to help keep you safe. I thought you had a real reason for getting Victor out—and that you were going to return him. Does it sound crazy? Yeah, but that's normal for you. You've always had good reasons for what you do." He sighed. "But this . . . this is crossing a line. Letting Strigoi go in order to chase some idea—some idea that couldn't possibly work—is ten times worse than what we did with Victor. A hundred times worse. Every day Dimitri walks the world is another day that people are going to die."

I collapsed against the wall and closed my eyes, feeling sick to my stomach. Eddie was right. I had screwed up. I'd promised myself that I would kill Dimitri if I faced him before we could pursue Robert's solution. It all should have ended today . . . but I had choked up. Again.

I opened my eyes and straightened up, needing to find a new purpose before I burst into tears in the middle of this casino.

"We have to find the others. They're out there unprotected."

It was probably the only thing that could have stopped Eddie's scolding just then. Instinctual duty kicked in. Protect Moroi.

"Can you tell where Lissa's at?"

My bond had kept me connected to her during our escape, but I hadn't allowed myself any deeper probing than confirming she was alive and okay. I expanded the link a little further now. "Across the street. At MGM." I'd seen the ginormous hotel when we ran into this one but hadn't realized Lissa was there. Now I could feel her, hiding out in a crowd like us, scared but not injured. I would have rather she and the others opted to hang out in the sun, but instinct had driven her to the shelter of walls.

Eddie and I spoke no more about Dimitri as we headed out and crossed the busy road. The sky was turning peach, but I still felt secure out there. Far more secure than in the Luxor's hallway. With the bond, I could always find Lissa, and without any hesitation, I led Eddie through MGM's twists and turns—honestly, the layout of these places just got more and more confusing—until we saw Lissa and Adrian standing near a row of slot machines. He was smoking. She spotted me, sprinted over, and threw her arms around me.

"Oh my God. I was so scared. I didn't know what had happened to you guys. I *hate* that one-way bond."

I forced a smile for her. "We're fine."

"In a bruised kind of way," mused Adrian, strolling over. I didn't doubt it. In the adrenaline of a fight, it was easy to not notice injuries and pain. Later, when the battle lust faded, you started to realize just what you'd put your body through.

I was so grateful to see Lissa okay that I missed what Eddie had already noticed. "You guys, where are Victor and Robert?"

Lissa's happy face crumpled, and even Adrian looked grim.

"Damn it," I said, needing no explanation.

Lissa nodded, eyes wide and distraught. "We lost them."

ELEVEN

WELL. HOW PERFECT.

It took us a while to decide our next course of action. We tossed around a few feeble ideas to track Robert and Victor, all of which we eventually shot down. Robert's phone was a cell, and while the CIA could trace those kinds of things, we certainly couldn't. Even if Robert's address was listed in the phone book, I knew Victor wouldn't have let them go back there. And while Adrian and Lissa could spot a spirit user's aura, we could hardly go wandering aimlessly in a city and expect to find something.

No, we were out of luck with those two. There was nothing to be done now but head back to Court and face whatever punishment awaited us. We—*I*—had screwed up.

With sunset approaching—and seeing as we no longer had a known criminal to get us in trouble—my group glumly decided to head to the Witching Hour to make our travel plans. Lissa and I had the potential to be recognized over there, but runaway girls weren't quite in the same category as fugitive traitors. We decided to roll the dice (no pun intended) and hang around guardians rather than risk more Strigoi attacks before we could get out of Vegas.

The Witching Hour was no different from any of the other casinos we'd been to—unless you knew what to look for. Humans there were too interested in the allure of the games and glitz to notice that a lot of the other patrons were uniformly tall, slim, and pale. As for the dhampirs? Humans couldn't tell that we weren't human. It was only the uncanny sense Moroi and dhampirs had that let us know who was who.

Sprinkled throughout the cheering, chattering, and—at times—wailing crowd were guardians. As in demand as guardians were, only a handful could be allocated full-time to a place like this. Fortunately, their numbers were reinforced by the wealthy and powerful who'd come to play. Excited Moroi whooped over slot machines or roulette while silent, watchful guardians hovered behind them, keeping an eye on everything. No Strigoi would come here.

"What now?" asked Lissa, almost yelling over the noise. It was the first time any of us had spoken since deciding to go here. We'd come to a halt near some blackjack tables, right in the thick of everything.

I sighed. My mood was so dark, I didn't even need any spirit side effects. *I lost Victor, I lost Victor.* My own mental accusations were on an endless loop.

"We find their business center and book tickets out of here," I said. "Depending on how long until we can catch a flight, we might have to get a room again."

Adrian's eyes were scanning the action around us, lingering longest on one of the many bars. "Wouldn't kill us to spend a little time here."

I snapped. "Really? After everything that's happened, that's all you can think about?"

His enraptured gaze turned back to me and became a frown. "There are cameras here. People who may recognize you. Getting hard proof that you were in this casino and *not* Alaska is a good thing."

"True," I admitted. I think Adrian's typical blasé air was masking discomfort. Aside from learning why I'd really come to Las Vegas, he'd also run into Strigoi—Dimitri among them. That was never an easy experience for any Moroi. "Though we've got no alibi for when we were actually *in* Alaska."

"So long as Victor doesn't get himself spotted around here, no one's going to make the connection." Adrian's voice became bitter. "Which really shows how stupid they all are."

"We helped put Victor away," said Lissa. "No one would think we'd be crazy enough to let him out."

Eddie, staying silent, gave me a pointed look.

"Then it's settled," said Adrian. "Somebody go book us tickets. I'm going to get a drink and try my hand at some games. The universe owes me some good luck."

"I'll get the tickets," said Lissa, scanning a sign that pointed out the directions for the pool, restrooms—and business center.

"I'll go with you," said Eddie. Whereas before his expression had been accusatory, he now seemed to be avoiding my eyes altogether.

"Fine," I said, crossing my arms. "Let me know when you're done, and we'll find you." That was to Lissa, meaning she'd tell me through the bond.

Convinced he was free, Adrian headed straight for the bar, me trailing after him.

"A Tom Collins," he told the Moroi bartender. It was like Adrian had a mental cocktail dictionary in his head and just checked them off one by one. I almost never saw him drink the same thing twice.

"You want it spiked?" the bartender asked. He wore a crisp white shirt and black bow tie and hardly appeared older than me.

Adrian made a face. "No."

The bartender shrugged and turned around to make the drink. "Spiked" was Moroi code for putting a shot of blood into the drink. There were a couple of doors behind the bar, ones that probably led to feeders. Glancing down the bar, I could see happy, laughing Moroi with red-tinged drinks. Some liked the thought of having blood with their alcohol. Most—like Adrian, apparently—wouldn't take blood unless it was "straight from the source." It supposedly didn't taste the same.

While we waited, an older Moroi standing next to Adrian glanced over at me and nodded with approval. "You got yourself a good one," he told Adrian. "Young, but that's the best way." The guy, who was either drinking red wine or pure blood, jerked his head toward the others standing at the bar. "Most of these are used and washed-up."

I followed his shrug, even through there was no need. Interspersed among the humans and Moroi were several dhampir women, dressed very glamorously in silk and velvet dresses that left little to the imagination. Most were older than me. Those who weren't had a weary look in their eyes, despite their flirtatious laughter. Blood whores. I glared at the Moroi.

"Don't you *dare* talk about them like that, or I'll smash that wineglass in your face."

The guy's eyes widened, and he looked at Adrian. "Feisty."

"You have no idea," said Adrian. The bartender returned with the Tom Collins. "She's had kind of a bad day."

The asshole Moroi guy didn't look back at me. He apparently didn't take my threat nearly as seriously as he should have. "Everyone's having kind of a bad day. You hear the news?"

Adrian looked relaxed and amused as he sipped his drink, but standing so close to him, I felt him stiffen a little. "What news?"

"Victor Dashkov. You know, that guy who kidnapped the Dragomir girl and was plotting against the queen? He escaped."

Adrian's eyebrows rose. "Escaped? That's crazy. I heard he was at some maximum-security place."

"He was. No one really knows what happened. There were supposedly humans involved . . . and then the story gets weird."

"How weird?" I asked.

Adrian slipped an arm around me, which I suspected was a silent message to let him do the talking. Whether that was because he believed that was "proper" blood whore behavior or because he was worried I'd punch the guy, I couldn't say.

"One of the guards was in on it—though he claims he was

being controlled. He also conveniently says it's all a haze and he can't remember much. I heard it from some royals who are helping with the investigation."

Adrian laughed, taking down a big gulp of his drink. "That *is* convenient. Sounds like an inside job to me. Victor'd have a lot of money. Easy enough to bribe a guard. That's what I think happened."

There was a pleasant smoothness to Adrian's voice, and as a slightly dopey smile came over the other guy's face, I realized Adrian had pulled a little compulsion. "I bet you're right."

"You should tell your royal friends," added Adrian. "An inside job."

The guy nodded eagerly. "I will."

Adrian held his gaze a few moments more and then finally glanced down to the Tom Collins. The glaze-eyed look faded from the man, but I knew Adrian's order to spread the "inside job" story would stick. Adrian gulped down the rest of the drink and set the empty glass on the bar. He was about to speak again when something across the room caught his attention. The Moroi man noticed too, and I followed both of their gazes to see what had them both so starstruck.

I groaned. Women, of course. At first I thought they were dhampirs since my kind seemed to be making up most of the eye candy here. A double take revealed a surprise: The women were Moroi. Moroi showgirls, to be precise. There were several of them, clad in similar short, low-cut sequined dresses. Only, each one wore a different jewel-toned color: copper, peacock blue . . . Feathers and rhinestones glittered in their hair, and they smiled and laughed as they passed through the gaping crowd, beautiful and sexy in a way different from my race.

Which wasn't a surprise. I tended to notice Moroi men ogling dhampir girls more often, simply because I was a dhampir. But naturally, Moroi men were attracted to and infatuated with their own women. It was how their race survived, and though Moroi men might want to fool around with dhampirs, they almost always ended up with their own kind in the end.

The showgirls were tall and graceful, and their fresh, brilliant appearances made me think they must be on their way to a performance. I could just imagine what a glittering display of dancing they must make. I could appreciate that, but Adrian clearly appreciated it more, judging from his wide-eyed look. I elbowed him.

"Hey!"

The last of the showgirls disappeared through the casino crowd, off toward a sign that said THEATER, just as I'd suspected. Adrian looked back at me, turning on a rogue smile.

"Nothing wrong with looking." He patted my shoulder.

The Moroi standing next to him nodded in agreement. "I think I might take in a show today." He swirled his drink around. "All this Dashkov business and that mess with the Dragomirs . . . makes me sad for poor Eric. He was a good guy."

I put on a dubious look. "You knew Lissa's fath—Eric Dragomir?"

"Sure." The Moroi gestured for a refill. "I've been a manager here for years. He was here all the time. Believe me, *he* had an appreciation for those girls."

"You're lying," I said coolly. "He adored his wife." I'd seen Lissa's parents together. Even at a young age, I'd been able to see how crazy in love they were.

"I'm not saying he *did* anything. Like your boyfriend said, nothing wrong with looking. But a lot of people knew the Dragomir prince liked to party it up wherever he went—especially if there was female company." The Moroi sighed and lifted his glass. "Damn shame what happened to him. Here's hoping they catch that Dashkov bastard and leave Eric's little girl alone."

I didn't like this guy's insinuations about Lissa's dad and was grateful she wasn't around. What made me uneasy was that we'd recently found out Lissa's brother Andre had also been kind of a party boy who fooled around and broke hearts. Did that kind of thing run in the family? What Andre had done wasn't right, but there was a big difference between a teenage boy's exploits and those of a married man. I didn't like to admit it, but even the most in-love guys still checked out other women without cheating. Adrian was proof. Still, I didn't think Lissa would like the idea of her dad flirting around with other women. The truth about Andre had been hard enough, and I didn't want anything to shatter the angelic memories of her parents.

I shot Adrian a look that said listening to this guy any longer really would come down to a fistfight. I didn't want to be standing here if Lissa came searching for us. Adrian, always more astute than he appeared, smiled down at me.

"Well, my sweet, shall we try our luck? Something tells me you're going to beat the odds—like always."

I cut him a look. "Cute."

Adrian winked at me and stood up. "Nice talking to you," he told the Moroi.

"You too," the man said. The thrall of compulsion was wearing off. "You should dress her better, you know."

"I'm not interested in putting clothes *on* her," Adrian called as he steered me away.

"Watch it," I warned through gritted teeth, "or you might be the one with a wineglass in your face."

"I'm playing a part, little dhampir. One that's going to make sure you stay out of trouble." We stopped near the casino's poker room, and Adrian gave me a head-to-toe assessment. "That guy was right about the clothes, though."

I gritted my teeth. "I can't believe he said those things about Lissa's dad."

"Gossip and rumors never go away—you of all people should know that. Doesn't matter if you're dead. Besides, that conversation was actually to our—by which I mean *your*—advantage. Somebody else is probably considering the inside-job theory already. If that guy can help get it around even more, it'll ensure no one even thinks the world's most dangerous guardian could have been involved."

"I suppose." Forcibly, I pushed my temper down. I had always been trigger-happy, and I knew for sure now that the bits of darkness I'd gleaned from Lissa in the last twenty-four hours were making things worse, as I'd feared. I changed the subject, steering to safer ground. "You're being pretty nice now, considering how mad you were earlier."

"I'm not all that happy, but I've done some thinking," Adrian said.

"Oh? Care to enlighten me?

"Not here. We'll talk later. We've got more important things to worry about."

"Like covering up a crime and getting out of this city without being attacked by Strigoi?"

"No. Like me winning money."

"Are you crazy?" Asking Adrian that was never a good idea. "We just escaped a bunch of bloodthirsty monsters, and all you can think about is gambling?"

"The fact that we're alive means we should live," he argued. "Especially if we've got the time, anyway."

"You don't need any more money."

"I will if my dad turns me out. Besides, it's really about enjoying the game."

By "enjoying the game," I soon realized that Adrian meant "cheating." If you considered using spirit cheating. Because there was so much mental power tied into spirit, its users were very good at reading people. Victor had been right. Adrian joked and kept ordering drinks, but I could tell he was paying close attention to the others. And even though he was careful not to say anything explicitly, his expressions spoke for him—confident, uncertain, annoyed. Without words, he was still able to project compulsion and bluff the other players.

"Be right back," I told him, feeling Lissa's call.

He waved me off, unconcerned. I wasn't worried about his safety either, seeing as there were a few guardians in the room. What concerned me was the possibility some casino official would notice his compulsion and throw us all out. Spirit users wielded it the most strongly, but all vampires had it to a certain extent. Using it was considered immoral, so it was banned among Moroi. A casino would definitely have reason to be on the lookout for it.

The business center turned out to be near the poker room, and I found Lissa and Eddie quickly. "What's the report?" I asked as we walked back.

"We've got a flight in the morning," said Lissa. She hesitated. "We could have gone out tonight, but . . ."

She didn't need to finish. After what we'd faced today, no one wanted to risk even the slightest chance of running into a Strigoi. Going to the airport would only require a taxi ride, but even still, that would mean we'd have to risk walking out into the darkness.

I shook my head and led them toward the poker room. "You did the right thing. We've got time to kill now. . . . Do you want to get a room and get some sleep?"

"No." She shivered, and I felt fear in her. "I don't want to leave this crowd. And I'm kind of afraid of what I'd dream. . . ."

Adrian might be able to act like he didn't care about the Strigoi, but those faces were still haunting Lissa—especially Dimitri's. "Well," I said, hoping to make her feel better, "staying up will help get us back on the Court's schedule. You can also watch Adrian get thrown out by casino security."

As I'd hoped, watching Adrian cheat with spirit did indeed distract Lissa—so much so that she grew interested in trying it herself. Great. I urged her to safer games and recapped how Adrian had planted the idea of an inside job in the Moroi guy's head. I left out the part about Lissa's father. The night miraculously passed without incident—either of the Strigoi or security type—and a couple of people even recognized Lissa, which would help our alibi. Eddie didn't speak to me the entire night.

We left the Witching Hour in the morning. None of us were happy about losing Victor or the attack, but the casino had soothed us all a little—at least until we got to the airport. At the casino, we'd been flooded with Moroi news, insulated from the human world. But while waiting for our plane, we couldn't help but watch the TVs that seemed to be everywhere.

The headline story that night was all about a mass killing over at the Luxor, one that had left no clues for the police. Most of the casino guards involved had died from broken necks, and no other bodies were found. My guess was that Dimitri had tossed his cronies outside, where the sun would turn them to ash. Meanwhile, Dimitri himself had slipped away, leaving no other witnesses behind. Even the cameras had recorded nothing, which didn't surprise me. If I could disable surveillance at a prison, Dimitri could certainly manage it at a human hotel.

Whatever mood-improvement we'd achieved instantly disappeared, and we didn't talk much. I stayed out of Lissa's mind because I didn't need her depressed feelings amplifying my own.

We'd arranged a direct flight to Philadelphia and would then catch a commuter flight back to the airport near Court. What we'd face once there . . . well, that was probably the least of our concerns.

I wasn't worried about Strigoi boarding our plane in the daytime, and without any prisoners to watch, I allowed myself to fall into much-needed sleep. I couldn't remember the last time I'd gotten any on this trip. I slept heavily, but my dreams were haunted by the fact that I'd let one of the Moroi's most dangerous criminals escape *and* allowed a Strigoi to walk free *and* gotten a bunch of humans killed. I held none of my friends responsible. This disaster was all on me.

TWELVE

WHICH WAS CONFIRMED WHEN WE finally stumbled back to the Royal Court.

I wasn't the only one in trouble, of course. Lissa was summoned to the queen for chastising, though I knew she'd suffer no actual punishment. Not like Eddie and me. We might be out of school, but we were technically under the jurisdiction of the official guardians now, which meant we faced as much trouble as any disobedient employee. Only Adrian escaped any consequences. He was free to do whatever he wanted.

And really, my punishment wasn't as bad as it could have been. Honestly, what did I have to lose at this point? My chances of guarding Lissa had already been sketchy, and no one had wanted me as a guardian except Tasha anyway. A crazy Vegas weekend—which was our cover story—was hardly enough to dissuade her from taking me on. It was enough, however, to make some of Eddie's prospects withdraw their requests for him to be their guardian. Enough still wanted him that he was in no danger of losing a good position, but I felt horribly guilty. He didn't breathe a word to anyone about what we'd done, but each time he looked at me, I could see the condemnation in his eyes.

And I saw a lot of him in the next couple days. It turned out guardians had a system in place to deal with those who were disobedient.

"What you did was so irresponsible that you might as well be back in school. Hell, elementary school, even."

We were in one of the offices in the guardians' headquarters, being yelled at by Hans Croft, the guy in charge of all the guardians at Court and someone who was instrumental in guardian assignments. He was a dhampir in his early fifties, with a bushy gray-and-white mustache. He was also an asshole. The scent of cigar smoke always encircled him. Eddie and I were sitting meekly before him while he paced with his hands behind his back.

"You could have gotten the last Dragomir killed—not to mention the Ivashkov boy. How do you think the queen would have reacted to the death of her great-nephew? And talk about timing! You go off party-hopping right when the guy who tried to kidnap the princess is running loose. Not that you would know that, seeing as you were probably too busy playing slot machines and using your fake IDs."

I winced at the reference to Victor, though I suppose I should have been relieved that we were above suspicion for his escape. Hans read my grimace as an admission of guilt.

"You might have graduated," he declared, "but that does *not* mean you are invincible."

This whole encounter reminded me of when Lissa and I had returned to St. Vladimir's, when we'd been chastised for the same thing: recklessly running off and endangering her. Only this time, there was no Dimitri to defend me. That memory made a lump form in my throat as I remembered his face, serious and gorgeous, those brown eyes intense and passionate as he spoke up for me and convinced the others of my value.

But no. No Dimitri here. It was just Eddie and me alone, facing the consequences of the real world.

"You." Hans pointed a stubby finger at Eddie. "You might be lucky enough to slide out of this without too many repercussions. Sure, you'll have a black mark on your record forever. And you've totally screwed up your chances of ever having an elite royal position with other guardians to support you. You'll get some assignment though. Working alone with some minor nobility, probably."

High-ranking royals had more than one guardian, which always made protection easier. Hans's point was that Eddie's assignment would be lowly—creating more work and danger for him. Casting him a sidelong glance, I saw that hard, determined look on his face again. It seemed to say he didn't care if he had to guard a family by himself. Or even ten families. In fact, he gave off the vibe that they could drop him alone into a nest of Strigoi and he'd take them all on.

"And *you*." Hans's sharp voice jerked my gaze back to him. "You will be lucky to ever have a job."

Like always, I spoke without thinking. I should have taken this silently like Eddie. "Of course I'll have one. Tasha Ozera wants me. And you're too short on guardians to keep me sitting around."

Hans's eyes gleamed with bitter amusement. "Yes, we

are short on guardians, but there's all sorts of work we need done—not just personal protection. Someone has to staff our offices. Someone has to sit and guard the front gates."

I froze. A desk job. Hans was threatening me with a desk job. All of my horrible imaginings had involved me guarding some random Moroi, someone I didn't know and would possibly hate. But in any of those scenarios, I would be out in the world. I would be in motion. I would be fighting and defending.

But this? Hans was right. Guardians were needed for the Court's administrative jobs. True, they only kept a handful—we were too valuable—but someone had to do it. One of those someones being me was too awful to comprehend. Sitting around all day for hours and hours . . . like the guards in Tarasov. Guardian life had all sorts of unglamorous—but necessary—tasks.

It truly, truly hit me then that I was in the real world. Fear slammed into me. I'd taken on the title of guardian when I graduated, but had I really understood what it meant? Had I been playing make-believe—enjoying the perks and ignoring the consequences? I was out of school. There would be no detention for this. This was real. This was life and death.

My face must have given away my feelings. Hans gave a small, cruel smile. "That's right. We've got all sorts of ways to tame troublemakers. Lucky for you, your ultimate fate's still being decided. And in the meantime, there's *a lot* of work that needs to be done around here that you two are going to be helping with."

That "work" over the next few days turned out to be menial manual labor. Honestly, it wasn't too different from detention, and I was pretty sure it had just been created to give wrongdoers like us something awful to do. We worked twelve hours a day, much of it outdoors hauling rocks and dirt to build some new, pretty courtyard for a set of royal town houses. Sometimes we were put on cleaning duty, scrubbing floors. I knew they had Moroi workers for these kinds of things, and probably they were being given a vacation right now.

Still, it was better than the other work Hans would give us: sorting and filing mountains and mountains of paper. That gave me a new appreciation for information going digital . . . and again made me worry about the future. Over and over, I kept thinking about that initial conversation with Hans. The threat that this could be my life. That I would never be a guardian—in the true sense—to Lissa or any other Moroi. Throughout my training, we'd always had a mantra: *They come first*. If I had really and truly screwed up my future, I'd have a new mantra: *A comes first. Then B, C, D . . .*

Those work days kept me away from Lissa, and the front-desk staff within our respective buildings went out of their way to keep us apart too. It was frustrating. I could keep track of her through the link, but I wanted to talk to her. I wanted to talk to anyone. Adrian stayed away too and didn't bother with dreams, making me wonder how he felt. We'd never had our "talk" after Las Vegas. Eddie and I often worked side by side, but he wasn't speaking to me, which left me with hours of being trapped with my own thoughts and guilt.

And believe me, I had plenty of things to intensify my guilt. Around Court, people didn't really notice workers. So whether I was inside or outside, people were always talking like I wasn't there. The biggest topic was Victor. Dangerous Victor Dashkov on the loose. How could it have happened? Did he have powers no one knew about? People were afraid, some even convinced he'd show up at Court and try to kill everyone in their sleep. The "inside job" theory was running rampant, which continued to keep us above suspicion. Unfortunately, it meant a lot of people now worried about traitors within our midst. Who knew who might be working for Victor Dashkov? Spies and rebels could be lurking at Court, planning all sorts of atrocities. I knew all the stories were exaggerated, but it didn't matter. They all came from one kernel of truth: Victor Dashkov was walking the world a free man. And only I—and my accomplices—knew it was all because of me.

Being seen in Las Vegas had continued to provide an alibi for the prison break and had made what we'd done seem even more rash. People were aghast that we'd let the Dragomir princess run off while there was a dangerous man on the loose—the man who'd assaulted her! Thank God, everyone said, that the queen had pulled us out of there before Victor found us. The Las Vegas trip had also opened up a whole new line of speculation—one that involved me personally.

"Well, that doesn't surprise me about Vasilisa," I overheard a woman say while I was working outdoors one day. She and some friends were strolling along toward the feeders' building and didn't even see me. "She's run away before, right? Those

Dragomirs can be wild ones. She'll probably go straight back to the first party she can find, once they catch Victor Dashkov."

"You're wrong," her friend said. "That's not why she went. She's actually pretty levelheaded. It's that dhampir that's always with her—the Hathaway girl. I heard she and Adrian Ivashkov went to Las Vegas to elope. The queen's people just barely got there in time to stop them. Tatiana's furious, especially since Hathaway declared nothing will keep her and Adrian apart."

Whoa. That was kind of a shock. I mean, I guessed it was better for people to think Adrian and I were running off than for them to accuse me of aiding and abetting a fugitive, but still . . . I was kind of amazed at how that conclusion had come about. I hoped Tatiana hadn't heard about our so-called elopement. I was pretty sure that would ruin whatever progress she and I had made.

My first real social contact came in the form of an unlikely source. I was shoveling dirt into a raised flower bed and sweating like crazy. It was nearing bedtime for Moroi, meaning the sun was out in full summer glory. We at least had a pretty site while working: the Court's giant church.

I'd spent a lot of time at the Academy's chapel but had rarely visited this church since it was set far from the main buildings of the Court. It was Russian Orthodox—the predominant Moroi religion—and reminded me a lot of some of the cathedrals I'd seen while actually in Russia, though not nearly as big. It was made of beautiful red stonework, its towers topped with green-tiled domes, which were in turn topped with golden crosses.

Two gardens marked the far boundaries of the church's extensive grounds, one of which we were working on. Near us was one of the Court's most remarkable sites: a giant statue of some ancient Moroi queen that was almost ten times my height. A matching statue of a king stood on the opposite side of the grounds. I could never remember their names but was pretty sure we'd gone over them in one of my history classes. They'd been visionaries, changing the Moroi world of their time.

A figure appeared in my periphery, and I assumed it was Hans coming to give us another awful chore. Looking up, I was astonished to see it was Christian.

"Figures," I said. "You know you'll get in trouble if someone sees you talking to me."

Christian shrugged and sat on the edge of a partially completed stone wall. "Doubt it. You're the one who'll get into trouble, and I really don't think things can get any worse for you."

"True," I grunted.

He sat there in silence for several moments, watching me shovel pile after pile of dirt. Finally, he asked, "Okay. So how and *why* did you do it?"

"Do what?"

"You know exactly what. Your little adventure."

"We got on a plane and flew to Las Vegas. Why? Hmm. Let's think." I paused to wipe sweat off my forehead. "Because where else are we going to find pirate-themed hotels and bartenders who don't card very much?"

Christian scoffed. "Rose, don't bullshit me. You did not go to Las Vegas."

"We've got plane tickets and hotel receipts to prove it, not to mention people who saw the Dragomir princess hit it big on slot machines."

My attention was on my work, but I suspected Christian was shaking his head in exasperation. "As soon as I heard three people had broken Victor Dashkov out of prison, I knew it had to be you. Three of you gone? No question."

Not far away, I saw Eddie stiffen and glance around uneasily. I did the same. I might have been desperate for social contact, but not at the risk of dangerous parties overhearing us. Our crimes getting out would make garden labor seem like a vacation. We were alone, but I still pitched my voice low and attempted an honest face.

"I heard they were humans hired by Victor." That was yet another theory running wild, as was this one: "Actually, I think he turned Strigoi."

"Right," Christian said snidely. He knew me too well to believe me. "And I also heard one of the guardians has no memory of what made him attack his friends. He swears he was under the control of someone. Anyone who had that kind of compulsion could probably make others see humans, mimes, kangaroos. . . ."

I refused to look at him and slammed the shovel hard into the ground. I bit my lip on any angry retort.

"She did it because she thinks Strigoi can be restored to

their original form."

My head shot up, and I stared at Eddie in disbelief, astonished he'd spoken. "What are you doing?"

"Telling the truth," replied Eddie, never stopping his work. "He's our friend. You think he's going to report us?"

No, rebel Christian Ozera was not going to report us. But that didn't mean I wanted this out. It's a fact of life: The more people who know a secret, the more likely it is to leak.

Unsurprisingly, Christian's reaction was not all that different from everyone else's. "*What*? That's impossible. Everyone knows that."

"Not according to Victor Dashkov's brother," said Eddie.

"Will you stop it?" I exclaimed.

"You can tell him or I will."

I sighed. Christian's pale blue eyes were staring at us, wide and shocked. Like most of my friends, he rolled with crazy ideas, but this was pushing the crazy line.

"I thought Victor Dashkov was an only child," Christian said.

I shook my head. "Nope. His dad had an affair, so Victor's got an illegitimate half-brother. Robert. And he's a spirit user."

"Only you," said Christian. "Only you would find something like this."

I ignored what appeared to be a return to his normal cynicism. "Robert claims to have healed a Strigoi—killed the undead part of her and brought her back to life."

"Spirit has limits, Rose. You might have been brought back, but Strigoi are *gone*."

"We don't know about spirit's full range," I pointed out. "Half of it is still a mystery."

"We know about St. Vladimir. If he could restore Strigoi, don't you think a guy like him would have been doing it? I mean, if that's not miraculous, what is? Something like that would have survived in the legends," argued Christian.

"Maybe. Maybe not." I retied my ponytail, replaying our encounter with Robert in my mind for the hundredth time. "Maybe Vlad didn't know how. It's not all that easy."

"Yeah," agreed Eddie. "This is the good part."

"Hey," I shot back at him. "I know you're mad at me, but with Christian here, we really don't need anyone else making snide comments."

"I don't know," said Christian. "For something like this, you actually might need two people. Now explain how this miracle is supposedly done."

I sighed. "By adding spirit to a stake, along with the other four elements."

Spirit charms were still a new concept to Christian too. "Never thought of that. I guess spirit would shake things up . . . but I can't imagine you staking a Strigoi with a spirit-charmed stake would be enough to bring them back."

"Well . . . that's the thing. According to Robert, *I* can't do it. It has to be done by a spirit user."

More silence. I'd rendered Christian speechless yet again.

At last he said, "We don't know that many spirit users. Let alone any who could fight *or* stake a Strigoi."

"We know two spirit users." I frowned, recalling Oksana in

Siberia and Avery locked away . . . where? A hospital? A place like Tarasov? "No, four. Five, counting Robert. But yeah, none of them can really do it."

"It doesn't matter because it can't be done," Eddie said.

"We don't know that!" The desperation in my own voice startled me. "Robert believes it. Victor even believes." I hesitated. "And Lissa does too."

"And she wants to do it," Christian said, catching on quickly. "Because she would do anything for you."

"She can't."

"Because she doesn't have the ability or because you won't let her?"

"Both," I cried. "I'm not letting her anywhere near a Strigoi. She's already . . ." I groaned, hating to reveal what I'd discovered in our time apart through the bond. "She got a hold of a stake and is trying to charm it. So far, she hasn't had much luck, thank God."

"If this *were* possible," began Christian slowly. "It could change our world. If she could learn . . . "

"What? No!" I'd been so eager to get Christian to believe me, and now I wished he hadn't. The one saving grace in all this was that with none of my friends thinking it was possible, none of them had given any thought to Lissa actually trying to fight a Strigoi. "Lissa's no warrior. No spirit user we know is, so unless we find one, I'd rather . . . " I winced. "I'd rather Dimitri died."

That finally made Eddie stop working. He threw down his shovel. "Really? I never would have guessed that."

Sarcasm to rival my own.

I spun around and strode toward him, my fists clenched. "Look, I can't take this anymore! I'm sorry. I don't know what else to say. I know I screwed up. I let Dimitri get away. I let Victor get away."

"You *let* Victor get away?" asked Christian, startled.

I ignored him and continued shouting at Eddie. "It was a mistake. With Dimitri . . . it was a weak moment. I failed in my training. I know I did. We both know it. But you know I didn't intend the damage I caused. If you're really my friend, you *have* to know it. If I could take it back . . ." I swallowed, surprised to feel my eyes burning. "I would. I swear I would, Eddie."

His face was perfectly still. "I believe you. I am your friend, and I know . . . I know you didn't mean for things to turn out like they did."

I sagged in relief, surprised at how truly worried I'd been about losing his respect and friendship. Looking down, I was startled to see my fists balled up. I relaxed them, unable to believe I'd been that upset. "Thank you. Thank you so much."

"What's all this shouting?"

We both turned and saw Hans heading toward us. And he looked pissed off. I also noticed then that Christian had practically vanished into thin air. Just as well.

"This isn't social time!" growled Hans. "You two still have another hour left today. If you're going to get distracted, then maybe you should be separated." He beckoned to Eddie. "Come on. There's some filing with your name on it."

I shot Eddie a sympathetic look as Hans led him away. Yet I was relieved it wasn't me off to do paperwork.

I continued my labors, my mind spinning with the same questions I'd had all week. I had meant what I said to Eddie. I wanted so badly for this dream of Dimitri being saved to be true. I wanted it more than anything—except Lissa risking her life. I shouldn't have hesitated. I should have just killed Dimitri. Victor wouldn't have escaped. Lissa wouldn't have given Robert's words a second thought.

Thinking of Lissa pushed me into her mind. She was in her room, doing some last-minute packing before going to bed. Tomorrow was her Lehigh visit. Unsurprisingly, my invitation to go with her had been revoked in light of recent events. Her birthday—something that had been horribly overlooked in this mess—was this weekend as well, and it didn't seem right for me to be apart from her during it. We should have been celebrating together. Her thoughts were troubled, and she was so consumed by them that a sudden knock at the door made her jump.

Wondering who could be visiting her at this hour, she opened the door and gasped to see Christian standing there. It was surreal to me too. Part of me still kept thinking we were in our school dorms, where rules—theoretically—kept guys and girls out of each other's rooms. But we were no longer there. We were technically adults now. He must have gone straight to her room after seeing me, I realized.

It was astonishing how quickly the tension ratcheted up between them. A bundle of emotions burst into Lissa's chest, the usual mix of anger, grief, and confusion.

"What are you doing here?" she demanded.

The same emotions were in his face. "I wanted to talk to you."

"It's late," she said stiffly. "Besides, I seem to remember you don't like talking."

"I want to talk about what happened with Victor and Robert."

That was enough to startle her out of her anger. She cast an anxious look into the hallway and then beckoned him inside. "How do you know about that?" she hissed, hastily shutting the door.

"I just saw Rose."

"How did you get to see her? *I* can't see her." Lissa was as frustrated as me over how our superiors had been keeping us apart.

Christian shrugged, careful to maintain a safe distance between them in the suite's small living room. Both of them had their arms crossed defensively, though I don't think they realized how they were mirroring each other. "I snuck into her prison camp. They've got her shoveling dirt for hours."

Lissa grimaced. With the way they'd kept us separated, she hadn't known much about my activities. "Poor Rose."

"She's managing. Like always." Christian's eyes turned toward the couch and her open suitcase, where a silver stake lay on top of a silk blouse. I doubted that shirt would survive the trip without a million wrinkles. "Interesting thing to bring on a college visit."

Lissa hastily shut the suitcase. "That's none of your business."

"Do you really believe it?" he asked, ignoring her comment. He took a step forward, his eagerness apparently making him forget about wanting to keep away. Even as distracted as she was by the situation, Lissa immediately became aware of their new proximity, the way he smelled, the way the light shone on his black hair. . . . "Do you think you could bring back a Strigoi?"

She turned her attention back to the conversation and shook her head. "I don't know. I really don't. But I feel like . . . I feel like I have to try. If nothing else, I want to know what spirit in a stake will do. That's harmless enough."

"Not according to Rose."

Lissa gave him a rueful smile, realized what she was doing, and promptly dropped it. "No. Rose doesn't want me going anywhere near this idea—even though she wants it to be real."

"Tell me the truth." His gaze burned to her. "Do you think you have any chance of staking a Strigoi?"

"No," she admitted. "I could barely throw a punch. But . . . like I said, I feel like I should try. I should try to learn. To stake one, I mean."

Christian pondered this for a few moments and then gestured toward the suitcase again. "You're going to Lehigh in the morning?"

Lissa nodded.

"And Rose got cut from the trip?"

"Of course."

"Did the queen offer to let you bring another friend?"

"She did," admitted Lissa. "In particular, she suggested Adrian. But he's sulking . . . and I'm not really sure if I'm in the mood for him."

Christian seemed pleased by this. "Then bring me."

My poor friends. I wasn't sure how much more shock any of them could handle today.

"Why the hell would I bring *you*?" she exclaimed. All her anger returned at his presumption. It was a sign of her agitation that she'd sworn.

"Because," he said, face calm, "I can teach you how to stake a Strigoi."

THIRTEEN

"THE HELL YOU CAN," I said aloud to no one.

"No, you can't," said Lissa, with an expression that matched my own incredulity. "I know you've been learning to fight with fire, but you haven't done any staking."

Christian's face was adamant. "I have—a little. And I can learn more. Mia's got some guardian friends here that have been teaching her physical combat, and I've learned some of it."

The mention of him and Mia working together didn't do much to improve Lissa's opinion. "You've barely been here a week! You make it sound like you've been training for years with some master."

"It's better than nothing," he said. "And where else are you going to learn? Rose?"

Lissa's outrage and disbelief dimmed a little. "No," she admitted. "Never. In fact, Rose would drag me away if she caught me doing it."

Damn straight I would. In fact, despite the obstacles and staff that kept blocking me, I was tempted to march over there right now.

"Then this is your chance," he said. His voice turned wry.

"Look, I know things aren't . . . great with us, but that's irrelevant if you're going to learn this. Tell Tatiana you want to bring me to Lehigh. She won't like it, but she'll let you. I'll show you what I know in our free time. Then, when we get back, I'll take you to Mia and her friends."

Lissa frowned. "If Rose knew . . ."

"That's why we'll start when you're away from Court. She'll be too far away from you to do anything."

Oh, for the love of God. I would give them some lessons about fighting—starting with a punch to Christian's face.

"And when we get back?" asked Lissa. "She'll find out. It's inevitable with the bond."

He shrugged. "If she's still on landscape duty, we'll be able to get away with it. I mean, she'll know, but she won't be able to interfere. Much."

"It may not be enough," Lissa said with a sigh. "Rose was right about that—I can't expect to learn in a few weeks what it took her years to do."

Weeks? *That* was her timeline on this?

"You have to try," he said, almost gentle. Almost.

"Why are you so interested in this?" Lissa asked suspiciously. "Why do you care so much about bringing Dimitri back? I mean, I know you liked him, but you don't quite have the same motivation here that Rose does."

"He was a good guy," said Christian. "And if there was a way to turn him back to a dhampir? Yeah, that'd be amazing. But it's more than that . . . more than just him. If there was a way to save all Strigoi, that would change our world. I mean, not that setting them on fire isn't cool after they've gone on killing sprees, but if we could stop those killing sprees in the first place? That's the key to saving us. All of us."

Lissa was speechless for a moment. Christian had spoken passionately, and there was a hope radiating off of him that she just hadn't expected. It was . . . moving.

He took advantage of her silence. "Besides, there's no telling what you'd do without any guidance. And I'd like to reduce the odds of you getting yourself killed, because even if Rose wants to deny it, I know you're going to keep pushing this."

Lissa stayed quiet yet again, pondering the situation. I listened to her thoughts, not liking at all where they were going.

"We're leaving at six," she said at last. "Can you meet me downstairs at five thirty?" Tatiana wouldn't be thrilled when she heard about the new guest choice, but Lissa was pretty sure she could do some fast talking in the morning.

He nodded. "I'll be there."

Back in my room, I was totally aghast. Lissa was going to attempt to learn to stake a Strigoi—*behind my back*—and she was going to get Christian to help her. Those two had been snarling at each other since the breakup. I should have felt flattered that sneaking around me was bringing them together, but I wasn't. I was pissed off.

I considered my options. The buildings Lissa and I were staying in didn't have the kind of front-desk curfew security that our school dorms had had, but the staff here had been instructed to tip off someone in the guardians' office if I got too social. Hans had also told me to stay away from Lissa until further notice. I pondered it all for a moment, thinking it might be worth Hans dragging me from Lissa's room, and then finally thought of an alternate plan. It was late but not *too* late, and I left my room for the one next door to mine. Knocking on the door, I hoped my neighbor was still awake.

She was a dhampir my age, a recent graduate from a different school. I didn't own a cell phone, but I'd seen her talking on one earlier today. She answered the door a few moments later and fortunately didn't appear to have been in bed.

"Hey," she said, understandably surprised.

"Hey, can I send a text from your phone?"

I didn't want to commandeer her phone with a conversation, and besides, Lissa might just hang up on me. My neighbor shrugged, stepped into the room, and returned with the phone. I had Lissa's number memorized and sent her the following note:

I know what you're going to do, and it is a BAD idea. I'm going to kick both your asses when I find you.

I handed the phone back to its owner. "Thanks. If anyone texts back, can you let me know?"

She told me she would, but I didn't expect any return texts. I got my message another way. When I returned to the room and Lissa's mind, I got to be there when her phone chimed. Christian had left, and she read my text with a rueful smile. My answer came through the link. She knew I was watching.

Sorry, Rose. It's a risk I'll have to take. I'm doing this.

* * *

I tossed and turned that night, still angry at what Lissa and Christian were trying to do. I didn't think I'd ever fall asleep, but when Adrian came to me in a dream, it became clear that my body's exhaustion had defeated my mind's agitation.

"Las Vegas?" I asked.

Adrian's dreams always occurred in different places of his choosing. Tonight, we stood on the Strip, very near where Eddie and I had rendezvoused with Lissa and him at the MGM Grand. The bright lights and neon of the hotels and restaurants gleamed in the blackness, but the whole setting was eerily silent compared to the reality. Adrian had not brought the cars or people of the real Las Vegas here. It was like a ghost town.

He smiled, leaning against a pole covered in paper ads for concerts and escort services. "Well, we didn't really get a chance to enjoy it while we were there."

"True." I stood a few feet away, arms crossed over my chest. I had on jeans and a T-shirt, along with my *nazar*. Adrian had apparently decided not to dress me tonight, for which I was grateful. I could have ended up like one of those Moroi show-girls, in feathers and sequins. "I thought you were avoiding me." I still wasn't entirely sure where our relationship stood, despite his flippant attitude back at the Witching Hour.

He snorted. "It's not by my choice, little dhampir. Those guardians are doing their best to keep you in solitary. Well, kind of."

"Christian managed to sneak in and talk to me earlier," I said, hoping to avoid the issue that had to be on Adrian's mind: that I'd risked lives to save my ex-boyfriend. "He's going to try to teach Lissa to stake a Strigoi."

I waited for Adrian to join in my outrage, but he appeared as lax and sardonic as usual. "Not surprised she's gonna try. What surprises me is that he'd actually be interested in helping with some crazy theory."

"Well, it's crazy enough to appeal to him . . . and can apparently overpower them hating each other lately."

Adrian tilted his head, making some of the hair fall over his eyes. A building with blue neon palm trees cast an eerie glow upon his face as he gave me a knowing look. "Come on, we both know why he's doing it."

"Because he thinks his after-school group with Jill and Mia qualifies him to teach that stuff?"

"Because it gives him an excuse to be around her—without making it look like he gave in first. That way, he can still seem manly."

I shifted slightly so that the lights of a giant sign advertising slot machines didn't shine in my eyes. "That's ridiculous." Especially the part about Christian being manly.

"Guys do ridiculous things for love." Adrian reached into his pocket and held up a pack of cigarettes. "Do you know how badly I want one of these right now? Yet I suffer, Rose. All for you."

"Don't turn romantic on me," I warned, trying to hide my smile. "We don't have time for that, not when my best friend wants to go monster hunting."

"Yeah, but how is she actually going to find him? That's kind of a problem." Adrian didn't need to elaborate on the "him."

"True," I admitted.

"And she hasn't been able to charm the stake yet anyway, so until she does, all the kung-fu skills in the world won't matter."

"Guardians don't do kung-fu. And how did you know about the stake?"

"She's asked for my help a couple of times," he explained.

"Huh. I didn't know that."

"Well, you've been kind of busy. Not that you've even spared a thought for your poor pining boyfriend."

With all my chores, I hadn't spent a huge amount of time in Lissa's head—just enough to check in with her. "Hey, I would have taken you over filing any day." I'd been so afraid that Adrian would be furious with me after Vegas, yet here he was, light and playful. A little *too* light. I wanted him to focus on the problem at hand. "What's your take on Lissa and the charms? Is she close to doing it?"

Adrian absentmindedly played with the cigarettes, and I was tempted to tell him to go ahead and have one. This was his dream, after all. "Unclear. I haven't taken to charms the way she has. It's weird having the other elements in there . . . makes it hard to manipulate spirit."

"Are you helping her anyway?" I asked suspiciously.

He shook his head in amusement. "What do you think?"

I hesitated. "I . . . I don't know. You help her with most spirit things, but helping her with this would mean . . ."

". . . Helping Dimitri?"

I nodded, not trusting myself to elaborate.

"No," Adrian said at last. "I'm not helping her, simply because I don't know how."

I exhaled with relief. "I really am sorry," I told him. "For everything . . . for lying about where I was and what I was doing. It was wrong. And I don't understand . . . well, I don't get why you're being so nice to me."

"Should I be mean?" He winked. "Is that the kind of thing you're into?"

"No! Of course not. But, I mean, you were so mad when you came to Vegas and found out what was going on. I just thought . . . I don't know. I thought you hated me."

The amusement faded from his features. He came over to me and rested his hands on my shoulders, his dark green eyes dead serious. "Rose, nothing in this world could make me hate you."

"Not even trying to bring my ex-boyfriend back from the dead?"

Adrian held onto me, and even in a dream, I could smell his skin and cologne. "Yeah, I'll be honest. If Belikov were walking around right now, alive like he used to be? There would be some problems. I don't want to think what would happen with us if . . . well, it's not worth wasting time on. He's not here."

"I still . . . I still want us to work," I said meekly. "I would still try, even if he were back. I just have a hard time letting someone I care about go."

"I know. You did what you did out of love. I can't be mad at you over that. It was stupid, but that's how love is. Do you have any idea what I'd do for you? To keep you safe?"

"Adrian . . ."

I couldn't meet his eyes. I suddenly felt unworthy. He was so easy to underestimate. The only thing I could do was lean my head against his chest and let him wrap his arms around me.

"I'm sorry."

"Be sorry you lied," he said, pressing a kiss to my forehead. "Don't be sorry you loved him. That's part of you, part you have to let go, yeah, but still something that's made you who you are."

Part you have to let go . . .

Adrian was right, and that was a damned scary thing to admit. I'd had my shot. I'd made my gamble to save Dimitri, and it had failed. Lissa wouldn't get anywhere with the stake, meaning I really did have to treat Dimitri the way everyone else did: He was dead. I had to move on.

"Damn it," I muttered.

"What?" asked Adrian.

"I hate it when you're the sane one. That's my job."

"Rose," he said, forcibly trying to keep a serious tone, "I can think of many words to describe you, *sexy* and *hot* being at the top of the list. You know what's not on the list? *Sane.*"

I laughed. "Okay, well, then my job is to be the less crazy one."

He considered. "That I can accept."

I brought my lips up to his, and even if there were still some shaky things in our relationship, there was no uncertainty in how we kissed. Kissing in a dream felt exactly like real life.

Heat blossomed between us, and I felt a thrill run through my whole body. He released my hands and wrapped his arms around my waist, bringing us closer. I realized that it was time to start believing what I kept saying. Life did go on. Dimitri might be gone, but I could have something with Adrian—at least until my job took me away. That was, of course, assuming I got one. Hell, if Hans kept me on desk duty here and Adrian continued his slothful ways, we could be together forever.

Adrian and I kissed for a long time, pressing closer and closer. At last I broke things off. If you had sex in a dream, did that mean you'd *really* done it? I didn't know, and I certainly wasn't going to find out. I wasn't ready for that yet.

I stepped back, and Adrian took the hint. "Find me when you get some freedom."

"Hopefully soon," I said. "The guardians can't punish me forever."

Adrian looked skeptical, but he let the dream dissolve without further comment. I returned to my own bed and my own dreams.

The only thing that stopped me from intercepting Lissa and Christian when they met up early in her lobby the next day was that Hans summoned me to work even earlier. He put me on paperwork duty—in the vaults, ironically enough—leaving me to file and stew over Lissa and Christian as I watched them through my bond. I took it as a sign of my multitasking skills that I was able to alphabetize and spy at the same time.

Yet my observations were interrupted when a voice said,

"Didn't expect to find you here again."

I blinked out of Lissa's head and looked up from my paperwork. Mikhail stood before me. In light of the complications that had ensued with the Victor incident, I'd nearly forgotten Mikhail's involvement in our "escape." I set the files down and gave him a small smile.

"Yeah, weird how fate works, huh? They actually *want* me here now."

"Indeed. You're in a fair amount of trouble, I hear."

My smile turned into a grimace. "Tell me about it." I glanced around, even though I knew we were alone. "*You* didn't get in any trouble, did you?"

He shook his head. "No one knows what I did."

"Good." At least one person had escaped this debacle unscathed. My guilt couldn't have handled him getting caught too.

Mikhail knelt so that he was eye level with me, resting his arms on the table I sat at. "Were you successful? Was it worth it?"

"That's a hard question to answer."

He arched an eyebrow.

"There were some . . . not so successful things that happened. But we did find out what we wanted to know—or, well, we think we did."

His breath caught. "How to restore a Strigoi?"

"I think so. If our informant was telling the truth, then yeah. Except, even if he was . . . well, it's not that easy to do. It's nearly impossible, really."

"What is it?"

I hesitated. Mikhail had helped us, but he wasn't in my circle of confidants. Yet even now, I saw that haunted look in his eyes, the one I'd seen before. The pain of losing his beloved still tormented him. It likely always would. Would I be doing more harm than good by telling him what I'd learned? Would this fleeting hope only hurt him more?

I finally decided to tell him. Even if he told others—and I didn't think he would—most would laugh it off anyway. There would be no damage there. The real trouble would come if he told anyone about Victor and Robert—but I didn't actually have to mention their involvement to him. Unlike Christian, it had apparently not occurred to Mikhail that the prison break so big in Moroi news had been pulled off by the teens he helped smuggle out. Mikhail probably couldn't spare a thought for anything that didn't involve saving his Sonya.

"It takes a spirit user," I explained. "One with a spirit-charmed stake, and then he . . . or she . . . has to stake the Strigoi."

"Spirit . . ." That element was still foreign to most Moroi and dhampirs—but not to him. "Like Sonya. I know spirit's supposed to make them more alluring . . . but I swear, she never needed it. She was beautiful on her own." As always, Mikhail's face took on that same sad look it did whenever Ms. Karp was mentioned. I'd never really seen him truly happy since meeting him and thought he'd be pretty good-looking if he ever genuinely smiled. He suddenly seemed embarrassed at his romantic lapse and returned to business. "What spirit user could do a staking?"

"None," I said flatly. "Lissa Dragomir and Adrian Ivashkov are the only two spirit users I even know—well, aside from Avery Lazar." I was leaving Oksana and Robert out of this. "Neither of them has the skill to do it—you know that as well as I do. And Adrian has no interest in it anyway."

Mikhail was sharp, picking up on what I didn't say. "But Lissa does?"

"Yes," I admitted. "But it would take her years to learn to do it. If not longer. And she's the last of her line. She can't be risked like that."

The truth of my words hit him, and I couldn't help but share his pain and disappointment. Like me, he'd put a lot of faith into this last-ditch effort to be reunited with his lost love. I had just affirmed that it was possible . . . yet impossible. I think it would have been easier on both of us to learn it had all been a hoax.

He sighed and stood up. "Well . . . I appreciate you going after this. Sorry your punishment is for nothing."

I shrugged. "It's okay. It was worth it."

"I hope . . ." His face turned hesitant. "I hope it ends soon and doesn't affect anything."

"Affect what?" I asked sharply, catching the edge in his voice.

"Just . . . well, guardians who disobey orders sometimes face long punishments."

"Oh. This." He was referring to my constant fear of being stuck with a desk job. I tried to play flippant and not to show

how much that possibility scared me. "I'm sure Hans was bluffing. I mean, would he really make me do this forever just because I ran away and—"

I stopped, my mouth hanging open when a knowing glint flashed in Mikhail's eyes. I'd heard long ago how he'd tried to track down Ms. Karp, but the logistics had never really hit me until now. No one would have condoned his search. He would have had to leave on his own, breaking protocol, and come skulking back when he finally gave up on locating her. He would have been in just as much trouble as me for going MIA.

"Is that . . ." I swallowed. "Is that why you . . . why you work down here in the vaults now?"

Mikhail didn't answer my question. Instead, he glanced down with a small smile and pointed at my stacks of paper. "*F* comes before *L*," he said before turning and leaving.

"Damn," I muttered, looking down. He was right. Apparently I couldn't alphabetize so well while watching Lissa. Still, once I was alone, that didn't stop me from tuning back into her mind. I wanted to know what she was doing . . . and I didn't want to think about how what I'd done would probably be considered worse than Mikhail's deeds in the eyes of the guardians. Or that a similar—or worse—punishment might be in store for me.

Lissa and Christian were at a hotel near Lehigh's campus. The middle of the vampiric day meant evening for the human university. Lissa's tour wouldn't start until their morning the next day, which meant she had to bide her time at the hotel now and try to adjust to a human schedule.

Lissa's "new" guardians, Serena and Grant, were with her,

along with three extras that the queen had sent as well. Tatiana had allowed Christian to come along and hadn't been nearly as opposed as Lissa had feared—which again made me question if the queen really was as awful as I'd always believed. Priscilla Voda, a close advisor of the queen that both Lissa and I liked, was also accompanying Lissa as she looked around the school. Two of the additional guardians stayed with Priscilla; the third stayed with Christian. They ate dinner as a group and then retired to their rooms. Serena was actually staying with Lissa in hers while Grant stood guard outside the door. Watching all this triggered a pang in me. Pair guarding—it was what I'd been trained for. What I'd been expecting my whole life to do for Lissa.

Serena was a picture-perfect example of guardian aloofness, being there but not there as Lissa hung up some of her clothes. A knock at the door immediately shot Serena into action. Her stake was in hand, and she strode to the door, looking out through its peephole. I couldn't help but admire her reaction time, though part of me would never believe anyone could guard Lissa as well as I could. "Get back," Serena said to Lissa.

A moment later, the tension in Serena faded a tiny bit, and she opened the door. Grant stood there with Christian beside him.

"He's here to see you," Grant said, like it wasn't obvious.

Lissa nodded. "Um, yeah. Come on in."

Christian stepped inside when Grant backed away. Christian gave Lissa a meaningful look as he did, making a small head nod toward Serena.

"Hey, um, would you mind giving us some privacy?" As soon as the words were out of Lissa's mouth, she turned bright pink. "I mean . . . we just . . . we just need to talk about some things, that's all."

Serena kept her face *almost* neutral, but it was clear she thought they were going to do more than talk. Average teen dating wasn't usually hot gossip in the Moroi world, but Lissa, with her notoriety, attracted a bit more attention with her romantic affairs. Serena would have known Christian and Lissa had gone out and broken up. For all she knew, they were back together now. Lissa inviting him on this trip certainly suggested it.

Serena glanced around warily. The balance of protection and privacy was always difficult with Moroi and guardians, and hotel rooms like this made it even harder. If they were on a vampiric schedule, with everyone sleeping during daylight hours, I didn't doubt Serena would have stepped into the hall with Grant. But it was dark outside, and even a fifth-floor window could be a Strigoi liability. Serena wasn't keen on leaving her new charge alone.

Lissa's hotel suite had an expansive living room and work area, with an adjacent bedroom accessible through frosted-glass French doors. Serena nodded toward them. "How about I just go in there?" A smart idea. Provided privacy but kept her close by. Then, Serena realized the implications, and *she* blushed. "I mean . . . unless you guys want to go in there and I'll—"

"No," exclaimed Lissa, growing more and more embarrassed. "This is fine. We'll stay in here. We're just *talking*."

I wasn't sure whose benefit that was for, Serena's or Christian's. Serena nodded and disappeared into the bedroom with a book, which reminded me eerily of Dimitri. She shut the door. Lissa wasn't sure how well noise traveled, so she turned the TV on.

"God, that was miserable," she groaned.

Christian seemed totally at ease as he leaned against the wall. He wasn't the formal type by any means, but he'd put on dress clothes for dinner earlier and still wore them. They looked good on him, no matter how much he always complained. "Why?"

"Because she thinks we're—she thinks we're—well, you know."

"So? What's the big deal?"

Lissa rolled her eyes. "You're a guy. Of course it doesn't matter to you."

"Hey, it's not like we *haven't*. Besides, better for her to think that than to know the truth."

The reference to their past sex life inspired a mix of emotions—embarrassment, anger, and longing—but she refused to let that show. "Fine. Let's just get this over with. We've got a big day, and our sleep's going to be all screwy as it is. Where do we start? Do you want me to get the stake?"

"No need yet. We should just practice some basic defensive moves." He straightened up and moved toward the center of the room, dragging a table out of the way.

I swear, if not for the context, watching the two of them attempt combat training on their own would have been hilarious.

"Okay," he said. "So you already know how to punch."

"What? I do not!"

He frowned. "You knocked out Reed Lazar. Rose mentioned it, like, a hundred times. I've never heard her so proud about something."

"I punched *one* person *once* in my life," she pointed out. "And Rose was coaching me. I don't know if I could do it again."

Christian nodded, looking disappointed—not in her skills but because he had an impatient nature and wanted to jump right into the really hard-core fighting stuff. Nonetheless, he proved a surprisingly patient teacher as he went over the fine art of punching and hitting. A lot of his moves were actually things he'd picked up from me.

He'd been a decent student. Was he at guardian levels? No. Not by a long shot. And Lissa? She was smart and competent, but she wasn't wired for combat, no matter how badly she wanted to help with this. Punching Reed Lazar had been a beautiful thing, but it didn't appear to be anything that would ever become natural for her. Fortunately, Christian started with simple dodging and watching one's opponent. Lissa was just a beginner at it but showed a lot of promise. Christian seemed to chalk it up to his instructive skills, but I'd always thought spirit users had a kind of preternatural instinct about what others might do next. I doubted it would work on Strigoi, though.

After a little of that, Christian finally returned to offense, and that's when things went bad.

Lissa's gentle, healing nature didn't mesh with that, and she refused to really strike out with her full force, for fear of hurting him. When he realized what was happening, his snarky temper started to rise.

"Come on! Don't hold back."

"I'm not," she protested, delivering a punch to his chest that didn't come close to budging him.

He raked a hand irritably through his hair. "You are too! I've seen you knock on a door harder than you're hitting me."

"That's a ridiculous metaphor."

"And," he added, "you aren't aiming for my face."

"I don't want to leave a mark!"

"Well, at the rate we're going, there's no danger of that," he muttered. "Besides, you can heal it away."

I was amused at their bickering but didn't like his casual encouragement of spirit use. I still hadn't shaken my guilt over the long-term damage that the prison break could have caused.

Reaching forward, Christian grabbed her by the wrist and jerked her toward him. He balled her fingers with his other hand and then slowly demonstrated how to swing a punch upward by pulling her fist toward his face. He was more interested in showing the technique and motion, so it only brushed against him.

"See? Arc upward. Make the impact right there. Don't worry about hurting me."

"It's not that simple. . . ."

Her protest died off, and suddenly, they both seemed to notice the situation they were in. There was barely any space between them, and his fingers were still wrapped around her wrist. They felt warm against Lissa's skin and were sending electricity through the rest of her body. The air between them seemed thick and heavy, like it might just wrap them up and pull them together. From the widening of Christian's eyes and sudden intake of breath, I was willing to bet he was having a similar reaction at being so close to her body.

Coming to himself, he abruptly released her hand and stepped back. "Well," he said roughly, though still clearly unnerved by the proximity, "I guess you aren't really serious about helping Rose."

That did it. Sexual tension notwithstanding, anger kindled up in Lissa at the comment. She balled her fist and totally caught Christian off guard when she swung out and socked him in the face. It didn't have the grace of her Reed punch, but it took Christian hard. Unfortunately, she lost her balance in the maneuver and stumbled forward into him. The two of them went down together, hitting the floor and knocking over a small table and lamp nearby. The lamp caught the table's corner and broke.

Meanwhile, Lissa had landed on Christian. His arms instinctively went out around her, and if the space between them before had been small, it was nonexistent now. They stared into each other's eyes, and Lissa's heart was pounding fiercely in her chest. That tantalizing electric feeling crackled around them again, and all the world for her seemed to focus on his lips. Both she and I wondered later if they might have kissed, but just then, Serena came bursting out of the bedroom.

She was on guardian high alert, body tense and ready to face an army of Strigoi with her stake in hand. She came screeching to a halt when she saw the scene before her: what appeared to be a romantic interlude. Admittedly, it was an odd one, what with the broken lamp and swelling red mark on Christian's face. It was pretty awkward for everyone, and Serena's attack mode faded to one of confusion.

"Oh," she said uncertainly. "Sorry."

Embarrassment flooded Lissa, as well as self-resentment at being affected so much by Christian. She was furious at him, after all. Hastily, she pulled away and sat up, and in her flustered state, she felt the need to make it clear that there was nothing romantic whatsoever going on.

"It . . . it's not what you think," she stuttered, looking anywhere except at Christian, who was getting to his feet and seemed just as mortified as Lissa. "We were fighting. I mean, practicing fighting. I want to learn to defend against Strigoi. And attack them. And stake them. So Christian was kind of helping me, that's all." There was something cute about her rambling, and it reminded me charmingly of Jill.

Serena visibly relaxed, and while she'd mastered that blank face all guardians excelled at, it was clear she was amused. "Well," she said, "it doesn't look like you're doing a very good job."

Christian turned indignant as he stroked his injured cheek. "Hey! We are too. I taught her this."

Serena still thought it was all funny, but a serious, considering glint was starting to form in her eyes. "That seems like it was more lucky than anything else." She hesitated, like she was on the verge of a big decision. At last she said, "Look, if you guys are serious about this, then you need to learn to do it the right way. I'll show you how."

No. Way.

I was seriously on the verge of escaping the Court and hitchhiking to Lehigh to *really* show them how to throw a punch—with Serena as my example—when something jolted me away from Lissa and back into my own reality. Hans.

I had a sarcastic greeting on my lips, but he didn't give me a chance. "Forget the filing and follow me. You've been summoned."

"I—what?" Highly unexpected. "Summoned where?"

His face was grim. "To see the queen."

FOURTEEN

THE LAST TIME TATIANA HAD wanted to yell at me, she'd simply taken me to one of her private sitting rooms. It had made for a weird atmosphere, like we were at teatime—except people didn't usually scream at other people during teatime. I had no reason to believe this would be any different . . . until I noticed my escort was leading me to the main business buildings of the Court, the places where all royal governing was conducted. Shit. This was more serious than I'd thought.

And indeed, when I was finally ushered into the room where Tatiana waited . . . well, I nearly came to a standstill and couldn't enter. Only a slight touch on my back from one of the guardians with me kept me moving forward. The place was packed.

I didn't know for sure which room I was in. The Moroi actually kept a bona fide throne room for their king or queen, but I didn't think this was it. This room was still heavily decorated, conveying an old-world royal feel, with painstakingly carved floral molding and shining gold candleholders on the walls. There were actually lit candles in them too. Their light reflected off the metallic decorations in the room. Everything glittered, and I felt like I'd stumbled into a stage production.

And really, I might as well have. Because after a moment's

surveying, I realized where I was. The people in the room were split. Twelve of them sat at a long table on a dais at what was clearly meant to be the focal point of the room. Tatiana herself sat at the middle of the table, with six Moroi on one side and five Moroi on the other. The other side of the room was simply set with rows of chairs—still elaborate and padded with satin cushions—which were also filled with Moroi. The audience.

The people sitting on either side of Tatiana were the tip-off. They were older Moroi, but ones who carried a regal air. Eleven Moroi for the eleven acting royal families. Lissa was not eighteen—though she was about to be, I realized with a start—and therefore had no spot yet. Someone was sitting in for Priscilla Voda. I was looking at the Council, the princes and princesses of the Moroi world. The oldest member of each family claimed the royal title and an advisory spot beside Tatiana. Sometimes the eldest waived the spot and gave it to someone the family felt was more capable, but the selectee was almost always at least forty-five. The Council elected the Moroi king or queen, a position held until death or retirement. In rare circumstances, with enough backing from the royal families, a monarch could be forcibly removed from office.

Each prince or princess on the Council was in turn advised by a family council, and glancing back at the audience, I recognized clusters of family members sitting together: Ivashkovs, Lazars, Badicas . . . The very back rows appeared to be observers. Tasha and Adrian sat together, and I knew for a fact they weren't members of the Royal Council or family councils. Still, seeing them set me at ease a little.

I remained near the entrance to the room, shifting uneasily from foot to foot, wondering what was in store. I hadn't just earned public humiliation; I'd apparently earned it in front of the most important Moroi in the world. Wonderful.

A gangly Moroi with patchy white hair stepped forward, around the side of the long table, and cleared his throat. Immediately, the hum of conversation died. Silence filled the room.

"This session of the Moroi Royal Council is now in order," he declared. "Her Royal Majesty, Tatiana Marina Ivashkov, is presiding." He gave a slight bow in her direction and then discretely backed off to the side of the room, standing near some guardians who lined the walls like decorations themselves.

Tatiana always dressed up at the parties I saw her at, but for a formal event like this, she was really channeling the queen look. Her dress was long-sleeved navy silk, and a glittering crown of blue and white stones sat atop her elaborately braided hair. In a beauty pageant, I would have written such gems off as rhinestones. On her, I didn't question for a moment that they were real sapphires and diamonds.

"Thank you," she said. She was also using her royal voice, resonant and impressive, filling the room. "We will be continuing our conversation from yesterday."

Wait . . . what? They'd been discussing me *yesterday* too? I noticed then that I'd wrapped my arms around myself in a sort of protective stance and immediately dropped them. I didn't want to look weak, no matter what they had in store for me.

"Today we will be hearing testimony from a newly made guardian." Tatiana's sharp gaze fell on me. The whole room's did. "Rosemarie Hathaway, will you please come forward?"

I did, keeping my head high and posture confident. I didn't exactly know where to stand, so I picked the middle of the room, directly facing Tatiana. If I was going to be paraded in public, I wished someone would have tipped me off to wear guardian black and white. Whatever. I'd show no fear, even in jeans and a T-shirt. I gave a small, proper bow and then met her eyes directly, bracing for what was to come.

"Will you please state your name?" she asked.

She'd already done it for me, but I still said, "Rosemarie Hathaway."

"How old are you?"

"Eighteen?"

"And how long have you been eighteen?"

"A few months."

She waited a couple moments to let it sink in, as though this were important information. "Miss Hathaway, we understand that around that time, you withdrew from St. Vladimir's Academy. Is this correct?"

That's what this was about? Not the Vegas trip with Lissa?

"Yes." I offered no more info. Oh God. I hoped she didn't get into Dimitri. She shouldn't have known about my relationship with him, but there was no telling what information could spread around here.

"You went to Russia to hunt Strigoi."

"Yes."

"As a type of personal revenge following the attack at St. Vladimir's?"

"Er . . . yes."

No one said anything, but my response definitely caused a stir in the room. People shifted uneasily and glanced at their neighbors. Strigoi always inspired fear, and someone actively seeking them out was still an unusual concept among us. Oddly, Tatiana seemed very pleased by this confirmation. Was it going to be used as more ammunition against me?

"We would assume then," she continued, "that you are one of those who believe in direct strikes against the Strigoi?"

"Yes."

"Many had different reactions to the terrible attack at St. Vladimir's," she said. "You aren't the only dhampir who wanted to strike back against the Strigoi—though you were certainly the youngest."

I hadn't known about others going on vigilante sprees—well, aside from some reckless dhampirs in Russia. If that was the story about my trip she was willing to believe, that was fine with me.

"We have reports from both guardians and Alchemists in Russia that you were successful." This was the first time I'd heard the Alchemists mentioned in public, but of course they'd be a common topic among the Council. "Can you tell me how many you killed?"

"I . . ." I stared in surprise. "I'm not sure, Your Majesty. At least . . ." I racked my brain. "Seven." It might have been more. She thought so too.

"That might be a modest estimate compared to what our sources say," she noted grandly. "Nonetheless, still an impressive number. Did you perform the kills by yourself?"

"Sometimes I did. Sometimes I had help. There were . . . some other dhampirs I worked with once in a while." Technically, I'd had Strigoi help as well, but I wasn't going to mention that.

"They were close to your age?"

"Yes."

Tatiana said no more, and as though receiving a cue, a woman beside her spoke up. I believed she was the Conta princess.

"When did you kill your first Strigoi?"

I frowned. "Last December."

"And you were seventeen?"

"Yes."

"Did you perform that kill yourself?"

"Well . . . mostly. A couple friends helped with distraction." I hoped they weren't going to push for more details. My first kill had occurred when Mason had died, and aside from the events surrounding Dimitri, that memory tormented me the most.

But Princess Conta didn't want too many other details. She and the others—who soon joined in the questioning—mostly wanted to know about my kills. They were slightly interested in knowing when other dhampirs had helped me—but didn't want to go into when I'd had Moroi help. They also glossed over my disciplinary record, which I found baffling. The rest of my academic details were mentioned—my exceptional combat grades, how I'd been one of the best when Lissa and I had run away our sophomore year and how quickly I'd made up for lost time to become top in my class again (at least as far as fighting went). They talked also about how I'd protected Lissa whenever we were out in the world alone and finally concluded with my exceptional trial scores.

"Thank you, Guardian Hathaway. You may leave."

Tatiana's dismissive voice left no room for doubt. She wanted me out of there. I was only too eager to comply, giving another bow, and then scurrying out. I cast a quick glance at Tasha and Adrian as I did, and the queen's voice rang out as I cleared the door, "That concludes our session today. We will convene again tomorrow."

I wasn't surprised when Adrian caught up with me a few minutes later. Hans hadn't ordered me to come back and work after the session, so I had decided to read that as freedom.

"Okay," I said, slipping my hand into Adrian's. "Enlighten me with your royal political wisdom. What was that all about?"

"No clue. I'm the last person to ask about political stuff," he said. "I don't even go to those things, but Tasha found me at the last minute and said to come with her. I guess she got a tip-off you'd be there—but she was just as confused."

Neither of us had said anything, but I realized I was leading him toward one of the buildings that housed commerce—restaurants, shops, etc. I was starving all of a sudden.

"I got the impression this was part of something they'd already been talking about—she mentioned their last session."

"It was closed. Like tomorrow's. No one knows what

they're discussing."

"Then why make this one public?" It didn't seem fair that the queen and Council could pick and choose what they shared with others. Everything should have been public.

He frowned. "Probably because they're going to hold a vote soon, and that'll be public. If your testimony plays some role, then the Council may want to make sure other Moroi witnessed it—so that everyone understands the decision when it comes." He paused. "But what do I know? I'm no politician."

"Makes it sound like it's already decided," I grumbled. "Why have a vote at all? And why would *I* have anything to do with government?"

He opened the door to a small café that sold light lunch food—burgers and sandwiches. Adrian had been raised with fancy restaurants and gourmet food. I think he preferred that, but he also knew I didn't like always being on display *or* being reminded that I was with a royal from an elite family. I appreciated that he'd known I'd just want something ordinary today.

Nonetheless, our being together earned us a few curious glances and whispers from the diner's patrons. At the school, we'd been a source of speculation, but here at Court? We were a main-stage attraction. Images were important at Court, and most dhampir-Moroi relationships were carried out in secret. Us being so open—especially considering Adrian's connections—was scandalous and shocking, and people weren't always discreet with their reactions. I'd heard all sorts of things since returning to Court. One woman had called me shameless. Another had speculated aloud why Tatiana hadn't simply "dealt with me."

Fortunately, most of our audience was content to stare today, making them easy to ignore. There was a small line of thought on Adrian's forehead as we sat down at a table. "Maybe they're voting to make you Lissa's guardian after all."

I was so astonished that I couldn't say anything for several seconds when the waitress suddenly appeared. I finally stammered out my order and then stared at Adrian with wide eyes.

"Seriously?" The session had been an examination of my skills, after all. It made sense. Except . . . "No. The Council wouldn't go to the trouble of holding sessions for one guardian assignment." My hopes fell.

Adrian gave a shrug of acknowledgment. "True. But this isn't an ordinary guardian assignment. Lissa's the last of her line. Everyone—including my aunt—has a special interest in her. Giving her someone like you who's . . ." I gave him a dangerous look as he grasped for a word. ". . . Controversial could upset some people."

"And that's why they actually wanted *me* there to describe what I've done. To convince people in person that I'm competent." Even as I spoke the words, I still didn't dare believe them. It was too good to be true. "I just can't imagine it, seeing as I seem to be in so much trouble with the guardians."

"I don't know," he said. "It's just a guess. Who knows? Maybe they do think the Las Vegas thing was just a harmless prank." There was a bitter tone in his voice over that. "And I told you that Aunt Tatiana was coming around to you. Maybe she wants you as Lissa's guardian now but needs to make a public display to justify it."

That was a startling thought. "But if I do get to come with Lissa, what are you going to do? Get respectable and come to college too?"

"I don't know," he said, green eyes thoughtful as he sipped his drink. "Maybe I will."

That was also unexpected, and my conversation with his mother returned to my mind. What if I was Lissa's guardian in college and he was with us for the next four years? I was fairly certain Daniella had thought we'd be splitting up this summer. I'd thought so too . . . and was surprised to feel how relieved I was that I might get to stay with him. Dimitri always left my heart full of pain and longing, but I still wanted Adrian in my life.

I grinned at him and rested my hand on his. "I'm not sure what I'd do with you if you were respectable."

He lifted my hand to his lips and kissed it. "I've got some suggestions," he told me. I didn't know if it was his words or the feel of his mouth on my skin that sent shivers through me. I was about to ask what those suggestions were when our interlude was interrupted . . . by Hans.

"Hathaway," he said, one eyebrow arched as he stood over us. "You and I have some very different ideas about the definition of 'punishment.'"

He had a point. In my mind, punishment involved easy things like lashings and starvation. Not filing.

Instead, I replied, "You didn't tell me to come back after I saw the queen."

He gave me an exasperated look. "I *also* didn't tell you to go off on a playdate. Come on. Back to the vaults."

"But I have a BLT coming!"

"You'll get your lunch break in another couple hours like the rest of us."

I tried to repress my outrage. They hadn't been feeding me bread crusts and water during my work detail, but the food hadn't tasted much better. Just then, the waitress returned with our food. I grabbed the sandwich before she even set the plates down and wrapped it in a napkin. "Can I take it to go?"

"If you can eat it before we get back." His voice was skeptical, seeing as the vault was pretty close. Clearly, he was underestimating my ability to consume food.

In spite of Hans's disapproving expression, I gave Adrian a kiss goodbye and a look that told him maybe we'd continue our conversation. He gave me a happy, knowing smile that I only saw for a second before Hans ordered me away. True to my expectations, I managed to get the sandwich down before we arrived back at the guardians' building, though I did feel a little nauseous for the next half hour or so.

My lunchtime was almost dinnertime for Lissa, out in the human world. Returning to my miserable punishment, I cheered up a little at the joy running through her via our bond. She'd spent the whole day on her campus tour of Lehigh, and it was everything she'd hoped it could be. She loved it all. She loved the beautiful buildings, the grounds, the dorms . . . and especially the classes. A glimpse at the course catalog opened up a world of subjects that even St. Vladimir's superior education hadn't offered us. She wanted to see and do everything that the school had to offer.

And even though she wished I was there, she was still excited about the fact that it was her birthday. Priscilla had given her some elaborate jewelry and had promised a fancy dinner that night. It wasn't exactly the type of celebration Lissa had hoped for, but the thrill of her eighteenth birthday was still intoxicating—particularly as she looked around at the dream school she'd be attending soon.

I confess, I felt a pang of jealousy. Despite Adrian's theory about why the queen had called me in today, I knew—as did Lissa—that the odds of me going to college with her were still probably nonexistent. Some petty part of me couldn't understand how Lissa could therefore be excited about it if I wasn't going to be along. Childish of me, I know.

I didn't have long to sulk, though, because once all the touring was done, Lissa's entourage returned to the hotel. Priscilla told them they could clean up for an hour or so before heading to dinner. For Lissa, this meant more fighting-practice time. My brooding mood immediately turned irate.

Things got worse when I realized that earlier in the day, Serena had told Grant about Lissa and Christian's desire to defend themselves. He apparently thought that it was a good idea too. It would figure. Lissa had two progressive guardians. Why couldn't she have gotten some stodgy, old-school person who would be horrified at the thought of a Moroi even *thinking* about fighting off a Strigoi?

So, while I sat helpless and unable to smack sense into any

of them, Lissa and Christian now had *two* instructors. Not only did this mean more learning opportunities, it also meant Serena had a competent partner to demonstrate certain moves with. She and Grant sparred, explaining maneuvers while Lissa and Christian watched wide-eyed.

Fortunately (well, not for Lissa), she and I soon noticed something. The guardians didn't know the true reason Lissa was interested in fighting. They had no idea—how could they have?—that she wanted to go hunt and stake a Strigoi in the feeble hope of bringing him back to life. They thought she just wanted to learn basic defense, something that seemed very sensible to them. So that was what they taught.

Grant and Serena also made Lissa and Christian practice on each other. I suspected there were a couple reasons for this. One was that Lissa and Christian didn't have the skill to do much damage to each other. The second reason was that it amused the guardians.

It did *not* amuse Lissa and Christian. There was still so much tension between them, both sexual and angry, that they resented being in such close contact. Grant and Serena stopped the two Moroi from doing any more face punching, but simple dodges often meant brushing against each other, fingers sliding against skin in the heat of the action. Every once in a while, the guardians would have someone play Strigoi—putting Lissa or Christian on the offensive. The two Moroi welcomed this to a certain extent; after all, direct attacks were what they wanted to learn.

But, when Christian (playing Strigoi) lunged at Lissa and

pushed her into a wall, learning offense suddenly didn't seem like such a good idea to her. The maneuver pressed them right up to each other, his arms holding hers. She could smell him and feel him and was overwhelmed by the fantasy of him just holding her there and kissing her.

"I think you two should go back to basic defense," said Grant, interrupting her traitorous feelings. He sounded like he was more worried about them hurting each other than the possibility that they might start making out.

It took Lissa and Christian a moment to even register his words, let alone part from each other. When they did, both avoided eye contact and returned to the couch. The guardians launched into more examples of how to avoid an attacker. Lissa and Christian had seen this so many times that they knew the lesson by heart, and their earlier attraction gave way to frustration.

Lissa was too polite to say anything, but after fifteen minutes of Serena and Grant showing how to block with your arms and dodge someone reaching for you, Christian finally spoke. "How do you stake a Strigoi?"

Serena froze at Christian's words. "Did you say *stake*?"

Rather than being shocked, Grant chuckled. "I don't think that's anything you need to worry about. You want to focus on getting *away* from a Strigoi, not getting closer."

Lissa and Christian exchanged an uneasy look.

"I helped kill Strigoi before," Christian pointed out. "I used fire at the school's attack. Are you saying that's not okay? That I shouldn't have done it?"

Now Serena and Grant traded glances. *Ha,* I thought. Those two weren't as progressive as I thought. They were coming from a defense point of view, not offense.

"Of course you should have," said Grant at last. "What you did was amazing. And in a similar situation? Sure. You wouldn't want to be helpless. But that's the point—you have your fire. If it came down to you fighting a Strigoi, your magic's going to be the way to go. You already know how to use it—and it'll keep you safely out of their range."

"What about me?" asked Lissa. "I don't have any kind of magic like that."

"You'll never get close enough to a Strigoi for it to be a problem," said Serena fiercely. "We won't let you."

"Besides," added Grant with amusement, "it's not like we just go around handing out stakes." I would have given anything for them to go take a look in her suitcase right then.

Lissa bit her lip and refused to make eye contact with Christian again, for fear of giving away their intentions. This was not going according to their crazy plan. Christian again took the lead.

"Can you at least demo it?" he asked, trying—and succeeding—to look like someone just seeking the sensational and exciting. "Is it hard to do? It seems like all you have to do is aim and hit."

Grant snorted. "Hardly. There's a bit more to it than that."

Lissa leaned forward, clasping her hands together as she followed Christian's lead. "Well, then don't worry about teaching us. Just show us."

"Yeah. Let's see." Christian shifted restlessly beside her. As he did, their arms brushed, and instantly they moved apart.

"It's not a game," Grant said. Nonetheless, he walked over to his coat and produced his stake. Serena stared incredulously.

"What are you going to do?" she asked. "Stake *me*?"

He gave that small chuckle of his and searched the room with his sharp eyes. "Of course not. Ah. There we are." He walked over to a small armchair that had a decorative pillow. He lifted it up and tested its width. It was fat and thickly filled with some sort of dense stuffing. He returned to Lissa and gestured for her to stand. To everyone's astonishment, he handed her his stake.

Locking his body into a rigid position, he gripped the pillow hard between his hands and extended it out a couple feet in front of him. "Go ahead," he said. "Aim and hit it."

"Are you crazy?" asked Serena.

"Don't worry," he said. "Princess Voda can afford the incidentals. I'm proving a point. Strike the pillow."

Lissa hesitated only a few more moments. An excitement that seemed unusually intense filled her. I knew she'd been anxious to learn this, but her desire for it seemed higher than before. Gritting her teeth, she stepped forward and awkwardly tried to impale the pillow with her stake. She was cautious—fearing she'd hurt Grant—but there was no need for her to worry. She didn't even budge him, and all she managed with the stake was a slight snagging of the fabric on the surface. She tried a few more times but achieved little more.

Christian, being who he was, said, "That's all you can do?"

Glaring, she handed him the stake. "You do better."

Christian stood, snarky smile disappearing as he studied the pillow critically and sized up his blow. As he did, Lissa glanced around and saw the humor in the guardians' eyes. Even Serena had relaxed. They were making their point, proving staking wasn't an easy thing to learn. I was glad, and my opinion of them rose.

Christian finally made his move. He did actually pierce the fabric, but the pillow and its stuffing proved too much to break through. And again, Grant wasn't shaken at all. After more failed attempts, Christian sat down again and handed the stake back. It was kind of fun to see Christian's cocky attitude shot down a little. Even Lissa enjoyed it, despite her own frustration over how difficult this was becoming.

"The stuffing's got too much resistance," Christian complained.

Grant handed his stake to Serena. "What, and you think a Strigoi's body is going to be easier to get through? With muscles and ribs in the way?"

Grant got back into his position, and without hesitation, Serena struck with the stake. Its point burst through the other side of the pillow, coming to a halt just in front of Grant's chest as tiny fluffy pieces of stuffing drifted to the ground. She jerked it out and handed it to him like it had been the simplest thing in the world.

Both Christian and Lissa stared in amazement. "Let me try again," he said.

By the time Priscilla called them to dinner, there wasn't a

pillow in that hotel room left untouched. Boy, she was going to be surprised when she got the bill. Lissa and Christian hacked away with the stake while the guardians looked on with a superior air, confident their message was being delivered. Staking Strigoi was not easy.

Lissa was finally getting it. She realized that in some ways, piercing a pillow—or a Strigoi—wasn't even about understanding the principle. Sure, she'd heard me talk about lining your shot up to get to the heart and miss the ribs, but this was more than knowledge. A lot of it was strength—strength she physically didn't have yet. Serena, though seemingly petite, had spent years building up her muscle and could get that stake through practically anything. One hour-long lesson wouldn't give Lissa that kind of strength, and she whispered as much to Christian when the group went out to dinner.

"You're quitting already?" he asked, voice equally low as they rode in the backseat of an SUV. Grant, Serena, and a third guardian were there too, but they were deep in discussion.

"No!" Lissa hissed back. "But I've got to, like, train before I can do it."

"Like lift weights?"

"I . . . I don't know." The others were still talking to each other, but Lissa's topic was too dangerous for her to risk them hearing. She leaned close to Christian, unnerved yet again at how his closeness and familiarity affected her. Swallowing, she tried to keep her face impassive and stick to the topic. "But I'm just not strong enough. It's physically impossible."

"Sounds like you're giving up."

"Hey! You didn't make it through any of the pillows either."

He flushed slightly. "I almost got through that green one."

"There was hardly anything in it!"

"I just need more practice."

"You don't need to do anything," she shot back, fighting to keep her voice quiet through her anger. "This isn't your fight. It's mine."

"Hey," he snapped, eyes glittering like pale blue diamonds, "you're crazy if you think I'm going to just let you go and risk—"

He cut himself off and actually bit his lip, as though will alone wasn't enough to stop him from talking. Lissa stared at him, and both of us began wondering how he would have finished. What wouldn't he risk? Her putting herself in danger? That was my guess.

Even without talk, he spoke volumes with his expression. Through Lissa's eyes, I saw him drinking in her features and trying to hide his emotions. At last, he jerked away and broke that intimate space between them, getting as far from her as he could.

"Fine. Do whatever you want. I don't care."

Neither of them spoke after that, and since it was lunchtime for me, I returned to my own reality and welcomed a filing break—only to be informed by Hans that I had to keep working.

"Come on! Isn't it lunchtime? You have to feed me," I exclaimed. "That's just beyond cruel. At least throw me some crumbs."

"I did feed you. Or, well, you fed yourself when you inhaled that sandwich. You wanted your lunch break then. You got it. Now you keep working."

I slammed my fists against the endless piles of paper before me. "Can't I at least do something else? Paint buildings? Haul rocks?"

"I'm afraid not." A smile twisted the corners of his lips. "There's a lot of filing we need done."

"How long? How long are you going to punish me?"

Hans shrugged. "Until someone tells me to stop."

He left me alone again, and I leaned back in my chair, forcibly trying not to flip the table in front of me over. I thought it would make me feel momentarily better, but it also meant I'd have to redo the work I'd done. With a sigh, I returned to my task.

Lissa was at dinner when I tuned back into her later. It might have technically been in honor of her birthday, but really, it was all royal conversation with Priscilla. That was no way to spend a birthday, I decided. I'd have to make this up to her whenever I earned freedom. We'd have a real party, and I'd be able to give her my birthday present: gorgeous leather boots that Adrian had helped me acquire back at school.

Being in Christian's head might have been more interesting, but since that wasn't an option, I returned to my own and mulled over my earlier talk with Adrian. Was this punishment finally going to end? Was an official royal decree going to put me and Lissa together at last, despite the guardians' normal policy?

Trying to figure it out was like being on a hamster wheel. A lot of work. No progress. But it got me through the dinner conversation, and before I knew it, Lissa's group was getting up and heading for the restaurant's door. It was dark out now, and Lissa couldn't help but feel the weirdness of being on a human schedule. Back at school or the Court, this would be the middle of the day. Instead, they were now heading back to their hotel and would be going to bed. Well, probably not right away. I had no doubt that if Lissa and Christian could get over their current huff, they'd be back to stabbing more pillows. As much as I wanted those two dating again, I couldn't help but think they were a lot safer apart.

Or maybe not.

The group had hung out at the restaurant far past the normal dinner hour, so the lot was mostly empty as they walked across it. The guardians hadn't exactly parked in the back, but they weren't near the main entrance either. They had, however, made a point of parking next to one of the street lamps illuminating the lot.

Except it wasn't lit now. The light had been broken.

Grant and Priscilla's guardian noticed it right away. It was the kind of little detail we were trained to notice: anything unusual, anything that might have changed. In a flash, the two of them had stakes out and were flanking the Moroi. It only took seconds for Serena and the guardian assigned to Christian to follow suit. That was something else we were trained to do. Be on guard. React. Follow your colleagues.

They were fast. All of them were fast. But it didn't matter.

Because suddenly, there were Strigoi everywhere.

I'm not entirely sure where they came from. Maybe they'd been behind the cars or on the parking lot's edges. If I'd had a bird-eye's view of the situation or been there myself with my "nausea alarm," I might have had a better sense of it all. But I was watching the scene through Lissa's eyes, and the guardians were going out of their way to block her from the Strigoi who seemed to have appeared out of thin air as far as she was concerned. Most of the actions were a blur to her. Her bodyguards were shoving her around, trying to keep her safe as white, red-eyed faces popped up everywhere. She saw it all through a fear-filled haze.

But before long, both of us could see people dying. Serena, just as fast and strong as she'd been in the hotel room, staked a male Strigoi cleanly through the heart. Then, in return, a female Strigoi leapt at Priscilla's guardian and broke his neck. Lissa was distantly aware of Christian's arm around her, pressing her against the SUV and shielding her with his own body. The remaining guardians were also still forming a protective ring as best they could, but they were distracted. Their circle was faltering—and they were dropping.

One by one, the Strigoi killed the guardians. It wasn't for lack of skill on the guardians' part. They were simply outnumbered. One Strigoi tore out Grant's throat with her teeth. Serena was backhanded hard against the asphalt, landing facedown and not moving. And, horror of horrors, the Strigoi didn't seem to be sparing Moroi either. Lissa—pushing so hard against the SUV that it seemed as though she might become one with it—stared wide-eyed as one Strigoi swiftly and efficiently ripped into Priscilla's neck, pausing to drink her blood. The Moroi woman didn't even have time to register surprise, but at least there had been no real suffering. The endorphins dimmed the pain as the blood and life were drained from her body.

Lissa's emotions shifted into something beyond fear, something that hardly felt like anything at all. She was in shock. Numbed. And with a cold, hard certainty, she knew that her death was coming and accepted it. Her hand found Christian's, squeezing it tightly, and turning toward him, she took small comfort in knowing the last sight she would see in life was the beautiful, crystalline blue of his eyes. From the look on his face, his thoughts were along similar themes. There was warmth in his eyes, warmth and love and—

Total and complete astonishment.

His eyes widened, focusing on something just behind Lissa. At that same moment, a hand grabbed Lissa's shoulder and whipped her around. *This is it*, a small voice inside her whispered. *This is where I die.*

Then, she understood Christian's astonishment.

She was facing Dimitri.

Like me, she had that surreal sense of it being Dimitri yet not being Dimitri. So many of his features were the same . . . and yet so many were different. She tried to say something, anything, but while the words formed on her lips, she just couldn't manage to get them out.

Intense heat suddenly flared behind her, and a brilliant

light lit Dimitri's pale features. Neither Lissa nor I needed to see Christian to know he had produced a ball of fire with his magic. Either the shock of seeing Dimitri or fear for Lissa had spurred Christian into action. Dimitri squinted slightly at the light, but then a cruel smile twisted his lips, and the hand resting on her shoulder slid up to her neck.

"Put it out," said Dimitri. "Put it out or she dies."

Lissa finally found her voice, even with her air cut off. "Don't listen to him," she gasped out. "He's going to kill us anyway."

But behind her, the heat died. Shadows fell across Dimitri's face once again. Christian wouldn't risk her, even though she was right. It hardly seemed to matter.

"Actually," said Dimitri, voice pleasant amid the grim scene, "I'd rather you two stay alive. At least for a little while longer."

I felt Lissa's face move to a frown. I wouldn't have been surprised if Christian's did too, judging from the confusion in his voice. He couldn't even manage a snarky comment. He could only ask the obvious: "Why?"

Dimitri's eyes gleamed. "Because I need you to be bait for Rose."

FIFTEEN

IN MY PANICKED MIND RIGHT then, getting up and running on foot to Lehigh—despite it being miles and miles away—seemed like a totally solid plan. A heartbeat later, I knew this was out of my league. Way, way out of my league.

As I shot up from my table and tore out of the room, I felt a sudden longing for Alberta. I'd seen her jump into action at St. Vladimir's and knew she could take charge of any situation. At this point in our relationship, she would respond to any threat I brought to her. The guardians at Court were still strangers to me. Who could I go to? Hans? The guy who hated me? He wouldn't believe me, not like Alberta or my mother would. Running down the quiet hallways, I dismissed all such worries. It didn't matter. I would make him believe. I would find anyone I could. Anyone who could get Lissa and Christian out of this.

Only you can, a voice hissed in my head. *You're the one Dimitri wants.*

I ignored that thought too, largely because in my distraction, I collided into someone rounding a corner.

I gave a muffled cry that sounded like "Oomph" as my face slammed into someone's chest. I looked up. Mikhail. I would have been relieved, except I was too pumped full of adrenaline and worry. I grabbed his sleeve and began tugging him toward the stairs.

"Come on! We have to get help!"

Mikhail remained were he was, not budging against my pull. He frowned, face calm. "What are you talking about?"

"Lissa! Lissa and Christian. They've been taken by Strigoi—by Dimitri. We can find them. I can find them. But we have to hurry."

Mikhail's confusion grew. "Rose . . . how long have you been down here?"

I didn't have time for this. Leaving him, I fled up the stairs to the main levels of the complex. A moment later I heard his footsteps behind me. When I reached the main office, I expected someone to chastise me for leaving my punishment, except . . . no one seemed to even notice me.

The office was in chaos. Guardians were running around, calls were being made, and voices rose to frantic levels. They knew, I realized. They already knew.

"Hans!" I called, pushing my way through the crowd. He was on the other side of the room and had just hung up on a cell call. "Hans, I know where they are. Where the Strigoi took Lissa and Christian."

"Hathaway, I don't have time for your—" His scowl faltered. "You have that bond."

I stared in astonishment. I'd been ready for him to dismiss me as a nuisance. I'd been ready for a long fight to convince him. I gave him a hasty nod.

"I saw it. I saw everything that happened." Now I frowned.

"How do you know already?"

"Serena," he said grimly.

"Serena's dead . . ."

He shook his head. "No, not yet. Though she certainly sounded like it on the phone. Whatever happened, it took everything she had to make that call. We have Alchemists coming to get her, and . . . clean up."

I replayed the events, remembering how Serena had been slammed against the asphalt. It had been a hard blow, and when she didn't move, I'd assumed the worst. Yet if she'd survived—and apparently she must have—I could just barely form a mental image of her dragging her cell phone out of her pocket with bloody hands. . . .

Please, please let her be alive, I thought, not sure who I was praying to.

"Come on," said Hans. "We need you. There are teams already forming."

There was another surprise. I hadn't expected him to bring me on so quickly. A new respect for Hans settled over me. He might act like an asshole, but he was a leader. When he saw an asset, he used it. In one swift motion, he was hurrying out the door, several guardians following him. I struggled to keep up with their longer strides and saw Mikhail coming as well.

"You're doing a rescue," I told Hans. "That's . . . rare." I hesitated to even speak the words. I certainly didn't want to discourage this. But Moroi rescues weren't normal. When Strigoi took them, they were often regarded as dead. The rescue we'd done after the Academy attack had been an oddity, one that had taken a lot of persuasion.

Hans gave me a wry look. "So is the Dragomir princess."

Lissa was precious to me, worth more than anything else in the world. And for the Moroi, I realized, she was precious too. Most Moroi captured by Strigoi might be regarded as dead, but she wasn't most Moroi. She was the last in her line, the last of one of twelve ancient families. Losing her wouldn't just be a hit to Moroi culture. It would be a sign, an omen that the Strigoi were truly defeating us. For her, the guardians would risk a rescue mission.

In fact, it appeared they would risk a lot of things. As we arrived at the garages where the Court's vehicles were stored, I saw masses of other guardians arriving—along with Moroi. I recognized a few. Tasha Ozera was among them, and like her, the others were fire users. If we'd learned anything, it was how valuable they were in a fight. It appeared the controversy of Moroi going to battle was being ignored right now, and I was amazed at how quickly this group had been summoned. Tasha's eyes met mine, her face grave and drawn. She said nothing to me. She didn't need to.

Hans was barking orders, splitting people into groups and vehicles. With every bit of self-control I could muster, I waited patiently near him. My restless nature made me want to jump in and start demanding to know what I could do. He would get to me, I assured myself. He had a role for me; I just had to wait.

My self-control was also being tested with Lissa. After Dimitri had taken her and Christian away, I'd left her mind. I couldn't go back, not yet. I couldn't stand to see them—to see Dimitri. I knew I'd have to once I began directing the guardians, but for now, I held off. I knew Lissa was alive. That was all that mattered for the time being.

Still, I was so wound up and filled with tension that when someone touched my arm, I nearly turned on them with my stake.

"Adrian . . ." I breathed. "What are you doing here?"

He stood there looking down at me, and his hand gently brushed my cheek. I had only ever seen such a serious, grim look on his face a couple of times. As usual, I didn't like it. Adrian was one of those people who should always be smiling.

"As soon as I heard the news, I knew where you'd be."

I shook my head. "It happened like . . . I don't know, ten minutes ago?" Time had blurred for me. "How could everyone know so soon?"

"It was radioed across the Court as soon as they found out. They've got an instant alert system. In fact, the queen's kind of in lockdown."

"What? Why?" Somehow that annoyed me. Tatiana wasn't the one in danger. "Why waste resources on *her*?" A nearby guardian gave me a critical look over that.

Adrian shrugged. "Strigoi attack relatively close by? They take it as a pretty serious security threat for us."

Relatively was the key word. Lehigh was about an hour and a half from Court. Guardians were always on alert, though with each passing second, I wished they'd move faster *and* be on alert. If Adrian hadn't shown up, I was pretty sure I would have lost my patience and told Hans to hurry.

"It's Dimitri," I said in a low voice. I hadn't been sure if I should tell anyone else that. "He's the one who took them. He's using them to lure me there."

Adrian's face grew darker. "Rose, you can't . . ." He trailed off, but I knew his meaning.

"What choice do I have?" I exclaimed. "I have to go. She's my best friend, and I'm the only one who can lead them to her."

"It's a trap."

"I know. And he knows I know."

"What will you do?" Again, I knew exactly what Adrian meant.

I glanced down at the stake I'd unconsciously pulled out earlier. "What I have to. I have to . . . I have to kill him."

"Good," said Adrian, relief flooding his features. "I'm glad."

For some reason, that irritated me. "God," I snapped. "Are you that eager to get rid of any competition?"

Adrian's face stayed serious. "No. I just know that as long as he's still alive—or, well, kind of alive—then you're in danger. And I can't stand that. I can't stand knowing that your life is in the balance. And it is, Rose. You'll never be safe until he's gone. I want you safe. I *need* you to be safe. I can't . . . I can't have anything happen to you."

My flare of anger vanished as quickly as it had come. "Oh, Adrian, I'm sorry. . . ."

I let him draw me into his arms. Resting my head against his chest, I felt his heartbeat and the softness of his shirt, I allowed myself a brief and fleeting moment of comfort. I just wanted to sink into him then and there. I didn't want to be consumed by these feelings of fear: fear for Lissa and fear *of* Dimitri. I went cold all over as a sudden realization slipped over me. No matter what happened, I would lose one of them tonight. If we rescued Lissa, Dimitri would die. If he survived, she would die. There was no happy ending for this story, nothing that could save my heart from being crushed into pieces.

Adrian brushed my forehead with his lips and then leaned down toward my mouth. "Be careful, Rose. No matter what happens, please, *please* be careful. I can't lose you."

I didn't know what to say to that, how to respond to all that emotion pouring from him. My own mind and heart were flooded with so many mixed feelings that I could barely form a coherent thought. Instead, I drew my lips to his and kissed him. In the midst of all the death tonight—the death that already had happened and that which was still to come—that kiss seemed more powerful than any he and I had ever shared. It was alive. I was alive, and I wanted to stay that way. I wanted to bring Lissa back, and I wanted to return to Adrian's arms again, return to his lips and all this life. . . .

"Hathaway! Good God, do I need to hose you down?"

I broke abruptly from Adrian and saw Hans glaring at me. Most of the SUVs were loaded up. Now it was my turn to act. I gave Adrian a look of farewell, and he forced a small smile that I think was supposed to be brave.

"Be careful," he repeated. "Bring them back—and bring yourself back too."

I gave him a quick nod and then followed an impatient Hans into one of the SUVs. The most bizarre sense of déjà vu settled over me as I slid into the backseat. This was so like the time Victor had kidnapped Lissa that I nearly froze up. Then, too, I had ridden in a similar black SUV, directing guardians toward Lissa's location. Only it had been Dimitri sitting beside me—the wonderful, brave Dimitri I'd known so long ago. Yet those memories were so etched into my mind and heart that I could picture every detail: the way he'd tucked his hair behind his ears, the fierce look in his brown eyes as he'd stepped on the gas to get us to Lissa faster. He'd been so determined, so ready to do what was right.

This Dimitri—Dimitri the Strigoi—was also determined. But in a very different way.

"You gonna be able to do this?" asked Hans from the front seat. A hand gently squeezed my arm, and I was startled to see Tasha beside me. I hadn't even noticed she was riding with us. "We're counting on you."

I nodded, wanting to be worthy of his respect. In best guardian fashion, I kept my emotions off my face, trying not to feel that conflict between the two Dimitris. Trying not to remember that the night we'd gone after Lissa and Victor had been the same night Dimitri and I had fallen prey to the lust charm. . . .

"Head toward Lehigh," I said in a cool voice. I was a guardian now. "I'll direct you when we get closer."

We'd only been on the road for about twenty minutes when I sensed Lissa's group coming to a halt. Dimitri had apparently chosen a hideout not too far from the university, which would make it easier for us to find than if they'd kept moving. Of course, I had to remind myself that Dimitri *wanted* to be found. Knowing that the guardians with me wouldn't need my directions until we were closer to Lehigh, I steeled myself and jumped into Lissa's head to see what was going on.

Lissa and Christian hadn't been harmed or attacked, aside from being pushed and dragged around. They sat in what looked like a storage room—a storage room that hadn't been used in a very long time. Dust coated everything in a heavy layer, so much that it was hard to make out some of the objects piled on the rickety shelves. Some tools, maybe. Paper here and there, as well as the occasional box. A bare lightbulb was the only light in the room, giving everything a harsh and dingy feel.

Lissa and Christian sat in straight-backed wooden chairs, their hands bound behind their backs with rope. For a moment, déjà vu hit again. I remembered last winter when I too, along with my friends, had been bound to chairs and held captive by Strigoi. They'd drunk from Eddie, and Mason had died. . . .

No. Don't think like that, Rose. Lissa and Christian are alive. Nothing's happened to them yet. Nothing will *happen to them.*

Lissa's mind was on the here and now, but a little probing let me see what the overall building had looked like when she'd been brought in. It had seemed to be a warehouse—an old, abandoned one—which made it a nice place for the Strigoi to hole up with their prisoners.

There were four Strigoi in the room, but as far as Lissa was concerned, only one really mattered. Dimitri. I understood her reaction. Seeing him as a Strigoi had been hard for me. Surreal, even. I'd adapted somewhat, simply because of all the time I'd spent with him. Still, even I was caught by surprise sometimes at seeing him like that. Lissa hadn't been prepared at all and was in total shock.

Dimitri's dark brown hair was worn loose around his chin today, a look I'd always loved on him, and he was pacing rapidly, causing his duster to swirl around him. A lot of the time, his back was to Lissa and Christian, which made it that much more troubling for her. Without seeing his face, she could almost believe it was the Dimitri she'd always known. He was arguing with the other three as he walked back and forth across the small space, agitation radiating off him in an almost palpable wave.

"If the guardians really are coming," snarled one Strigoi, "then we should be posted outside." She was a tall, gangly redhead who appeared to have been Moroi when turned. Her tone implied that she did *not* think guardians were actually coming, though.

"They're coming," said Dimitri in a low voice, that lovely accent making my heart ache. "I know they are."

"Then let me get out there and be useful!" she snapped. "You don't need us to babysit these two." Her tone was dismissive. Scornful, even. It was understandable. Everyone in the vampire world knew Moroi didn't fight back, and Lissa and Christian were firmly bound.

"You don't know them," said Dimitri. "They're dangerous. I'm not even sure this is enough protection."

"That's ridiculous!"

In one smooth motion, Dimitri turned and backhanded her. The hit knocked her back a few feet, her eyes widening in fury and shock. He resumed his pacing as though nothing had happened.

"You will stay here, and you will guard them as long as I tell you to, do you understand?" She glared back and gingerly touched her face but said nothing. Dimitri glanced at the others. "And you'll stay too. If the guardians actually make it this far inside, you'll be needed for more than just guard duty."

"How do you know?" demanded another Strigoi, a black-haired one who might have been human once. A rarity among Strigoi. "How do you know they'll come?"

Strigoi had amazing hearing, but with their bickering, Lissa had a brief opportunity to speak undetected to Christian. "Can you burn my ropes?" she murmured in a nearly inaudible voice. "Like with Rose?"

Christian frowned. When he and I had been captured, it was what he'd done to free me. It had hurt like hell and left blisters on my hands and wrists. "They'll notice," he breathed back. The conversation went no further because Dimitri came to an abrupt halt and turned toward Lissa.

She gasped at the sudden and unexpected movement. Swiftly approaching her, he knelt down before her and peered into her eyes. She trembled in spite of her best efforts. She had never been this close to a Strigoi, and the fact that it was Dimitri was that much worse. The red rings around his pupils seemed to burn into her. His fangs looked poised to attack.

His hand snaked out and gripped her neck, tilting her face up so he could get an even better look into her eyes. His fingers dug into her skin, not enough to cut off her air but enough that she would have bruises later. If there was a later.

"I know the guardians will come because Rose is watching," said Dimitri. "Aren't you, Rose?" Loosening his hold a little, he ran his fingertips over the skin of Lissa's throat, so gently . . . yet there was no question he had the power to snap her neck.

It was like he was looking into *my* eyes at the moment. My soul. I even felt like he was stroking *my* neck. I knew it was impossible. The bond existed between Lissa and me. No one else could see it. Yet, just then, it was like no one else existed but *him* and me. It was like there was no Lissa between us.

"You're in there, Rose." A pitiless half smile played over his mouth. "And you won't abandon either of them. You also aren't foolish enough to come alone, are you? Maybe once you would have—but not anymore."

I jerked out of her head, unable to stare into those eyes—and see them staring back at me. Whether it was my own fear or a mirroring of Lissa's, I discovered my body was also trembling. I forced it to stop and tried to slow my racing heart. Swallowing, I glanced around to see if anyone had noticed, but they were all preoccupied with discussing strategy—except for Tasha.

Her cool blue gaze studied me, her face drawn with concern. "What did you see?"

I shook my head, unable to look at her either. "A nightmare," I murmured. "My worst nightmare coming true."

SIXTEEN

I DIDN'T HAVE A PRECISE count of how many Strigoi were with Dimitri's group. So much of what I'd seen through Lissa had been blurred with confusion and terror. The guardians, knowing we were expected, had simply had to make a best guess about how many to send. Hans had hoped overwhelming force would make up for us losing the element of surprise. He'd dispatched as many guardians as he could reasonably clear from the Court. Admittedly, the Court was protected by wards, but it still couldn't be left entirely undefended.

Having the new grads there had helped. Most of them had been left behind, allowing the seasoned guardians to go on our hunting party. That left us with forty or so. It was as unusual as large groups of Strigoi banding together. Guardians were usually sent out in pairs, maybe groups of three at most, with Moroi families. This large of a force had the potential to bring about a battle rivaling that of the Academy attack.

Knowing that sneaking through the dark wouldn't work, Hans stopped our convoy a little ways from the warehouse the Strigoi were holed up at. The building was situated on a service road cutting off from the highway. It was an industrial area, hardly a deserted path in the woods, but all the businesses and factories were shut down this late at night. I stepped out of the

SUV, letting the warm evening wrap around me. It was humid, and the moisture in the air felt especially oppressive when I was already smothered with fear.

Standing beside the road, I felt no nausea. Dimitri hadn't posted Strigoi this far, which meant our arrival was still—kind of—a surprise. Hans walked over to me, and I gave him the best estimate I could on the situation, based on my limited information.

"But you can find Vasilisa?" he asked.

I nodded. "As soon as I'm in the building, the bond will lead me straight to her."

He turned, staring off into the night as cars sped by on the nearby highway. "If they're already waiting outside, they'll smell and hear us long before we see them." Passing headlights briefly illuminated his face, which was lined in thought. "You said there are three layers of Strigoi?"

"As far as I could tell. There are some on Lissa and Christian, then some outside." I paused, trying to think what Dimitri would do in this situation. Surely I knew him well enough, even as a Strigoi, to calculate his strategy. "Then another layer inside the building—before you get to the storage room." I didn't know this for certain, but I didn't tell Hans. The assumption was made on my own instincts, drawn from what I would do and what I thought Dimitri would do. I figured it would be best if Hans planned for three waves of Strigoi.

And that's exactly what he did. "Then we go in with three groups. You'll lead the group going in for the extraction. Another team will accompany yours and eventually split off.

They'll fight whoever's right inside, letting your group head for the captives."

It sounded so . . . militaristic. *Extraction. Captives.* And me . . . a team leader. It made sense with the bond, but always in the past, they'd simply used my knowledge and left me on the sidelines. *Welcome to being a guardian, Rose.* At school, we'd conducted all sorts of exercises, running as many different Strigoi scenarios as our instructors could dream up. Yet, as I stared up at the warehouse, all of those drills seemed like playacting, a game that could in no way measure up to what I was about to face. For half a second, the responsibility of it all seemed daunting, but I quickly shoved aside such concerns. This was what I had been trained to do, what I had been born to do. My own fears didn't matter. *They come first*. Time to prove it.

"What are we going to do since we can't sneak up on them?" I asked. Hans had a point about the Strigoi detecting us in advance.

An almost mischievous smile flickered on his face, and he explained his plan to the group while also dividing us into our teams. His approach tactic was bold and reckless. My kind of plan.

And like that, we were off. An outsider analyzing us might have said we were on a suicide mission. Maybe we were. It honestly didn't matter. The guardians wouldn't abandon the last Dragomir. And I wouldn't have abandoned Lissa even if there were a million Dragomirs.

So, with sneaking having been ruled out, Hans opted for a full-on attack. Our group loaded back into the eight SUVs and tore off down the street at illegal speeds. We took up the entire width of the road, gambling on no oncoming traffic. Two SUVs led the charge side by side, then two rows of three. We shot to the end of the road, came to a halt with screeching tires at the front of the warehouse, and spilled out of our cars. If slow stealth wasn't an option, we'd gain surprise by going fast and furious.

Some of the Strigoi were indeed surprised. Clearly, they'd seen our approach, but it had happened so fast that they'd had only a little time to react. Of course, when you were as fast and deadly as Strigoi, a little time was all you needed. A group of them surged at us, and Hans's "outside team" charged back, those guardians putting themselves between my group and the other going inside. The Moroi fire users had been assigned to the outside group, for fear of setting the building on fire if they went inside.

My team moved around the battle, inevitably running into a few Strigoi who hadn't fallen to the first team's distraction. With well-practiced determination, I ignored the nausea sweeping through me from being this close to Strigoi. Hans had strictly ordered me not to stop unless any Strigoi were directly in my path, and he and another guardian were beside me to cover any threats that might come at me. He wanted nothing to delay me from leading them to Lissa and Christian.

We fought our way into the warehouse, entering a dingy hall blocked by Strigoi. I'd been right in my guess that Dimitri would have layers of security. A bottleneck formed in the small space, and for a few moments things were chaotic. Lissa was so close. It was like she was calling to me, and I burned with impatience as I waited for the hall to clear. My team was in the back, letting the other group do the fighting. I saw Strigoi and guardians alike fall and tried not to let it distract me. Fight now, grieve later. Lissa and Christian. I had to focus on them.

"There," said Hans, tugging my arm. A gap had formed ahead of us. There were still plenty of Strigoi, but they were distracted enough that my companions and I slipped through. We took off down the hall, which opened into a large empty space that made up the warehouse's heart. A few pieces of trash and debris were all that was left of the goods once stored here.

Doors led off of the room, but now I didn't need the bond to tell me where Lissa was. Three Strigoi stood guard outside a doorway. So. Four layers of security. Dimitri had one-upped me. It didn't matter. My group had ten people. The Strigoi snarled, bracing in anticipation as we charged them. Through an unspoken signal, half of my group engaged them. The rest of us busted down the door.

Despite my intense focus on reaching Lissa and Christian, one tiny thought had always been dancing in the back of my brain. Dimitri. I hadn't seen Dimitri in any of the Strigoi we'd encountered. With my full attention on our attackers, I hadn't slipped into Lissa's head to verify the situation, but I felt totally confident that he was still inside the room. He would have stayed with her, knowing I would come. He would be waiting to face me.

One of them dies tonight. Lissa or Dimitri.

Having reached our goal, I no longer needed extra protection. Hans pulled out his stake on the first Strigoi he encountered, pushing past me and jumping into the fray. The rest of my group did likewise. We poured into the room, and if I thought there'd been chaos earlier, it was nothing compared to what we faced. All of us—guardians and Strigoi—just barely fit inside the room, which meant we were fighting in very, very close quarters. A female Strigoi—the one Dimitri had slapped earlier—came at me. I fought on autopilot, barely aware of my stake piercing her heart. In this room, full of shouting and death and colliding, there were only three people in the world that mattered to me now: Lissa, Christian, and Dimitri.

I'd found him at last. Dimitri was with my two friends against the far wall. No one was fighting him. He stood with arms crossed, a king surveying his kingdom as his soldiers battled the enemy. His eyes fell on me, his expression amused and expectant. This was where it would end. We both knew it. I shoved my way through the crowd, dodging Strigoi. My colleagues pushed into the fray beside me, dispatching whomever stood in my way. I left them to their fight, moving toward my objective. All of this, everything happening, had led to this moment: the final showdown between Dimitri and me.

"You're beautiful in battle," said Dimitri. His cold voice carried to me clearly, even above the roar of combat. "Like an avenging angel come to deliver the justice of heaven."

"Funny," I said, shifting my hold on the stake. "That *is* kind of why I'm here."

"Angels fall, Rose."

I'd almost reached him. Through the bond, I felt a brief surge of pain from Lissa. A burning. No one was harming her yet, but when I saw her arms move out of the corner of my eye, I realized what had happened. Christian had done what she'd asked: He'd burned her ropes. I saw her move to untie him in return, and then my attention shifted back to Dimitri. If Lissa and Christian were free, then so much the better. It would make their escape easier, once we cleared out the Strigoi. *If* we cleared out the Strigoi.

"You've gone to a lot of trouble to get me here," I told Dimitri. "A lot of people are going to die—yours and mine."

He shrugged, unconcerned. I was almost there. In front of me, a guardian battled a bald Strigoi. That lack of hair was *not* attractive with his chalk white skin. I moved around them.

"It doesn't matter," said Dimitri. He tensed as I approached. "None of them matter. If they die, then they obviously aren't worthy."

"Prey and predator," I murmured, recalling what he'd said to me while holding me prisoner.

I'd reached him. No one stood between us now. This was different from our past fights, where we'd had lots of room to size each other up and plan our attacks. We were still crammed into the room, and in keeping our distance from the others, we'd closed the gap between us. That was a disadvantage for me. Strigoi outmatched guardians physically; extra room helped us compensate with more maneuverability.

I didn't need to maneuver quite yet, though. Dimitri was trying to wait me out, wanting me to make the first move. He kept a good position, though, one that blocked me from getting a clear shot on his heart. I could do some damage if I cut him elsewhere with the stake, but he would likely get a hit in on me that would be packed with power in this proximity. So I tried to wait him out as well.

"All this death is because of you, you know," he said. "If you'd let me awaken you . . . let us be together . . . well, none of this would have happened. We'd still be in Russia, in each other's arms, and all of your friends here would be safe. None of them would have died. It's your fault."

"And what about the people I'd have to kill in Russia?" I demanded. He'd shifted his weight a little. Was that an opening? "They wouldn't be safe if I—"

A crashing sound off to my left startled me. Christian, now freed, had just slammed his chair into a Strigoi engaged with a guardian. The Strigoi shrugged Christian off like a fly. Christian flew backward, slamming into a wall and landing on the floor with a slightly stunned look. In spite of myself, I spared him a glance and saw Lissa running to his side. And so help me, she had a stake in her hand. How she'd managed that, I had no idea. Maybe she'd picked it up from a fallen guardian. Maybe none of the Strigoi had thought to search her when she came in. After all, why on earth would a Moroi be carrying a stake?

"Stop it! Stay out of the way!" I yelled at them, turning back to Dimitri. Letting those two distract me had cost me. Realizing Dimitri was about to attack, I managed to dodge without even seeing what he was doing. It turned out he'd been reaching for my neck, and my imprecise evasion had spared me the full damage. Still, his hand caught me on the shoulder, knocking me back almost as far as Christian had gone. Unlike my friend, though, I had years of training that had taught me to recover from something like that. I'd honed a lot of balance and recovery skills. I staggered only a little, then quickly regained my footing.

I could only pray Christian and Lissa would listen to me and not do anything stupid. My attention had to stay on Dimitri, or I'd get myself killed. And if I died, Lissa and Christian died for sure. My impression while fighting our way inside had been that the guardians outnumbered the Strigoi, though that meant little sometimes. Still, I had to hope my colleagues would finish our foes off, leaving me to do what I had to do.

Dimitri laughed at my dodge. "I'd be impressed if that wasn't something a ten-year-old could do. Now your friends . . . well, they're also fighting at a ten-year-old level. And for Moroi? That's actually pretty good."

"Yeah, well, we'll see what your assessment is when I kill you," I told him. I made a small feint to test how much he was paying attention. He sidestepped with hardly any notice at all, as graceful as a dancer.

"You can't, Rose. Haven't you figured that out by now? Haven't you *seen* it? You can't defeat me. You can't kill me. Even if you could, you can't bring yourself to do it. You'll hesitate. Again."

No, I wouldn't. That's what he didn't realize. He'd made a mistake bringing Lissa here. She increased the stakes—no pun intended—on everything. She was here. She was real. Her life was on the line, and for that . . . for that, I wouldn't hesitate.

Dimitri must have grown tired of waiting for me. He leapt out, hand again going for my neck. And again I evaded, letting my shoulder take the brunt of the hit. This time he held on to my shoulder. He jerked me toward him, triumph flaring in those red eyes. In the sort of space we were in, this was probably all he needed to kill me. He had what he wanted.

Apparently, though, he wasn't the only one who wanted me. Another Strigoi, maybe thinking he'd help Dimitri, pushed toward us and reached for me. Dimitri bared his fangs, giving the other Strigoi a look of pure hatred and fury.

"Mine!" Dimitri hissed, hitting the other Strigoi in a way that he had clearly not expected.

And that was my opening. Dimitri's brief distraction had caused him to loosen his grip on me. That same close proximity which made him so lethal to me now made me just as dangerous. I was by his chest, by his heart, and I had my stake in hand.

I'll never be able to say for sure just how long the next series of events took. In some ways, it felt like only one heartbeat passed. At the same moment, it was as though we were frozen in time. Like the entire world had stopped.

My stake was moving toward him, and as Dimitri's eyes fell on me once more, I think he finally believed I would kill him. I was not hesitating. This was happening. My stake was there—

And then it wasn't.

Something hit me hard on my right side, pushing me away

from Dimitri and ruining my shot. I stumbled, barely avoiding hitting anyone. While I always tried to be vigilant regarding all things around me in a fight, I'd let my guard down in that direction. The Strigoi and guardians were on my left. The wall—and Lissa and Christian—were on my right.

And it was Lissa and Christian who had shoved me out of the way.

I think Dimitri was as astonished as I was. He was also equally astonished when Lissa came toward him with that stake in her hand. And like lightning through the bond, I read what she had very, very carefully kept from me the last day: She had managed to charm the stake with spirit. It was the reason she'd been so keyed up during her last stake-practice session with Grant and Serena. Knowing she had the tool she needed had fueled her desire to use it. Her hiding all of that information from me was a feat on par with charming the stake.

Not that it mattered right now. Charmed stake or no, she couldn't get near Dimitri. He knew it too, and his surprise immediately changed to delighted amusement—almost indulgent, like the way one watches a child do something adorable. Lissa's attack was awkward. She wasn't fast enough. She wasn't strong enough.

"No!" I screamed, leaping toward them, though pretty certain I wasn't going to be fast enough either.

Suddenly, a blazing wall of heat and flame appeared before me, and I barely had the presence of mind to back up. That fire had shot up from the floor, forming a ring around Dimitri that kept me from him. It was disorienting, but only for a moment.

I knew Christian's handiwork.

"Stop it!" I didn't know what to do, if I should attack Christian or leap into the fire. "You'll burn us all alive!" The fire was fairly controlled—Christian had that much skill—but in a room this size, even a controlled fire was deadly. Even the other Strigoi backed away.

The flames were closing in on Dimitri, growing tighter and tighter. I heard him scream, could see the look of agony, even through the fire. It began to consume his coat, and smoke poured out from the blaze. Some instinct told me I needed to stop this . . . and yet, what did it matter? I'd come to kill him. Did it matter if someone else did it for me?

And that's when I noticed Lissa was still on the offensive. Dimitri was distracted, screaming as the flames wrapped around him. I was screaming too . . . for him, for her . . . it's hard to say. Lissa's arm shot through the flames, and again, pain surged through the bond—pain that dwarfed the earlier singe from Christian burning her ropes. Yet she kept going, ignoring the fiery agony. Her alignment was right. She had the stake aimed at the heart.

The stake went in, piercing him.

Well, kind of.

Just like when she'd practiced with the pillow, she didn't quite have the strength to get the stake where it needed to go. I felt her steel herself, felt her summon up every ounce of strength she had. Throwing her full weight into it, she shoved again, using both hands. The stake went in further. Still not enough. This delay would have cost her

her life in a normal situation. This was not a normal situation. Dimitri had no means to block her, not with the fire slowly eating him. He did manage a small struggle that loosened the stake, undoing what little progress she'd made. Grimacing, she tried again, pushing the stake back to its former position.

Still, it wasn't enough.

I came to my senses then, knowing I needed to stop this. Lissa was going to burn herself up if she kept trying to stake him. She lacked the skill. Either I needed to stake him or we just needed to let the fire finish him off. I moved forward. Lissa caught sight of me in her periphery and sent out a blast of compulsion at me.

No! Let me do this!

The command hit me hard, an invisible wall that made me come to a halt. I stood there dazed, both from the compulsion itself and the realization that she'd used it on me. It only took a moment for me to shake it off. She was too distracted to put her full power into the order, and I was pretty compulsion-resistant anyway.

Yet, that slight delay had stopped me from reaching her. Lissa seized her last chance, knowing she'd get no other.

One more time, fighting through the fire's searing pain, she threw everything she had into shoving the stake all the way into Dimitri's heart. Her strike was still awkward, still requiring a little more wiggling and pushing than the clean hit a trained guardian would make. Clumsy or not, the stake finally made it. It pierced his heart. And as it did, I felt magic flood our bond, the familiar magic I'd felt so many times when she performed a healing.

Except . . . this was a hundred times more powerful than anything I'd ever felt before. It froze me up as neatly as her compulsion had. I felt as though all of my nerves were exploding, like I'd just been struck by lightning.

White light suddenly burst out around her, a light that dwarfed the fire's brightness. It was like someone had dropped the sun into the middle of that room. I cried out, my hand rising instinctively to shield my eyes as I stepped backward. From the sounds in the room, everyone else was having a similar reaction.

For a moment, it was as if there was no bond anymore. I felt nothing from Lissa—no pain, no magic. The bond was as colorless and empty as the white light filling the room. The power she'd used had over-flooded and overwhelmed our bond, numbing it.

Then the light simply disappeared. No fade-out. Just . . . gone in an eye blink. Like a switch had been flipped. There was silence in the room, save for a few murmurings of discomfort and confusion. That light must have been toxic to sensitive Strigoi eyes. It was hard enough for me. Starbursts danced in my sight. I couldn't focus on anything as the afterimage of that brilliance burned across my vision.

At last—with a little squinting—I could vaguely see again. The fire was gone, though black smudges on the wall and ceiling marked its presence, as did some lingering smoke. By my estimation, there should have been a lot more damage. I could spare no time for that miracle, though, because there was another one taking place in front of me.

Not just a miracle. A fairy tale.

Lissa and Dimitri were both on the floor. Their clothes were burned and singed. Angry red and pink patches marked her beautiful skin from where the fire had hit hardest. Her hands and wrists were particularly bad. I could see spots of blood where the flames had actually burned some of her skin away. Third-degree burns, if I was recalling my physiology classes correctly. Yet she seemed to feel no pain, nor did the burns affect her hands' movement.

She was stroking Dimitri's hair.

While she sat in some semblance of an upright position, he was in an ungainly sprawl. His head rested in her lap, and she was running her fingers through his hair in a gentle, repetitive motion—like one does to comfort a child or even an animal. Her face, even marred with the fire's terrible damage, was radiant and filled with compassion. Dimitri had called me an avenging angel, but she was an angel of mercy as she gazed down at him and crooned soothing, nonsense words.

With the state of his clothes and what I'd seen in the fire, I'd expected him to be burned to a crisp—some sort of blackened, skeletal nightmare. Yet when he shifted his head, giving me my first full view of his face, I saw that he was completely unharmed. No burns marked his skin—skin that was as warm and tanned as it had been the first day I'd met him. I caught only a glimpse of his eyes before he buried his face against Lissa's knee. I saw endless depths of brown, the depths I'd fallen into so many times. No red rings.

Dimitri . . . was not a Strigoi.

And he was weeping.

SEVENTEEN

THE ENTIRE ROOM SEEMED to hold its breath.

Yet even in the face of miracles, guardians—or Strigoi, for that matter—were hard to distract. Fights that had paused now resumed with just as much fury. The guardians had the upper hand, and those of them who weren't engaged with the last surviving Strigoi suddenly leapt toward Lissa, trying to pull her away from Dimitri. To everyone's surprise, she held on to him tightly and made a few feeble attempts to fight off those crowding around her. She was fierce and protective, again putting me in mind of a mother defending her child.

Dimitri was holding on to her just as intently, but both he and Lissa were outmatched. The guardians finally pried them apart. There were confused shouts as guardians tried to determine whether they should kill Dimitri. It wouldn't have been hard. He was helpless now. He could barely stand when they jerked him to his feet.

That woke me up. I'd simply been staring, frozen and dumbstruck. Shaking off my daze, I sprang forward, though I wasn't sure who I was going for: Lissa or Dimitri.

"No! Don't!" I yelled, seeing some of the guardians move in with stakes. "He's not what you think! He's not Strigoi! Look at him!"

Lissa and Christian were shouting similar things. Someone grabbed me and pulled me back, telling me to let the others handle this. Without even thinking, I turned and punched my captor in the face, discovering too late it was Hans. He fell back a little, seeming more surprised than offended. Attacking him was enough to attract the attention of others, however, and soon I had my own group of guardians to fight off. My efforts didn't do any good, partially because I was outnumbered and partially because I couldn't take them on the same way I'd attacked Strigoi.

As the guardians hauled me out, I noticed then that Lissa and Dimitri had already been removed from the room. I demanded to know where they were, yelling that I had to see them. No one listened to me. They dragged me away, out of the warehouse, passing a disturbing amount of bodies. Most were Strigoi, but I recognized a few faces from the guardian regiment at the Court. I grimaced, even though I hadn't known them well. The battle was over, and our side had won—but at a great cost. The surviving guardians would be doing cleanup now. I wouldn't have been surprised if Alchemists showed up, but at the moment, none of that was my concern.

"Where's Lissa?" I kept demanding as I was shoved inside one of the SUVs. Two guardians slid in with me, one sitting on each side. I didn't know either of them. "Where's Dimitri?"

"The princess has been taken to safety," one of the guardians said crisply. He and the other guy stared straight ahead, and I realized neither was going to acknowledge the question about Dimitri. He might as well not exist for any of them.

"Where's Dimitri?" I repeated, speaking more loudly in the hopes that might get an answer. "Is he with Lissa?"

That got a reaction. "Of course not," said the guardian who'd spoken before.

"Is he . . . is he alive?" It was one of the hardest questions I'd ever asked, but I had to know. I hated to admit it, but if I were in Hans's place, I wouldn't have been looking for miracles. I would have been exterminating anything I perceived as a threat.

"Yes," said the driver at last. "He . . . it . . . is alive."

And that was all I could get out of them, no matter how much I argued and demanded to be released from the car—and believe me, I did a lot of that. Their ability to ignore me was pretty impressive, really. To be fair, I'm not even sure that they knew what had happened. Everything had occurred so fast. The only thing these two knew was that they'd been ordered to escort me out of the building.

I kept hoping someone I knew might join us in our SUV. Nope. Only more unknown guardians. No Christian or Tasha. Not even Hans—of course, that was understandable. He was probably afraid I'd accidentally punch him again.

When we were loaded up and on the road, I finally gave up my badgering and sank back into the seat. Other SUVs had left with ours, but I had no clue whether my friends were in them.

The bond between Lissa and me was still numb. After that initial shock where I'd felt nothing, I'd slowly regained a slight sense of her, telling me we were still connected and that she was alive. That was about it. With all that power that had blasted through her, it was almost like the bond had been temporarily fried. The magic between us was fragile. Each time I tried to use the bond to check on her, it was as though I'd stared too brightly at something and was still blinded. I just had to assume it would reestablish itself soon because I needed her insight on what had happened.

No, scratch insight. I needed to know what had happened, period. I was still in a bit of shock, and the long ride back to Court allowed me time to process what few facts I had access to. I immediately wanted to jump to Dimitri but needed to start at the beginning if I really wanted to analyze all that had occurred.

First: Lissa had charmed a stake and withheld the info from me. When? Before her college trip? At Lehigh? While captive? It didn't matter.

Second, in spite of her failed pillow attempts, she had gotten the stake into Dimitri's heart. It had been a struggle, but Christian's fire had made it possible. I winced, recalling the burns Lissa had suffered during that ordeal. I'd felt the pain of those before the bond blanked out, and I'd also seen the marks on her. Adrian wasn't the world's best healer, but hopefully his magic would be enough to take care of her injuries.

The third and final fact here . . . well . . . was it a fact? Lissa had stabbed Dimitri and used the same magic she would for a healing . . . and then? That was the big question. What had happened, aside from what felt like a nuclear explosion of magic through our bond? Had I really seen what I thought I'd seen?

Dimitri had . . . changed.

He was no longer a Strigoi. I felt it in my heart, even though I'd only had that brief glimpse of him. It had been enough to allow me to see the truth. The Strigoi features were gone. Lissa had done everything Robert had sworn she needed to do to restore a Strigoi, and certainly after all that magic . . . well, it was easy to believe anything was possible. That image of Dimitri came back to me, clinging to Lissa with tears running down his face. I'd never seen him so vulnerable. Somehow, I didn't believe Strigoi cried.

Something in my heart twisted painfully, and I blinked rapidly to stop from crying too. Glancing around, I tuned back into my surroundings. Outside the car, the sky was lightening. It was nearly sunrise. The guardians with me had signs of weariness on their faces, yet the alert expressions in their eyes never faltered. I'd lost track of the time, but my internal clock told me we'd been on the road for a while. We had to almost be back at Court.

Tentatively, I touched the bond and found it was back but still fragile. It was like it flickered in and out, still reestablishing itself. That was enough to put me at ease, and I breathed a sigh of relief. When the bond had first come about years ago, it had been so strange . . . surreal. Now I'd accepted it as part of my life. Its absence today had felt unnatural.

Looking through Lissa's eyes, at the SUV she rode in, I immediately hoped I'd see Dimitri with her. That one glimpse at the warehouse hadn't been enough. I needed to see him again, needed to see if this miracle had truly happened. I wanted to drink in those features, to gaze at the Dimitri from so long ago. The Dimitri I loved.

But he wasn't with Lissa. Christian was there, however, and he glanced over at her as she stirred. She'd been asleep and still felt groggy. That, combined with the aftereffect of that searing power earlier, kept our connection a little hazy. Things shifted out of focus for me off and on, but overall, I could follow what was happening.

"How do you feel?" asked Christian. His voice and his eyes as he peered at her were filled with so much affection that it seemed impossible she didn't notice. But then, she was a little preoccupied right now.

"Tired. Worn out. Like . . . I don't know. Like I've been thrown around in a hurricane. Or run over by a car. Pick something horrible, and that's what I feel like."

He gave her a small smile and gently touched her cheek. Opening myself to her senses more, I felt the pain of her burns and that he was tracing the skin near one, though being careful to keep away from it.

"Is it awful?" she asked him. "Is all my skin melted off? Do I look like some alien?"

"No," he said, with a small laugh. "There's not that much. You're beautiful, like always. It would take a lot for that to change."

The throbbing pain she felt made her think that there was more damage than he was admitting to, but the compliment and the way he'd said it went a long way to soothe her. For a moment, her whole existence focused on his face and the way the rising sun was starting to light it up.

Then the rest of her world came crashing down on her.

"Dimitri! I need to see Dimitri!"

There were guardians in the car, and she glanced around at them as she spoke. As with me, no one seemed willing to acknowledge him or what had happened.

"Why can't I see him? Why'd you take him away?" This was directed to anyone who would answer, and at last, Christian did.

"Because they think he's dangerous."

"He's not. He's just . . . He needs me. He's hurting inside."

Christian's eyes suddenly went wide, his face filling with panic. "He's not . . . You aren't bonded to him, are you?"

I guessed by the look on his face that Christian was recalling Avery and how bonding with multiple people had pushed her over the edge. Christian hadn't been there for Robert's explanation of the soul going to the world of the dead and how restored Strigoi didn't get bonded.

Lissa shook her head slowly. "No . . . I just know. When I . . . when I healed him, we had this connection, and I felt it. What I had to do . . . I can't explain it." She ran a hand through her hair, frustrated that she couldn't put her magic into words. Weariness was starting to overtake her. "It was like I had to do surgery on his soul," she said at last.

"They think he's dangerous," repeated Christian gently.

"He's not!" Lissa glared around at the rest of the car's occupants, all of whom were looking somewhere else. "He's not Strigoi anymore."

"Princess," began one of the guardians uneasily, "no one

really knows what happened. You can't be sure that—"

"I am sure!" she said, voice too loud for the small space. There was a regal, commanding air to it. "*I know.* I saved him. I brought him back. I know with every single part of me that he's no longer Strigoi!"

The guardians looked uncomfortable, again not speaking. I think they were just confused, and really, how could they not be? There was no precedent for this.

"Shh," said Christian, putting his hand on hers. "There's nothing you can do until we're back at Court. You're still hurt and exhausted—it's written all over you."

Lissa knew he was right. She *was* hurt, and she *was* exhausted. That magic had ripped her apart. At the same time, what she had done for Dimitri had created a bond to him—not a magical one, but a psychological one. She really was like a mother. She felt desperately protective and concerned.

"I need to see him," she said.

She did? What about me?

"You will," said Christian, sounding more certain than I suspected he was. "But just try to rest now."

"I can't," she said, even while stifling a yawn.

That smile flickered back across his lips, and he slipped his arm around her, pulling her as close as the seat belts would allow. "Try," he told her.

She rested her head against his chest, and his closeness was a type of healing in and of itself. Worry and concern for Dimitri still coursed through her, but her body's needs were stronger for the moment. At last, she drifted into sleep in Christian's embrace, just barely hearing him murmur, "Happy birthday."

Twenty minutes later, our convoy arrived back at Court. I thought this meant instant freedom, but my guardians took their time in getting out, waiting for some signal or directions that no one had bothered to tell me about. It turned out they were waiting for Hans.

"No," he said, firmly putting a hand on my shoulder as I shot out of the car and tried to race away to . . . well, I wasn't sure where. Wherever Dimitri was. "Hold on."

"I have to see him!" I exclaimed, trying to push past. Hans was like a brick wall. Considering he'd actually fought a lot more Strigoi than me tonight, you'd have thought he'd be tired. "You have to tell me where he is."

To my surprise, Hans did. "Locked away. Far, far out of your reach. Or anyone else's. I know he used to be your teacher, but it's better if he's kept away for now."

My brain, weary from the night's activities and overwrought with emotion, took a moment to process this. Christian's words came back to me. "He's not dangerous," I said. "He's not a Strigoi anymore."

"How can you be so certain?"

The same question Lissa had been asked. How could we really answer that? We knew because we'd gone to incredible pains to find out how to transform a Strigoi, and when we'd completed those steps, there'd been an atom bomb of magic. Wasn't that enough proof for anyone? Hadn't Dimitri's *appearance* been enough?

Instead, my answer was like Lissa's. "I just know."

Hans shook his head, and now I could see he actually was exhausted. "No one knows what's going on with Belikov. Those of us that were there . . . well, I'm not sure what I saw. All I do know is that he was leading Strigoi a little while ago, and now he's out in the sun. It doesn't make any sense. No one knows what he is."

"He's a dhampir."

"And until we do," he continued, ignoring my comment, "Belikov has to stay locked up while we examine him." *Examine?* I didn't like the sound of that. It made Dimitri seem like a lab animal. It made my temper flare, and I nearly started yelling at Hans. A moment later, I got myself under control.

"Then I need to see Lissa."

"She's been taken to the medical center for treatment—which she needs very badly. You can't go there," he added, anticipating my next response. "Half the guardians are there. It's chaos, and you'd be in the way."

"Then what the hell am I supposed to do?"

"Go get some sleep." He gave me a wry look. "I still think you've got a bad attitude, but after what I saw back there . . . well, I'll say this. You know how to fight. We need you—probably for more than paperwork. Now go take care of yourself."

And that was that. The dismissal in his voice was clear, and as the guardians hurried around, it was like I didn't exist. Whatever trouble I'd been in before seemed long forgotten. No more filing in the wake of this. But what was I supposed to do? Was Hans crazy? How could I sleep? I had to do something. I had to see Dimitri—but I didn't know where they'd taken him.

Probably the same jail Victor had been kept in, which was inaccessible to me. I also needed to see Lissa—but she was deep in the medical center. I had no power here. I needed to appeal to someone with influence.

Adrian!

If I went to Adrian, maybe he could pull some strings. He had his royal connections. Hell, the queen loved him, in spite of his slacker ways. As much as it killed me to accept, I was realizing that getting in to see Dimitri right away was going to be nearly impossible. But the medical center? Adrian might be able to get me in to see Lissa, even if it was crowded and chaotic. The bond was still blurry, and talking to her directly would allow me to score faster answers about Dimitri. Plus, I wanted to see for myself that she was all right.

Yet when I reached the housing Adrian stayed in at Court, I was informed by the doorman that Adrian had already left a little while ago to—ironically enough—go to the medical center. I groaned. Of course he'd already be there. With his healing abilities, they would have summoned him out of bed. Weak or not, he could definitely help.

"Were you there?" the doorman asked me as I started to turn away.

"What?" For a minute I thought he was talking about the medical center.

"The battle with the Strigoi! The rescue. We've been hearing all sorts of things."

"Already? What did you hear?"

The guy's eyes were wide and excited. "They say almost

every guardian died. But that you captured a Strigoi and brought him back."

"No, no . . . there were more injuries than deaths. And the other . . ." For a moment, I couldn't breathe. What had happened? What had really happened with Dimitri? "A Strigoi was changed back to a dhampir."

The doorman stared. "Were you hit on the head?"

"I'm telling the truth! Vasilisa Dragomir did it. With her spirit power. Spread *that* around."

I left him with his mouth hanging open. And like that, I had no more options, no one else to get information from. I went back to my room feeling defeated but far too keyed up to sleep. At least, that's what I initially thought. After some pacing, I sat on the bed to try to come up with a plan. Yet before long, I felt myself falling into a heavy sleep.

I awoke with a start, confused and aching in parts of my body that I hadn't realized had taken hits in the fight. I peered at the clock, astonished at how long I'd slept. In vampire time, it was late morning. Within five minutes, I had showered and put on non-torn, non-bloody clothes. Just like that, I was out the door.

People were out and about their daily business, yet every couple or group I passed seemed to be talking about the battle at the warehouse—and about Dimitri.

"You know she can heal," I heard one Moroi guy say to his wife. "Why not Strigoi? Why not the dead?"

"It's insane," the woman countered. "I've never believed in this spirit thing anyway. It's a lie to cover up the fact that the

Dragomir girl never specialized."

I didn't hear the rest of their conversation, but others I passed had similar themes. People were either convinced the whole thing was a scam or were regarding Lissa as a saint already. Every so often, I'd heard something weird, like that the guardians had captured a bunch of Strigoi to experiment on. In all the speculation, though, I never heard Dimitri's name come up or knew what was really happening to him.

I followed the only plan I had: Go to the guardian building that held the Court's jail, though I was unsure what I'd actually do when I got there. I wasn't even entirely sure that was where Dimitri still was, but it seemed the most likely place. When I passed a guardian along the way, it took me several seconds to realize I knew him. I came to a halt and turned.

"Mikhail!" He glanced back and, seeing me, walked over. "What's going on?" I asked, relieved to see a friendly face. "Have they let Dimitri out?"

He shook his head. "No, they're still trying to figure out what happened. Everyone's confused, even though the princess still swore up and down after she saw him that he's not Strigoi anymore."

There was a wonder in Mikhail's voice—and wistfulness too. He was hoping that it was true, that there might be a chance for his beloved to be saved. My heart ached for him. I hoped he and Sonya could have a happy ending just like—

"Wait. What did you say?" His words drew my romantic musings to a halt. "Did you say Lissa saw him? You mean after the fight?" I immediately reached for the bond. It was gradually growing clearer—but Lissa was asleep, so I learned nothing.

"He asked for her," Mikhail explained. "So they let her in—guarded, of course."

I stared, my jaw nearly dropping to the ground. Dimitri was seeing visitors. They were actually letting him see visitors. The knowledge lit up the dark mood that had been building in me. I turned away. "Thanks, Mikhail."

"Wait, Rose—"

But I didn't stop. I ran to the guardians' holding building at a full-out sprint, oblivious to the looks I got. I was too excited, too invigorated with this new info. I could see Dimitri. I could finally be with him, back the way he was supposed to be.

"You can't see him."

I literally came to a halt when the guardian on duty in the front reception area stopped me.

"Wh-what? I need to see Dimitri."

"No visitors."

"But Lissa—er, Vasilisa Dragomir got to see him."

"He asked for her."

I stared incredulously. "He must have asked for me too."

The guardian shrugged. "If he did, no one's told me."

The anger I'd kept back last night finally awoke. "Then go find someone who knows! Dimitri wants to see me. You have to let me in. Who's your boss?"

The guardian scowled at me. "I'm not going anywhere until my shift is over. If you've got clearance, someone will let you know. Until then, no one without special permission is allowed to go down there."

After taking out a fair portion of Tarasov's security, I felt pretty confident I could easily dispatch this guy. However, I felt equally confident that once I got to the depths of the jail cells, I'd run into a lot more guardians. For a second, taking them out seemed very reasonable. It was Dimitri. I would do anything for him. A slight stirring in the bond made me see reason. Lissa had just woken up.

"Fine," I said. I lifted my chin and gave him a haughty look. "Thanks for the 'help.'" I didn't need this loser. I'd go to Lissa.

She was staying at almost the opposite end of the Court's grounds from the holding area, and I covered the distance at a light jog. When I finally reached her and she opened the door to her room, I saw that she'd gotten ready almost as quickly as I had. In fact, I could feel that she'd been pretty close to leaving. Studying her face and hands, I was relieved to see that almost all of the burns were gone. A few red spots lingered on her fingers, but that was it. Adrian's handiwork. No doctor could have made that happen. In a pale blue tank top, with her blond hair pulled back, she didn't look at all like anyone who'd been through such a major ordeal less than twenty-four hours ago.

"Are you okay?" she asked. In spite of everything else that had happened, she'd never stopped worrying about me.

"Yeah, fine." Physically, at least. "You?"

She nodded. "Fine."

"You look good," I said. "Last night . . . I mean, I was pretty scared. With the fire . . ." I couldn't quite finish.

"Yeah," she said, looking away from me. She seemed nervous and uncomfortable. "Adrian's been pretty great healing people."

"Is that where you're going?" There was agitation and restlessness in the bond. It would make sense if she wanted to hurry over to the medical center and help out too. Except . . . further probing gave me the startling truth. "You're going to see Dimitri!"

"Rose—"

"No," I said eagerly. "It's perfect. I'll go with you. I was just over there, and they wouldn't let me in."

"Rose—" Lissa looked very uncomfortable now.

"They gave me some bullshit about how he'd asked for you and not me and that that's why they couldn't let me in. But if you're going, they'll have to let me."

"Rose," she said firmly, finally breaking through my chatter. "You can't go."

"I—what?" I replayed her words, just in case I'd misheard them. "Of course I can. I need to see him. You know I do. And he needs to see me."

She slowly shook her head, still looking nervous—but also sympathetic. "That guardian was right," she said. "Dimitri *hasn't* been asking for you. Only me."

All my eagerness, all that fire, froze up. I was dumbstruck, confused more than anything. "Well . . ." I recalled how he'd clung to her last night, that desperate look on his face. I hated to admit it, but it kind of made sense why he would have asked for her first. "Of course he'd want to see you. Everything's so new and strange, and you're the one who saved him. Once he comes around more, he'll want to see me too."

"Rose, you can't go." This time the sadness in Lissa's voice was mirrored through the bond, flooding into me. "It's not just that Dimitri didn't ask to see you. He asked specifically *not* to see you."

EIGHTEEN

THE THING THAT REALLY SUCKS about being psychically linked to someone is that you have a pretty good idea when they're lying—or, in this case, not lying. Still, my response was immediate and instinctive.

"That's not true."

"Isn't it?" She gave me a pointed look. She too knew that I could feel the truth in her words.

"But that . . . it can't . . . " I wasn't at a loss for words very often—and certainly not with Lissa. So frequently in our relationship, I'd been the one being assertive and explaining to *her* why things had to be the way they were. Somewhere along the way, with me not realizing it, Lissa had lost that fragility.

"I'm sorry," she said, voice still kind but also firm. The bond betrayed how much she hated telling me unpleasant things. "He asked me . . . told me specifically not to let you come. That he doesn't want to see you."

I stared at her pleadingly, my voice almost childlike. "But why? Why would he say that? Of course he wants to see me. He must be confused. . . ."

"I don't know, Rose. All I know is what he told me. I'm so sorry." She reached for me like she might hug me, but I stepped away. My head was still reeling.

"I'll go with you anyway. I'll wait upstairs with the other guardians. Then, when you tell Dimitri I'm there, he'll change his mind."

"I don't think you should," she said. "He seemed really serious about you not coming—almost frantic. I think knowing you're there would upset him."

"Upset him? *Upset him?* Liss, it's me! He *loves* me. He needs me."

She winced, and I realized I'd been shouting at her. "I'm just going on what he said. It's all so confusing . . . please. Don't put me in this position. Just . . . wait and see what happens. And if you want to know what's going on, you can always . . ."

Lissa didn't finish, but I knew what she was suggesting. She was offering to let me see her meeting with Dimitri through the bond. It was a big gesture on her part—not that she could have stopped me if I wanted to do it. Still, she didn't usually like the idea of being "spied" on. This was the best thing she could think of to make me feel better.

Not that it really did. All of this was still crazy. Me being denied access to Dimitri. Dimitri allegedly not wanting to see me! What the hell? My gut reaction was to ignore everything she'd just said and go along with her, demanding access when she arrived. The feelings in the bond were begging me not to, though. She didn't want to create trouble. She might not understand Dimitri's wishes either, but she felt they should be honored until the situation could be better assessed.

"Please," she said. The plaintive word finally cracked me.

"Okay." It killed me to say it. It was like admitting defeat. *Think of it as a tactical retreat.*

"Thank you." This time she did hug me. "I swear I'll get more information and figure out what's going on, okay?"

I nodded, still dejected, and we walked out of the building together. With grim reluctance, I parted with her when the time came, letting her go off to the guardians' building while I headed toward my room. As soon as she was out of my sight, I immediately slipped into her head, watching through her eyes as she walked through the perfectly manicured grass. The bond was still a little hazy but growing clearer by the minute.

Her feelings were a jumble. She felt bad for me, guilty that she'd had to refuse me. At the same time, she was anxious to visit Dimitri. She needed to see him too—but not in the same way I did. She still had that feeling of responsibility for him, that burning urge to protect him.

When she arrived at the building's main office, the guardian who'd stopped me gave her a nod of greeting and then made a quick phone call. A few moments later, three guardians entered and gestured for Lissa to follow them into the depths of the building. They all looked unusually grim, even for guardians.

"You don't have to do this," one of them told her. "Just because he keeps asking . . ."

"It's fine," she said with the cool, dignified air of any royal. "I don't mind."

"There'll be plenty of guards around just like last time. You don't need to worry about your safety."

She gave all of them a sharp look. "I was never worried about it to begin with."

Their descent into the building's lower levels brought back painful memories of when Dimitri and I had visited Victor. That had been the Dimitri I'd had a perfect union with, the Dimitri who understood me entirely. And after the visit, he'd been enraged at Victor's threats against me. Dimitri had loved me so much that he'd been willing to do anything to protect me.

A key card–protected door finally allowed access to the holding level, which consisted mostly of a long hallway lined with cells. It didn't have the depressing feel that Tarasov had had, but this place's stark and steel-lined industrial air didn't exactly inspire warm and fuzzy feelings.

Lissa could hardly walk down the hall because it was so crowded with guardians. All that security for one person. It wasn't impossible for a Strigoi to break through a cell's steel bars, but Dimitri was no Strigoi. Why couldn't they see that? Were they blind?

Lissa and her escort made their way through the crowd and came to a stop in front of his cell. It was as cold looking as everything else in this prison area, with no more furnishings than were absolutely required. Dimitri sat on the narrow bed, his legs drawn up to him as he leaned into a corner of the wall and kept his back to the cell's entrance. It wasn't what I had expected. Why wasn't he beating at the bars? Why wasn't he demanding to be released and telling them he wasn't a Strigoi? Why was he taking this so quietly?

"Dimitri."

Lissa's voice was soft and gentle, filled with a warmth that stood out against the harshness of the cell. It was the voice of an angel.

And as Dimitri slowly turned around, it was obvious he thought so too. His expression transformed before our eyes, going from bleakness to wonder.

He wasn't the only one filled with wonder. My mind might have been tied to Lissa's, but back across Court, my own body nearly stopped breathing. The glimpse I'd gotten of him last night had been amazing. But this . . . this full-on view of him looking at Lissa—at me—was awe-inspiring. It was a wonder. A gift. A miracle.

Seriously. How could anyone think he was a Strigoi? And how could I have possibly let myself believe the Dimitri I'd been with in Siberia was *this* one? He'd cleaned up from the battle and wore jeans and a simple black T-shirt. His brown hair was tied back into a short ponytail, and a faint shadow across his lower face showed that he needed to shave. Probably no one would let him get near a razor. Regardless, it almost made him look sexier—more real, more dhampir. More *alive.* His eyes were what really pulled it all together. His death white skin—now gone—had always been startling, but those red eyes had been the worst. Now they were perfect. Exactly as they used to be. Warm and brown and long-lashed. I could have gazed at them forever.

"Vasilisa," he breathed. The sound of his voice made my chest tighten. God, I'd missed hearing him speak.

"You came back."

As soon as he began approaching the bars, the guardians around Lissa started closing rank, ready to stop him should he indeed bust through. "Back off!" she snapped in a queenly tone, glaring at everyone around her. "Give us some space." No one reacted right away, and she put more power into her voice. "I mean it! Step back!"

I felt the slightest trickle of magic through our link. It wasn't a huge amount, but she was backing her words with a little spirit-induced compulsion. She could hardly control such a large group, but the command had enough force to make them clear out a little and create space between her and Dimitri. She turned her attention back to him, demeanor instantly changing from fierce to kind.

"Of course I came back. How are you? Are they . . ." She cast a dangerous look at the guardians in the hall. "Are they treating you okay?"

He shrugged. "Fine. Nobody's hurting me." If he was anything like his old self, he would have never admitted if anyone *was* hurting him. "Just a lot of questions. So many questions." He sounded weary, again . . . very unlike a Strigoi who never needed rest. "And my eyes. They keep wanting to examine my eyes."

"But how do you *feel*?" she asked. "In your mind? In your heart?" If the whole situation hadn't been so sobering, I would have been amused. It was very much a therapist's line of questioning—something both Lissa and I had experienced a lot of. I'd hated being asked those questions, but now I truly wanted to know how Dimitri felt.

His gaze, which had so intently focused on her, now drifted away and grew unfocused. "It's . . . it's hard to describe. It's like I've woken up from a dream. A nightmare. Like I've been watching someone else act through my body—like I was at a movie or a play. But it wasn't someone else. It was *me*. All of it was me, and now here I am, and the whole world has shifted. I feel like I'm relearning everything."

"It'll pass. You'll get more used to it, once you settle back into your old self." That was a guess on her part, but one she felt confident of.

He inclined his head toward the gathered guardians. "They don't think so."

"They will," she said adamantly. "We just need more time." A small silence fell, and Lissa hesitated before speaking her next words. "Rose . . . wants to see you."

Dimitri's dreamy, morose attitude snapped in a heartbeat. His eyes focused back on Lissa, and I got my first glimpse of true, intense emotion from him. "No. Anyone but her. I *can't* see her. Don't let her come here. *Please.*"

Lissa swallowed, unsure how to respond. The fact that she had an audience made it harder. The best she could do was lower her voice so the others wouldn't hear. "But . . . she loves you. She's worried about you. What happened . . . with us being able to save you? Well, a lot of it was because of her."

"You saved me."

"I only did the final piece. The rest . . . well, Rose did, um, a lot." Say, like, organizing a prison break and releasing fugitives.

Dimitri turned from Lissa, and the fire that had briefly lit his features faded. He walked over to the side of the cell and leaned against the wall. He closed his eyes for a few seconds, took a deep breath, and then opened them.

"Anyone but her," he repeated. "Not after what I did to her. I did a lot of things . . . horrible things." He turned his hands palm-up and stared at them for a moment, like he could see blood. "What I did to her was worst of all—especially because it *was* her. She came to save me from that state, and I . . ." He shook his head. "I did terrible things to her. Terrible things to others. I can't face her after that. What I did was unforgivable."

"It's not," said Lissa urgently. "It wasn't you. Not really. She'll forgive you."

"No. There's no forgiveness for me—not after what I did. I don't deserve her, don't deserve to even be around her. The only thing I can do . . ." He walked back over to Lissa, and to the astonishment of both of us, he fell to his knees before her. "The only thing I can do—the only redemption I can try for—is to pay you back for saving me."

"Dimitri," she began uneasily, "I told you—"

"I felt that power. In that moment, I felt you bring my soul back. I felt you heal it. That's a debt I can't ever repay, but I swear I'll spend the rest of my life trying." He was looking up at her, that enraptured look back on his face.

"I don't want that. There's nothing to repay."

"There's everything to pay," he argued. "I owe you my life—my soul. It's the only way I can come close to ever redeeming myself for all the things I did. It's still not enough . . . but it's all

I can do." He clasped his hands. "I swear, whatever you need, anything—if it's in my power—I'll do it. I'll serve and protect you for the rest of my life. I'll do whatever you ask. You have my loyalty forever."

Again, Lissa started to say she didn't want that, but then a canny thought came to mind. "Will you see Rose?"

He grimaced. "Anything but that."

"Dimitri—"

"Please. I'll do anything else for you, but if I see her . . . it'll hurt too much."

That was probably the only reason that could have made Lissa drop the subject. That and the desperate, dejected look on Dimitri's face. It was one she had never seen before, one I'd never seen before either. He'd always been so invincible in my eyes, and this sign of vulnerability didn't make him seem weaker to me. It simply made him more complex. It made me love him more—and want to help him.

Lissa could only give him a small nod as answer before one of the guardians in charge said she had to leave. Dimitri was still on his knees as they escorted her out, staring after her with an expression that said she was the closest to any hope he had left in this world.

My heart twisted with both sorrow and jealousy—and a bit of anger too. I was the one he should have looked at that way. How dare he? How dare he act like Lissa was the greatest thing in the world? She'd done a lot to save him, true, but *I* was the one who'd traveled around the globe for him. *I* was the one who had continually risked my life for him. Most importantly,

I was the one who loved him. How could he turn his back on that?

Both Lissa and I were confused and upset as she left the building. Both of us were distraught over Dimitri's state. Despite how angry I was over his refusal to see me, I still felt horrible at seeing him so low. It killed me. He'd never acted that way before. After the Academy's attack, he had certainly been sad and had grieved over that loss. This was a different kind of despair. It was a deep sense of depression and guilt that he didn't feel he could escape from. Both Lissa and I were shocked by that. Dimitri had always been a man of action, someone ready to get up after a tragedy and fight the next battle.

But this? This was unlike anything we'd ever seen in him, and Lissa and I had wildly varying ideas on how to solve it. Her gentler, sympathetic approach was to keep talking to him while also calmly persuading Court officials that Dimitri was no longer a threat. My solution to this problem was to go to Dimitri, no matter what he claimed he wanted. I'd busted in and out of a prison. Getting into a jail cell should be cake. I was still certain that once he saw me, he'd have a change of heart about all this redemption stuff. How could he truly think I wouldn't forgive him? I loved him. I understood. And as far as convincing officials that he wasn't dangerous . . . well, my method there was a little fuzzy still, but I had a feeling it would involve a lot of yelling and beating on doors.

Lissa knew perfectly well that I had observed her encounter with Dimitri, so she didn't feel obligated to come see me, not when she knew they could still use her over at the medical center. She'd heard Adrian had nearly collapsed with all the magic he'd wielded to help others. It seemed so uncharacteristic of him, so unselfish . . . he'd done amazing deeds, at great cost to himself.

Adrian.

There was a problem. I hadn't had a chance to see him since getting back after the warehouse fight. And aside from hearing about him healing others, I really hadn't thought about him at all. I'd said that if Dimitri really could be saved, it didn't mean the end of Adrian and me. Yet, Dimitri had barely been back twenty-four hours, and here I was, already obsessing ov—

"Lissa?"

Despite the fact that I'd pulled back to my own mind, part of me was still absentmindedly following along with Lissa. Christian was standing outside the medical center, leaning against its wall. From his posture, it appeared as though he'd been there for a while waiting for something—or rather, someone.

She came to a halt, and inexplicably, all thoughts of Dimitri vanished from her mind. Oh, come *on*. I wanted those two to patch things up, but we had no time for this. Dimitri's fate was a lot more important than bantering with Christian.

Christian didn't look like he was in a snarky mood, though. His expression was curious and concerned as he regarded her. "How are you feeling?" he asked. They hadn't talked to each other since the ride back, and she'd been largely incoherent during a lot of it.

"Fine." She touched her face absentmindedly. "Adrian healed me."

"I guess he is good for something." Okay, maybe Christian was feeling a little snarky today. But only a little.

"Adrian's good for lots of things," she said, though she couldn't help a small smile. "He ran himself into the ground here all night."

"What about you? I know how you are. As soon as you were up and around, you were probably right there beside him."

She shook her head. "No. After he healed me, I went to see Dimitri."

All mirth disappeared from Christian's face. "You've talked to him?"

"Twice now. But yeah. I have."

"And?"

"And what?"

"What's he like?"

"He's like Dimitri." She suddenly frowned, reconsidering her words. "Well . . . not quite like Dimitri."

"What, does he still have some Strigoi in him?" Christian straightened up, blue eyes flashing. "If he's still dangerous, you have no business going near—"

"No!" she exclaimed. "He's not dangerous. And . . ." She took a few steps forward, returning his glare. "Even if he was, *you* have no business telling me what I can or can't do!"

Christian sighed dramatically. "And here I thought Rose was the only one who threw herself into stupid situations, regardless of whether they might kill her."

Lissa's anger flared up rapidly, likely because of all the spirit she'd been using. "Hey, you didn't have any issues helping me stake Dimitri! You trained me for it."

"That was different. We were in a bad situation already, and if things went wrong . . . well, I could have incinerated him." Christian regarded her from head to toe, and there was something in his gaze . . . something that seemed like more than just objective assessment. "But I didn't have to. You were amazing. You made the hit. I didn't know if you could, but you did . . . and the fire . . . You didn't flinch at all, but it must have been awful. . . ."

There was a catch in his voice as he spoke, like he was only now truly assessing the consequences of what might have happened to Lissa. His concern and admiration made her flush, and she tilted her head—an old trick—so that the pieces of hair that had escaped from her ponytail would fall forward and hide her face. There was no need for it. Christian was now staring pointedly at the ground.

"I had to do it," she said at last. "I had to see if it was possible."

He looked up. "And it was . . . right? There really isn't any trace of Strigoi?"

"None. I'm positive. But no one believes it."

"Can you blame them? I mean, I helped out with it and I wanted it to be true . . . but I'm not sure I ever really, *truly* thought someone could come back from that." He glanced away again, his gaze resting on a lilac bush. Lissa could smell its scent, but the distant and troubled look on his face told her that his thoughts weren't on nature. Neither were they on Dimitri, I realized. He was thinking about his parents. What if there'd been spirit users around when the Ozeras had turned Strigoi? What if there had been a way to save them?

Lissa, not guessing what I had, remarked, "I don't even know that I believed either. But as soon as it happened, well . . . I knew. I *know*. There's no Strigoi in him. I have to help him. I have to make others realize it. I can't let them lock him up forever—or worse." Getting Dimitri out of the warehouse without the other guardians staking him had been no easy feat for her, and she shivered recalling those first few seconds after his change when everyone had been shouting to kill him.

Christian turned back and met her eyes curiously. "What did you mean when you said he was like Dimitri but not like Dimitri?"

Her voice trembled a little when she spoke. "He's . . . sad."

"Sad? Seems like he should be happy he was saved."

"No . . . you don't understand. He feels awful about everything he did as a Strigoi. Guilty, depressed. He's punishing himself for it because he doesn't think he can be forgiven."

"Holy shit," said Christian, clearly caught off guard. A few Moroi girls had walked by just then and looked scandalized at his swearing. They hurried off, whispering among themselves. Christian ignored them. "But he couldn't help it—"

"I know, I know. I already went over it with him."

"Can Rose help?"

"No," Lissa said bluntly.

Christian waited, apparently hoping she'd elaborate. He

grew annoyed when she didn't. "What do you mean she can't? She should be able to help us more than anyone!"

"I don't want to get into it." My situation with Dimitri bothered her a lot. That made two of us. Lissa turned toward the medical building. It looked regal and castle-like on the outside, but it housed a facility as sterile and modern as any hospital. "Look, I need to get inside. And don't look at me like that."

"Like what?" he demanded, taking a few steps toward her.

"That disapproving, pissed-off look you get when you don't get your way."

"I don't have that look!"

"You have it right now." She backed away from him, moving toward the center's door. "If you want the whole story, we can talk later, but I don't have the time . . . and honestly . . . I don't really feel like telling it."

That pissed-off look—and she was right, he *did* have it—faded a little. Almost nervously, he said, "Okay. Later then. And Lissa . . ."

"Hmm?"

"I'm glad you're all right. What you did last night . . . well, it really was amazing."

Lissa stared at him for several heavy seconds, her heart rate rising slightly as she watched a light breeze ruffle his black hair. "I couldn't have done it without your help," she said at last. With that, she turned and went inside, and I returned completely to my own head.

And like earlier, I was at a loss. Lissa would be busy the rest of the day, and standing and yelling in the guardians' office wouldn't really help me get to Dimitri. Well, I supposed there was the off chance I might annoy them so much that they'd throw *me* in jail too. Then Dimitri and I would be next to each other. I promptly dismissed that plan, fearing the only thing it would land me with was more filing.

What could I do? Nothing. I needed to see him again but didn't know how. I *hated* not having a plan. Lissa's encounter with Dimitri hadn't been nearly long enough for me, and anyway, I felt it was important to take him in through my eyes, not hers. And oh, that sadness . . . that utter look of hopelessness. I couldn't stand it. I wanted to hold him, to tell him everything would be okay. I wanted to tell him I forgave him and that we'd make everything like it used to be. We could be together, just the way we planned . . .

The thought brought tears to my eyes, and left alone with my frustration and inactivity, I returned to my room and flounced onto the bed. Alone, I could finally let loose the sobs I'd been holding in since last night. I didn't even entirely know what I was crying for. The trauma and blood of the last day. My own broken heart. Dimitri's sorrow. The cruel circumstances that had ruined our lives. Really, there were a lot of choices.

I stayed in my room for a good part of the day, lost in my own grief and restlessness. Over and over, I replayed Lissa's meeting with Dimitri, what he'd said and how he looked. I lost track of time, and it took a knock at the door to snap me out of my own suffocating emotions.

Hastily rubbing an arm over my eyes, I opened the door to find Adrian standing out there. "Hey," I said, a little surprised by his presence—not to mention guilty, considering I'd been moping over another guy. I wasn't ready to face Adrian yet, but it appeared I had no choice now. "Do you . . . do you want to come in?"

"Wish I could, little dhampir." He seemed to be in a hurry, not like he'd come to have a relationship talk. "But this is just a drop-by visit to issue an invitation."

"Invitation?" I asked. My mind was still on *Dimitri. Dimitri, Dimitri, Dimitri.*

"An invitation to a party."

NINETEEN

"ARE YOU CRAZY?" I ASKED.

He gave me the same wordless look he always did when I asked that question.

I sighed and tried again. "A *party*? That's pushing it, even for you. People just died! Guardians. Priscilla Voda." Not to mention, people had just come back from the dead. Probably best to leave that part out. "This isn't the time to get trashed and play beer pong."

I expected Adrian to say that it was always a good time for beer pong, but he remained serious. "Actually, it's *because* people died that there's going to be a party. It's not a kegger type. Maybe party's not even the right word. It's a . . ." He frowned, grasping at words. "A special event. An elite one."

"All royal parties are elite ones," I pointed out.

"Yeah, but not every royal is invited to this. It's the . . . well, elite of the elite."

That really wasn't helping. "Adrian—"

"No, listen." He made that familiar gesture of his that indicated frustration, running his hand through his hair. "It's not so much a party as a ceremony. An old, old tradition from . . . I don't know. Romania, I think. They call it the Death Watch.

But it's a way to honor the dead, a secret that's been passed on through the oldest bloodlines."

Flashbacks of a destructive secret society at St. Vladimir's came back to me. "This isn't some Mânã thing, is it?"

"No, I swear. Please, Rose. I'm not all that into it either, but my mom's making me go, and I'd really like it if you were there with me."

Elite and *bloodline* were warning words to me. "Will there be other dhampirs there?"

"No." He then added quickly, "But I made arrangements for some people you'll approve of to be there. It'll make it better for both of us."

"Lissa?" I guessed. If ever there was an esteemed bloodline, hers was it.

"Yeah. I just ran into her at the medical center. Her reaction was about like yours."

That made me smile. It also piqued my interest. I wanted to talk to her more about what had happened during her visit to Dimitri and knew she'd been avoiding me because of it. If going to some silly royal ritual or whatever it was could get me to her, then so much the better.

"Who else?"

"People you'll like."

"Fine. Be mysterious. I'll go to your cult meeting."

That earned me a return smile. "Hardly a cult, little dhampir. It really *is* a way to pay last respects to the people killed in that fight." He reached out and ran a hand along my cheek. "And I'm glad . . . God, I'm so glad you weren't one of them.

You don't know. . . ." His voice caught, the flippant smile trembling for a moment before stabilizing again. "You don't know how worried I was. Every minute you were gone, every minute I didn't know what had happened to you . . . it was agony. And even after I heard you were okay, I kept asking everyone at the medical center what they knew. Had they seen you fight, did you get hurt . . ."

I felt a lump in my throat. I hadn't been able to see Adrian when I'd returned, but I should have sent a message, at least. I squeezed his hand and tried to make a joke of something that really wasn't funny. "What'd they say? That I was a badass?"

"Yeah, actually. They couldn't stop talking about how amazing you were in battle. Word got back to Aunt Tatiana too about what you did, and even she was impressed."

Whoa. That was a surprise. I started to ask more, but his next words brought me up short.

"I also heard you were yelling at anyone you could to find out about Belikov. And that you were beating down the guardians' doors this morning."

I looked away. "Oh. Yeah. I . . . Look, I'm sorry, but I had to—"

"Hey, hey." His voice was heavy and earnest. "Don't apologize. I understand."

I looked up at him. "You do?"

"Look, it's not like I didn't expect this if he came back."

I glanced back at him hesitantly, studying his serious expression. "I know. I remember what you said before. . . ."

He nodded, then gave me another rueful smile. "Of course, I

didn't actually expect any of this to work. Lissa tried to explain the magic she used . . . but good God. I don't think I could ever do anything like she did."

"Do you believe?" I asked. "Do you believe he's no longer Strigoi?"

"Yeah. Lissa said he's not, and I believe her. And I saw him from a distance out in the sun. But I'm not sure it's a good idea for you to try to see him."

"That's your jealousy talking." I had absolutely no right to sound accusing, considering the way my heart was all tangled up over Dimitri.

"Of course it's jealousy," said Adrian nonchalantly. "What do you expect? The former love of your life comes back—from the dead, no less. That's not something I'm really excited about. But I don't blame you for feeling confused."

"I told you before—"

"I know, I know." Adrian didn't sound particularly upset. In fact, there was a surprisingly patient tone in his voice. "I know you said him coming back wouldn't affect things between us. But saying one thing before it happens and then actually having that thing happen are two different things."

"What are you getting at?" I asked, kind of confused.

"I want you, Rose." He squeezed my hand more tightly. "I've always wanted you. I want to be with you. I'd like to be like other guys and say I want to take care of you too, but . . . well. When it comes down to it, you'd probably be the one taking care of me."

I laughed in spite of myself. "Some days I think you're in

more danger from yourself than anyone else. You smell like cigarettes, you know."

"Hey, I have never, ever said I was perfect. And you're wrong. You're probably the most dangerous thing in my life."

"Adrian—"

"Wait." With his other hand, he pressed his fingers over my lips. "Just listen. It'd be stupid for me to think that your old boyfriend coming back isn't going to have any effect on you. So do I like you wanting to see him? No, of course not. That's instinct. But there's more, you know. I do believe that he's a dhampir again. Absolutely. But . . ."

"But what?" Adrian's words had me more curious than ever now.

"But just because he isn't a Strigoi doesn't mean it's entirely gone from him. Hold on." Adrian could see my mouth opening in outrage. "I'm not saying he's evil or means to be evil or anything like that. But what he went through . . . It's huge. Epic. We really don't know much about the changing process. What effect did that kind of life have on him? Are there violent parts of him that might suddenly lash out? That's what I'm worried about Rose. I know you. I know you aren't going to be able to help yourself. You'll have to see him and talk to him. But is it safe? That's what no one knows. We don't know anything about this. We don't know if he's dangerous."

Christian had said the same thing to Lissa. I examined Adrian intently. It sounded like a convenient excuse to keep Dimitri and me apart. Yet, I saw truth in those deep green eyes. He meant it. He was nervous about what Dimitri might do.

Adrian had also been honest about being jealous, which I had to admire. He hadn't ordered me not to see Dimitri or tried to dictate my behavior. I liked that too. I extended my hand and laced my fingers with Adrian's.

"He's not dangerous. He's . . . sad. Sad for what he's done. The guilt's killing him."

"I can imagine. I probably wouldn't forgive myself either if I suddenly realized I'd been brutally killing people for the last four months." Adrian pulled me to him and kissed the top of my head. "And for everyone's sake—yes, even his—I really hope he is exactly the way he was. Just be careful, okay?"

"I will," I said, kissing his cheek. "Inasmuch as I ever am."

He grinned and released me. "That's the best I can hope for. For now, I've got to head back to my parents' for a little bit. I'll come back for you at four, okay?"

"Okay. Is there anything I should wear to this secret party?"

"Nice dress clothes are fine."

Something occurred to me. "If this is so elite and prestigious, how are you going to get a lowly dhampir like me in?"

"With this." Adrian reached for a bag he'd set down upon entering. He handed it to me.

Curiously, I opened the bag and gaped at what I saw. It was a mask, one that just covered the top half of the face around the eyes. It was intricately worked with gold and green leaves and bejeweled flowers.

"A mask?" I exclaimed. "We're wearing masks to this thing? What is this, Halloween?"

He winked. "See you at four."

* * *

We didn't actually put on the masks until we arrived at the Death Watch. As part of the secret nature of it all, Adrian said we didn't want to call any attention to ourselves while going to it. So we walked across the Court's grounds dressed up—I wore the same dress I'd worn to dinner at his parents'—but not getting much more notice than the two of us usually did when we were together. Besides, it was late, and a lot of the Court was getting ready for bed.

Our destination surprised me. It was one of the buildings that non-royal Court workers lived in, one that was very near Mia's. Well, I supposed the last place you'd look for a royal party would be at the home of a commoner. Except we didn't go to any of the apartments inside. Once we stepped into the building's lobby, Adrian indicated we should put our masks on. He then took me over to what appeared to be a janitor's closet.

It wasn't. Instead, the door opened to a staircase leading down into darkness. I couldn't see the bottom, which put me on high alert. I instinctively wanted to know the details of every situation I entered. Adrian seemed calm and confident as he headed down, so I took it on faith he wasn't leading me to some sacrificial altar. I hated to admit it, but curiosity over this Death Watch thing was temporarily taking my mind off Dimitri.

Adrian and I eventually reached another door, and this one had two guards. Both men were Moroi, both masked like Adrian and me. Their postures were stiff and defensive. They said nothing but simply looked at us expectantly. Adrian said a few words that sounded like Romanian, and a moment later, one of the men unlocked the door and gestured us inside.

"Secret password?" I murmured to Adrian as we swept past.

"Passwords, actually. One for you and one for me. Every guest has a unique one."

We stepped into a narrow tunnel lit only by torches embedded in the walls. Their dancing flames cast fanciful shadows as we passed by. From far ahead, the low murmur of conversation reached us. It sounded surprisingly normal, like any conversation you'd hear at a party. Based on Adrian's description, I'd half-expected to hear chanting or drums.

I shook my head. "I knew it. They keep a medieval dungeon under the Court. I'm surprised there aren't chains on the walls."

"Scared?" Adrian teased, clasping hold of my hand.

"Of this? Hardly. I mean, on the Rose Hathaway Scale of Scariness, this is barely a—"

We emerged out of the hall before I could finish. An expansive room with vaulted ceilings spread out before us, something that boggled my spatially challenged brain as I tried to recall just how far underground we'd gone. Wrought-iron chandeliers holding lit candles hung from the ceiling, casting the same ghostly light the torches had. The walls were made of stone, but it was a very artful, pretty stone: gray with reddish flecks, polished into smooth round pieces. Someone had wanted to keep the Old World dungeon feel but still have the place look stylish. It was a typical line of royal thinking.

Fifty or so people were milling around the room, some huddled in groups. Like Adrian and me, they wore formal clothing and half masks. All the masks were different. Some had a floral theme like mine, while others were decorated with animals. Some simply had swirls or geometric designs. Even though the masks only covered half the guests' faces, the sketchy lighting went a long way to obscure any other identifying features. I scrutinized them carefully, hoping I might pick out details that would give someone away.

Adrian led me out of the entryway and over toward a corner. As my view of the area expanded, I could see a large fire pit in the middle of the room, embedded in the stone floor. No fire burned in it, but everyone kept well away. For a moment, I had a disorienting flash of déjà vu, thinking back to my time in Siberia. I'd been to a type of memorial ceremony there too—though hardly one with masks or passwords—and everyone had sat around a bonfire outdoors. It had been in Dimitri's honor, as all those who had loved him sat and told stories about him.

I tried to get a better look at the fire, but Adrian was intent on keeping us behind the bulk of the crowd. "Don't bring attention to yourself," he warned.

"I was just looking."

"Yeah, but anyone who looks too close is going to realize you're the shortest person here. It'd be pretty obvious you're a dhampir. This is elite old blood, remember?"

I frowned at him as much as I could through the mask.

"But I thought you said you'd made arrangements for me to be here?" I groaned when he didn't answer. "Does 'making arrangements' mean just sneaking me in? If so, those guys were kind of crap security."

Adrian scoffed. "Hey, we had the right passwords. That's all it takes. I stole—er, borrowed them off my mom's list."

"Your mom's one of the people who helped organize this?"

"Yup. Her branch of the Tarus family's been deep inside this group for centuries. They apparently had a really big ceremony here after the school attack."

I turned all of this over in my mind, trying to decide how I felt. I hated when people were obsessed with status and appearances, yet it was hard to fault them wanting to honor those who had been killed—particularly when a majority of them had been dhampirs. The Strigoi attack on St. Vladimir's was a memory that would forever haunt me. Before I could ponder much further, a familiar sensation swept me.

"Lissa's here," I said, looking around. I could feel her nearby but didn't spot her immediately in the sea of masks and shadows. "There."

She stood apart from some of the others, wearing a rose-hued dress and a white and gold mask with swans on it. Through our link, I felt her searching for anyone she knew. I impulsively started to go to her, but Adrian held me back, telling me to wait while he retrieved her.

"What is all this?" she asked when she reached me.

"I figured you'd know," I told her. "It's all top secret royal stuff."

"Too top secret for me," she said. "I got my invite from the queen. She told me it was part of my heritage and to keep it to myself, and then Adrian came and said I had to come for your sake."

"Tatiana invited you directly?" I exclaimed. Maybe I shouldn't have been surprised. Lissa would have hardly needed sneaking in like I did. I figured someone would have made sure she got an invitation, but I'd assumed it had all been Adrian's doing. I glanced around uneasily. "Is Tatiana here?"

"Likely," said Adrian, voice annoyingly casual. As usual, his aunt's presence didn't have the same impact on him that it did the rest of us. "Oh, hey. There's Christian. With the fire mask."

I didn't know how Adrian spotted Christian, aside from the not-so-subtle mask metaphor. With his height and dark hair, Christian easily blended in with the other Moroi around him and had even been chatting with a girl standing nearby, which seemed out of character. "No way did *he* get a legit invite," I said. If any Ozeras had been deemed special enough to come to this, Christian wouldn't have been one of them.

"He didn't," agreed Adrian, making a small gesture for Christian to join us. "I gave him one of the passwords I stole from Mom."

I gave Adrian a startled look. "How many did you steal?"

"Enough to—"

"Let us come to attention."

A man's booming voice rang out through the room, halting both Adrian's words and Christian's steps. With a grimace,

Christian returned to where he'd been standing, cut off from us now on the other side of the room. It looked like I wouldn't have the chance to ask Lissa about Dimitri after all.

Without any direction, the others in the room began forming a circle around the fire pit. The room wasn't big enough for us to make a single-layered circle, so I was still able to stay behind other Moroi as I watched the spectacle. Lissa stood by me, but her attention was fixated across from us, on Christian. She was disappointed that he hadn't been able to join us.

"Tonight we come to honor the spirits of those who died fighting the great evil that has plagued us for so long." This was the same man who had called us to attention. The black mask he wore glittered with silver swirls. He wasn't anyone special that I recognized. It was probably safe to assume that he was someone from an important bloodline who happened to have a good voice for bringing people together. Adrian confirmed it.

"That's Anthony Badica. They always recruit him as an emcee."

Anthony seemed more like a religious leader than an emcee right now, but I didn't want to answer back and attract anyone's notice.

"Tonight we honor them," continued Anthony.

I flinched as almost everyone around us repeated those words. Lissa and I exchanged startled looks. Apparently, there was a script we hadn't been told about.

"Their lives were taken from us too soon," continued Anthony.

"Tonight we honor them."

Okay, this script might not be so hard to follow after all. Anthony kept talking about how terrible the tragedy was, and we repeated the same response. The whole idea of this Death Watch still weirded me out, but Lissa's sadness permeated the bond and began to affect me too. Priscilla had always been good to her—and polite to me. Grant might have only been Lissa's guardian a short time, but he had protected her and helped her. In fact, if not for Grant's work with Lissa, Dimitri might still be a Strigoi. So, slowly, the gravity of it all began to hit me, and even if I thought there were better ways to mourn, I appreciated the acknowledgment the dead were getting.

After a few more refrains, Anthony gestured someone forward. A woman in a glittering emerald mask came forward with a torch. Adrian shifted beside me. "My darling mother," he murmured.

Sure enough. Now that he'd pointed it out, I could clearly make out Daniella's features. She tossed her torch into the fire pit, and it lit up like the Fourth of July. Someone must have doused that wood with either gasoline or Russian vodka. Maybe both. No wonder the other guests had kept their distance. Daniella melted into the crowd, and another woman came forward holding a tray with golden goblets. Walking around the circle, she handed a cup to each person. When she ran out, another woman appeared with a tray.

As the goblets were distributed, Anthony explained, "Now we will toast and drink to the dead, so that their spirits will move on and find peace."

I shifted uncomfortably. People talked about restless spirits and the dead finding peace without really knowing what that meant. Being shadow-kissed came with the ability to see the restless dead, and it had taken me a long time to gain control so that I *didn't* see them. They were always around me; I had to work to keep them blocked out. I wondered what I'd see now if I let down my walls. Would the ghosts of those killed the night of Dimitri's attack be hovering around us?

Adrian sniffed his cup as soon as he got it and scowled. For a moment, I felt panic until I sniffed mine too. "Wine. Thank God," I whispered to him. "From your face, I thought it was blood." I recalled how much he hated blood that wasn't straight from the source.

"Nah," he murmured back. "Just a bad vintage."

When everyone had their wine, Anthony raised his cup over his head with both hands. With the fire behind him, it gave him an almost sinister, otherworldly look. "We drink to Priscilla Voda," he said.

"We drink to Priscilla Voda," everyone repeated.

He brought the goblet down and took a sip. So did everyone else—well, except for Adrian. He gulped half his down, bad vintage or not. Anthony raised his cup over his head again.

"We drink to James Wilket."

As I repeated the words, I realized James Wilket was one of Priscilla's guardians. This crazy group of royals really was showing respect to dhampirs. We went through the other guardians one by one, but I kept my sips small, wanting to keep a level head tonight. I was pretty sure that by the end of the name list, Adrian was faking his sips because he'd run out.

When Anthony finished naming all who had died, he held his cup up again and approached the blazing fire, which had begun to make the small room uncomfortably hot. The back of my dress was growing damp with sweat.

"To all those lost by the great evil, we honor your spirits and hope they will move on in peace to the next world." He then dumped the remainder of his wine into the flames.

All this talk of spirits lingering in the world certainly didn't go along with the usual Christian afterlife beliefs that dominated Moroi religion. It made me wonder just how old this ceremony really was. Once more, I had an urge to drop my barriers and see if any of this had really drawn ghosts to us, but I feared what I'd find. Besides, I promptly got distracted when everyone else in the circle began dumping their wine into the fire as well. One by one, going clockwise, each person approached. All was silent as this happened, save for the crackling in the fire pit and shifting of logs. Everyone watched respectfully.

When my turn came, I fought hard not to tremble. I hadn't forgotten that Adrian had sneaked me in here. Lowly Moroi weren't allowed, let alone dhampirs. What would they do? Declare the space violated? Mob me? Cast me into the fire?

My fears proved unfounded. No one said or did anything unusual as I poured out my wine, and a moment later, Adrian stepped forward for his turn. I melted back beside Lissa. When the entire circle had gone up, we were led into a moment of silence for the departed. Having witnessed Lissa's kidnapping and subsequent rescue, I had a lot of dead to ponder. No amount of silence would ever do them justice.

Another unspoken signal seemed to pass through the room. The circle dispersed, and the tension lifted. People again fell into small chatty groups, just like at any other party, though I did see tears on the faces of some.

"A lot of people must have liked Priscilla," I observed.

Adrian turned toward a table that had mysteriously been arranged during the ceremony. It sat against the back wall and was filled with fruit, cheese, and more wine. Naturally, he poured a glass.

"They aren't *all* crying for her," he said.

"I find it hard to believe they're crying for the dhampirs," I pointed out. "No one here even knew them."

"Not true," he said.

Lissa quickly caught his meaning. "Most of the people who went on the rescue would have been guardians assigned to Moroi. They couldn't all be Court guardians."

She was right, I realized. We'd had too many people with us at the warehouse. Many of these Moroi had undoubtedly lost guardians that they'd become close to. Despite the disdain I often had for these types of royals, I knew some had probably formed legitimate friendships with and attachments to their bodyguards.

"This is a lame party," a voice suddenly said. We turned and saw that Christian had finally made his way over to us. "I couldn't tell if we were supposed to be having a funeral or summoning the devil. It was kind of a half-assed attempt at both."

"Stop it," I said, surprising myself. "Those people died for *you* last night. Whatever this is, it's still out of respect for them."

Christian's face grew sober. "You're right."

Beside me, I'd felt Lissa light up inside when she saw him. The horrors of their ordeal had brought them closer together, and I recalled the tenderness they'd shared on the ride back. She offered him a warm look and got a tentative smile in return. Maybe some good would come of all that had happened. Maybe they'd be able to fix their problems.

Or maybe not.

Adrian broke into a grin. "Hey. Glad you could make it."

For a moment, I thought he was speaking to Christian. Then I looked and saw a girl in a peacock mask had joined us. With the mingling people and masks, I hadn't noticed that she was purposely standing near us. I peered at her, seeing only blue eyes and golden curls before I finally recognized her. Mia.

"What are you doing here?" I asked.

She grinned. "Adrian got me a password."

"Adrian apparently got passwords for half the party."

He seemed very pleased with himself. "See?" he said, smiling at me. "I told you I'd make this worth your while. The whole gang's here. Nearly."

"This is one of the weirdest things I've ever seen," said Mia, glancing around. "I don't see why it has to be a secret that the people who got killed were heroes. Why can't they wait for the group funeral?"

Adrian shrugged. "I told you, this is an ancient ceremony.

It's a holdover from the Old Country, and these people think it's important. From what I know, it used to be a lot more elaborate. This is the modernized version."

It occurred to me then that Lissa hadn't said a single word since we'd noticed Christian had come with Mia. I opened myself to the bond, feeling a flood of jealousy and resentment. I still maintained Mia was one of the last people Christian would be involved with. (Okay, it was hard for me to imagine him involved with *anyone*. His getting together with Lissa had been monumental.) Lissa couldn't see that, though. All she saw was him continually hanging out with other girls. As our conversation continued, Lissa's attitude grew frostier, and the friendly looks he'd been giving her began to fade.

"So is it true?" Mia asked, oblivious to the drama unfolding around her. "Is Dimitri really . . . back?"

Lissa and I exchanged glances. "Yes," I said firmly. "He's a dhampir, but no one believes it yet. Because they're idiots."

"It just happened, little dhampir." Adrian's tone was gentle, though the topic clearly made him uncomfortable too. "You can't expect everyone to get on board with it right away."

"But they *are* idiots," said Lissa fiercely. "Anyone who talks to him can tell he's not a Strigoi. I'm pushing for them to let him out of his cell so that people can actually see for themselves."

I wished she would push a little harder for *me* to get to see him, but now wasn't the time to talk about that. Eyeing the room, I wondered if some people would have trouble accepting Dimitri because of his role in the deaths of their loved ones. He hadn't been in control of himself, but that wasn't enough to bring back the dead.

Still uncomfortable around Christian, Lissa was growing restless. She also wanted to leave and check on Dimitri. "How long do we have to stay here? Is there more to—"

"Who the hell are you?"

Our little cluster turned as one and found Anthony standing by us. Considering most of us were here illicitly, he could have been speaking to anyone. But, based on where his gaze was fixed, there was no question who he meant.

He was talking to me.

TWENTY

"YOU'RE NOT MOROI!" HE CONTINUED. He wasn't shouting, but we'd definitely gotten the attention of the people standing near us. "You're Rose Hathaway, aren't you? How dare you and your impure blood invade the sanctity of our—"

"That's enough," a lofty voice suddenly said. "I'll take it from here."

Even with her face covered, there was no mistaking that voice. Tatiana swept in beside the guy, wearing a silver flowered mask and a long-sleeved gray dress. I'd probably seen her earlier in the crowd and not even realized it. Until she spoke, she blended in with everyone else.

The whole room was quiet now. Daniella Ivashkov scurried up behind Tatiana, her eyes widening behind her mask when she recognized me. "Adrian—" she began.

But Tatiana was seizing the situation. "Come with me."

There was no question that the order was for me or that I would obey. She turned and walked swiftly toward the room's entrance. I hurried behind her, as did Adrian and Daniella.

As soon as we were out in the torch-lit hall, Daniella turned on Adrian. "What were you thinking? You know I don't mind you bringing Rose to certain events, but this was—"

"Inappropriate," said Tatiana crisply. "Although, perhaps it is fitting that a dhampir see how much the sacrifices of her people are respected."

That shocked us all into a moment of silence. Daniella recovered herself first. "Yes, but tradition states that—"

Tatiana interrupted her again. "I'm well aware of the tradition. It's a bad breach of etiquette, but Rosemarie being here certainly doesn't ruin our intentions. Losing Priscilla . . ." Tatiana didn't choke up, exactly, but she lost some of her normal composure. I didn't think of someone like her as having a best friend, but Priscilla pretty much had been. How would I act if I'd lost Lissa? Not nearly so controlled.

"Losing Priscilla is something I'll feel for a very, very long time," Tatiana managed at last. Her sharp eyes were on me. "And I hope you really do understand how much we need and value you and all the other guardians. I know sometimes your race feels underappreciated. You aren't. Those who died have left a gaping hole in our ranks, one that leaves us even more undefended, as I'm sure you must know."

I nodded, still surprised Tatiana wasn't shrieking for me to get out. "It's a big loss," I said. "And it makes the situation worse because numbers are what harm us half the time—especially when the Strigoi form large groups. We can't always match that."

Tatiana nodded, seeming pleasantly surprised we'd agreed on something. That made two of us. "I knew you'd understand. Nonetheless . . ." She turned toward Adrian. "You shouldn't have done this. Some lines of propriety need to be maintained."

Adrian was surprisingly meek. "Sorry, Aunt Tatiana. I just thought it was something Rose should see."

"You'll keep this to yourself, won't you?" asked Daniella, turning back to me. "A lot of the guests are very, very conservative. They wouldn't want this getting out."

That they met by firelight and played dress-up? Yeah, I could see them wanting that kept a secret.

"I won't tell anyone," I assured them.

"Good," said Tatiana. "Now, you should still probably leave before—is that Christian Ozera?" Her eyes had drifted back toward the crowded room.

"Yes," both Adrian and I said.

"He didn't get an invitation," exclaimed Daniella. "Is that your fault too?"

"It's not my fault so much as my genius," said Adrian.

"I doubt anyone will know, so long as he behaves himself," said Tatiana with a sigh. "And I'm sure he'd take any opportunity he can to talk to Vasilisa."

"Oh," I said, without thinking. "That's not Lissa." Lissa had actually turned her back toward Christian and was speaking to someone else while casting anxious looks out the door at me.

"Who is it?" asked Tatiana.

Crap. "That's, um, Mia Rinaldi. She's a friend of ours from St. Vladimir's." I'd almost considered lying and giving her a royal name. Some families were so big that it was impossible to keep track of everyone.

"Rinaldi." Tatiana frowned. "I think I know a servant with that name." I was actually pretty impressed that she knew the people who worked for her. Yet again, my opinion of her shifted.

"A servant?" asked Daniella, giving her son a warning look. "Is there anyone else I should know about?"

"No. If I'd had more time, I probably could have got Eddie here. Hell, maybe even Jailbait."

Daniella looked scandalized. "Did you just say Jailbait?"

"It's just a joke," I said hastily, not wanting to make this situation worse. I was afraid of how Adrian might answer. "It's what we sometimes call our friend Jill Mastrano."

Neither Tatiana nor Daniella seemed to think that was a joke at all.

"Well, no one seems to realize they don't belong," said Daniella, nodding toward Christian and Mia. "Though the gossips here will no doubt be running wild with how Rose interrupted this event."

"Sorry," I said, feeling bad that I might have gotten her in trouble.

"Nothing to be done for it now," said Tatiana wearily. "You should leave now so that everyone thinks you were severely chastised. Adrian, you come back with us and make sure your other 'guests' don't raise any attention. And do *not* do something like this again."

"I won't," he said, almost convincingly.

The three began to turn away, leaving me to skulk off, but Tatiana paused and glanced back. "Wrong or not, don't forget what you saw here. We really do need guardians."

I nodded, a flush of pride running through me at her acknowledgment. Then she and the others returned to the room. I watched them wistfully, hating that everyone in there thought I'd been kicked out in disgrace. Considering it could have gone a lot worse for me, I decided to count my blessings. I removed the mask, having nothing more to hide, and made the trek back upstairs and outdoors.

I hadn't gotten very far when someone stepped out in front of me. It was a sign of my preoccupation that I nearly leapt ten feet in the air.

"Mikhail," I exclaimed. "You scared me half to death. What are you doing out here?"

"Actually, I've been looking for you." There was an anxious, nervous look about him. "I went by your building earlier, but you weren't around."

"Yeah, I was at the Masquerade of the Damned."

He stared at me blankly.

"Never mind. What's up?"

"I think we might have a chance."

"Chance for what?"

"I heard you tried to see Dimitri today."

Ah, yes. The topic I definitely wanted to think more about. "Yeah. 'Try' is pretty optimistic. *He* doesn't want to see me, never mind the army of guardians blocking me out."

Mikhail shifted uncomfortably, peering around like a frightened animal. "That's why I came to find you."

"Okay, I'm really not following any of this." I was also

starting to get a headache from the wine.

Mikhail took a deep breath and exhaled. "I think I can sneak you in to see him."

I waited for a moment, wondering if there was a punch line coming or if maybe this was all some delusion born out of my wound-up emotions. Nope. Mikhail's face was deadly serious, and while I still didn't know him that well, I'd picked up enough to realize he didn't really joke around.

"How?" I asked. "I tried and—"

Mikhail beckoned for me to follow. "Come on, and I'll explain. We don't have much time."

I wasn't about to waste this chance and hurried after him. "Has something happened?" I asked, once I'd caught up to his longer stride. "Did . . . did he ask for me?" It was more than I dared to hope for. Mikhail's use of the word *sneak* didn't really support that idea anyway.

"They've lightened his guard," Mikhail explained.

"Really? How many?" There had been about a dozen down there when Lissa visited, including her escort. If they'd come to their senses and realized they only needed a guy or two on Dimitri, then that boded well for everyone accepting that he was no longer Strigoi.

"He's down to about five."

"Oh." Not great. Not horrible. "But I guess even that means they're a little closer to believing he's safe now?"

Mikhail shrugged, keeping his eyes on the path ahead of us. It had rained during the Death Watch, and the air, while still humid, had cooled a little. "Some of the guardians do. But it'll take a royal decree from the Council to officially declare what he is."

I almost came to a halt. "*Declare what he is*?" I exclaimed. "He's not a what! He's a person. A dhampir like us."

"I know, but it's out of our hands."

"You're right. Sorry," I grumbled. No point in shooting the messenger. "Well, I hope they get off their asses and come to a decision soon."

The silence that followed spoke legions. I gave Mikhail a sharp glare.

"What? What aren't you telling me?" I demanded.

He shrugged. "The rumor is that there's some other big thing being debated in the Council right now, something that takes priority."

That enraged me too. What in the world could take priority over Dimitri? *Calm, Rose. Stay calm. Focus. Don't let the darkness make this worse.* I always fought to keep it buried, but it often exploded in times of stress. And this? Yeah, this was a pretty stressful time. I shifted back to the original topic.

We reached the holding building, and I took the steps up two at a time. "Even if they've lightened the guardians on Dimitri, they still won't let me in. The ones that are there would know I was ordered to keep away."

"A friend of mine's covering the front shift right now. We won't have long, but he'll tell the guardians in the holding area that you were authorized to come down."

Mikhail was about to open the door, and I stopped him, putting my hand on his arm. "Why are you doing this for me?

The Moroi Council might not think Dimitri's a big deal, but the guardians do. You could get in big trouble."

He looked down at me, again with that small, bitter smile. "Do you have to ask?"

I thought about it. "No," I said softly.

"When I lost Sonya . . ." Mikhail closed his eyes for a heartbeat, and when he opened them, they seemed to be staring off into the past. "When I lost her, I didn't want to go on living. She was a good person—really. She turned Strigoi out of desperation. She saw no other way to save herself from spirit. I would give anything—*anything*—for a chance to help her, to fix things between us. I don't know if that'll ever be possible for us, but it *is* possible for you right now. I can't let you lose this."

With that, he let us in, and sure enough, there was a different guardian on duty. Just as Mikhail had said, the guy called down to tell the jail guardians Dimitri had a visitor. Mikhail's friend seemed incredibly nervous about it all, which was understandable. Still, he was willing to help. It was amazing, I thought, what friends would do for each other. These last couple of weeks were undeniable proof of that.

Just like at Lissa's visit, two guardians showed up to escort me downstairs. I recognized them from when I'd been in her head, and they seemed surprised to see me. If they'd overheard Dimitri adamantly saying he didn't want me to visit, then my presence would indeed be shocking. But as far as they knew, someone in power had condoned me being here, so they asked no questions.

Mikhail trailed us as we wound our way down, and I felt my heartbeat and breathing grow rapid. Dimitri. I was about to see Dimitri. What would I say? What would I do? It was almost too much to comprehend. I had to keep mentally slapping myself to focus, or else I was going to slide into dumbstruck shock.

When we reached the hallway that held the cells, I saw two guardians standing in front of Dimitri's cell, one at the far end, and two others by the entrance we'd come through. I stopped, uneasy about the thought of others overhearing me talk to Dimitri. I didn't want an audience like Lissa had had, but with the emphasis on security here, I might not have a choice.

"Can I get a little privacy?" I asked.

One of my escorts shook his head. "Official orders. Two guardians have to be posted at the cell at all times."

"She's a guardian," pointed out Mikhail mildly. "So am I. Let us go. The rest can wait by the door."

I flashed Mikhail a grateful look. I could handle having him nearby. The others, deciding we would be safe enough, moved discreetly to the ends of the hall. It wasn't total and complete privacy, but they wouldn't hear everything.

My heart felt ready to burst from my chest as Mikhail and I walked over to Dimitri's cell and faced it. He was seated almost as he had been when Lissa arrived: on the bed, curled up into himself, back facing us.

Words stuck in my throat. Coherent thought fled from my mind. It was like I'd totally forgotten the reason I'd come here.

"Dimitri," I said. At least, that's what I tried to say. I choked up a little, so the sounds that came out of my mouth were garbled. It was apparently enough, though, because Dimitri's back suddenly went rigid. He didn't turn around.

"Dimitri," I repeated, more clearly this time. "It's . . . me."

There was no need for me to say any more. He'd known from that first attempt at his name who I was. I had a feeling he would have known my voice in any situation. He probably knew the sound of my heartbeat and breathing. As it was, I think I stopped breathing while I waited for his response. When it came, it was a little disappointing.

"No."

"No what?" I asked. "As in, no, it's not me?"

He exhaled in frustration, a sound almost—but not quite—like the one he used to make when I did something particularly ridiculous in our trainings. "No, as in I don't want to see you." His voice was thick with emotion. "They weren't supposed to let you in."

"Yeah. Well, I kind of found a work-around."

"Of course you did."

He still wouldn't face me, which was agonizing. I glanced over at Mikhail, who gave me a nod of encouragement. I guessed I should be glad that Dimitri was talking to me at all.

"I had to see you. I had to know if you were okay."

"I'm sure Lissa's already updated you."

"I had to see for myself."

"Well, now you see."

"All I see is your back."

It was maddening, yet every word I got out of him was a gift. It felt like a thousand years since I'd heard his voice. Like before, I wondered how I could have ever confused the Dimitri in Siberia with this one. His voice had been identical in both places, the same pitch and accent, yet as a Strigoi, his words had always left a chill in the air. This was warm. Honey and velvet and all sorts of wonderful things wrapping around me, no matter the terrible things he was saying.

"I don't want you here," said Dimitri flatly. "I don't want to see you."

I took a moment to assess strategy. Dimitri still had that depressed, hopeless feel around him. Lissa had approached it with kindness and compassion. She'd gotten through his defenses, though a lot of that was because he regarded her as his savior. I could try a similar tactic. I could be gentle and supportive and full of love—all of which were true. I loved him. I wanted to help him so badly. Yet I wasn't sure that particular method would work for me. Rose Hathaway was not always known for the soft approach. I did, however, play on his sense of obligation.

"You can't ignore me," I said, trying to keep my volume out of range of the other guardians. "You owe me. I saved you."

A few moments of silence passed. "Lissa saved me," he said carefully.

Anger burned within my chest, just it had when I'd watched Lissa visit him. How could he hold her in such high regard but not *me*?

"How do you think she got to that point?" I demanded. "How do you think she learned how to save you? Do you have any idea what we—what *I*—had to go through to get that information? You think me going to Siberia was crazy? Believe me, you haven't even come close to seeing crazy. You know me. You know what I'm capable of. And I broke my own records this time. You. Owe. Me."

It was harsh, but I needed a reaction from him. Some kind of emotion. And I got it. He jerked around, eyes glinting and power crackling through his body. As always, his movements were both fierce and graceful. Likewise, his voice was a mix of emotions: anger, frustration, and concern.

"Then the best thing I can do is—"

He froze. The brown eyes that had been narrowed with aggravation suddenly went wide with . . . what? Amazement? Awe? Or perhaps that stunned feeling I kept having when I saw him?

Because suddenly, I was pretty sure he was experiencing the same thing I had earlier. He'd seen me plenty of times in Siberia. He'd seen me just the other night at the warehouse. But now . . . now he was truly viewing me with his own eyes. Now that he was no longer Strigoi, his whole world was different. His outlook and feelings were different. Even his soul was different.

It was like one of those moments when people talked about their lives flashing before their eyes. Because as we stared at one another, every part of our relationship replayed in my mind's eye. I remembered how strong and invincible he'd been when we first met, when he'd come to bring Lissa and me back to the folds of Moroi society. I remembered the gentleness of his touch when he'd bandaged my bloodied and battered hands. I remembered him carrying me in his arms after Victor's daughter Natalie had attacked me. Most of all, I remembered the night we'd been together in the cabin, just before the Strigoi had taken him. A year. We'd known each other only a year, but we'd lived a lifetime in it.

And he was realizing that too, I knew, as he studied me. His gaze was all-powerful, taking in every single one of my features and filing them away. Dimly, I tried to recall what I looked like today. I still wore the dress from the secret meeting and knew it looked good on me. My eyes were probably bloodshot from crying earlier, and I'd only had time for a quick brushing of my hair before heading off with Adrian.

Somehow, I doubted any of it mattered. The way Dimitri was looking at me . . . it confirmed everything I'd suspected. The feelings he'd had for me before he'd been turned—the feelings that had become twisted while a Strigoi—were all still there. They *had* to be. Maybe Lissa was his savior. Maybe the rest of the Court thought she was a goddess. I knew, right then, that no matter how bedraggled I looked or how blank he tried to keep his face, I was a goddess to him.

He swallowed and forcibly gained control of himself, just like he always had. Some things never changed. "Then the best thing I can do," he continued calmly, "is to stay away from you. That's the best way to repay the debt."

It was hard for me to keep control and maintain some sort of logical conversation. I was as awestruck as he was. I was also outraged. "You offered to repay Lissa by staying by her side forever!"

"I didn't do the things . . ." He averted his eyes for a moment, again struggling for control, and then met mine once more. "I didn't do the things to her that I did to you."

"You weren't you! I don't care." My temper was starting to burn again

"How many?" he exclaimed. "How many guardians died last night because of what I did?"

"I . . . I think six or seven." Harsh losses. I felt a small pang in my chest, recalling the names read off in that basement room.

"Six or seven," Dimitri repeated flatly, anguish in his voice. "Dead in one night. Because of me."

"You didn't act alone! And I told you, you weren't you. You couldn't control yourself. It doesn't matter to me—"

"It matters to me!" he shouted, his voice ringing through the hallway. The guardians at each end shifted but didn't approach. When Dimitri spoke again, he kept his voice lower, but it was still trembling with wild emotions. "It matters to me. That's what you don't get. You can't understand. You can't understand what it's like knowing what I did. That whole time being Strigoi . . . it's like a dream now, but it's one I remember clearly. There can be no forgiveness for me. And what happened with you? I remember that most of all. Everything I did. Everything I *wanted* to do."

"You're not going to do it now," I pleaded. "So let it go. Before—before everything happened, you said we could be together. That we'd get assignments near each other and—"

"Roza," he interrupted, the nickname piercing my heart. I think he'd slipped up, not truly meaning to call me that. There was a twisted smile on his lips, one without humor. "Do you really think they're going to ever let me be a guardian again? It'll be a miracle if they let me live!"

"That's not true. Once they realize you've changed and that you're really your old self . . . everything'll go back to how it was."

He shook his head sadly. "Your optimism . . . your belief that you can make anything happen. Oh, Rose. It's one of the amazing things about you. It's also one of the most infuriating things about you."

"I believed that you could come back from being a Strigoi," I pointed out. "Maybe my belief in the impossible isn't so crazy after all."

This conversation was so grave, so heartbreaking, yet it still kept reminding me of some of our old practice sessions. He'd try to convince me of some serious point, and I'd counter it with Rose-logic. It would usually earn me a mix of amusement and exasperation. I had the feeling that were the situation just a little different, he'd have that same attitude now. But this was not a practice session. He wouldn't smile and roll his eyes. This was serious. This was life and death.

"I'm grateful for what you did," he said formally, still struggling to master his feelings. It was another trait we shared, both of us always working to stay in control. He'd always been better at it than me. "I do owe you. And it's a debt I can't pay. Like I said, the best thing I can do is stay out of your life."

"If you're part of Lissa's, then you can't avoid me."

"People can exist around each other without . . . without

there being any more than that," he said firmly. It was such a Dimitri thing to say. Logic fighting emotion.

And that's when I lost it. Like I said, he was always better at keeping control. Me? Not so much.

I threw myself against the bars, so rapidly that even Mikhail flinched. "But I love you!" I hissed. "And I know you love me too. Do you really think you can spend the rest of your life ignoring that when you're around me?"

The troubling part was that for a very long time at the Academy, Dimitri had been convinced he could do exactly that. And he had been prepared to spend his life not acting on his feelings for me.

"You love me," I repeated. "I know you do." I stretched my arm through the bars. It was a long way from touching him, but my fingers reached out desperately, as though they might suddenly grow and be able to make contact. That was all I needed. One touch from him to know he still cared, one touch to feel the warmth of his skin and—

"Isn't it true," said Dimitri quietly, "that you're involved with Adrian Ivashkov?"

My arm dropped.

"Wh—where did you hear that?"

"Things get around," he said, echoing Mikhail.

"They certainly do," I muttered.

"So are you?" he asked more adamantly.

I hesitated before answering. If I told him the truth, he'd have more ground to make his point about us keeping apart. It was impossible for me to lie to him, though.

"Yes, but—"

"Good." I'm not sure how I expected him to react. Jealousy? Shock? Instead, as he leaned back against the wall, he looked . . . relieved. "Adrian's a better person than he gets credit for. He'll be good to you."

"But—"

"That's where your future is, Rose." A bit of that hopeless, world-weary attitude was returning. "You don't understand what it's like coming through what I did—coming back from being a Strigoi. It's changed everything. It's not just that what I did to you is unforgiveable. All my feelings . . . my emotions for you . . . they changed. I don't feel the way I used to. I might be a dhampir again, but after what I went through . . . well, it's scarred me. It altered my soul. I can't love anyone now. I can't—*I don't*—love you. There's nothing more between you and me."

My blood turned cold. I refused to believe his words, not after the way he'd looked at me earlier. "No! That's not true! I love you and you—"

"Guards!" Dimitri shouted, his voice so loud that it was a wonder the whole building didn't shake. "Get her out of here. *Get her out of here!*"

With amazing guardian reflexes, the guards were down at the cell in a flash. As a prisoner, Dimitri wasn't in a position to make requests, but the authorities here certainly weren't going to encourage a situation that would create a commotion. They began herding Mikhail and me out, but I resisted.

"No, wait—"

"Don't fight it," murmured Mikhail in my ear. "Our time's running out, and you couldn't have accomplished anything else today anyway."

I wanted to protest, but the words stuck on my lips. I let the guardians direct me out, but not before I gave Dimitri one last, lingering look. He had a perfect, guardian-blank look on his face, but the piercing way he stared at me made me certain there was a lot going on within him.

Mikhail's friend was still on duty upstairs, which let us slip out without getting in—much—more trouble. As soon as we were outdoors, I came to a halt and kicked one of the steps angrily.

"Damn it!" I yelled. A couple of Moroi across the courtyard—probably coming home from some late party—gave me startled looks.

"Calm down," said Mikhail. "This was the first time you've seen him since the change. There are only so many miracles you can expect right away. He'll come around."

"I'm not so sure," I grumbled. Sighing, I looked up at the sky. Little wispy clouds moved lazily about, but I barely saw them. "You don't know him like I do."

Because while part of me thought that a lot of what Dimitri had said was indeed a reaction to the shock of returning to himself, there was another part of me that wondered. I knew Dimitri. I knew his sense of honor, his adamant beliefs about what was right and wrong. He stood by those beliefs. He lived his life by them. If he truly, truly believed that the right thing to do was to avoid me and let any relationship between us fade, well . . . there was a good chance he might very well act on that idea, no matter the love between us. As I'd recalled earlier, he'd certainly shown a lot of resistance back at St. Vladimir's.

As for the rest . . . the part about him no longer loving me or being able to love anyone . . . well, that would be a different problem all together if it were true. Both Christian and Adrian had worried there would be some piece of Strigoi left in him, but their fears had been about violence and bloodshed. No one would have guessed this: that living as a Strigoi had hardened his heart, killing any chance of him loving anyone.

Killing any chance of him loving *me*.

And I was pretty sure that if that was the case, then part of me would die too.

TWENTY-ONE

THERE WAS LITTLE MORE MIKHAIL and I could say to each other after that. I didn't want him to get in trouble for what he'd done, and I let him lead us out of the guardians' building in silence. As we emerged outside, I could see the sky purpling in the east. The sun was nearly up, signaling the middle of our night. Briefly flipping into Lissa's mind, I read that the Death Watch had finally ended, and she was on her way back to her room—worried about me and still annoyed that Christian had shown up with Mia.

I followed Lissa's example, wondering if sleep might ease the agony that Dimitri had left in my heart. Probably not. Still, I thanked Mikhail for his help and the risk he'd taken. He merely nodded, like there was nothing to thank him for. It was exactly what he would have wanted me to do for him if our roles had been reversed and Ms. Karp had been the one behind bars.

I feel into a heavy sleep back in my bed, but my dreams were troubled. Over and over, I kept hearing Dimitri tell me he couldn't love me anymore. It beat into me over and over, smashing my heart into little pieces. At one point, it became more than a dreamlike beating. I heard real beating. Someone was pounding on my door, and slowly, I dragged myself out of my awful dreams.

Bleary-eyed, I went to the door and found Adrian. The scene was almost a mirror of last night when he'd come to invite me to the Death Watch. Only this time, his face was much grimmer. For a second, I thought he'd heard about my visit to Dimitri. Or that maybe he'd gotten in a lot more trouble than we'd realized for sneaking half of his friends into a secret funeral.

"Adrian . . . this is early for you. . . ." I glanced over at a clock, discovering that I'd actually slept in pretty late.

"Not early at all," he confirmed, face still serious. "Lots of stuff going on. I had to come tell you the news before you heard it somewhere else."

"What news?"

"The Council's verdict. They finally passed that big resolution they've been debating. The one you came in for."

"Wait. They're done?" I recalled what Mikhail had said, that a mystery issue had been keeping the Council busy. If it was finished, then they could move on to something else—say, like, officially declaring Dimitri a dhampir again. "That's great news." And if this really was tied into when Tatiana had had me come describe my skills . . . well, was there really a chance I might be named Lissa's guardian? Could the queen have really come through? She'd seemed friendly enough last night.

Adrian regarded me with something I'd never seen from him: pity. "You have no idea, do you?"

"No idea about what?"

"Rose . . ." He gently rested a hand on my shoulder. "The

Council just passed a decree lowering the guardian age to sixteen. Dhampirs'll graduate when they're sophomores and then go out for assignments."

"What?" Surely I'd misheard.

"You know how panicked they've been about protection and not having enough guardians, right?" He sighed. "This was their solution to increasing your numbers."

"But they're too young!" I cried. "How can anyone think sixteen-year-olds are ready to go out and fight?"

"Well," said Adrian, "because you testified that they were."

My mouth dropped, everything freezing around me. *You testified that they were . . .* No. It couldn't be possible.

Adrian gently nudged my arm, trying to shake me out of my stupor. "Come on, they're still wrapping up. They made the announcement in an open session, and some people are . . . a little upset."

"Yeah, I'll say." He didn't need to tell me twice. I immediately started to follow, then realized I was in my pajamas. I quickly changed and brushed my hair, still scarcely able to believe what he'd just said. My preparation only took five minutes, and then we were out the door. Adrian wasn't overly athletic, but he kept a pretty good pace as we headed toward the Council's hall.

"How did this happen?" I asked. "You don't really mean that . . . that what I said played a role?" I'd meant my words to be a demand, but they came out with more of a pleading note.

He lit a cigarette without breaking stride, and I didn't bother chastising him for it. "It's apparently been a hot topic for a while. It was a pretty close vote. The people pushing for it knew they'd need to show a lot of evidence to win. You were their grand prize: a teen dhampir slaying Strigoi left and right, long before graduation."

"Not that long," I muttered, my fury kindling. Sixteen? Were they serious? It was ludicrous. The fact that *I* had been unknowingly used to support this decree made me sick to my stomach. I'd been a fool, thinking they'd all ignored my rule breaking and had simply paraded me in to praise me. They'd used me. *Tatiana* had used me.

When we reached it, the Council hall was in as much chaos as Adrian had implied. True, I hadn't spent a lot of time in these kinds of meetings, but I was pretty sure that people standing up in clusters and yelling at each other wasn't normal. The Council's herald probably didn't usually scream himself hoarse trying to bring order to the crowd either.

The only spot of calm was Tatiana herself, sitting patiently in her seat at the center of the table, just as Council etiquette dictated. She looked very pleased with herself. The rest of her colleagues had lost all sense of propriety and were on their feet like the audience, arguing amongst themselves or anyone else ready to pick a fight. I stared in amazement, unsure what to do in all this disorder.

"Who voted for what?" I asked.

Adrian studied the Council members and ticked them off on his fingers. "Szelsky, Ozera, Badica, Dashkov, Conta, and Drozdov. They were against it."

"Ozera?" I asked in surprise. I didn't know the Ozera

princess—Evette—very well, but she'd always seemed pretty stiff and unpleasant. I had new respect for her now.

Adrian nodded over to where Tasha was furiously addressing a large group of people, eyes flashing and arms waving wildly. "Evette was persuaded by some of her family members."

That made me smile too, but only for a moment. It was good that Tasha and Christian were being acknowledged amongst their clan again, but the rest of our problem was still alive and kicking. I could deduce the rest of the names.

"So . . . Prince Ivashkov voted for it," I said. Adrian shrugged by way of apology for his family. "Lazar, Zeklos, Tarus, and Voda." That the Voda family would vote for extra protection wasn't entirely a surprise, considering the recent slaughter of one of their members. Priscilla wasn't even in her grave yet, and the new Voda prince, Alexander, seemed clearly unsure what to do with his sudden promotion.

I gave Adrian a sharp look. "That's only five to six. Oh." Realization dawned. "Shit. Royal tiebreaker."

The Moroi voting system had been set up with twelve members, one for each family, and then whoever the reigning king or queen was. True, it often meant one group got two votes, since the monarch rarely voted against his or her own family. It had been known to happen. Regardless, the system should have had thirteen votes, preventing ties. Except . . . a recent problem had developed. There were no Dragomirs on the Council anymore, meaning ties could occur. In that rare event, Moroi law dictated that the monarch's vote carried extra weight. I'd heard that had always been controversial, and yet at the same time, there wasn't much to be done for it. Ties in the Council would mean nothing ever got settled, and since monarchs were elected, many took it on faith that they would act in the best interests of the Moroi.

"Tatiana's was the sixth," I said. "And hers swayed it." Glancing around, I saw a bit of anger on the faces of those from the families who had voted against the decree. Apparently, not everyone believed Tatiana had acted in the best interest of the Moroi.

Lissa's presence sang to me through the bond, so her arrival a few moments later was no surprise. News had spread fast, though she didn't yet know the fine details. Adrian and I waved her over. She was as dumbfounded as we were.

"How could they do that?" she asked.

"Because they're too afraid that someone might make *them* learn to defend themselves. Tasha's group was getting too loud."

Lissa shook her head. "No, not just that. I mean, why were they even in session? We should be in mourning after what happened the other day—publicly. The whole Court, not just some secret part of it. One of the Council members even died! Couldn't they wait for the funeral?" In her mind's eye, I could see the images from that grisly night, where Priscilla had died right before Lissa's eyes.

"But was easily replaceable," a new voice said. Christian had joined us. Lissa took a few steps away from him, still annoyed about Mia. "And actually, it's the perfect time. The people who wanted this had to jump at their chance. Every time there's a big Strigoi fight, everyone panics. Fear'll make a lot of people get on board with this. And if any Council members were undecided before this, that battle probably pushed them over."

That was pretty wise reasoning for Christian, and Lissa was impressed, despite her troubled feelings for him right now. The Council's herald finally managed to make his voice heard over the shouts of the audience. I wondered if the group would have quieted down if Tatiana herself had started yelling at them to shut up. But no. That was probably beneath her dignity. She was still sitting there calmly, like nothing unusual was going on.

Nonetheless, it took several moments for everyone to settle down and take their seats. My friends and I hurriedly grabbed the first ones we could find. With peace and quiet achieved at last, the weary-looking herald yielded the floor to the queen.

Smiling grandly at the assembly, she addressed them in her most imperious voice. "We'd like to thank everyone for coming today and expressing your . . . opinions. I know some are still unsure about this decision, but Moroi law has been followed here—laws that have been in place for centuries. We will have another session soon to listen to what you have to say in an *orderly* fashion." Something told me that was an empty gesture. People could talk all they wanted; she wouldn't listen. "This decision—this *verdict*—will benefit the Moroi. Our guardians are already so excellent." She gave a condescending nod toward the ceremonial guardians standing along the room's walls. They wore typically neutral faces, but I was guessing that, like me, they probably wanted to punch half the Council. "They are so excellent, in fact, that they train their students to be ready to defend us at an early age. We will all be safer from tragedies like that which recently occurred."

She lowered her head a moment in what must have been a show of grieving. I recalled last night when she'd choked up over Priscilla. Had that been an act? Was her best friend's death a convenient way for Tatiana to push forward with her own agenda. Surely . . . surely, she wasn't that cold.

The queen lifted her head and continued. "And again, we're happy to listen to you register your opinions, although by our own laws, this matter *is* settled. Further sessions will have to wait until an adequate period of mourning has passed for the unfortunate departed."

Her tone and body language implied that this was indeed the end of the discussion. Then, an impertinent voice suddenly broke the room's silence.

My voice.

"Well, I'd kind of like to register my opinion now."

Inside my head, Lissa was shouting: *Sit down, sit down!* But I was already on my feet, moving toward the Council's table. I stopped at a respectful distance, one that would let them notice me but not get me tackled by guardians. And oh, they noticed me. The herald flushed bright red at my rule breaking.

"You are out of line and in violation of all Council protocol! Sit down right now before you are removed." He glanced over at the guardians, like he expected them to come charging forward right then. None of them moved. Either they didn't perceive me as a threat, or they were wondering what I was going to do. I was also wondering this.

With a small, delicate hand gesture, Tatiana waved the herald back. "I daresay there's been so much breach of protocol today that one more incident won't make a difference." She fixed me with a kind smile, one that was apparently intended to make us look like friends. "Besides, Guardian Hathaway is one of our most valuable assets. I'm always interested in what she has to say."

Was she really? Time to find out. I addressed my words to the Council.

"This thing you've just passed is utterly and totally insane." I considered it a great feat on my part that I didn't use any swear words there because I had some adjectives in mind that were much more fitting. Who said I didn't understand Council etiquette? "How can any of you sit there and think it's okay to send sixteen-year-olds out to risk their lives?"

"It's only two years' difference," said the Tarus prince. "It's not like we're sending ten-year-olds."

"Two years is a lot." I thought for a moment about when I'd been sixteen. What had happened in those two years? I'd run off with Lissa, watched friends die, traveled around the world, fallen in love. . . . "You can live a lifetime in two years. And if you want us to keep being on the front lines—which most of us willingly do when we graduate—then you owe us those two years."

This time, I glanced back at the audience. The reactions

were mixed. Some clearly agreed with me, nodding along. Some looked as though nothing in the world would change their minds about the decree being just. Others wouldn't meet my eyes. . . . Had I swayed them? Were they undecided? Embarrassed at their own selfishness? They might be the keys.

"Believe me, I would love to see your people enjoy their youth." This was Nathan Ivashkov speaking. "But right now, that's not an option we have. The Strigoi are closing in. We're losing more Moroi and guardians every day. Getting more fighters out there will stop this, and really, we're just letting those dhampirs' skills go to waste by waiting a couple years. This plan will protect *both* our races."

"It'll kill mine off faster!" I said. Realizing I might start shouting if I lost control, I took a deep breath before going on. "They won't be ready. They won't have all the training they need."

And that was where Tatiana herself made her master play. "Yet, by your own admission, you were certainly prepared at a young age. You killed more Strigoi before you were eighteen than some guardians kill their entire lives."

I fixed her with a narrow-eyed look. "I," I said coldly, "had an excellent instructor. One that you currently have locked up. If you want to talk about skills going to waste, then go look in your own jail."

There was a slight stirring in the audience, and Tatiana's *we're pals* face grew a little cold. "That is *not* an issue we are addressing today. Increasing our protection is. I believe you have even commented in the past that the guardian ranks are lacking in numbers." My own words, thrown back at me from last night. "They need to be filled. You—and many of your companions—have proven you're able to defend us."

"We were exceptions!" It was egotistical, but it was the truth. "Not all novices have reached that level."

A dangerous glint appeared in her eye, and her voice grew silky smooth again. "Well, then, perhaps we need more excellent training. Perhaps we should send *you* to St. Vladimir's or some other academy so that you can improve your young colleagues' education. My understanding is that your upcoming assignment will be a permanent administrative one here at Court. If you wanted to help make this new decree successful, we could change that assignment and make you an instructor instead. It might speed up your return to a bodyguard assignment."

I gave her a dangerous smile of my own. "Do not," I warned, "try to threaten, bribe, or blackmail me. Ever. You won't like the consequences."

That might have been going too far. People in the audience exchanged startled looks. Some of their expressions were disgusted, as though they could expect nothing better of me. I recognized a few of those Moroi. They were ones I'd overheard talking about my relationship with Adrian and how the queen hated it. I also suspected a number of royals from last night's ceremony were here too. They'd seen Tatiana lead me out and no doubt thought my outburst and disrespect today were a type of revenge.

The Moroi weren't the only ones who reacted. Regardless

of whether they shared my opinions, a few guardians stepped forward. I made sure to stay exactly where I was, and that, along with Tatiana's lack of fear, kept them in place.

"We're getting weary of this conversation," Tatiana said, switching to the royal *we*. "You can speak more—and do so in the proper manner—when we have our next meeting and open the floor to comments. For now, whether you like it or not, this resolution has been passed. It's law."

She's letting you off! Lissa's voice was back in my head. *Back away from this before you do something that'll get you in real trouble. Argue later.*

It was ironic because I'd been on the verge of exploding and letting my full rage out. Lissa's words stopped me—but not because of their content. It was Lissa herself. When Adrian and I had discussed the results earlier, I'd noted one piece of faulty logic.

"It wasn't a fair vote," I declared. "It wasn't legal."

"Are you a lawyer now, Miss Hathaway?" The queen was amused, and her dropping of my guardian title now was a blatant lack of respect. "If you're referring to the monarch's vote carrying more weight than others on the Council, then we can assure you that that has been Moroi law for centuries in such situations." She glanced at her fellow Council members, none of whom raised a protest. Even those who'd voted against her couldn't find fault with her point.

"Yeah, but the entire Council didn't vote," I said. "You've had an empty spot in the Council for the last few years—but not anymore." I turned and pointed at where my friends were sitting. "Vasilisa Dragomir is eighteen now and can fill her family's spot." In all of this chaos, her birthday had been overlooked, even by me.

The eyes in the room turned on Lissa—something she did *not* like. However, Lissa was used to being in the public eye. She knew what was expected of a royal, how to look and carry herself. So, rather than cringing, she sat up straight and stared ahead with a cool, regal look that said she could walk up to that table right now and demand her birthright. Whether it was that magnificent attitude alone or maybe a little spirit charisma, she was almost impossible to look away from. Her beauty had its usual luminous quality, and around the room, a lot of the faces held the same awe for her that I'd observed around Court. Dimitri's transformation was still an enigma, but those who believed in it were indeed regarding her as some kind of saint. She was becoming larger than life in so many people's eyes, both with her family name and mysterious powers—and now the alleged ability to restore Strigoi.

Smug, I looked back at Tatiana. "Isn't eighteen the legal voting age?" *Checkmate, bitch.*

"Yes," she said cheerfully. "If the Dragomirs had a quorum."

I wouldn't say my stunning victory exactly shattered at that point, but it certainly lost a little of its luster. "A what?"

"A quorum. By law, for a Moroi family to have a Council vote, they must have a family. She does not. She's the only one."

I stared in disbelief. "What, you're saying she needs to go have a kid to get a vote?"

Tatiana grimaced. "Not now, of course. Someday, I'm sure. For a family to have a vote, they must have at least two members, one of whom must be over eighteen. It's Moroi law—again, a law that's been in the books for centuries."

A few people were exchanging confused and surprised looks. This was clearly not a law many were familiar with. Of course, this situation—a royal line reduced to one person—wasn't one that had occurred in recent history, if it had ever occurred at all.

"It's true," said Ariana Szelsky reluctantly. "I've read it."

Okay, *that* was when my stunning victory shattered. The Szelsky family was one I trusted, and Ariana was the older sister of the guy my mom protected. Ariana was a pretty bookish kind of person, and seeing as she'd voted against the guardian age change, it seemed unlikely she'd offer this piece of evidence if it weren't true.

With no more ammunition, I resorted to old standbys.

"That," I told Tatiana, "is the most fucked-up law I have ever heard."

That did it. The audience broke into shocked chatter, and Tatiana gave up on whatever pretense of friendliness she'd been clinging to. She beat the herald to any orders he might have given.

"Remove her!" shouted Tatiana. Even with the rapidly growing noise, her voice rang clearly through the room. "We will not tolerate this sort of vulgar behavior!"

I had guardians on me in a flash. Honestly, with how often I'd been dragged away from places lately, there was almost something comfortably familiar about it. I didn't fight the guardians as they led me to the door, but I also didn't let them take me without a few parting words.

"You could change the quorum law if you wanted, you sanctimonious bitch!" I yelled back. "You're twisting the law because you're selfish and afraid! You're making the worst mistake of your life. You'll regret it! Wait and see—you'll wish you'd never done it!"

I don't know if anyone heard my tirade because by then, the hall was back to the chaos it had been in when I entered. The guardians—three of them—didn't let go of me until we were outside. Once they released me, we all stood around awkwardly for a moment.

"What now?" I asked. I tried to keep the anger out of my voice. I was still furious and worked up, but it wasn't these guys' fault. "Are you going to lock me up?" Seeing as it would bring me back to Dimitri, it would almost be a reward.

"They only said to remove you," one of the guardians pointed out. "No one said what to do with you after that."

Another guardian, old and grizzled but still fierce looking, gave me a wry look. "I'd take off while you can, before they really have a chance to punish you."

"Not that they won't find you if they really want to," added the first guardian.

With that, the three of them headed back inside, leaving me confused and upset. My body was still revved for a fight, and I was filled with the frustration I always experienced whenever I was faced with a situation I felt powerless in. All that yelling for nothing. I'd accomplished nothing.

"Rose?"

I shifted from my churning emotions and looked up at the building. The older guardian hadn't gone inside and still stood in the doorway. His face was stoic, but I thought I saw a twinkle in his eye. "For what it's worth," he told me, "I thought you were fantastic in there."

I didn't feel much like smiling, but my lips betrayed me. "Thanks," I said.

Well, maybe I'd accomplished one thing.

TWENTY-TWO

I DIDN'T TAKE THE GUY'S advice and tear off out of there, though I didn't exactly sit on the front step either. I lingered nearby in a cluster of cherry trees, figuring it would only be a matter of time before the assembly ended and people spilled out the doors. After several minutes passed and nothing happened, I flipped into Lissa's mind and discovered things were still in full force. Despite Tatiana declaring twice now that the session was over, people were still standing around and arguing in groups.

Tasha was standing in one such group with Lissa and Adrian, making one of the impassioned speeches she was so good at. Tasha might not be as coldly calculating as Tatiana was when it came to political moves, but Tasha did have a keen sense of ripples in the system and recognized opportunities when they came. She was against the age-lowering decree. She was for teaching Moroi to fight. Neither of those was getting her very far, so she jumped on the next best thing: Lissa.

"Why are we arguing among ourselves about how best to kill Strigoi when we can save them?" Tasha put one arm around Lissa and one around Adrian, drawing them both forward. Lissa still wore her serenely confident look, but Adrian looked ready to bolt if given half a chance. "Vasilisa—who, by the way, is indeed being denied her fair voice here, thanks to an archaic law—has shown that Strigoi can be brought back."

"That hasn't been proven," exclaimed one man in the crowd.

"Are you kidding?" asked a woman beside him. "My sister was with the group that brought him back. She says he's definitely a dhampir. He was even out in the sun!"

Tasha nodded in approval at the woman. "I was there as well. And now we have two spirit users capable of doing this for other Strigoi."

As much as I respected Tasha, I wasn't entirely with her on this. The amount of power—not to mention effort involved in the staking—that Lissa had required with Dimitri had been staggering. It had even temporarily hurt the bond. That didn't mean she couldn't do it again. Nor did it mean she wouldn't *want* to again. She was just naively compassionate enough to throw herself into the line of fire to help others. But I knew the more power a spirit user wielded, the quicker they'd travel down the road to insanity.

And Adrian . . . well, he was almost a nonissue here. Even if he wanted to go staking Strigoi, he didn't have the kind of healing power it would take to restore one—at least not now. It's wasn't uncommon for Moroi to use their elements in different ways. Some fire users, like Christian, had skilled control of flame itself. Others could only use their magic to, say, warm the air in a room. Likewise, Lissa and Adrian had their strengths with spirit. His greatest healing triumph was mending a fracture, and she still couldn't walk dreams, no matter how much she practiced.

So, really, Tasha had one spirit user capable of saving Strigoi, and that one could hardly transform legions of those monsters. Tasha did seem to recognize this a little.

"The Council shouldn't be wasting time with age laws," she continued. "We need to sink our resources into finding more spirit users and recruiting them to help save Strigoi." She fixed her gaze on someone in the crowd. "Martin, didn't your brother get turned against his will? With enough work, we could bring him back to you. Alive. Just like you knew him. Otherwise, he's just going to get staked when guardians find him—and of course he'll be slaughtering innocents along the way."

Yeah, Tasha was good. She could paint a good image and nearly brought that Martin guy to tears. She didn't really mention people who'd turned Strigoi willingly. Lissa, still standing with her, wasn't sure how she felt about the idea of a Strigoi-saving spirit army, but she did recognize how this was all part of several other plans Tasha had—including one to get Lissa voting rights.

Tasha played up Lissa's abilities and character, scoffing at what was clearly an outdated law from an era that never could have foreseen this situation. Tasha further pointed out that a full Council of twelve families would send a message to Strigoi everywhere about Moroi unity.

I didn't want to hear any more. I'd let Tasha wield her

political magic and talk more to Lissa later. I was still so agitated about what had happened when I'd yelled at the Council that I couldn't stand to see that room anymore. I left her mind and returned to my own, yelping when I saw a face right in front of mine.

"Ambrose!"

One of the best-looking dhampirs on the planet—after Dimitri, of course—flashed me a gleaming, movie-star smile. "You were so still, I thought maybe you were trying to be a dryad."

I blinked. "A what?"

He gestured to the cherry trees. "Nature spirits. Beautiful women who become one with trees."

"I'm not sure if that was a compliment or not," I said. "But it's good to see you again."

Ambrose was a true oddity in our culture: a male dhampir who had neither taken guardian vows nor run off to hide among humans. Female dhampirs often chose not to join the guardians in order to focus on raising families. That's why we were so rare. But men? They had no excuse, as far as most people were concerned. Rather than skulk off in disgrace, however, Ambrose had chosen to stay and simply work for the Moroi another way. He was essentially a servant—a high-class one who served drinks at elite parties and gave massages to royal women. He also, if rumors were true, served Tatiana in physical ways. That was so creepy, though, I promptly put it out of my mind.

"You too," he told me. "But if you aren't communing with

nature, what *are* you doing?"

"It's a long story. I kind of got thrown out of a Council meeting."

He looked impressed. "Literally thrown out?"

"Dragged, I guess. I'm surprised I haven't seen you around," I mused. "Of course, I've kind of been, um, distracted this last week."

"So I've heard," he said, giving me a sympathetic look. "Although, I actually have been away. Just got back last night."

"Just in time for the fun," I muttered.

The guileless look on his face told me hadn't heard about the decree yet. "What are you doing now?" he asked. "This doesn't look like punishment. Did you finish your sentence?"

"Something like that. I'm kind of waiting for someone now. Was just going to hang out in my room."

"Well, if you're killing time, why don't you come see Aunt Rhonda?"

"Rhonda?" I scowled. "No offense, but your aunt didn't really impress me with her abilities last time."

"None taken," he said cheerfully. "But she's been wondering about you. And Vasilisa. So, if you're just hanging around . . ."

I hesitated. He was right that I had nothing better to do right now. I was stuck on options with both Dimitri and the Council's idiotic resolutions. Yet Rhonda—his fortune-telling Moroi aunt—wasn't someone I really wanted to see again. Despite my glib words, the truth was that in retrospect, some of Rhonda's predictions *had* come true. I just didn't like what they'd been.

"Fine," I said, trying to look bored. "Make it fast."

He smiled again, like he could see through my ruse, and led me off to a building I'd been to once before. It housed a luxurious salon and spa frequented by royal Moroi. Lissa and I had had our nails done there, and as Ambrose and I wound our way through it to Rhonda's lair, I felt a strange pang within me. Manicures and pedicures . . . they seemed like the most trivial things in the world. But on that day, they'd been wonderful. Lissa and I had laughed and grown closer . . . just before the school was attacked and everything fell apart. . . .

Rhonda told fortunes in a back room that was far from the busy spa. Despite the seedy feel of it, she did a pretty brisk business and even had her own receptionist. Or, well, she used to. This time, the desk was empty, and Ambrose led me straight through to Rhonda's room. It looked exactly the same as before, like being inside a heart. Everything was red: the wallpaper, the decorations, and the cushions covering the floor.

Rhonda herself sat on the floor, eating a cup of yogurt, which seemed terribly ordinary for someone who allegedly wielded mystical powers. Curly black hair cascaded around her shoulders, making the large gold hoops in her ears gleam.

"Rose Hathaway," she said happily, setting the yogurt aside. "What a nice surprise."

"Shouldn't you have seen me coming?" I asked dryly.

Her lips twitched with amusement. "That's not my power."

"Sorry to interrupt your dinner," Ambrose said, gracefully folding his muscled body as he sat down. "But Rose isn't easy to catch hold of."

"I imagine not," she said. "I'm impressed you got her to come at all. What can I do for you today, Rose?"

I shrugged and sank down beside Ambrose. "I don't know. I'm only here because Ambrose talked me into it."

"She didn't think your last reading was very good," he said.

"Hey!" I shot him a chastising look. "That's not exactly what I said."

Last time, Lissa and Dimitri had been with me. Rhonda's tarot cards had shown Lissa crowned with power and light—no surprise. Rhonda had said Dimitri would lose what he valued most, and he had: his soul. And me? Rhonda had bluntly told me that I'd kill the undead. I'd scoffed at that, knowing I had a lifetime of Strigoi-killing ahead of me. Now I wondered if "undead" meant the Strigoi part of Dimitri. Even if I hadn't driven the stake, I'd certainly played a major role.

"Maybe another reading would help the other one make more sense?" she offered.

My mind was putting together another fraud psychic joke, which was why it was so astonishing when my mouth said, "That's the problem. The other one *did* make sense. I'm afraid . . . I'm afraid of what else the cards will show."

"The cards don't make the future," she said gently. "If something's meant to be, it'll be, regardless of whether you see it here. And even then . . . well, the future is always changing. If we had no choices, there'd be no point in living."

"See now," I said flippantly, "that's the kind of vague gypsy response I was hoping for."

"*Roma,*" she corrected. "Not gypsy." Despite my snark, she

still seemed to be in a good mood. Easygoing attitudes must have run in their family. "Do you want the cards or not?"

Did I? She was right about one thing—the future would unfold with or without me seeing it in the cards. And even if the cards showed it, I probably wouldn't understand it until afterward.

"Okay," I said. "Just for fun. I mean, last time was probably a lucky guess."

Rhonda rolled her eyes but said nothing as she began shuffling her tarot deck. She did it with such precision that the cards seemed to move themselves. When she finally stopped, she handed the deck to me to cut. I did, and she put it back together.

"We did three cards before," she said. "We've got time to do more if you'd like. Five, perhaps?"

"The more there are, the more likely it is that anything can get explained."

"If you don't believe in them, then it shouldn't be an issue."

"Okay, then. Five."

She grew serious as she flipped out the cards, her eyes carefully studying them. Two of the cards had come out upside down. I didn't take that as a good sign. Last time, I'd learned that it made seemingly happy cards . . . well, not so happy.

The first one was one the Two of Cups, showing a man and a woman together in a grassy, flower-filled field while the sun shone above them. Naturally, it was upside down.

"Cups are tied to emotions," Rhonda explained. "The Two of Cups shows a union, a perfect love and blossoming of joyous emotions. But since it's inverted—"

"You know what?" I interrupted. "I think I'm getting the hang of this. You can skip that one. I have a good idea what it means." It might as well have been Dimitri and me on that card, the cup empty and full of heartache. . . . I really didn't want to hear Rhonda analyze what was already tearing my heart up.

So she went on to the next one: the Queen of Swords, also upside down.

"Cards like this refer to specific people," Rhonda told me. The Queen of Swords looked very imperious, with auburn hair and silver robes. "The Queen of Swords is clever. She thrives on knowledge, can outwit her enemies, and is ambitious."

I sighed. "But upside down . . ."

"Upside down," said Rhonda, "all of those traits get twisted. She's still smart, still trying to get her way . . . but she's doing it through insincere ways. There's a lot of hostility and deception here. I'd say you have an enemy."

"Yeah," I said, eyeing the crown. "I think I can guess who. I just called her a sanctimonious bitch."

Rhonda didn't comment and moved on to the next one. It was facing the right way, but I kind of wished it wasn't. It had a whole bunch of swords stuck in the ground and a woman tied and blindfolded to one. Eight of Swords.

"Oh, come on," I exclaimed. "What is it with me and swords? You gave me one this depressing last time." It had shown a woman weeping in front of a wall of swords.

"That was the Nine of Swords," she agreed. "It could

always be worse."

"I have a hard time believing that."

She picked up the rest of the deck and scanned through it, finally pulling out one card. The Ten of Swords. "You could have drawn this." It showed a dead guy lying on the ground with a bunch of swords driven through him.

"Point taken," I said. Ambrose chuckled beside me. "What's the nine mean?"

"The nine is being trapped. Unable to get out of a situation. It can also mean slander or accusation. Summoning courage to escape something." I glanced back at the queen, thinking of the things I'd said in the Council room. Those would definitely count as accusations. And being trapped? Well, there was always the possibility of a lifetime of paperwork . . .

I sighed. "Okay, what's the next one?" It was the best-looking one in the bunch, the Six of Swords. It had a bunch of people in a boat, rowing off over moonlit water.

"A journey," she said.

"I was just on a journey. A few of them." I eyed her suspiciously. "Man, this isn't, like, some kind of a spiritual journey is it?"

Ambrose laughed again. "Rose, I wish you'd get tarot readings every day."

Rhonda ignored him. "If it were in cups, maybe. But swords are tangible. Action. A true, out-and-about journey."

Where on earth would I go? Did it mean I was traveling to the Academy like Tatiana had suggested? Or was it possible that, in spite of all my rule breaking and calling her royal highness names, I might actually get an assignment after all? One away from Court?

"You could be looking for something. It may be a physical journey combined with a spiritual journey," she said, which sounded like a total way to cover her ass. "This last one . . ." Her eyebrows knitted into a frown at the fifth card. "This is hidden from me."

I peered at it. "The Page of Cups. Seems pretty obvious. It's a page with, um, cups."

"Usually I have a clear vision. . . . The cards speak to me in how they connect. This one's not clear."

"The only thing that's not clear is whether it's a girl or a boy." The person on the card looked young but had hair and an androgynous face that made the gender impossible to determine. The blue tights and tunic didn't help, though the sunny field in the background seemed promising.

"It can be either," Rhonda said. "It's the lowest in rank of the cards that represent people in each suit: King, Queen, Knight, and then Page. Whoever the page is, it's someone trustworthy and creative. Optimistic. It could mean someone who goes on the journey with you—or maybe the reason for your journey."

Whatever optimism or truth I'd had in the cards pretty much disappeared with that. Given that she'd just said about a hundred things it could be, I didn't really consider it authoritative. Usually, she noticed my skepticism, but her attention was still on the card as she frowned.

"But I just can't tell. . . . There's a cloud around it. Why? It doesn't make sense."

Something about her confusion sent a chill down my spine. I always told myself this was fake, but if she'd been making it all up . . . well, wouldn't she have made something up about the Page of Cups? She wasn't putting on a very convincing act if this last card was making her question herself. The thought that maybe there was some mystical force out there blocking her sobered up my cynical attitude.

With a sigh, she looked up at last. "Sorry that's all I can tell you. Did the rest help?"

I scanned the cards. Heartache. An enemy. Accusations. Entrapment. Travel. "Some of it tells me things I already know. The rest leaves me with more questions."

She smiled knowingly. "That's how it usually is."

I thanked her for the reading, secretly glad I didn't have to pay for it. Ambrose walked me out, and I tried to shake off the mood Rhonda's fortune had left me in. I had enough problems in my life without letting a bunch of stupid cards bother me.

"You going to be okay?" he asked when we finally emerged. The sun was climbing higher. The Royal Court would be going to bed soon, ending what had been a turbulent day. "I . . . I wouldn't have brought you if I'd known how much it would upset you."

"No, no," I said. "It's not the cards. Not exactly. There's a bunch of other things going on . . . one you should probably know about."

I hadn't wanted to bring up the decree when we'd first run into each other, but as a dhampir, he had a right to hear about what had happened. His face was perfectly still as I spoke, save for his dark brown eyes, which grew wider while the story progressed.

"There's some mistake," he said at last. "They wouldn't do that. They wouldn't do that to sixteen-year-olds."

"Yeah, well, I didn't think so either, but they were apparently serious enough about it to throw me out when I, um, questioned it."

"I can just imagine your 'questioning.' All this'll do is make more dhampirs drop out of the guardians . . . unless, of course, being that young makes them more open for brainwashing."

"Kind of a sensitive area for you, huh?" I asked. After all, he too was a guardian drop-out.

He shook his head. "Staying in this society was nearly impossible for me. If any of those kids do decide to drop out, they won't have the powerful friends I did. They'll be outcasts. That's all this'll do. Either kill off teens or cut them off from their own people."

I wondered what powerful friends he'd had, but this was hardly the time to learn his life history. "Well, that royal bitch doesn't seem to care."

The thoughtful, distracted look in his eyes suddenly sharpened. "Don't call her that," he warned with a glare. "This isn't her fault."

Whoa. Cue surprise. I'd almost never seen sexy, charismatic Ambrose be anything but friendly. "Of course it's her fault! She's the supreme ruler of the Moroi, remember?"

His scowl deepened. "The Council voted too. Not her alone."

"Yeah, but she voted in *support* of this decree. She swayed the vote."

"There must have been a reason. You don't know her like I do. She wouldn't want this kind of thing."

I started to ask if he was out of his mind but paused when I remembered his relationship with the queen. Those romantic rumors made me queasy, but if they were true, I supposed he might have legitimate concern for her. I also decided it was probably best that I *didn't* know her the way he did. The bite marks on his neck certainly indicated some sort of intimate activity.

"Whatever's going on between you is your business," I told him calmly, "but she's used it to trick you into thinking she's someone she isn't. She did it to me too, and I fell for it. It's all a scam."

"I don't believe it," he said, still stone-faced. "As queen, she's put into all sorts of tough situations. There must be more to it—she'll change the decree, I'm certain of it."

"As queen," I said, imitating his tone, "she should have the ability to—"

My words fell off as a voice spoke in my head. Lissa's.

Rose, you're going to want to see this. But you have to promise not to cause any trouble. Lissa flashed a location to me, along with a sense of urgency.

Ambrose's hard look shifted to one of concern. "Are you okay?"

"I—yeah. Lissa needs me." I sighed. "Look, I don't want us to fight, okay? Obviously we've each got different views of the situation . . . but I think we both agree on the same key point."

"That kids shouldn't be sent off to die? Yeah, we can agree on that." We smiled tentatively at each other, and the anger between us diffused. "I'll talk to her, Rose. I'll find out the real story and let you know, okay?"

"Okay." I had a hard time believing anyone could really have a heart-to-heart with Tatiana, but again, there might be more to their relationship than I realized. "Thanks. It was good seeing you."

"You too. Now go—go to Lissa."

I needed no further urging. Along with the sense of urgency, Lissa had passed one other message through the bond that sent my feet flying: *It's about Dimitri.*

TWENTY-THREE

I DIDN'T NEED THE BOND to find Lissa. The crowd tipped me off to where she—and Dimitri—were.

My first thought was that some kind of stoning or medieval mobbing was going on. Then I realized that the people standing around were simply watching something. I pushed through them, heedless of the dirty looks I got, until I stood in the front row of the onlookers. What I found brought me to a halt.

Lissa and Dimitri sat side by side on a bench while three Moroi and—yikes—Hans sat opposite them. Guardians stood scattered around them, tense and ready to jump in if things went bad, apparently. Before I even heard a word, I knew exactly what was going on. This was an interrogation, an investigation to determine what Dimitri was exactly.

Under most circumstances, this would be a weird place for a formal investigation. It was, ironically, one of the courtyards Eddie and I had worked on, the one that stood in the shadow of the statue of the young queen. The Court's church stood nearby. This grassy area wasn't exactly holy ground, but it was close enough to the church that people could run to it in an emergency. Crucifixes didn't hurt Strigoi, but they couldn't cross over into a church, mosque, or any other sacred place. Between that and the morning sun, this was probably as safe a location and time as officials could muster up to question Dimitri.

I recognized one of the Moroi questioners, Reece Tarus. He was related to Adrian on his mom's side but had also spoken in favor of the age decree. So I took an instant dislike to him, particularly considering the haughty tone he used toward Dimitri.

"Do you find the sun blinding?" asked Reece. He had a clipboard in front of him and appeared to be going down a checklist.

"No," said Dimitri, voice smooth and controlled. His attention was totally on his questioners. He had no clue I was there, and I kind of liked it that way. I wanted to just gaze at him for a moment and admire his features.

"What if you stare into the sun?"

Dimitri hesitated, and I'm not sure anyone but me caught the sudden glint in his eyes—or knew what it meant. The question was stupid, and I think Dimitri—maybe, just maybe—wanted to laugh. With his normal skill, he maintained his composure.

"Anyone would go blind staring into the sun long enough," he replied. "I'd go through what anyone else here would."

Reece didn't seem to like the answer, but there was no fault in the logic. He pursed his lips together and moved on to the next question. "Does it scald your skin?"

"Not at the moment."

Lissa glanced over at the crowd and noticed me. She couldn't feel me the way I could through our bond, but sometimes it seemed she had an uncanny sense of when I was around. I think she sensed my aura if I was close enough, since all spirit users claimed the field of light around shadow-kissed people was very distinct. She gave me a small smile before turning back to the questioning.

Dimitri, ever vigilant, noticed her tiny movement. He looked over to see what had distracted her, caught sight of me, and faltered a little on Reece's next question, which was, "Have you noticed whether your eyes occasionally turn red?"

"I . . ." Dimitri stared at me for several moments and then jerked his head back toward Reece. "I haven't been around many mirrors. But I think my guards would have noticed, and none of them have said anything."

Nearby, one of the guardians made a small noise. He barely managed to keep a straight face, but I think he too had wanted to snicker at the ridiculous line of questioning. I couldn't recall his name, but when I'd been at Court long ago, he and Dimitri had chatted and laughed quite a bit when together. If an old friend was starting to believe Dimitri was a dhampir again, then that had to be a good sign.

The Moroi next to Reece glared around, trying to figure out where the noise had come from, but discovered nothing. The questioning continued, this time having to do with whether Dimitri would step into the church if they asked him to.

"I can go right now," he told them. "I'll go to services tomorrow if you want." Reece made another note, no doubt wondering if he could get the priest to douse Dimitri in holy water.

"This is all a distraction," a familiar voice said in my ear. "Smoke and mirrors. That's what Aunt Tasha says." Christian now stood beside me.

"It needs to be done," I murmured back. "They have to see that he isn't Strigoi anymore."

"Yeah, but they've barely signed the age law. The queen gave the go-ahead for this as soon as the Council's session let out because it's sensational and will make people pay attention to something new. It was how they finally got the hall cleared. 'Hey, go look at the sideshow!'"

I could almost hear Tasha saying that word for word. Regardless, there was truth to it. I felt conflicted. I wanted Dimitri to be free. I wanted him to be the way he used to be. Yet I didn't appreciate Tatiana doing this for her own political gain and not because she actually cared about what was right. This was possibly the most monumental thing to happen in our history. It needed to be treated as such. Dimitri's fate shouldn't be a convenient "sideshow" to distract everyone from an unfair law.

Reece was now asking both Lissa and Dimitri to describe exactly what they'd experienced the night of the raid. I had a feeling this was something they'd recounted quite a bit. Although Dimitri had been the picture of nonthreatening composure so far, I still sensed that gray feel to him, the guilt and torment he felt over what he had done as a Strigoi. Yet, when he turned to listen to Lissa tell her version of the story, his face lit up with wonder. Awe. Worship.

Jealousy flashed through me. His feelings weren't romantic,

but it didn't matter. What mattered was that he had rejected me but regarded her as the greatest thing in the world. He'd told me never to talk to him again and sworn he'd do anything for her. Again I felt that petulant sense of being wronged. I refused to believe that he couldn't love me anymore. It wasn't possible, not after all he and I had been through together. Not after everything we'd felt for each other.

"They sure seem close," Christian noted, a suspicious note in his voice. I had no time to tell him his worries were unfounded because I wanted to hear what Dimitri had to say.

The story of his change was hard for others to follow, largely because spirit was still so misunderstood. Reece got as much out of it as he could and then turned the questioning over to Hans. Hans, ever practical, had no need for extensive interrogation. He was a man of action, not words. Gripping a stake in his hand, he asked Dimitri to touch it. The standing guardians tensed, probably in case Dimitri tried to grab the stake and go on a rampage.

Instead, Dimitri calmly reached out and held the top of the stake for a few moments. There was a collective intake of breath as everyone waited for him to scream in pain since Strigoi couldn't touch charmed silver. Instead, Dimitri looked bored.

Then he astonished them all. Drawing his hand back, he held out the bottom of his muscled forearm toward Hans. With the sunny weather, Dimitri was wearing a T-shirt, leaving the skin there bare.

"Cut me with it," he told Hans.

Hans arched an eyebrow. "Cutting you with this will hurt no matter what you are."

"It would be unbearable if I were a Strigoi," Dimitri pointed out. His face was hard and determined. He was the Dimitri I'd seen in battle, the Dimitri who never backed down. "Do it. Don't go easy on me."

Hans didn't react at first. Clearly, this was an unexpected course of action. Decision finally flashed across his features, and he struck out, swiping the stake's point against Dimitri's skin. As Dimitri had requested, Hans didn't hold back. The point dug deep, and blood welled up. Several Moroi, not used to seeing blood (unless they were drinking it), gasped at the violence. As one, we all leaned forward.

Dimitri's face showed he definitely felt pain, but charmed silver on a Strigoi wouldn't just hurt—it would burn. I'd cut a lot of Strigoi with stakes and heard them scream in agony. Dimitri grimaced and bit his lip as the blood flowed over his arm. I swear, there was pride in his eyes at his ability to stay strong through that.

When it became obvious he wouldn't start flailing, Lissa reached toward him. I sensed her intentions; she wanted to heal him.

"Wait," said Hans. "A Strigoi would heal from this in minutes."

I had to give Hans credit. He'd worked two tests into one. Dimitri shot him a grateful look, and Hans gave a small nod of acknowledgment. Hans believed, I realized. Whatever his faults, Hans truly thought Dimitri was a dhampir again. I would love him forever for that, no matter how much filing he made me do.

So, we all stood there watching poor Dimitri bleed. It was kind of sick, really, but the test worked. It was obvious to everyone that the cut wasn't going anywhere. Lissa was finally given leave to heal it, and that caused a bigger reaction among the crowd. Murmurs of wonder surrounded me, and those enraptured goddess-worshipping looks showed on people's faces.

Reece glanced at the crowd. "Does anyone have any questions to add to ours?"

No one spoke. They were all dumbfounded by the sights before them.

Well, someone had to step forward. Literally.

"I do," I said, striding toward them.

No, Rose, begged Lissa.

Dimitri wore an equally displeased look. Actually, so did almost everyone sitting near him. When Reece's gaze fell on me, I had a feeling he was seeing me in the Council room all over again, calling Tatiana a sanctimonious bitch. I put my hands on my hips, not caring what they thought. This was my chance to force Dimitri to acknowledge me.

"When you *used to be* Strigoi," I began, making it clear that I believed that was in the past, "you were very well connected. You knew about the whereabouts of lots of Strigoi in Russia and the U.S., right?"

Dimitri eyed me carefully, trying to figure out where I was going. "Yes."

"Do you still know them?"

Lissa frowned. She thought I was going to inadvertently implicate Dimitri as still being in contact with other Strigoi.

"Yes," he said. "So long as none of them have moved." The answer came more swiftly this time. I wasn't sure if he'd guessed my tactic or if he just trusted that my Rose-logic would go somewhere useful.

"Would you share that information with the guardians?" I asked. "Would you tell us all the Strigoi hideouts so that we could strike out against them?"

That got a reaction. Proactively seeking Strigoi was as hotly debated as the other issues going around right now, with strong opinions on all sides. I heard those opinions reiterated behind me in the crowd, some people saying I was suggesting suicide while others acknowledged we had a valuable tool.

Dimitri's eyes lit up. It wasn't the adoring look he often gave Lissa, but I didn't care. It was similar to the ones we used to share, in those moments where we understood each other so perfectly, we didn't even need to vocalize what we were thinking. That connection flashed between us, as did his approval—and gratitude.

"Yes," he replied, voice strong and loud. "I can tell you everything I know about Strigoi plans and locations. I'd face them with you or stay behind—whichever you wanted."

Hans leaned forward in his chair, expression eager. "That could be invaluable." More points for Hans. He was on the side of hitting out at Strigoi before they came to us.

Reece flushed—or maybe he was just feeling the sun. In

their efforts to see if Dimitri would burn up in the light, the Moroi were exposing themselves to discomfort. "Now hold on," Reece exclaimed over the increasing noise. "That has never been a tactic we endorse. Besides, he could always lie—"

His protests were cut off by a feminine scream. A small Moroi boy, no more than six, had suddenly broken from the crowd and run toward us. It was his mother who had screamed. I moved in to stop him, grabbing his arm. I wasn't afraid that Dimitri would hurt him, only that the boy's mother would have a heart attack. She came forward, face grateful.

"I have questions," the boy, obviously trying to be brave, said in a small voice.

His mother reached for him, but I held up my hand. "Hang on a sec." I smiled down at him. "What do you want to ask? Go ahead." Behind him, fear flashed over his mother's face, and she cast an anxious look at Dimitri. "I won't let anything happen to him," I whispered, though she had no way of knowing I could back that up. Nonetheless, she stayed where she was.

Reece rolled his eyes. "This is ridic—"

"If you're Strigoi," the boy interrupted loudly, "then why don't you have horns? My friend Jeffrey said Strigoi have horns."

Dimitri's eyes fell not on the boy but on me for a moment. Again, that spark of knowing shot between us. Then, face smooth and serious, Dimitri turned to the boy and answered, "Strigoi don't have horns. And even if they did, it wouldn't matter because I'm not Strigoi."

"Strigoi have red eyes," I explained. "Do his eyes look red?"

The boy leaned forward. "No. They're brown."

"What else do you know about Strigoi?" I asked.

"They have fangs like us," the boy replied.

"Do you have fangs?" I asked Dimitri in a singsong voice. I had a feeling this was already-covered territory, but it took on a new feel when asked from a child's perspective.

Dimitri smiled—a full, wonderful smile that caught me off guard. Those kinds of smiles were so rare from him. Even when happy or amused, he usually only gave half smiles. This was genuine, showing all his teeth, which were as flat as those of any human or dhampir. No fangs.

The boy looked impressed. "Okay, Jonathan," said his mother anxiously. "You asked. Let's go now."

"Strigoi are super strong," continued Jonathan, who possibly aspired to be a future lawyer. "Nothing can hurt them." I didn't bother correcting him, for fear he'd want to see a stake shoved through Dimitri's heart. In fact, it was kind of amazing that Reece hadn't already requested that. Jonathan fixed Dimitri with a piercing gaze. "Are *you* super strong? Can you be hurt?"

"Of course I can," replied Dimitri. "I'm strong, but all sorts of things can still hurt me."

And then, being Rose Hathaway, I said something I really shouldn't have to the boy. "You should go punch him and find out."

Jonathan's mother screamed again, but he was a fast little bastard, eluding her grasp. He ran up to Dimitri before anyone could stop him—well, I could have—and pounded his tiny fist against Dimitri's knee.

Then, with the same reflexes that allowed him to dodge enemy attacks, Dimitri immediately feinted falling backward, as though Jonathan had knocked him over. Clutching his knee, Dimitri groaned as though he were in terrible pain.

Several people laughed, and by then, one of the other guardians had caught hold of Jonathan and returned him to his near-hysterical mother. As he was being dragged away, Jonathan glanced over his shoulder at Dimitri. "He doesn't seem very strong to me. I don't think he's a Strigoi."

This caused more laughter, and the third Moroi interrogator, who'd been quiet, snorted and rose from his seat. "I've seen all I need to. I don't think he should walk around unguarded, but he's no Strigoi. Give him a real place to stay and just keep guards on him until further decisions are made."

Reece shot up. "But—"

The other man waved him off. "Don't waste any more time. It's hot, and I want to go to bed. I'm not saying I understand what happened, but this is the least of our problems right now, not with half the Council wanting to rip the other half's heads off over the age decree. If anything, what we've seen today is a good thing—miraculous, even. It could alter the way we've lived. I'll report back to Her Majesty."

And like that, the group began dispersing, but there was wonder on some of their faces. They too were beginning to realize that if what had happened to Dimitri was real, then everything we'd ever known about Strigoi was about to change. The guardians stayed with Dimitri, of course, as he and Lissa rose. I immediately moved toward them, eager to bask in our victory. When he'd been "knocked over" by Jonathan's tiny punch, Dimitri had given me a small smile, and my heart had leapt. I'd known then that I'd been right. He did still have feelings for me. But now, in the blink of an eye, that rapport was gone. Seeing me walk toward them, Dimitri's face grew cold and guarded again.

Rose, said Lissa through the bond. *Go away now. Leave him alone.*

"The hell I will," I said, both answering her aloud and addressing him. "I just furthered your case."

"We were doing fine without you," said Dimitri stiffly.

"Oh yeah?" I couldn't believe what I was hearing. "You seemed pretty grateful a couple minutes ago when I thought up the idea of you helping us against Strigoi."

Dimitri turned to Lissa. His voice was low, but it carried to me. "I don't want to see her."

"You have to!" I exclaimed. A few of the departing people paused to see what the racket was about. "You can't ignore me."

"Make her go away," Dimitri growled.

"I'm not—"

ROSE!

Lissa shouted in my head, shutting me up. Those piercing jade eyes stared me down. *Do you want to help him or not? Standing here and yelling at him is going to make him even more upset! Is that what you want? Do you want people to see that? See him get mad and yell back at you just so you don't feel invisible?*

They need to see him calm. They need to see him . . . normal. It's true—you did just help. But if you don't walk away right now, you could ruin everything.

I stared at them both aghast, my heart pounding. Her words had all been in my mind, but Lissa might as well have strode up to me and chewed me out aloud. My temper shot up even more. I wanted to go rant at both of them, but the truth of her words penetrated through my anger. Starting a scene would not help Dimitri. Was it fair that they were sending me away? Was it fair that the two of them were teaming up and ignoring what I'd just done? No. But I wasn't going to let my hurt pride screw up what I'd just achieved. People had to accept Dimitri.

I shot them both looks that made my feelings clear and then stormed away. Lissa's feelings immediately changed to sympathy through the bond, but I blocked them out. I didn't want to hear it.

I'd barely cleared the church's grounds when I ran into Daniella Ivashkov. Sweat was starting to smudge her beautifully applied makeup, making me think she'd been out here for a while watching the Dimitri-spectacle too. She appeared to have a couple friends with her, but they kept their distance and chatted amongst themselves when she stopped in front of me. Swallowing my anger, I reminded myself she'd done nothing to piss me off. I forced a smile.

"Hi, Lady Ivashkov."

"Daniella," she said kindly. "No titles."

"Sorry. It's still a weird thing."

She nodded toward where Dimitri and Lissa were departing

with his guards. "I saw you there, just now. You helped his case, I think. Poor Reece was pretty flustered."

I recalled that Reece was related to her. "Oh . . . I'm sorry. I didn't mean to—"

"Don't apologize. Reece is my uncle, but in this case, I believe in what Vasilisa and Mr. Belikov are saying."

Despite how angry Dimitri had just made me, my gut instinct resented the dropping of his "guardian" title. Yet I could forgive her, considering her attitude.

"You . . . you believe Lissa healed him? That Strigoi can be restored?" I was realizing there were lots of people who believed. The crowd had just demonstrated as much, and Lissa was still building her following of devotees. Somehow, my line of thinking always tended to assume all royals were against me. Daniella's smile turned wry.

"My own son is a spirit user. Since accepting that, I've had to accept a lot of other things I didn't believe were possible."

"I suppose you would," I admitted. Beyond her, I noticed a Moroi man standing near some trees. His eyes occasionally fell on us, and I could have sworn I'd seen him before. Daniella's next words turned my attention back to her.

"Speaking of Adrian . . . he was looking for you earlier. It's short notice now, but some of Nathan's relatives are having a late cocktail party in about an hour, and Adrian wanted you to go." Another party. Was that all anyone ever did here at Court? Massacres, miracles . . . it didn't matter. Everything was cause for a party, I thought bitterly.

I'd probably been with Ambrose and Rhonda when Adrian

went searching. It was interesting. In passing on the invitation, Daniella was also saying that she wanted me to go. Unfortunately, I had a hard time being as open to it. Nathan's family meant the Ivashkovs, and they wouldn't be so friendly.

"Will the queen be there?" I asked suspiciously.

"No, she has other engagements."

"Are you sure? No unexpected visits?"

She laughed. "No, I'm certain of it. Rumor has it that you two being in the same room together . . . isn't such a good idea."

I could only imagine the stories going around about my Council performance, particularly since Adrian's father had been there to witness it.

"No, not after that ruling. What she did . . ." The anger I'd felt earlier began to blaze again. "It was unforgivable." That weird guy by the tree was still waiting around. Why?

Daniella didn't confirm or deny my statement, and I wondered where she stood on the issue. "She's still quite fond of you."

I scoffed. "I have a hard time believing that." Usually, people who yelled at you in public weren't too "fond" of you, and even Tatiana's cool composure had cracked near the end of our spat.

"It's true. This will blow over, and there might even be a chance for you to be assigned to Vasilisa."

"You can't be serious," I exclaimed. I should have known better. Daniella Ivashkov didn't really seem like the joking type, but I really did believe I'd crossed the line with Tatiana.

"After everything that's happened, they don't want to

waste good guardians. Besides, she doesn't want there to be animosity between you."

"Yeah? Well, I don't want her bribery! If she thinks putting Dimitri out there and dangling a royal job is going to change my mind, she's wrong. She's a lying, scheming—"

I stopped abruptly. My voice had gone loud enough that Daniella's nearby friends were now staring. And I really didn't want to say the names I thought Tatiana deserved in front of Daniella.

"Sorry," I said. I attempted civility. "Tell Adrian I'll come to the party . . . but do you really want me to go? After I crashed the ceremony the other night? And after, um, other things I've done?"

She shook her head. "What happened at the ceremony is as much Adrian's fault as it is yours. It's done, and Tatiana let it go. This party's a much more lighthearted event, and if he wants you there, then I want him to be happy."

"I'll go shower and change now and meet him at your place in an hour."

She was tactful enough to ignore my earlier outburst. "Wonderful. I know he'll be happy to hear that."

I declined to tell her that I was actually happy about the thought of flaunting myself in front of some Ivashkovs in the hopes that it would get back to Tatiana. I no longer believed for an instant that she accepted what was going on with Adrian and me or that she would let my outburst blow over. And truthfully, I did want to see him. We hadn't had much time to talk recently.

After Daniella and her friends left, I figured it was time to get to the bottom of things. I headed straight over to the Moroi who'd been lurking around, hands on my hips.

"Okay," I demanded. "Who are you, and what do you want?"

He was only a few years older than me and didn't seem at all fazed by my tough-girl attitude. He crooked me a smile, and I again pondered where I'd seen him.

"I've got a message for you," he said. "And some gifts."

He handed over a tote bag. I looked inside and found a laptop, some cords, and several pieces of paper. I stared up at him in disbelief.

"What's this?"

"Something you need to get a move on—and not let anyone else know about. The note will explain everything."

"Don't play spy movie with me! I'm not doing anything until you—" His face clicked. I'd seen him back at St. Vladimir's, around the time of my graduation—always hovering in the background. I groaned, suddenly understanding the secretive nature—and cocky attitude. "You work for Abe."

TWENTY-FOUR

THE MAN GRINNED. "YOU MAKE that sound like a bad thing."

I made a face and looked back into the techno-bag with new appreciation. "What's going on?"

"I'm the messenger. I just run errands for Mr. Mazur."

"Is that a nice way of saying you spy for him? Find out everyone's dirty secrets so that he can use them against people and keep playing his games?" Abe seemed to know everything about everyone—especially royal politics. How else could he manage it without having eyes and ears everywhere? Say, at Court? For all I knew, he had my room wired with microphones.

"Spying's a harsh word." I notice the guy didn't deny it. "Besides, he pays well. And he's a good boss." He turned from me, job done, but gave one last warning. "Like I said—it's time sensitive. Read the note as soon as you can."

I had half a mind to throw it at the guy. I was getting used to the idea of being Abe's daughter, but that didn't mean I wanted to get tied up in some wacky scheme of his. A bag of hardware seemed foreboding.

Nonetheless, I hauled it back to my suite and emptied the contents onto my bed. There were a few sheets of paper, the top one being a typed cover letter.

Rose,

I hope Tad was able to get this to you in a timely manner. And I hope you weren't too mean to him. I'm doing this on behalf of someone who wants to speak to you about an urgent matter. However, it's a conversation that no one else must hear. The laptop and satellite modem in this bag will allow you to have a private discussion, so long as you're in a private location. I've included step-by-step instructions on how to configure it. Your meeting will take place at 7 a.m.

There was no name at the bottom, but I didn't need one. I set the letter down and stared at the jumble of cords. Seven was less than an hour away.

"Oh, come *on*, old man," I exclaimed.

To Abe's credit, the accompanying papers did have very basic directions that didn't require a computer engineer's insight. The only problem was, there were a lot of them, detailing where each cord went, what password to log in with, how to configure the modem, and so on. For a moment I considered ignoring it all. Yet when someone like Abe used the word *urgent*, it made me think maybe I shouldn't be so hasty in my dismissal.

So, bracing myself for some technical acrobatics, I set to following his instructions. It took almost the entire time I had, but I managed to hook up the modem and camera and access the secure program that would allow me to videoconference with Abe's mysterious contact. I finished with a few minutes to spare and waited the time out by staring at a black window in the middle of the screen, wondering what I'd gotten myself into.

At exactly seven, the window came to life, and a familiar—but unexpected—face appeared.

"Sydney?" I asked in surprise.

The video had that same, slightly jerky feel most Internet feeds had, but nonetheless, the face of my (kind of) friend Sydney Sage smiled back at me. Hers was a dry-humored smile, but that was typical of her.

"Good morning," she said, stifling a yawn. From the state of her chin-length blond hair, it was likely she'd just gotten out of bed. Even in the poor resolution, the golden lily tattoo on her cheek gleamed. All Alchemists had that same tattoo. It consisted of ink and Moroi blood, imparting Moroi good health and longevity to the wearer. It also had a bit of compulsion mixed in to keep the Alchemists' secret society from revealing anything they shouldn't about vampires.

"Evening," I said. "Not morning."

"We can argue your messed-up unholy schedule some other time," she said. "That's not what I'm here for."

"What *are* you here for?" I asked, still astonished to see her. The Alchemists did their jobs almost reluctantly, and while Sydney liked me better than most Moroi or dhampirs, she wasn't the type to make friendly phone (or video) calls. "Wait . . . you can't be in Russia. Not if it's morning . . ." I tried to remember the time change. Yes, for humans over there, the sun would be down or about to be right now.

"I'm back in my native country," she said with mock grandeur. "Got a new post in New Orleans."

"Whoa, nice." Sydney had hated being assigned to Russia, but my impression had been she was stuck there until finishing her Alchemist internship. "How'd you manage that?"

Her small smile turned to an expression of discomfort. "Oh, well. Abe, um, kind of did me a favor. He made it happen."

"You made a deal with him?" Sydney must have *really* hated Russia. And Abe's influence must have really been deep if he could affect a human organization. "What did you give him in return? Your soul?" Making a joke like that to someone as religious as her wasn't very appropriate. Of course, I think she thought Moroi and dhampirs ate souls, so maybe my comment wasn't too out there.

"That's the thing," she said. "It was kind of an 'I'll let you know when I need a favor in the future' arrangement."

"Sucker," I said.

"Hey," she snapped. "I don't have to be doing this. I'm actually doing *you* a favor by talking to you."

"Why *are* you talking to me exactly?" I wanted to question her more about her open-ended deal with the devil but figured that would get me disconnected.

She sighed and brushed some hair out of her face. "I need to ask you something. And I swear I won't tell on you . . . I just need to know the truth so that we don't waste our time on something."

"Okay . . ." *Please don't ask me about Victor,* I prayed.

"Have you broken into any place lately?"

Damn. I kept my face perfectly neutral. "What do you mean?"

"The Alchemists had some records stolen recently," she explained. She was all business-serious now. "And everyone's going crazy trying to figure out who did it—and why."

Mentally, I breathed a sigh of relief. Okay. It wasn't about Tarasov. Thank God there was one crime I wasn't guilty of. Then the full meaning of her words hit me. I glared.

"Wait. You guys get robbed, and I'm the one you suspect? I thought I was off your list of evil creatures?"

"No dhampir is off my list of evil creatures," she said. That half smile of hers had returned, but I couldn't tell if she was joking or not. It faded quickly, showing what a big deal this was for her. "And believe me, if anyone could break into our records, you could. It's not easy. Practically impossible."

"Um, thank you?" I wasn't sure if I should feel flattered or not.

"Of course," she continued scornfully, "they only stole paper records, which was stupid. Everything's backed up digitally nowadays, so I'm not sure why they'd go digging through dinosaur filing cabinets."

I could give her a lot of reasons why someone would do that, but finding out why I was her number-one suspect was more important. "That is stupid. So why do you think I'd do it?"

"Because of what was stolen. It was information about a Moroi named Eric Dragomir."

"I—what?"

"That's your friend, right? His daughter, I mean."

"Yeah . . ." I was almost speechless. Almost. "You have files on Moroi?"

"We have files on everything," she said proudly. "But when I tried to think who could commit a crime like this *and* would be interested in a Dragomir . . . well, your name popped into my head."

"I didn't do it. I do a lot of things, but not that. I didn't even know you had those kinds of records."

Sydney regarded me suspiciously.

"It's the truth!"

"Like I said before," she told me, "I won't turn you in. Seriously. I just want to know so that I can get people to stop wasting time on certain leads." Her smugness sobered. "And, well, if you did do it . . . I need to keep the attention off you. I promised Abe."

"Whatever it takes for you to believe me, I didn't do it! But now *I* want to know who did. What did they steal? Everything on him?"

She bit her lip. Owing Abe a favor might mean she'd go behind her own people's backs, but she apparently had limits on how much she'd betray.

"Come on! If you've got digital backup, you have to know what was taken. This is Lissa we're talking about." An idea came to me. "Could you send me copies?"

"No," she said swiftly. "Absolutely not."

"Then please . . . just a hint of what they were about! Lissa's my best friend. I can't let anything happen to her."

I fully braced myself for rejection. Sydney didn't seem

very personable. Did she have friends? Could she understand what I felt?

"Mostly bio stuff," she said at last. "Some of his history and observations we'd made."

"Observ—" I let it go, deciding I really didn't want to know more than I had to about Alchemists spying on us. "Anything else?"

"Financial records." She frowned. "Particularly about some large deposits he made to a bank account in Las Vegas. Deposits he went out of his way to cover up."

"Las Vegas? I was just there. . . ." Not that it was relevant.

"I know," she said. "I saw some Witching Hour security tapes of your adventure. The fact that you'd run off like that is part of why I suspected you. It seemed in character." She hesitated. "The guy with you . . . the tall Moroi with dark hair . . . is that your boyfriend?"

"Er, yeah."

It took a long time and great effort for her to concede the next statement. "He's cute."

"For an evil creature of the night?"

"Of course." She hesitated again. "Is it true you guys went there to elope?"

"What? No! These stories get to you guys too?" I shook my head, almost laughing at how ridiculous this all was, but knowing I needed to get back to the facts. "So, Eric had an account in Vegas he was moving money into?"

"It wasn't his. It was some woman's."

"What woman?"

"No one—well, no one we can track. She was just down as 'Jane Doe.'"

"Original," I muttered. "Why would he be doing that?"

"That we don't know. Or really care about. We just want to know who broke in and stole our stuff."

"The only thing I know about that is that it wasn't me." Seeing her scrutinizing look, I threw up my hands. "Come on! If I wanted to know about him, I'd just ask Lissa. Or steal our own records."

Several moments of silence passed.

"Okay. I believe you," she said.

"Really?"

"Do you want me to not believe you?"

"No, it was just easier than I thought convincing you."

She sighed.

"I want to know more about these records," I said fiercely. "I want to know who Jane Doe is. If you could get me other files—"

Sydney shook her head. "Nope. This is where I cut you off. You know too much already. Abe wanted me to keep you out of trouble, and I've done that. I've done my part."

"I don't think Abe's going to let you go so easily. Not if you made an open-ended deal."

She didn't acknowledge that, but the look in her brown eyes made me think she agreed. "Good night, Rose. Morning. Whatever."

"Wait, I—"

The screen went black.

"Damn," I growled, shutting the laptop more forcefully than I should have.

Every part of that conversation had been a shock, starting with Sydney and ending with someone stealing Alchemist records about Lissa's father. Why would anyone care about a dead man? And why steal the records at all? To learn something? Or to try to hide information? If that last one was true, then Sydney was right that it had been a failed effort.

I replayed it all in my head as I got ready for bed, staring at my reflection while brushing my teeth. Why, why, why? Why do it? And who? I needed no more intrigue in my life, but anything involving Lissa had to be treated seriously. Unfortunately, it soon became clear I wouldn't figure out anything tonight, and I fell asleep with all those questions spinning around in my head.

I woke up the next morning feeling a little less overwhelmed—but still short on answers. I debated whether or not to tell Lissa about what I'd learned and finally decided I should. If someone was gathering information on her father, she had a right to know, and besides, this was hardly the same as rumors about his—

A thought startled me in the middle of scrubbing shampoo into my hair. I'd been too tired and surprised to string together the pieces last night. That guy at the Witching Hour had said Lissa's dad was there a lot. Now Sydney's records reported that he'd made large deposits into an account in Las Vegas. Coincidence? Maybe. But as time went on, I was starting not to believe in coincidences anymore.

Once presentable, I set out toward Lissa's side of Court—but didn't get very far. Adrian was waiting for me down in my building's foyer, slumped back into an armchair.

"It's early for you, isn't it?" I teased, coming to a stop in front of him.

I expected a smile in return, but Adrian didn't look particularly cheerful this morning. In fact, he appeared kind of bedraggled. His hair lacked its usual styling care, and his clothing—unusually dressy for this time of day—was wrinkled. The scent of clove cigarettes hung around him.

"Easy to be early when you don't get much sleep," he responded. "I was up a lot of the night waiting for someone."

"Waiting for—oh. God." The party. I'd totally forgotten the party his mother had invited me to. Abe and Sydney had distracted me. "Adrian, I'm so sorry."

He shrugged and didn't touch me when I sat down on the arm of his chair. "Whatever. I probably shouldn't be surprised anymore. I'm starting to realize I've been deluding myself."

"No, no. I was going to go, but then you won't believe what—"

"Save it. Please." His voice was weary, his eyes bloodshot. "It's not necessary. My mom told me she saw you over at Dimitri's questioning."

I frowned. "But that's not why I missed the party. There was this guy—"

"That's not the point, Rose. The point is that you managed to make time for that—and a visit to his cell, if what I heard is true. Yet, you couldn't bother showing up at something you said you'd do with me—or even send a message. That was all you had to do; say you couldn't go. I waited over an hour for you at my parents' house before giving up."

I started to say he could have tried to contact me, but honestly, why should he have? It wasn't his responsibility. I was the one who'd told Daniella I'd meet him there. It was my fault for not showing up.

"Adrian, I'm sorry." I clasped his hand, but he didn't squeeze back. "Really, I meant to, but—"

"No," he interrupted again. "Ever since Dimitri came back . . . no, scratch that. Ever since you became obsessed with changing him, you've been torn over me. No matter what's happened between us, you've never really given yourself over to our relationship. I wanted to believe what you told me. I thought you were ready . . . but you weren't."

Protests rose to my lips, but once more, I stopped them. He was right. I'd said I'd give dating him a fair shot. I'd even sunk into the comfortable role of his girlfriend, yet the whole time . . . the whole time, part of me had been consumed with Dimitri. I'd known it too but had kept living split lives. A weird flashback to my time with Mason popped into my head. I'd led the same double life with him, and he'd died for it. I was a mess. I didn't know my own heart.

"I'm sorry," I said again. "I really do want us to have something. . . ." Even to me, the words sounded so lame. Adrian gave me a knowing smile.

"I don't believe that. Neither do you." He stood up and ran

his hand over his hair, not that it did any good. "If you really want to be with me, then you've got to mean it this time."

I hated seeing him so grim. I especially hated being the reason. I followed him to the door. "Adrian, wait. Let's talk more."

"Not now, little dhampir. I need some sleep. I just can't handle playing this game right now."

I could have gone after him. I could have tackled him to the ground. But it wouldn't have been worth it . . . because I had no answers to give him. He'd been right about everything, and until I could make up my own confused mind, I had no right to force a talk. Besides, considering the state he was in, I doubted any further conversation would have been productive.

Yet as he started to step outside, I couldn't help my next words. "Before you go—and I understand why you have to—there's something I've got to ask you. Something that's not about us. It affects—it affects Lissa."

This slowly brought him to a halt. "Always a favor." With a world-weary sigh, he glanced at me over his shoulder. "Make it fast."

"Someone broke into the Alchemists' records and stole information about Lissa's dad. Some of it was ordinary life history stuff, but there were some documents about him making secret deposits into a bank account in Las Vegas. Some woman's bank account."

Adrian waited a few moments. "And?"

"And I'm trying to figure out why someone would do that. I don't want anyone snooping around her family. Do you have any idea what her dad would have been doing?"

"You heard the guy at the casino. Her dad was there a lot. Maybe he had gambling debts and was paying off a loan shark."

"Lissa's family's always had money," I pointed out. "He couldn't have gotten into that much debt. And why would anyone care enough to steal that info?"

Adrian threw up his hands. "I don't know. That's all I've got, at least this early in the morning. I don't have the brain power for intrigue. I can't really picture any of that being a threat to Lissa, though."

I nodded, disappointed. "Okay. Thanks."

He continued on his way, and I watched him go. Lissa lived near him, but I didn't want him to think I was following him. When he'd put enough distance between us, I stepped outdoors as well and started to head in the same direction. The faint sound of bells brought me to a halt. I hesitated, suddenly unsure where to go.

I wanted to talk to Lissa and tell her what Sydney had told me. Lissa was alone for a change; this was the perfect opportunity. And yet . . . the bells. It was Sunday morning. Mass was about to start at the Court's church. I had a hunch about something, and in spite of everything that had happened—including with Adrian—I had to see if I was right.

So I sprinted off toward the church, going in the opposite direction of Lissa's building. The doors were shut when I reached my destination, but a few other latecomers were trying to quietly slip in. I entered with them, pausing to get my bearings. Clouds of incense hung in the air, and my eyes took a moment to adjust from sunlight to candlelight. Since this church dwarfed St. Vladimir's chapel, it was packed with a lot more people than I was used to seeing at mass. Most of the seats were full.

But not all of them.

My hunch had been right. Dimitri sat in one of the back pews. A few guardians sat near him, of course, but that was it. Even in a crowded church, no one else had joined him on the bench. Reece had asked Dimitri if he'd step inside the church yesterday, and Dimitri had gone one step further, saying he'd even go to Sunday services.

The priest had already begun to speak, so I moved down Dimitri's pew as quietly as I could. Silence didn't matter, though, because I still attracted a fair amount of attention from nearby people who were astonished to see me sitting next to the Strigoi-turned-dhampir. Eyes stared and several hushed conversations broke out.

The guardians had left some space near Dimitri, and when I sat beside him, the look on his face showed he was both surprised and not surprised by this.

"Don't," he said in a hushed voice. "Don't start—not in here."

"Wouldn't dream of it, comrade," I murmured back. "Just came for the good of my soul, that's all."

He didn't need to say a word to convey to me that he doubted I was here for any holy reasons. I stayed quiet throughout the service, though. Even I respected some boundaries. After several minutes, the tension in Dimitri's body eased a little.

He'd grown wary when I joined him but must have eventually decided I'd be on good behavior. His attention shifted off of me and focused on the singing and the praying, and I did my best to watch him without being obvious.

Dimitri used to go to the school's chapel because it brought him peace. He had always said that even though the killing he did destroyed evil in the world, he still felt the need to come think about his life and seek forgiveness for his sins. Seeing him now, I realized that was truer than ever.

His expression was exquisite. I was so used to seeing him hide emotions that it was a bit startling for him to suddenly have a host of them on his face. He was absorbed in the priest's words, his gorgeous face completely focused. And I realized he was taking everything the priest was saying about sin personally. Dimitri was replaying all the awful things he'd done as a Strigoi. From the despair on his face, you'd think that Dimitri himself was responsible for all the sins of the world the priest spoke of.

For a moment, I thought I saw hope on Dimitri's face too, just a spark of it mixed in with his guilt and sorrow. No, I realized. Not hope. Hope implies that you think you have a chance at something. What I saw in Dimitri was longing. Wistfulness. Dimitri wished that by being here in this holy place and listening to the messages conveyed, he might find redemption for what he had done. Yet . . . at the same time, it was clear he didn't believe that was possible. He wanted it but could never have it as far as he was concerned.

Seeing that in him hurt me. I didn't know how to react to

that kind of bleak attitude. He thought there was no hope for him. Me? I couldn't imagine a world without hope.

I also never would have imagined I'd quote back a church lesson, but when the rest of the crowd stood up to take communion, I found myself saying to Dimitri: "Don't you think that if God can supposedly forgive you, it's kind of egotistical for you not to forgive yourself?"

"How long have you been waiting to use that line on me?" he asked.

"Actually, it just came to me. Pretty good, huh? I bet you thought I wasn't paying attention."

"You weren't. You never do. You were watching me."

Interesting. To know that I was watching him, would Dimitri have had to have watched me watching him? It boggled the mind. "You didn't answer my question."

He kept his eyes on the communion line while composing his answer. "It's irrelevant. I don't have to forgive myself even if God does. And I'm not sure He would."

"That priest just said God would. He said God forgives *everything*. Are you calling the priest a liar? That's pretty sacrilegious."

Dimitri groaned. I never thought I'd take joy in tormenting him, but the frustrated look on his face wasn't because of his personal grief. It was because of me being impertinent. I'd seen this expression a hundred times on him, and the familiarity of it warmed me, as crazy as that sounds.

"Rose, you're the one being sacrilegious. You're twisting these people's faith for your own purposes. You've never believed in any of this. You still don't."

"I believe that the dead can come back to life," I said seriously. "The proof is sitting right next to me. If that's true, then I think you forgiving yourself isn't that much more of a leap."

His gaze hardened, and if he was praying for anything right then, it was that the communion process would speed up so that he could get out of here and away from me. We both knew he had to wait this church service out. If he ran out, it would make him look Strigoi.

"You don't know what you're talking about," he said.

"Don't I?" I hissed, leaning closer. I did it to drive home my point, but all it did (for me, at least) was give me a better view of the way the candlelight shone on his hair and how long and lean his body was. Someone had apparently decided he could be trusted to shave, and his face was smooth, showing its wonderful, perfect lines.

"I know exactly what I'm talking about," I continued, trying to ignore how his presence affected me. "I know that you've been through a lot. I know that you did terrible things—I *saw* them. But it's in the past. It was beyond your control. It's not like you're going to do it again."

A strange, haunted look crossed his face. "How do you know? Maybe the monster didn't leave. Maybe there's still something Strigoi lurking in me."

"Then you need to defeat it by moving on with your life! And not just through your chivalrous pledge to protect Lissa. You need to live again. You need to open yourself up to people who love you. No Strigoi would do that. That's how you'll save yourself."

"I can't have people loving me," he growled. "I'm incapable of loving anyone in return."

"Maybe you should try instead of just feeling sorry for yourself!"

"It's not that easy."

"Da—" I just barely stopped myself from swearing in a church. "Nothing we've ever done has been easy! Our life before—before the attack wasn't easy, and we made it through that! We can make it through this too. We can make it through anything together. It doesn't matter if you put your faith in this place. I don't care. What matters is that you put your faith in *us*."

"There is no us. I've already told you that."

"And you know I'm not a very good listener."

We were keeping our voices low, but I think our body language clearly indicated an argument. The other churchgoers were too distracted to notice, but Dimitri's guardians were regarding us carefully. Again, I reminded myself about what Lissa and Mikhail had both said. Getting Dimitri angry in public was not going to do him any favors. The problem was, I had yet to say anything that *didn't* make him angry.

"I wish you hadn't come here," he said at last. "It's really better for us to stay apart."

"That's funny because I could have sworn you once said we were meant to be together."

"I want you to stay away from me," he said, ignoring my comment. "I don't want you to keep trying to bring back feelings that are gone. *That's* the past. None of that's going to happen again. Not ever. It's better for us if we act like strangers. It's better for *you*."

The loving, compassionate feelings he had stirred within me heated up—to fury. "If you're going to tell me what I can or can't do," I growled in as low a tone as I could manage, "then at least have the courage to say it to my face!"

He spun around so quickly that he might have indeed still been Strigoi. His face was filled with . . . what? Not that earlier depression. Not rage either, though there was a bit of anger. There was more, though . . . a mingling of desperation, frustration, and maybe even fear. Underscoring all of it was pain, like he suffered from terrible, exquisite agony.

"I don't want you here," he said, eyes blazing. The words hurt, but something about it all thrilled me, just as his earlier agitation at my flippant comments had. This wasn't the cold and calculating Strigoi. This wasn't the defeated man in the cell. This was my old instructor, my lover, who attacked everything in life with intensity and passion. "How many times do I have to tell you that? You need to stay away from me."

"But you aren't going to hurt me. I know that."

"I've already hurt you. Why can't you understand that? How many times do I have to say it?"

"You told me . . . you told me before you left that you loved me." My voice trembled. "How can you let that go?"

"Because it's too late! And it's easier than being reminded of what I did to you!" His control snapped, his voice echoing through the back of the church. The priest and those still taking communion didn't notice, but we'd definitely gotten the attention of those in the back half of the church. A few of the guardians stiffened, and again, I had to repeat the warning to myself. No matter how furious I was at Dimitri, no matter how betrayed I felt that he'd turned away from me . . . I could *not* risk others thinking he was dangerous. Dimitri hardly looked like he was going to snap someone's neck, but he was clearly upset, and one might confuse his frustration and pain for something more sinister.

I turned from him, trying to calm my churning emotions. When I looked back, our eyes locked, power and electricity burning between us. Dimitri could ignore it all he wanted, but that connection—that deep calling of our souls—was still in there. I wanted to touch him, not just with this brushing of my leg but with everything. I wanted to wrap him in my arms and hold him against me, reassuring him that we could do anything together. Without even realizing it, I reached toward him, needing that touch. He sprang up like I was a snake, and all of his guardians shot forward, braced for what he might do.

But he did nothing. Nothing except stare at me with a look that made my blood run cold. Like I was something strange and bad. "Rose. Please stop. Please stay away." He was working hard to stay calm.

I shot up, now as angry and frustrated as him. I had a feeling if I stayed, we'd both snap. In an undertone, I murmured, "This isn't over. I won't give up on you."

"I've given up on you," he said back, voice also soft. "Love fades. Mine has."

I stared at him in disbelief. All this time, he'd never phrased it like that. His protests had always been about some greater good, about the remorse he felt over being a monster or how it had scarred him from love. *I've given up on you. Love fades. Mine has.*

I backed up, the sting of those words hitting me as hard as if he'd slapped me. Something shifted in his features, like maybe he knew how much he'd hurt me. I didn't stick around to see. Instead, I pushed my way out of the aisle and ran out the doors in the back, afraid that if I stayed any longer, everyone in the church would see me cry.

TWENTY-FIVE

I DIDN'T WANT TO SEE anyone after that. I trekked back to my room as quickly as I could, hardly noticing the obstacles and people in my path. Over and over, Dimitri's words played in my head: *Love fades. Mine has.* Somehow, that was the worst thing he could have said. Don't get me wrong: The rest wasn't easy either. Having him tell me he was going to avoid me and ignore our past relationship made me feel awful too. Yet, within that, no matter how much it hurt, was the tiny hope that there was still some spark of love between us. That he still loved me.

But . . . love fades.

That was something else altogether. It meant that what we had would die, going pale until it crumbled and drifted away like dried up leaves in the wind. The thought of it caused a pain in my chest and stomach, and I curled up on my bed, wrapping my arms around myself as though that might lessen the hurt. I couldn't accept what he had said. I couldn't accept that somehow, after his ordeal, his love for me had gone away.

I wanted to stay in my room for the rest of the day, curled up in the darkness of my covers. I forgot about Sydney's conversation and my earlier concerns about Lissa's dad. I even let go of Lissa herself. She had a few errands today, but every so often, a message would flit to me through the bond: *Come join me?*

When I didn't contact her, she began to grow worried. I was suddenly afraid that she—or someone else—might come seeking me in my room. So I decided to leave. I had no real destination; I just had to keep moving. I walked around the Court, scouting places I'd never seen before. It was filled with more statues and fountains than I'd realized. Their beauty was lost on me, though, and when I returned to my room hours later, I was exhausted from all the walking. Oh well. At least I'd dodged having to talk to anyone.

Or had I? It was late, past my usual bedtime, when a knock came at my door. I was hesitant to answer. Who would be coming by so late? Did I want the distraction or did I want to keep my solitude? I had no idea who it could be, save that it wasn't Lissa. God. For all I knew, it was Hans, demanding to know why I hadn't been showing up for my work detail. After much thinking (and more persistent knocking), I decided to open it.

It was Adrian.

"Little dhampir," he said with a small, weary smile. "You look like you've seen a ghost."

Not a ghost, exactly. Believe me, I knew ghosts when I saw them. "I just . . . I just didn't really expect to see you after this morning. . . ."

He entered and sat down on my bed, and I was glad to see he'd cleaned up since our earlier talk. He wore fresh clothes, and his hair was back to its normal perfection. I still caught the lingering scent of cloves, but after what I'd put him through, he was entitled to his vices.

"Yeah, well, I didn't expect to come by either," he admitted. "But you . . . well . . . you got me thinking about something."

I sat down beside him, keeping a healthy distance. "Us?"

"No. Lissa."

"Oh." I'd accused Dimitri of being egotistic, but here I was, naturally assuming love for me was all that could have driven Adrian over.

His green eyes turned speculative. "I kept thinking about what you'd said, about her dad. And you were right—right about the gambling thing. He'd have the money to pay off any debt. He wouldn't have had to keep it a secret. So I went and asked my mom."

"What?" I exclaimed. "No one's supposed to know that—"

"Yeah, yeah, I figured your information had been top secret. Don't worry. I told her that when we were in Vegas, we heard some people talking about it—about Lissa's dad making secret deposits."

"What'd she say?"

"The same thing I did. Well, actually, she snapped at me first. She said Eric Dragomir was a good man and that I shouldn't spread rumors about the dead. She suggested that maybe he had a gambling problem, but if so, people shouldn't focus on that, when he did so many great things. After the Death Watch, I think she's afraid of me causing more public scenes."

"She's right. About Eric," I said. Maybe someone had stolen those records as some part of a slander campaign. Admittedly, spreading rumors about the dead was pointless, but maybe someone wanted to blacken the Dragomir reputation and get rid of any chance of the voting law being changed for Lissa? I was about to say as much to Adrian when he interrupted with something even more shocking.

"And then my dad overheard us, and he was like, 'He was probably funding some mistress. You're right—he was a nice guy. But he liked to flirt. And he liked the ladies.'" Adrian rolled his eyes. "That's a direct quote: 'He liked the ladies.' My dad is such an ass. He sounds twice his age."

I gripped Adrian's arm without realizing it. "What did he say after that?"

Adrian shrugged but left my hand where it was. "Nothing. My mom got mad and said the same thing to him that she said to me, that it was cruel to spread stories no one could prove."

"Do you think it's true? Do you think Lissa's dad had a mistress? Was that what he was paying out for?"

"Don't know, little dhampir. Honestly? My dad's the type who would jump on any rumor he could. Or make one up. I mean, we know Lissa's dad liked to party. It's easy to jump to conclusions from there. Probably he had some dirty secret. Hell, we all do. Maybe whoever stole those files just wanted to exploit that."

I told him my theory about it being used against Lissa. "Or," I said, reconsidering, "maybe someone who supports her took it. So that it wouldn't get out."

Adrian nodded. "Either way, I don't think Lissa's in mortal danger."

He started to rise, and I pulled him back. "Adrian, wait . . . I . . ." I swallowed. "I wanted to apologize. The way I've been treating you, what I've been doing . . . it wasn't fair to you. I'm sorry."

He looked away from me, eyes focused on the ground. "You can't help the way you feel."

"The thing is . . . I don't know how I feel. And that sounds stupid, but it's the truth. I care about Dimitri. I was stupid to think I'd be unaffected by him being back. But I realize now . . ." *Love fades. Mine has.* "I realize now that it's over with him. I'm not saying that's easy to get past. It'll take a while, and I'd be lying to both of us if I said it wouldn't."

"That makes sense," Adrian said.

"It does?"

He glanced at me, a flicker of amusement in his eyes. "Yes, little dhampir. Sometimes you make sense. Go on."

"I . . . well, like I said . . . I've got to heal from him. But I do care about you. . . . I think I even love you a little." That got a small smile. "I want to try again. I really do. I like having you in my life, but I may have jumped into things too soon before. You don't have any reason to want me after the way I've dragged you around, but if you want to get together again, then I want to."

He studied me for a long time, and my breath caught. I'd meant what I said: He had every right to end things with us . . . and yet, the thought that he might terrified me.

At last, he pulled me against him and lay back against the bed. "Rose, I have all sorts of reasons to want you. I haven't been able to stay away from you since I saw you at the ski lodge."

I shifted closer to Adrian on the bed and pressed my head against his chest. "We can make this work. I know we can. If I screw up again, you can leave."

"If only it were that easy," he laughed. "You forget: I have an addictive personality. I'm addicted to you. Somehow I think you could do all sorts of bad things to me, and I'd still come back to you. Just keep things honest, okay? Tell me what you're feeling. If you're feeling something for Dimitri that's confusing you, tell me. We'll work it out."

I wanted to tell him that—regardless of my feelings—he had nothing to worry about with Dimitri because Dimitri had rejected me a number of times now. I could chase after Dimitri all I wanted, and it wouldn't do any good. *Love fades.* Those words still stung, and I couldn't bear to give voice to that pain. But as Adrian held me and I thought about how understanding he was about all of this, some wounded part of me acknowledged that the opposite was true as well: *Love grows.* I would try with him. I really would.

I sighed. "You're not supposed to be this wise. You're supposed to be shallow and unreasonable and . . . and . . ."

He pressed a kiss to my forehead. "And?"

"Mmm . . . ridiculous."

"Ridiculous I can manage. And the others . . . but only on special occasions."

We were wrapped close together now, and I tilted my head to study him, the high cheekbones and artfully messy hair that made him so gorgeous. I remembered his mother's words, that regardless of what we wanted, he and I would eventually have to part ways. Maybe this was how my life was going to be. I'd always lose the men I loved.

I pulled him hard against me, kissing his mouth with a force that caught even him by surprise. If I had learned anything about life and love, it was that they were tenuous things that could end at any moment. Caution was essential—but not at the cost of wasting your life. I decided I wasn't going to waste it now.

My hands were already tugging at Adrian's shirt before that thought was fully formed. He didn't question it or hesitate in taking my clothes off in return. He might have moments of profoundness and understanding, but he was still . . . well, Adrian. Adrian lived his life in the now, doing the things he wanted without much second-guessing. And he had wanted me for a very long time.

He was also very good at this sort of thing, which was why my clothes came off faster than his. His lips were hot and eager against my throat, but he was careful to never once let his fangs brush my skin. I was a little less gentle, surprising myself when I dug my nails into the bare skin of his back. His lips moved lower, tracing the line of my collarbone while he deftly took off my bra one-handed.

I was a little astonished at my body's reaction as we both fought to get the other's jeans off first. I'd convinced myself that I'd never want sex again after Dimitri, but right now? Oh, I wanted it. Maybe it was some psychological reaction to Dimitri's rejection. Maybe it was an impulse to live for the moment. Maybe it was love for Adrian. Or maybe it was just lust.

Whatever it was, it made me powerless beneath his hands and mouth, which seemed intent on exploring every part of me. The only time he paused was when all my clothes were finally off and I lay there naked with him. He was almost naked too, but I hadn't quite gotten to his boxers yet. (They were silk because, honestly, what else would Adrian wear?). He cupped my face in his hands, his eyes filled with intensity and desire—and a bit of wonder.

"What are you, Rose Hathaway? Are you real? You're a dream within a dream. I'm afraid touching you will make me wake up. You'll disappear." I recognized a little of the poetic trance he sometimes fell into, the spells that made me wonder if he was catching a little of the spirit-induced madness.

"Touch me and find out," I said, drawing him to me.

He didn't hesitate again. The last of his clothes came off, and my whole body heated at the feel of his skin and the way his hands slid over me. My physical needs were rapidly trampling over any logic and reason. There was no thought, just us, and the fierce urgency bringing us together. I was all burning need and desire and sensation and—

"Oh, shit."

It came out as kind of a mumble since we'd been kissing, our lips eagerly seeking out the other's. With guardian reflexes, I barely managed to shift away, just as our hips started to come together. Losing the feel of him was shocking to me, more so for him. He was stunned, simply staring in astonishment as I wriggled further from him and finally managed a sitting position on the bed.

"What . . . what's wrong? Did you change your mind?"

"We need protection first," I said. "Do you have any condoms?"

He processed this for a few seconds and then sighed. "Rose, only you would pick this instant to remember that."

That was a fair point. My timing kind of sucked. Still, it was better than remembering it *afterward.* In spite of my body's rampant desire—and it was still there, believe me—I suddenly had a startling, vivid image of Dimitri's sister Karolina. I'd met her in Siberia, and she'd had a baby that was about six months old. The baby was adorable, as babies often are, but by God, she had been so much work. Karolina had a waitressing job, and as soon as she was home from that, her attention went to the baby. When she was at work, Dimitri's mother took care of the baby. And the baby always needed something: food, changing, rescue from choking on a small object. His sister Sonya had been on the verge of having a baby too, and with the way I'd left things with his youngest sister, Viktoria, I wouldn't be surprised to find she was pregnant before long. Huge life changes made from small, careless actions.

So I was pretty confident I didn't want a baby in my life right now, not this young. With Dimitri, it hadn't been a concern, thanks to dhampir infertility. With Adrian? It was an issue, as was the fact that while disease was rare among both our races, I wasn't the first girl Adrian had been with. Or the second. Or the third . . .

"So do you have any?" I asked impatiently. Just because I was in responsible mode, it didn't mean I wanted sex any less.

"Yes," said Adrian, sitting up as well. "Back in my bedroom."

We stared at each other. His bedroom was far away, over in the Moroi section of Court.

He slid nearer, putting his arm around me and nibbling my earlobe. "The odds of anything bad happening are pretty low."

I closed my eyes and tipped my head back against him. He wrapped his hands around my hips and stroked my skin. "What are you, a doctor?" I asked.

He laughed softly, his mouth kissing the spot just behind my ear. "No. I'm just someone willing to take a risk. You can't tell me you don't want this."

I opened my eyes and pulled away so that I could look at him directly. He was right. I did want this. Very, very badly. And the part of me—which was pretty much all of me—that burned with lust was attempting to win me over. The odds probably were low, right? Weren't there people who tried forever to get pregnant and couldn't? My desire had an okay argument, so it was kind of a surprise when my logic won.

"*I* can't take the risk," I said.

Now Adrian studied me, and at last, he nodded. "Okay. Another time then. Tonight we'll be . . . responsible."

"That's all you're going to say?"

He frowned. "What else would I say? You said no."

"But you . . . you could have compelled me."

Now he was really astonished. "Do you *want* me to compel you?"

"No. Of course not. It just occurred to me that . . . well, that you could have."

Adrian cupped my face in his hands. "Rose, I cheat at cards and buy liquor for minors. But I would never, ever force you into something you don't want. Certainly not this—"

His words were cut off because I'd pressed myself against him and started kissing him again. Surprise must have kept him from doing anything right away, but soon, he pushed me away with what seemed like great reluctance.

"Little dhampir," he said dryly, "if you want to be responsible, this is not a good way to do it."

"We don't have to let this go. And we *can* be responsible."

"All of those stories are—"

He came screeching to a halt when I tossed my hair out of the way and offered my neck to him. I managed to turn slightly so that I could meet his eyes, but I said nothing. I didn't have to. The invitation was obvious.

"Rose . . ." he said uncertainly—though I could see the longing spring up in his face.

Drinking blood wasn't the same as sex, but it was a yearning all vampires had, and doing it while aroused—so I'd heard—was a mind-blowing experience. It was also taboo and hardly ever done, so people claimed. It was where the definition of blood whore had originated: dhampirs who gave their blood during sex. The idea of dhampirs yielding blood at all was considered disgraceful, but I'd done it before: with Lissa when she needed food and with Dimitri when he'd been Strigoi. And it had been glorious.

He tried again, his voice steadier this time. "Rose, do you know what you're asking?"

"Yes," I said firmly. I gently ran a finger along his lips and then slipped in to touch his fangs. I threw his own words back at him. "You can't tell me you don't want this."

He did want it. In a heartbeat, his mouth was at my neck and his fangs were piercing my skin. I cried out at the sudden pain, a sound that softened to a moan as the endorphins that came with every vampire bite flooded into me. An exquisite bliss consumed me. He pulled me hard against him as he drank, almost onto his lap, pressing my back against his chest. I was distantly aware of his hands all over me again, of his lips upon my throat. Mostly, all I knew was that I was drowning in pure, ecstatic sweetness. The perfect high.

When he pulled away, it was like losing part of myself. Like being incomplete. Confused, needing him back, I reached for him. He gently pushed my hand away, smiling as he licked his lips.

"Careful, little dhampir. I went longer than I should have. You could probably grow wings and fly off right now."

It actually didn't sound like a bad idea. In a few more moments, though, the intense, crazy part of the high faded, and I settled back to myself. I still felt wonderful and dizzy; the endorphins had fed my body's desire. My reasoning slowly came back to me, allowing (kind of) coherent thought to penetrate that happy haze. When Adrian was convinced I was sober enough, he relaxed and lay down on the bed. I joined him a moment later, curling up against his side. He seemed as content as I was.

"That," he mused, "was the best not-sex ever."

My only response was a sleepy smile. It was late, and the more I crashed down from the endorphin rush, the drowsier I felt. Some tiny part of me said that even though I'd wanted this and cared about Adrian, the whole act had been wrong. I hadn't done it for the right reasons, instead letting myself get carried away by my own grief and confusion.

The rest of me decided that wasn't true, and the nagging voice soon faded into exhaustion. I fell asleep against Adrian, getting the best night of sleep I'd had in a long time.

I wasn't entirely surprised that I was able to get out of bed, shower, get dressed, and even blow-dry my hair without Adrian waking up. My friends and I had spent many a morning trying to drag him out of bed in the past. Hungover or sober, he was a heavy sleeper.

I spent more time on my hair than I had in a while. The telltale mark of a vampire bite was fresh on my neck. So I wore my hair down, careful to style it with a part so that the long waves hung heavy on the bite side. Satisfied the bruise would stay camouflaged, I pondered what to do next. In an hour or so, the Council was going to listen to arguments from factions with varying ideas on the new age decree, Moroi fighting, and the Dragomir vote. Provided they let me in the hall, I had no intention of missing the debates on the hottest issues in our world right now.

I didn't want to wake up Adrian, though. He was tangled up in my sheets and slept peacefully. If I woke him up, I'd feel obligated to stick around while he got ready. Through the bond, I felt Lissa sitting alone at a café table. I wanted to see her and have breakfast, so I decided Adrian could fend for himself. I left him a note about where I was, told him the door would lock on his way out, and drew lots of *x*'s and *o*'s.

When I was halfway to the café, though, I sensed something that ruined my breakfast plan. Christian had sat down with Lissa.

"Well, well," I muttered. With everything else going on, I hadn't paid much attention to Lissa's personal life. After what had happened at the warehouse, I wasn't entirely surprised to see them together, though her feelings told me there had been no romantic reconciliation . . . yet. This was an uneasy attempt at friendship, a chance to get over their constant jealousy and distrust.

Far be it from me to intrude on love at work. I knew another place near the guardians' buildings that also had coffee and doughnuts. It would do, provided no one there remembered that I was technically still on probation and had made a scene in a royal hall.

The odds on that probably weren't good.

Still, I decided to give it a try and headed over, eyeing the overcast sky uneasily. Rain wouldn't help my mood any. When I got to the café, I discovered I didn't have to worry about anyone paying attention to me. There was a bigger draw: Dimitri.

He was out with his personal guard, and even though I was glad he had some freedom, the attitude that he needed close watching still angered me. At least there was no giant crowd today. People who came in for breakfast couldn't help but stare, but few lingered. He had five guardians with him this time, which was a significant reduction. That was a good sign. He sat alone at a table, coffee and a half-eaten glazed doughnut in front of him. He was reading a paperback novel that I would have bet my life was a Western.

No one sat with him. His escort simply maintained a ring of protection, a couple near the walls, one at the entrance, and two at nearby tables. The security seemed pointless. Dimitri was completely engrossed in his book, oblivious to the guards and occasional spectators—or he was simply making a good show of not caring. He seemed very harmless, but Adrian's words came back to me. Was there any Strigoi left in him? Some dark part? Dimitri himself claimed he still carried the piece that prevented him from ever truly loving anyone.

He and I had always had this uncanny awareness of each other. In a crowded room, I could always find him. And in spite of his preoccupation with the book, he looked up when I walked toward the café's counter. Our eyes met for a millisecond. There was no expression on his face . . . and yet, I had the feeling he was waiting for something.

Me, I realized with a start. Despite everything, despite our fight in the church . . . he still thought I would pursue and make some pledge of my love. Why? Did he just expect me to be that unreasonable? Or was it possible . . . was it possible he *wanted* me to approach him?

Well, whatever the reason, I decided I wouldn't give it to him. He'd hurt me too many times already. He'd told me to stay away, and if that was all part of some elaborate game to toy with my feelings, I wasn't going to play. I gave him a haughty look and turned away sharply as I walked up to the counter. I ordered chai and a chocolate éclair. After a moment's consideration, I ordered a second éclair. I had a feeling it was going to be one of those days.

My plan had been to eat outside, but as I glanced toward the tinted windows, I could just barely make out the pattern of raindrops hitting the panes. Damn. I briefly considered fighting the weather and going somewhere else with my food, but I decided I wasn't going to let Dimitri scare me off. Spying a table far from him, I headed toward it, going out of my way not to look at or acknowledge him.

"Hey Rose. Are you going to the Council today?"

I came to a halt. One of Dimitri's guardians had spoken, giving me a friendly smile as he did. I couldn't recall the guy's name, but he'd seemed nice whenever we passed each other. I didn't want to be rude, and so, reluctantly, I answered back—even though it meant staying near Dimitri.

"Yup," I said, making sure my attention was only on the guardian. "Just grabbing a bite before I do."

"Are they going to let you in?" asked another of the guardians. He too was smiling. For a moment, I thought they were mocking my last outburst. But no . . . that wasn't it. Their faces showed approval.

"That's an excellent question," I admitted. I took a bite of my éclair. "But I figure I should give it a try. I'll also try to be on good behavior."

The first guardian chuckled. "I certainly hope not. That group deserves all the grief you can give them over that stupid age law." The other guardians nodded.

"What age law?" asked Dimitri.

Reluctantly, I looked over at him. As always, he swept my breath away. *Stop it, Rose,* I scolded myself. *You're mad at him, remember? And now you've chosen Adrian.*

"The decree where royals think sending sixteen-year-old dhampirs out to fight Strigoi is the same as sending eighteen-year-olds," I said. I took another bite.

Dimitri's head shot up so quickly, I nearly choked on my food. "Which sixteen-year-olds are fighting Strigoi?" His guardians tensed but did nothing else.

It took me a moment to get the bite of éclair down. When I could finally speak, I was almost afraid to. "That's the decree. Dhampirs graduate when they're sixteen now."

"When did this happen?" he demanded.

"Just the other day. No one told you?" I glanced over at the other guardians. One of them shrugged. I had the impression that they might believe Dimitri was truly a dhampir but that they weren't ready to get chatty with him. His only other social contact would have been Lissa and his interrogators.

"No." Dimitri's brow furrowed as he pondered the news.

I ate my éclair in silence, hoping it would push him to talk more. It did.

"That's insane," he said. "Morality aside, they aren't ready that young. It's suicide."

"I know. Tasha gave a really good argument against it. I did too."

Dimitri gave me a suspicious look at that last part, particularly when a couple of his guardians smiled.

"Was it a close vote?" he asked. He spoke to me interrogation style, in the serious and focused way that had so defined him as a guardian. It was a lot better than depression, I decided. It was also better than him telling me to go away.

"Very close. If Lissa could have voted, it wouldn't have passed."

"Ah," he said, playing with the edges of his coffee cup. "The quorum."

"You know about that?" I asked in surprise.

"It's an old Moroi law."

"So I hear."

"What's the opposition trying to do? Sway the Council back or get Lissa the Dragomir vote?"

"Both. And other things."

He shook his head, tucking some hair behind his ear. "They can't do that. They need to pick one cause and throw their weight behind it. Lissa's the smartest choice. The Council needs the Dragomirs back, and I've seen the way people look at her when they put me on display." Only the slightest edge of bitterness laced his words, indicating how he felt about that.

Then it was back to business. "It wouldn't be hard to get support for that—if they don't divide their efforts."

I started in on my second éclair, forgetting about my earlier resolution to ignore him. I didn't want to distract him from the topic. It was the first thing that had brought the old fire back to his eyes, the only thing he seemed truly interested in—well, aside from pledging lifelong devotion to Lissa and telling me to stay out of his life. I liked this Dimitri.

It was the same Dimitri from long ago, the fierce one who was willing to risk his life for what was right. I almost wished he'd go back to being annoying, distant Dimitri, the one who told me to stay away. Seeing him now brought back too many memories—not to mention the attraction I thought I'd smashed. Now, with that passion all over him, he seemed sexier than ever. He'd worn that same intensity when we'd fought together. Even when we'd had sex. This was the way Dimitri was supposed to be: powerful and in charge. I was glad and yet . . . seeing him the way I loved only made my heart feel that much worse. He was lost to me.

If Dimitri guessed my feelings, he didn't show it. He looked squarely at me, and, like always, the power of that gaze wrapped around me. "The next time you see Tasha, will you send her to me? We need to talk about this."

"So, Tasha can be your friend, but not me?" The sharp words were out before I could stop them. I flushed, embarrassed that I'd lapsed in front of the other guardians. Dimitri apparently didn't want an audience either. He looked up at the one who had initially addressed me.

"Is there any way we could have some privacy?"

His escort exchanged looks, and then, almost as one being, they stepped back. It wasn't a considerable distance, and they still maintained a ring around Dimitri. Nonetheless, it was enough that all of our conversation wouldn't be overheard. Dimitri turned back to me. I sat down.

"You and Tasha have completely different situations. She can safely be in my life. You can't."

"And yet," I said with an angry toss of my hair, "it's apparently okay for me to be in your life when it's convenient—say, like, running errands or passing messages."

"It doesn't really seem like you need me in your life," he noted dryly, inclining his head slightly toward my right shoulder.

It took me a moment to grasp what had happened. In tossing my hair, I'd exposed my neck—and the bite. I tried not to blush again, knowing I had nothing to feel embarrassed about. I pushed the hair back.

"That's none of your business," I hissed, hoping the other guardians hadn't seen.

"Exactly." He sounded triumphant. "Because you need to live your own life, far away from me."

"Oh, for God's sake," I exclaimed. "Will you stop with the—"

My eyes lifted from his face because an army suddenly descended upon us.

Okay, it wasn't exactly an army, but it might as well have been. One minute it was just Dimitri, me, and his security, and then suddenly—the room was swarming with guardians. And not just any guardians. They wore the black-and-white outfits guardians often did for formal occasions, but a small red button on their collars marked them as guardians specifically attached to the queen's guard. There had to be at least twenty of them.

They were lethal and deadly, the best of the best. Throughout history, assassins who had attacked monarchs had found themselves quickly taken down by the royal guard. They were walking death—and they were all gathering around us. Dimitri and I both shot up, unsure what was happening but certain the threat here was directed at us. His table and its chairs were between us, but we still immediately fell into the standard fighting stance when surrounded by enemies: Go back-to-back.

Dimitri's security wore ordinary clothing and seemed a bit astonished to see their brethren, but with guardian efficiency, the escort promptly joined the advancing queen's guard. There were no more smiles or jokes. I wanted to throw myself in front of Dimitri, but in this situation, it was kind of difficult.

"You need to come with us right now," one of the queen's guards said. "If you resist, we'll take you by force."

"Leave him alone!" I yelled, looking from face to face. That angry darkness exploded within me. How could they still not believe? Why were they still coming after him? "He hasn't done anything! Why can't you guys accept that he's really a dhampir now?"

The man who'd spoken arched an eyebrow. "I wasn't talking to *him*."

"You're . . . you're here for me?" I asked. I tried to think of any new spectacles I might have caused recently. I considered the crazy idea that the queen had found out I'd spent the night with Adrian and was pissed off about it. That was hardly enough to send the palace guard for me, though . . . or was it? Had I really gone too far with my antics?

"What for?" demanded Dimitri. That tall, wonderful body of his—the one that could be so sensual sometimes—was filled with tension and menace now.

The man kept his gaze on me, ignoring Dimitri. "Don't make me repeat myself: Come with us quietly, or we will make you." The glimmer of handcuffs showed in his hands.

My eyes went wide. "That's crazy! I'm not going anywhere until you tell me how the hell this—"

That was the point at which they apparently decided I wasn't coming quietly. Two of the royal guardians lunged for me, and even though we technically worked for the same side, my instincts kicked in. I didn't understand anything here except that I would *not* be dragged away like some kind of master criminal. I shoved the chair I'd been sitting in earlier at one of the guardians and aimed a punch at the other. It was a sloppy throw, made worse because he was taller than me. That height difference allowed me to dodge his next grab, and when I kicked hard at his legs, a small grunt told me I'd hit home.

I heard a few scattered screams. The people working at the café ducked behind their counter like they expected automatic weapons to come out. The other patrons who'd been eating breakfast hurriedly sprang from their tables, heedlessly knocking over food and dishes. They ran for the exits—exits that were blocked by still more guardians. This brought more screams, even though the exits were being cut off because of me.

Meanwhile, other guardians were joining the fray. Although I got a couple of good punches in, I knew the numbers were too overwhelming. One guardian caught hold of my arm and began trying to put the cuffs on me. He stopped when another set of hands grabbed me from the other side and jerked me away.

Dimitri.

"Don't touch her," he growled.

There was a note in his voice that would have scared me if it had been directed toward me. He shoved me behind him, putting his body protectively in front of mine with my back to the table. Guardians came at us from all directions, and Dimitri began dispatching them with the same deadly grace that had once made people call him a god. He didn't kill any of the ones he fought, but he made sure they were out of action. If anyone thought his ordeals as a Strigoi or being locked up had diminished his fighting ability, they were terribly mistaken. Dimitri was a force of nature, managing to take on both impossible odds and stop me each time I tried to join the fight. The queen's guards might have been the best of the best, but Dimitri . . . well, my former lover and instructor was in a category all his own. His fighting skills were beyond anyone else's, and he was using them all in defense of me.

"Stay back," he ordered me. "They aren't laying a hand on you."

At first, I was overwhelmed by his protectiveness—even though I hated not being part of a fight. Watching him fight again was also entrancing. He made it look beautiful and lethal at the same time. He was a one-man army, the kind of warrior that protected his loved ones and brought terror to his enemies—

And that's when a horrible revelation hit me.

"Stop!" I suddenly yelled. "I'll come! I'll come with you!"

No one heard me at first. They were too involved with the fight. Guardians kept trying to sneak behind Dimitri, but he seemed to sense them and would shove chairs or anything else he could get a hold of at them—while still managing to kick and punch those coming at us head-on. Who knew? Maybe he really could have taken on an army by himself.

But I couldn't let him.

I shook Dimitri's arm. "Stop," I repeated. "Don't fight anymore."

"Rose—"

"Stop!"

I was pretty sure I'd never screamed any word so loudly in my life. It rang through the room. For all I knew, it rang through the entire Court.

It didn't exactly make everyone come to a halt, but many of the guardians slowed down. A few of the cowering café workers peered over the counter at us. Dimitri was still in motion, still ready to take everyone on, and I had to practically throw myself at him to get him to notice me.

"Stop." This time, my voice was a whisper. An uneasy silence had fallen over everyone. "Don't fight them anymore. I'm going to go with them."

"No. I won't let them take you."

"You have to," I begged.

He was breathing hard, every part of him braced and ready to attack. We locked gazes, and a thousand messages seemed to flow between us as the old electricity crackled in the air. I just hoped he got the right message.

One of the guardians tentatively stepped forward—having to go around the unconscious body of his colleague—and Dimitri's tension snapped. He started to block the guardian and defend me again, but I instead put myself between them, clasping Dimitri's hand and still looking into his eyes. His skin was warm and felt so, so right touching mine.

"Please. No more."

I saw then that he finally understood what I was trying to say. People were still afraid of him. No one knew what he was. Lissa had said him behaving calmly and normally would soothe fears. But this? Him taking on an army of guardians? That was not going to get him points for good behavior. For all I knew, it was already too late after this, but I had to attempt damage control. I couldn't let them lock him up again—not because of me.

As he looked at me, he seemed to send a message of his own: that he would still fight for me, that he would fight until he collapsed to keep them from taking me.

I shook my head and gave his hand a parting squeeze. His fingers were exactly as I remembered, long and graceful, with calluses built up from years of training. I let go and turned to face the guy who had originally spoken. I assumed he was some sort of leader.

I held out my hands and slowly stepped forward. "I'll go quietly. But, please . . . don't lock him back up. He just thought . . . he just thought I was in trouble."

The thing was, as the handcuffs were clamped onto my wrists, *I* was starting to think I was in trouble too. As the guardians helped each other up, their leader took a deep breath and made the proclamation he'd been trying to make since entering. I swallowed, waiting to hear Victor's name.

"Rose Hathaway, you are under arrest for high treason."

Not quite what I'd expected. Hoping my submission had earned me points, I asked, "What kind of high treason?"

"The murder of Her Royal Majesty, Queen Tatiana."

TWENTY-SIX

MAYBE IT WAS SOMEONE'S SICK sense of humor, but I ended up in Dimitri's now-vacated cell.

I had come quietly after that guardian laid the charges before me. In fact, I'd become comatose because too much of what he'd said was impossible to process. I couldn't even really get to the part about me. I couldn't feel outrage or indignation over the accusation because I was still stuck on the part about Tatiana being dead.

Not just dead. Murdered.

Murdered?

How had that happened? How had that happened around here? This Court was one of the most secure places in the world, and Tatiana in particular was always guarded—by the same group that had descended on Dimitri and me so quickly. Unless she'd left Court—and I was pretty sure she hadn't—no Strigoi could have killed her. With the constant threats we faced, murder among dhampirs and Moroi was almost unheard of. Sure, it happened. It was inevitable in any society, but with the way ours was hunted, we rarely had time to turn on each other (shouting in Council meetings aside). That was part of why Victor had been so condemned. His crimes were about as bad as things got.

Until now.

Once I got past the impossible idea of Tatiana being dead, I was able to ask the real question: Why me? Why were they accusing me? I was no lawyer, but I was pretty sure calling someone a sanctimonious bitch was *not* hard evidence in a trial.

I tried getting more details from the guards outside my cell, but they remained hard-faced and silent. After making my voice hoarse from shouting, I slumped onto the bed and went to Lissa's mind, where I was certain I'd get more information.

Lissa was frantic, trying to get answers from anyone she could. Christian was still with her, and they stood inside the foyer of one of the administrative buildings, which was filled with a flurry of activity. Dhampirs and Moroi alike ran everywhere, some frightened of this new government instability and others hoping to take advantage of it. Lissa and Christian stood in the midst of it all, like leaves swept along in a storm's fury.

While Lissa was now technically an adult, she had still always been under the wing of some older person at Court—usually Priscilla Voda, and occasionally even Tatiana. Neither of them was available now, for obvious reasons. While many royals respected her, Lissa had no real source to turn to.

Seeing her agitation, Christian clasped her hand. "Aunt Tasha will know what's going on," he said. "She'll turn up sooner or later. You know she won't let anything happen to Rose."

Lissa knew there was a bit of uncertainty in that statement

but didn't mention it. Tasha might not *want* anything to happen to me, but she certainly wasn't all-powerful.

"Lissa!"

Adrian's voice caused both Lissa and Christian to turn around. Adrian had just entered, along with his mother. Adrian looked as though he had literally gone straight from my bedroom to here. He wore yesterday's clothes, slightly rumpled, and his hair was styled with none of his usual care. By comparison, Daniella looked polished and put together, the perfect picture of a businesswoman who hadn't lost her femininity.

At last! Here were people who might have answers. Lissa rushed over to them gratefully.

"Thank God," Lissa said. "No one will tell us what's happened . . . except that the queen is dead and Rose is locked up." Lissa looked up at Daniella's face pleadingly. "Tell me there's been some kind of mistake."

Daniella patted Lissa's shoulder and gave as comforting a look as she could manage, given the circumstances. "I'm afraid not. Tatiana was killed last night, and Rose is their main suspect."

"But she would never have done that!" exclaimed Lissa.

Christian joined her in righteous fury. "Her yelling at the Council that day isn't enough to convict her for murder." Ah, Christian and I had the same line of reasoning. It was almost scary. "Neither is crashing the Death Watch."

"You're right. It's not enough," agreed Daniella. "But it doesn't make her look good either. And apparently, they have other evidence they say proves her guilt."

"What kind of evidence?" Lissa demanded.

Daniella turned apologetic. "I don't know. That's still part of the investigation. They'll have a hearing to present the evidence and question her whereabouts, possible motives . . . that kind of thing." She glanced around at the people rushing by. "If they even get that far. This kind of thing . . . it hasn't happened in ages. The Council gains absolute control until a new monarch is elected, but there's still going to be chaos. People are afraid. I won't be surprised if the Court goes under martial law."

Christian turned to Lissa, hope on his face. "Did you see Rose last night? Was she with you?"

Lissa frowned. "No. I think she was in her room. The last time I saw her was the day before yesterday."

Daniella didn't look happy about that. "That's not going to help. If she was alone, then she has no alibi."

"She wasn't alone."

Three sets of eyes turned in Adrian's direction. It was the first time he'd spoken since first calling to Lissa. Lissa hadn't focused on him too much yet, meaning I hadn't either. She'd only observed his superficial appearance when he arrived, but now she could see the little details. Worry and distress had left their marks, making him look older than he was. When she tuned in to his aura, she saw the usual gold of a spirit user, but it and its other colors were muddied and tinged with darkness. There was a flickering there too, a warning of spirit's instability taking hold. This had all come about too quickly for him to react, but I suspected he'd hit the cigarettes and liquor as soon as he had a free moment. It was how Adrian coped with this sort of thing.

"What are you saying?" Daniella asked sharply.

Adrian shrugged. "She wasn't alone. I was with her all night."

Lissa and Christian did a good job of maintaining neutral expressions, but Daniella's face registered the shock that any parent would have upon hearing about her child's sex life. Adrian noticed her reaction as well.

"Save it," he warned. "Your morals, your opinions . . . none of it matters right now." He gestured toward a group of panicked people running by, screaming about how Victor Dashkov must have surely come to Court to kill them all. Adrian shook his head and turned back to his mother. "I was with Rose. That proves she didn't do it. We'll deal with your motherly disapproval about my love life later."

"That's not what worries me! If they do have hard evidence and you get mixed up in this, you could be under suspicion too." The composure Daniella had entered with was beginning to crack.

"She was my aunt," cried Adrian incredulously. "Why on earth would Rose and I kill her?"

"Because she disapproved of you dating. And because Rose was upset over the age ruling." This came from Christian. Lissa glared, but he merely shrugged. "What? I'm just stating the obvious. Someone else would if I didn't. And we all heard the stories—people have been making up things that are extreme even for Rose." A strong comment indeed.

"When?" asked Daniella, clutching Adrian's sleeve. "When were you with Rose? When did you get there?"

"I don't know. I don't remember," he said.

She tightened her grip. "Adrian! Take this seriously. This is going to make a huge difference on how things proceed. If you got there before Tatiana was killed, then you won't be tied to it. If you were with Rose afterward—"

"Then she has an alibi," he interrupted. "And there's no problem."

"I hope that's true," murmured Daniella. Her eyes didn't seem focused on my friends anymore. The wheels in her head were spinning, her thoughts jumping ahead as she tried to think how best to protect her son. I had been an unfortunate case for her. He was, understandably, a red-alert emergency for her. "We're still going to have to get you a lawyer. I'll talk to Damon. I have to find him before the hearing tonight. And Rufus will have to know about this too. Damn." Adrian arched an eyebrow at that. I had the impression Lady Ivashkov didn't swear very often. "We *have* to find out what time you were there."

Adrian still wore his distress around him like a cloak and looked as though he might fall over if he didn't get nicotine or alcohol soon. I hated to see him like that, particularly over me. There was strength within him, no question, but his nature—and the sketchy effects of spirit—made coping with this hard. Yet, through his agitation, he managed to pull up a memory to help his frantic mother.

"There was someone in the building lobby when I came in . . . a janitor or something, I think. No one at the front desk, though." Most buildings usually kept a staff member around for emergencies or concierge services.

Daniella's face lit up. "That's it. That's what we'll need. Damon will find out the time you were there so that we can get you free and clear of this."

"*And* so he can defend me if things turn bad?"

"Of course," she answered swiftly.

"What about Rose?"

"What about her?"

Adrian still looked ready to fall apart, but there was seriousness and focus in his green eyes. "If you find out Aunt Tatiana was killed before I was there, and Rose is thrown to the wolves alone, will Damon be her lawyer?"

His mother faltered. "Oh, well, darling . . . Damon doesn't really do that sort of thing. . . ."

"He will if you ask him to," said Adrian sternly.

"Adrian," she said wearily, "you don't know what you're talking about. They say the evidence against her is bad. If our family's shown supporting—"

"It's not like we're supporting murder! You met Rose. You liked her. Can you look me in the eye and say it's okay for her to go in with whatever half-assed defense they dredge up for her? *Can you?*"

Daniella blanched, and I swear, she actually cringed away. I don't think she was used to such fierce resoluteness from her devil-may-care son. And though his words were perfectly sane, there was kind of a crazy desperation in his voice and attitude that was a little scary. Whether that was caused by spirit or just his own emotion, I couldn't say.

"I . . . I'll speak to Damon," Daniella said at last. She'd had to swallow a few times before actually getting the words out.

Adrian let out a deep breath and some of that fury went with it. "Thank you."

She scurried away, melting into the crowd and leaving Adrian alone with Christian and Lissa. The two of them looked only a little less stunned than Daniella had.

"Damon Tarus?" Lissa guessed. Adrian nodded.

"Who's that?" asked Christian.

"My mom's cousin," said Adrian. "The family lawyer. A real shark. Kind of sleazy too, but he can pretty much get anyone out of anything."

"That's something, I suppose," mused Christian. "But is he good enough to fight this so-called hard evidence?"

"I don't know. I really don't know." Adrian absentmindedly reached for his pocket, the usual cigarette spot, but he had none today. He sighed. "I don't know what their evidence is or how Aunt Tatiana even died. All I heard was that they found her dead this morning."

Lissa and Christian exchanged grimaces. Christian shrugged, and Lissa turned back to Adrian, taking on the role of messenger.

"A stake," said Lissa. "They found her in bed with a silver stake through her heart."

Adrian said nothing, and his expression didn't really

change. It occurred to Lissa that in all this talk about innocence, evidence, and lawyers, everyone had kind of overlooked the fact that Tatiana had been Adrian's great-aunt. He hadn't approved of some of her decisions and had made plenty of jokes about her behind her back. But she was still his family, someone he'd known his entire life. He had to be feeling the pain of her death on top of everything else. Even I felt a little conflicted. I hated her for what she'd done to me, but I'd never wanted her dead. And I couldn't help but remember that she'd occasionally spoken to me like I was a real person. Maybe it had been faked, but I was pretty sure she'd been sincere the night she'd stopped by the Ivashkovs'. She'd been weary and thoughtful, mostly just concerned about bringing peace to her people.

Lissa watched Adrian go, sympathy and sorrow flooding through her. Christian gently tapped her arm. "Come on," he said. "We've found out what we needed to know. We're just in the way here."

Feeling helpless, Lissa let him lead her outside, dodging more panicked crowds. The orange of a low sun gave every leaf and tree a golden, warm feel. There had been a lot of people out when we returned from the warehouse with Dimitri, but it was nothing compared to this. People were buzzing with fear, hurrying to pass the news. Some were already in mourning, clad in black, with tears on their faces. I wondered how much of that was real. Even in the midst of tragedy and crime, royals would be scrambling for power.

And each time she heard my name, Lissa would grow more

and more angry. It was the bad anger too, the kind that felt like black smoke in our bond and often made her lash out. It was spirit's curse.

"I can't believe this!" she exclaimed to Christian. I noticed, even if she didn't, that he was hurriedly taking her somewhere where there weren't people. "How could anyone think that about Rose? It's a set up. It *has* to be."

"I know, I know," he said. He knew spirit's danger signs too and was trying to calm her down. They'd reached a small, grassy area in the shade of a large hazelnut tree and settled onto the ground. "We know she didn't do it. That's all there is to it. We'll prove it. She can't be punished for something she didn't do."

"You don't know this group," grumbled Lissa. "If someone's out to get her, they can make all sorts of things possible." With only the faintest awareness, I drew a little of that darkness from her into me, trying to calm her down. Unfortunately, it just made me angrier.

Christian laughed. "You forget. I grew up around this group. I went to school with this group's kids. I know them—but we're not panicking until we know more, okay?"

Lissa exhaled, feeling much better. I was going to take too much darkness if I wasn't careful. She gave Christian a small, tentative smile.

"I don't remember you being this reasonable before."

"It's because everyone has different definitions of 'reasonable.' Mine's just misunderstood, that's all." His voice was lofty.

"I think you must be misunderstood a lot," she laughed.

His eyes held hers, and the smile on his face transformed into something warmer and softer. "Well, I hope this isn't misunderstood. Otherwise, I might get punched."

Leaning over, he brought his lips to hers. Lissa responded with no hesitation or thought whatsoever, losing herself in the sweetness of the kiss. Unfortunately, I was swept along with it. When they pulled away, Lissa felt her heart rate increase and her cheeks flush.

"What exactly was that the definition of?" she asked, reliving how his mouth had felt.

"It means 'I'm sorry,'" he said.

She looked away and nervously plucked at some of the grass. Finally, with a sigh, she looked back up. "Christian . . . was there ever . . . was there ever anything between you and Jill? Or Mia?"

He stared in surprise. "What? How could you think that?"

"You spent so much time with them."

"There is only one person I have ever wanted," he said. The steadiness of his gaze, of those crystal blue eyes, left no question as to who that person was. "No one else has ever come close. In spite of everything, even with Avery—"

"Christian, I'm so sorry for that—"

"You don't have to—"

"I do—"

"Damn it," he said. "Will you let me finish a sent—"

"No," Lissa interrupted. And she leaned over and kissed him, a hard and powerful kiss that burned through her body, one that told her there was no one else in the world for her either.

Well. Apparently Tasha had been right: I was the only one who could bring them back together. I just somehow hadn't expected my arrest to play a role.

I pulled away from her head to give them some privacy and save myself from watching them make out. I didn't begrudge them their moment. There was nothing either could do for me right now, and they deserved their reunion. Their only course of action was to wait for more information, and really, their method of passing time was a lot healthier than whatever Adrian was probably doing.

I lay down on the bed and stared up at the ceiling. There was nothing but plain metal and neutral colors around me. It drove me crazy. I had nothing to watch, nothing to read. I felt like an animal trapped in a cage. The room seemed to grow smaller and smaller. All I could do was replay what I'd learned via Lissa, analyzing every word of what had been said. I had questions about everything, of course, but the one thing that stuck with me was Daniella mentioning a hearing. I needed to know more about that.

I got my answer—hours later.

I'd fallen into sort of a numb haze by then and almost didn't recognize Mikhail standing in front of my cell door. I leapt from my bed to the bars and saw that he was unlocking the door. Hope surged through me.

"What's going on?" I asked. "Are they letting me go?"

"I'm afraid not," he said. His point was proven when, after

opening the door, he promptly put my hands in cuffs. I didn't fight it. "I'm here to take you to your hearing."

Stepping into the hall, I saw other guardians gathered. My own security detail. A mirror of Dimitri's. Lovely. Mikhail and I walked together, and mercifully, he spoke along the way instead of maintaining that awful silence that seemed to be common treatment for prisoners.

"What's the hearing exactly? A trial?"

"No, no. Too soon for a trial. A hearing decides whether you're going to trial."

"That sounds kind of like a waste of time," I pointed out. We emerged from the guardians' building, and that fresh, damp air was the sweetest thing I'd ever tasted.

"It's a bigger waste of time if you go to a full-fledged trial, and they realize there was no case to stand on. At the hearing, they'll lay out all the evidence they have, and a judge—or, well, someone acting as a judge—will decide if you should have a trial. The trial makes it official. That's where they pass the verdict and dole out the punishment."

"Why'd they take so long for the hearing? Why'd they make me wait in that cell all day?"

He laughed, but not because he thought it was funny. "This is fast, Rose. Very fast. It can take days or weeks to get a hearing, and if you do go to trial, you'll stay locked up until then."

I swallowed. "Will they move fast on that too?"

"I don't know. No monarch's been murdered in almost a hundred years. People are running wild, and the Council wants to establish order. They're already making huge plans for the queen's funeral—a giant spectacle that'll distract everyone. Your hearing is also an attempt to establish order."

"What? How?"

"The sooner they convict the murderer, the safer everyone will feel. They think this case against you is so solid, they want to rush it through. They *want* you to be guilty. They want to bury her knowing her killer is moving toward justice, so that everyone can sleep easy when the new king or queen is elected."

"But I didn't—" I let my denial go. There was no point.

Ahead of us, the building that housed the courtroom loomed. It had seemed forbidding the first time I'd been here for Victor's trial, but that had been owing to fear of the memories he sparked in me. Now . . . now it was my own future on the line. And apparently not just my own future—the Moroi world was watching and waiting, hoping I was a villain who could be safely put away forever. Swallowing, I gave Mikhail a nervous look.

"Do you think . . . do you think they'll send me to trial?"

He didn't answer. One of the guards held the door open for us.

"Mikhail?" I urged. "Will they really put me on trial for murder?"

"Yes," he said sympathetically. "I'm pretty sure they will."

TWENTY-SEVEN

WALKING INTO THE COURTROOM was one of the most surreal experiences of my life—and not just because I was the one being accused here. It just kept reminding me of Victor's trial, and the idea that I was now in his place was almost too weird to comprehend.

Entering a room with a troop of guardians makes people stare—and believe me, there were a lot of people packed in there—so naturally, I didn't skulk or look ashamed. I walked with confidence, my head held high. Again, I had that eerie flashback to Victor. He too had walked in defiantly, and I'd been appalled that someone who had committed his crimes could behave that way. Were these people thinking the same thing about me?

On the dais at the front of the room sat a woman I didn't recognize. Among the Moroi, a judge was usually a lawyer who had been appointed to the position for the purposes of the hearing or whatever. The trial itself—at least a big one like Victor's—had been presided over by the queen. She had been the one to ultimately decide the final verdict. Here, the Council members would be the ones to decide if I even reached that stage. *The trial makes it official. That's where they pass the verdict and dole out the punishment.*

My escort took me to the front seating of the room, past the bar that separated the key players from the audience, and motioned me toward a spot next to a middle-aged Moroi in a very formal and very designer black suit. The suit screamed, *I'm sorry the queen is dead, and I'm going to look fashionable while showing my grief.* His hair was a pale blond, lightly laced with the first signs of silver. Somehow, he made it look good. I presumed this was Damon Tarus, my lawyer, but he didn't say a word to me.

Mikhail sat beside me as well, and I was glad they'd chosen him to be the one who literally didn't leave my side. Glancing back, I saw Daniella and Nathan Ivashkov sitting with other high-ranking royals and their families. Adrian had chosen not to join them. He sat farther back, with Lissa, Christian, and Eddie. All of their faces were filled with worry.

The judge—an elderly, gray-haired Moroi who looked like she could still kick ass—called the room to attention, and I twisted around to face forward again. The Council was entering, and she announced them one by one. Two sets of benches had been arranged for them, two rows of six with a thirteenth in back raised. Of course, only eleven of the spots were filled, and I tried not to scowl. Lissa should have been sitting there.

When the Council was settled, the judge turned to face the rest of us and spoke in a voice that rang through the room. "This hearing is now in order, in which we will determine whether there is enough evidence to—"

A commotion at the door cut her off, and the audience

craned their necks to see what was going on.

"What's this disturbance about?" the judge demanded.

One of the guardians had the door partially open and was leaning out, apparently speaking to whoever was in the hall. He ducked back into the room. "The accused's lawyer is here, Your Honor."

The judge glanced at Damon and me and then delivered a frown to the guardian. "She already has a lawyer."

The guardian shrugged and appeared comically helpless. If there had been a Strigoi out there, he would have known what to do. This bizarre interruption of protocol was beyond his skill set. The judge sighed.

"Fine. Send whoever it is up here and let's get this settled."

Abe walked in.

"Oh dear lord," I said out loud.

I didn't have to scold myself for speaking out of turn because a hum of conversation immediately filled the room. My guess was that half were in awe because they knew Abe and his reputation. The other half were probably just stunned by his appearance.

He wore a gray cashmere suit, considerably lighter than Damon's grim black. Underneath it was a dress shirt that was so bright a white, it seemed to glow—particularly next to the brilliant crimson silk tie he wore. Other spots of red were scattered about his outfit—a handkerchief in the pocket, ruby cuff links. Naturally, it was all as perfectly tailored and expensive as Damon's outfit. But Abe didn't look like he was in mourning. He didn't even look like he was coming to a trial. It was more like he'd been interrupted on his way to a party. And of course, he sported his usual gold hoop earrings and trimmed black beard.

The judge silenced the room with a hand motion as he strutted up to her.

"Ibrahim Mazur," she said, with a shake of her head. There were equal parts amazement and disapproval in her voice. "This is . . . unexpected."

Abe swept her a gallant bow. "It's lovely to see you again, Paula. You haven't aged a day."

"We aren't at a country club, Mr. Mazur," she informed him. "And while here, you will address me by my proper title."

"Ah. Right." He winked. "My apologies, Your Honor." Turning, he glanced around until his eyes rested on me. "There she is. Sorry to have delayed this. Let's get started."

Damon stood up. "What is this? Who *are* you? I'm her lawyer."

Abe shook his head. "There must have been some mistake. It took me a while to get a flight here, so I can see why you would have appointed a community lawyer to fill in."

"Community lawyer!" Damon's face grew red with indignation. "I'm one of the most renowned lawyers among American Moroi."

"Renowned, community." Abe shrugged and leaned back on his heals. "I don't judge. No pun intended."

"Mr. Mazur," interrupted the judge, "are *you* a lawyer?"

"I'm a lot of things, Paula—Your Honor. Besides, does it matter? She only needs someone to speak for her."

"And she has someone," exclaimed Damon. "Me."

"Not anymore," said Abe, his demeanor still very pleasant. He had never stopped smiling, but I thought I saw that dangerous glint in his eyes that frightened so many of his enemies. He was the picture of calm, while Damon looked like he was ready to have a seizure.

"Your Honor—"

"Enough!" she said in that resounding voice of hers. "Let the girl choose." She fixed her brown eyes on me. "Who do you want to speak for you?"

"I . . ." My mouth dropped open at how abruptly the attention shifted to me. I'd been watching the drama between the two men like a tennis match, and now the ball had hit me in the head.

"Rose."

Startled, I turned slightly. Daniella Ivashkov had crept over in the row behind me. "Rose," she whispered again, "you have no idea who that Mazur man is." Oh, didn't I? "You want nothing to do with him. Damon's the best. He's not easy to get."

She moved back to her seat, and I looked between my two potential lawyers' faces. I understood Daniella's meaning. Adrian had talked her into getting Damon for me, and then she had talked Damon into actually doing it. Rejecting him would be an insult to her, and considering she was one of the few royal Moroi who'd been nice to me about Adrian, I certainly didn't want to earn her dislike. Besides, if this was some setup by royals, having one of them on my side was probably my best chance at getting off.

And yet . . . there was Abe, looking at me with that clever smile of his. He was certainly very good at getting his way, but a lot of that was by force of his presence and reputation. If there really was some absurd evidence against me, Abe's attitude wouldn't be enough to make it go away. Of course, he was sly, too. The serpent. He could make the impossible happen; he'd certainly pulled a lot of strings for me.

That did not, however, change the fact that he wasn't a lawyer.

On the other hand, he was my father.

He was my father, and although we still barely knew each other, he'd gone to great lengths to get here and saunter in with his gray suit to defend me. Was it fatherly love gone bad? Was he really all that good a lawyer? And at the end of the day, was it true that blood ran thicker than water? I didn't know. I actually didn't like that saying. Maybe it worked for humans, but it made no sense with vampires.

Anyway, Abe was staring at me intently with dark brown eyes nearly identical to mine. *Trust me,* he seemed to say. But could I? Could I trust my family? I would have trusted my mother if she were here—and I knew she trusted Abe.

I sighed and gestured toward him. "I'll take him." In an undertone, I added, "Don't let me down, Zmey."

Abe's smile grew broader as shocked exclamations filled the audience, and Damon protested in outrage. Daniella might have had to persuade him to take me on in the beginning, but now this case had become a matter of pride for him. His reputation had just been sullied by me passing him up.

But I'd made my choice, and the exasperated judge would hear no more arguments about it. She shooed Damon away, and Abe slid into his seat. The judge began with the standard opening speech, explaining why we were here, etc., etc. As she spoke, I leaned toward Abe.

"What have you gotten me into?" I hissed to him.

"Me? What have *you* gotten yourself into? Couldn't I have just picked you up at the police station for underage drinking, like most fathers?"

I was beginning to understand why people got irritated when I made jokes in dangerous situations.

"My fucking future's on the line! They're going to send me to trial and convict me!"

Every trace of humor or cheer vanished from his face. His expression grew hard, deadly serious. A chill ran down my spine.

"That," he said in a low, flat voice, "is something I swear to you is never, ever going to happen."

The judge turned her attention back to us and the prosecuting lawyer, a woman called Iris Kane. Not a royal name, but she still looked pretty hard-core. Maybe that was just a lawyer thing.

Before the evidence against me was laid out, the queen's murder was also described in all its grisly detail. How'd she'd been found this morning in bed, a silver stake through her heart and a profound look of horror and shock on her face. Blood had been everywhere: on her nightgown, the sheets, her skin . . . The pictures were shown to everyone in the room, triggering a variety of reactions. Gasps of surprise. More fear and panic. And some . . . some people wept. Some of those tears were undoubtedly because of the whole terrible situation, but I think many cried because they'd loved or liked Tatiana. She'd been cold and stiff at times, but for the most part, her reign had been a peaceful and just one.

After the pictures, they called me up. The hearing didn't run the way a normal trial did. There was no formal switching back of lawyers as they questioned witnesses. They each just sort of stood there and took turns asking questions while the judge kept order.

"Miss Hathaway," began Iris, dropping my title. "What time did you return to your room last night?"

"I don't know the exact time. . . ." I focused on her and Abe, not the sea of faces out there. "Somewhere around 5 a.m., I think. Maybe 6."

"Was anyone with you?"

"No, well—yes. Later." Oh, God. *Here it comes*. "Um, Adrian Ivashkov visited me."

"What time did he arrive?" asked Abe.

"I'm not sure of that either. A few hours after I got back, I guess."

Abe turned his charming smile on Iris, who was rustling through some papers. "The queen's murder has been pretty accurately narrowed down to between seven and eight. Rose wasn't alone—of course, we would need Mr. Ivashkov to testify to that effect."

My eyes flicked briefly to the audience. Daniella looked

pale. This was her nightmare: Adrian getting involved. Glancing farther over, I saw that Adrian himself seemed eerily calm. I really hoped he wasn't drunk.

Iris held up a sheet of paper triumphantly. "We have a signed statement from a janitor who says Mr. Ivashkov arrived at the defendant's building at approximately nine twenty."

"That's pretty specific," said Abe. He sounded amused, like she'd said something cute. "Do you have any desk staff to confirm that?"

"No," Iris said icily. "But this is enough. The janitor remembers because he was about to take his break. Miss Hathaway was alone when the murder took place. She has no alibi."

"Well," said Abe, "at least according to some questionable 'facts.'"

But no more was said about the time. The evidence was admitted into the official records, and I took a deep breath. I hadn't liked that line of questioning, but it had been expected, based on the earlier conversations I'd heard via Lissa. The no-alibi thing wasn't good, but I kind of shared Abe's vibe. What they had so far still didn't seem strong enough to send me to trial. Plus, they hadn't asked anything else about Adrian, which left him out of this.

"Next exhibit," said Iris. There was smug triumph all over her face. She knew the time thing was sketchy, but whatever was coming up, she thought it was gold.

But actually, it was silver. A silver stake.

So help me, she had a silver stake in a clear plastic container. It gleamed in the incandescent lighting—except for its tip. That was dark. With blood.

"This is the stake used to kill the queen," declared Iris. "Miss Hathaway's stake."

Abe actually laughed. "Oh, come on. Guardians are issued stakes all the time. They have an enormous, identical supply."

Iris ignored him and looked at me. "Where is your stake right now?"

I frowned. "In my room."

She turned and glanced out over the crowd. "Guardian Stone?"

A tall dhampir with a bushy black mustache rose from the crowd. "Yes?"

"You conducted the search of Miss Hathaway's room and belongings, correct?"

I gaped in outrage. "You searched my—"

A sharp look from Abe silenced me.

"Correct," said the guardian.

"And did you find any silver stakes?" asked Iris.

"No."

She turned back to us, still smug, but Abe seemed to find this new information even more ridiculous than the last batch. "That proves nothing. She could have lost the stake without realizing it."

"Lost it in the queen's heart?"

"Miss Kane," warned the judge.

"My apologies, Your Honor," said Iris smoothly. She turned to me. "Miss Hathaway, is there anything special about your stake? Anything that would distinguish it from others?"

"Y-yes."

"Can you describe that?"

I swallowed. I had a bad feeling about this. "It has a pattern etched near the top. A kind of geometric design." Guardians had engraving done sometimes. I'd found this stake in Siberia and kept it. Well, actually, Dimitri had sent it to me after it had come loose from his chest.

Iris walked over to the Council and held out the container so that each of them could examine it. Returning to me, she gave me my turn. "Is this your pattern? Your stake?"

I stared. It was indeed. My mouth opened, ready to say *yes*, but then I caught Abe's eye. Clearly, he couldn't talk directly to me, but he sent a lot of messages in that gaze. The biggest one was to be careful, be sly. What would a slippery person like Abe do?

"It . . . it looks *similar* to the design on mine," I said at last. "But I can't say for sure if it's the exact same one." Abe's smile told me I'd answered correctly.

"Of course you can't," Iris said, as though she'd expected no better. She handed off the container to one of the court clerks. "But now that the Council has seen that the design matches her description and is *almost* like her stake, I would like to point out that testing has revealed"—she held up more papers, victory all over her face—"that her fingerprints are on it."

There, it was. The big score. The "hard evidence."

"Any other fingerprints?" asked the judge.

"No, Your Honor. Just hers."

"That means nothing," said Abe with a shrug. I had a

feeling that if I stood and suddenly confessed to the murder, he would still claim it was dubious evidence. "Someone steals her stake and wears gloves. Her fingerprints would be on it because it's *hers*."

"That's getting kind of convoluted, don't you think?" asked Iris.

"The evidence is still full of holes," he protested. "That's what's convoluted. How could she have gotten into the queen's bedroom? How could she have gotten through the guards?"

"Well," mused Iris, "those would be questions best explored in trial, but considering Miss Hathaway's extensive record of breaking into and out of places, as well as the countless other disciplinary marks she has, I don't doubt she could have found any number of ways to get inside."

"You have no proof," said Abe. "No theory."

"We don't need it," said Iris. "Not at this point. We have more than enough to go to trial, don't we? I mean, we haven't even gotten to the part where countless witnesses heard Miss Hathaway tell the queen she'd regret establishing the recent guardian law. I can find the transcript if you like—not to mention reports of other 'expressive' commentary Miss Hathaway made in public."

A memory came back to me, of standing outside with Daniella while I ranted—with others watching—about how the queen couldn't buy me off with an assignment. Not a good decision on my part. Neither was busting in on the Death Watch or complaining about the queen being worth protecting when Lissa had been captured. I'd given Iris a lot of material.

"Oh yes," Iris continued. "We also have accounts of the queen declaring her extreme disapproval of Miss Hathaway's involvement with Adrian Ivashkov, particularly when the two ran off to elope." I opened my mouth at that, but Abe silenced me. "There are countless other records of Her Majesty and Miss Hathaway sparring in public. Would you like me to find those papers too, or are we able to vote on a trial now?"

This was directed at the judge. I had no legal background, but the evidence was pretty damning. I would have said that there was definitely reason to consider me a murder suspect, except . . .

"Your Honor?" I asked. I think she'd been about to give her declaration. "Can I say something?"

The judge thought about it, then shrugged. "I see no reason not to. We're collecting all the evidence there is."

Oh, me freelancing was *not* in Abe's plan at all. He strode to the stand, hoping to stop me with his wise counsel, but he wasn't fast enough.

"Okay," I said, hoping I sounded reasonable and wasn't going to lose my temper. "You've put up a lot of suspicious stuff here. I can see that." Abe looked pained. It was not an expression I'd seen on him before. He didn't lose control of situations very often. "But that's the thing. It's *too* suspicious. If I were going to murder someone, I wouldn't be that stupid. Do you think I'd leave my stake stuck in her chest? Do you think I wouldn't wear gloves? Come on. That's insulting. If I'm as crafty as you claim my record says I am, then why would I do it this way? I mean, seriously? If I did it, it'd be a lot better.

You'd never even peg me as a suspect. This is all really kind of an insult to my intelligence."

"Rose—" began Abe, a dangerous note in his tone. I kept going.

"All this evidence you've got is so painfully obvious. Hell, whoever set this up might as well have painted an arrow straight to me—and someone *did* set me up, but you guys are too stupid to even consider that." The volume of my voice was rising, and I consciously brought it back to normal levels. "You want an easy answer. A quick answer. And you especially want someone with no connections, no powerful family to protect them . . ." I hesitated there, unsure how to classify Abe. "Because that's how it always is. That's how it was with that age law. No one was able to stand up for the dhampirs either because this goddamned system won't allow it."

It occurred to me then that I had strayed pretty far off the subject—and was making myself look more guilty by slamming the age law. I reined myself back in.

"Um, anyway, Your Honor . . . what I'm trying to say is that this evidence shouldn't be enough to accuse me or send me to trial. I wouldn't plan a murder this badly."

"Thank you, Miss Hathaway," said the judge. "That was very . . . informative. You may take your seat now while the Council votes."

Abe and I returned to our bench. "What in the world were you thinking?" he whispered.

"I was telling it like it is. I was defending myself."

"I wouldn't go that far. You're no lawyer."

I gave him a sidelong look. "Neither are you, old man."

The judge asked the Council to vote on whether they believed there was enough evidence to make me a viable suspect and send me to trial. They did. Eleven hands went up. Just like that, it was over.

Through the bond, I felt Lissa's alarm. As Abe and I rose to leave, I looked out in the audience, which was starting to disband and buzzing with talk over what would happen now. Her light green eyes were wide, her face unusually pale. Beside her, Adrian too looked distressed, but as he stared at me, I could see love and determination radiating. And in the back, behind both of them . . .

Dimitri.

I hadn't even known he was here. His eyes were on me too, dark and endless. Only I couldn't read what he was feeling. His face betrayed nothing, but there was something in his eyes . . . something intense and intimidating. The image of him ready to take down that group of guardians flashed through my mind, and something told me that if I asked, he would do it again. He would fight his way to me through this courtroom and do everything in his power to rescue me from it.

A brushing of my hand distracted me from him. Abe and I had started to exit, but the aisle ahead of us was packed with people, bringing us to a halt. The touch against my hand was a small piece of paper shoved between my fingers. Glancing over, I saw Ambrose was sitting near the aisle, staring straight ahead. I wanted to ask what was going on, but some instinct kept me silent. Seeing as the line still wasn't moving, I hastily opened the paper, keeping it out of Abe's sight.

The paper was tiny, its elegant cursive almost impossible to read.

Rose,

If you're reading this, then something terrible has happened. You probably hate me, and I don't blame you. I can only ask that you trust that what I did with the age decree was better for your people than what others had planned. There are some Moroi who want to force all *dhampirs into service, whether they want it or not, by using compulsion. The age decree has slowed that faction down.*

However, I write to you with a secret you must put right, and it is a secret you must share with as few as possible. Vasilisa needs her spot on the Council, and it can be done. She is not the last Dragomir. Another lives, the illegitimate child of Eric Dragomir. I know nothing else, but if you can find this son or daughter, you will give Vasilisa the power she deserves. No matter your faults and dangerous temperament, you are the only one I feel can take on this task. Waste no time in fulfilling it.

—Tatiana Ivashkov

I stared at the piece of paper, its writing swirling before me, but its message burning into my mind. *She is not the last Dragomir. Another lives.*

If that was true, if Lissa had a half-brother or half-sister . . . it would change everything. She would get a vote on the Council. She would no longer be alone. *If* it was true. *If* this was from Tatiana. Anyone could sign her name to a piece of paper. It didn't make it real. Still, I shivered, troubled at the thought of getting a letter from a dead woman. If I allowed myself to see the ghosts around us, would Tatiana be there, restless and vengeful? I couldn't bring myself to let down my walls and look. Not yet. There had to be other answers. Ambrose had given me the note. I needed to ask him . . . except we were moving down the aisle again. A guardian nudged me along.

"What's that?" asked Abe, always alert and suspicious.

I hastily folded the note back up. "Nothing."

The look he gave me told me he didn't believe that at all. I wondered if I should tell him. *It is a secret you must share with as few as possible.* If he was one of the few, this wasn't the place. I tried to distract him from it and shake the dumbstruck look that must have been on my face. This note was a big problem—but not quite as big as the one immediately facing me.

"You told me I wouldn't go to trial," I said to Abe. My earlier annoyance returned. "I took a big chance with you!"

"It wasn't a big chance. Tarus couldn't have got you out of this either."

Abe's easy attitude about all this infuriated me further. "Are you saying you knew this hearing was a lost cause from the beginning?" It was what Mikhail had said too. How nice to have such faith from everyone.

"This hearing wasn't important," Abe said evasively. "What happens next is."

"And what is that exactly?"

He gave me that dark, sly gaze again. "Nothing you need to worry about yet."

One of the guardians put his hand on my arm, telling me

I needed to move. I resisted his pull and leaned toward Abe.

"The hell I don't! This is my life we're talking about," I exclaimed. I knew what would come next. Imprisonment until the trial. And then more imprisonment if I was convicted. "This is serious! I don't want to go to trial! I don't want to spend the rest of my life in a place like Tarasov."

The guard tugged harder, pushing us forward, and Abe fixed me with a piercing gaze that made my blood run cold.

"You will *not* go to trial. You will *not* go to prison," he hissed, out of the guards' hearing. "I won't allow it. Do you understand?"

I shook my head, confused over so much and not knowing what to do about any of it. "Even you have your limits, old man."

His smile returned. "You'd be surprised. Besides, they don't even send royal traitors to prison, Rose. Everyone knows that."

I scoffed. "Are you insane? Of course they do. What else do you think they do with traitors? Set them free and tell them not to do it again?"

"No," said Abe, just before he turned away. "They execute traitors."

Many thanks to all the friends and family who have lent their considerable support to me as I worked on this, especially my amazing and patient husband. I know I couldn't get through this without you! Special thanks also to my pal Jen Ligot and her eagle eyes.

On the publishing side, I'm always grateful for the hard work of my agent Jim McCarthy, as well as everyone else at Dystel & Goderich Literary Management—including Lauren Abramo, who helps spread Vampire Academy around the world. Thank you also to the gang at Penguin Books—Jessica Rothenberg, Ben Schrank, Casey McIntyre, and so many others—who work a lot of magic for this series. My publishers outside the U.S. are also doing wonderful things for getting the word out about Rose, and I'm constantly amazed to see the growing international response. Thank you so much for all you do.

A last shout-out to my readers, whose continued enthusiasm still overwhelms me. Thank you for reading and loving these characters as much as I do.